Through Time and Crown

A novel by
LeAnn Rhodes

Through Time and Crown

Paperback ISBN: 979-8-9934211-0-0
Kindle eBook ISBN: 979-8-9934211-1-7

Author's Disclaimer

This is a work of fiction. Names, characters, places, and events are either products of the author's imagination or are used fictiously. While certain elements may be inspired by historical figures, locations, or occurrences, they have been adapted for narrative purposes and should not be interpreted as accurate representations of real people or events.

Any resemblance to actual persons, living or dead, historical or contemporary, or to other fictional characters, settings, or storylines is purely coincidental and unintentional.

AI Usage Disclaimer

This manuscript was created with the assistance of AI-based tools. The author provided detailed scene outlines, character profiles, thematic direction, and original dialogue, which were used to guide the AI in drafting narrative text. While the author edited and refined the output extensively, portions of the manuscript were generated by an AI tool and should be considered AI-generated content.

The author's creative process blended human intention with technological support, and every scene reflects the author's original vision, voice, and storytelling goals.

To my nieces, Kaileigh and Serenity.

Bread before bells.

Mercy with order.

Worth over birth.

Stone and paint remember.

Chapters

Through Time

- 1 -

King Alaric

Sunset's orange glow filters through the high lancet windows of the Council Chamber, casting long shadows across the stone floor. King Alaric leans back in his carved chair at the head of the long oak table. To his left, Lord Reginald's papers are spread out as he gives the King the granary report.

"The granaries at Redwyke hold well. Three months' stores remain, and the roads south show green shoots pushing through the mud. The kingdom has weathered winter well, Your Majesty."

"Good tidings." Alaric responds then nods toward Archbishop Anselm, "And the parishes?"

"Few deaths this winter past, Sire. Father Jerome reports the coastal villages weathered the recent storms without losing boats or life."

To the King's right, Lord Geoffrey, the Council's youngest advisor recently assigned to merchant management, shifts in his seat. "The merchants speak of trade routes opening early. If the rains hold off—"

A sharp humming cuts through his words, like a thousand bees swarming in the rafters. The sound grows louder until the very air seems to vibrate. Alaric's hand moves instinctively toward his sword hilt as the humming gives life to the very air around them.

Light erupts near the vaulted ceiling, bright as summer lightning. The snap that follows echoes off the stone walls like a coachman's whip cracking. The light retreats as three figures tumble from the ceiling's empty air.

They fall in a tangle of limbs and strange leather that stretches across their figures and glimmers as they impact the stone floor.

The largest figure, a man in black and grey, rolls clear of another man, clad in blue, who lands on an iron candle stand. The third, a woman also dressed in that same blue, lands on her feet and mirrors the grey man's movement. Small glass squares on their left forearms flicker from some foreign fire underneath.

Before Alaric has time to compose his senses, the woman lunges at the grey clad man. He sidesteps while sending a fist whistling past her ear. She spins away as the blue clad man vaults over the ruined candle stand, still moving despite the fall that should have shattered bones.

They circle each other like wolves, oblivious to the five men gaping from the oak table.

"By all the saints! Guards, hold!" Alaric snaps as steel scrapes from scabbards at the chamber's entrance.

Ralf Godwin stumbles backward, his face white as parchment. Archbishop Anselm grips his jeweled cross, lips moving in silent prayer. Lord Reginald's ink pot has overturned, black liquid spreading across his ledgers.

The three strange warriors continue their deadly dance, moving at speeds faster than Alaric's fastest mount. Their strange garments wrap them in lightning in response to each landed strike. The grey man flows like water around the blue clad figures, he their clear target.

The woman lunges but the grey man catches her wrist and uses her momentum to spin her toward her companion. But she plants her foot against a stone column and launches herself backward, driving her elbow toward the grey man's ribs. He twists away, the blow glancing off his strange armor. The blue clad man vaults over an overturned side table, his boots silent on stone as he lands behind the grey figure.

"They fight as if blades are an afterthought," Geoffrey murmurs, his voice barely audible above the sound of bodies colliding with furniture.

"Or as if blades slow them," Alaric answers, watching the woman duck under a sweeping arm and drive her knee upward.

The grey man blocks with crossed forearms, the impact causing the strange armor's lightening to come alive again. The woman spins away, snatching a wooden cleaning bucket from beside a tapestry. She hurls it, hitting her mark with deadly precision.

But the grey man's arm sweeps up, batting the bucket aside. It splinters against the stone wall, but the glass square on his forearm dims and the fire within wavers like a candle in wind.

"Their leathers fit like a second skin," Alaric notes, studying how the strange garments move with each fighter's body, never binding or catching.

"What leathers look like that?" Geoffrey questions.

The blue clad figures circle their grey adversary like well acquainted dancers, their movements coordinated without words or glances. One feints left while the other attacks from the right, forcing their opponent to choose.

"That woman," Ralf whispers from behind them, his voice cracking.

Alaric's jaw tightens. The impropriety of witnessing a woman's form in such garments, her curves outlined as brazenly as any tavern wench, compounds with the impossibility of seeing her fight with a man's skill and station. These three are far from ordinary. Certainly not English, possibly not even from the continent.

They fight as if the very air belongs to them. Their movements unhindered by their body's weight.

The grey man's elbow drives deep into the woman's stomach, doubling her over. His knee snaps upward toward her chin, but she twists aside, taking the blow on her shoulder instead. She staggers, gasping. While before her suit shimmered with every landed hit, this time it did not.

Does the lightning protect them? Alaric's mind races to keep up, to understand.

The blue clad man flows forward like water spilled over stone. His shoulder drives into their grey opponent's ribs, sending him stumbling backward into the overturned side table that splinters under the force of his weight.

The woman straightens, one hand pressed to her shoulder where the elbow struck. Her eyes sweep the chamber in a quick assessment, moving across the long oak table to where five men stand frozen by their abandoned chairs.

Her gaze locks on Alaric's crown. Her eyes hold the calculating assessment of someone who understands power, who knows exactly what she sees. The recognition sends a chill through Alaric's chest.

"Adrian. Company," she calls, her voice clipped short by pain and controlled breathing.

"Copy," the man returns without shifting his attention from their grey adversary, who rolls to his feet among the table's broken planks.

For the first time since their violent arrival, all three fighters seem aware they are not alone. The woman's stance shifts subtly, her weight balanced differently now that she knows witnesses surround them.

The grey man's head turns slightly right then left, his peripheral vision catching the robes at the table and the steel at the door.

"Steel won't help ignorance," Archbishop Anselm says evenly, his voice cutting through the tension as guards near the door advance forward. "Look before you strike."

The guards halt mid-stride, though their hands remain tight on sword hilts. Alaric watches the Archbishop's face. Calm, thoughtful, as if strange warriors tumbling from light itself merely require careful consideration rather than immediate action.

Lord Geoffrey steps between Alaric and the three fighters, his hand finding his dagger though he lacks the skill to use it. Across the oak table, Lord Reginald and Ralf edge toward the door with cautious steps.

The grey man straightens, his attention shifting between Geoffrey's protective stance and Alaric's crown. The gleaming glass square on his forearm pulses weakly before breathing its last breath and the strange light within dies out.

Anselm's words echo in Alaric's mind. *Steel won't help ignorance.* The Archbishop speaks as if he recognizes something. Not the strangers themselves, perhaps, but their nature. The Church guards its own secrets, knowledge gathered across centuries that could indeed kill a curious man faster than any blade.

"Your Grace," Alaric projects his voice over the scene, hoping to give Anselm an opening for negotiation, "what do you see?"

The blue clad figures maintain their combat stances, but their focus has shifted. They watch the guards, the exits, the positioning of everyone in the chamber. Professional assessment, not panic.

"Patience, Sire," Anselm murmurs. "Some arrivals require interpretation."

The grey man's head tilts slightly, as if listening to something beyond normal hearing. His stance shifts, weight redistributing, and Alaric realizes with uncomfortable certainty that this warrior could reach Geoffrey and him before any guard could intervene.

The chamber holds its collective breath, balanced on the knife's edge between violence and revelation.

The grey man moves like a striking snake and finds his prey.

Geoffrey's hand barely clears his dagger hilt before the warrior flows around him, one arm snaking around Geoffrey's shoulder while his free hand plucks Geoffrey's dagger from its sheath.

The dagger's steel grazes Geoffrey's neck as the grey man drags him backward, using Geoffrey's body as a shield between himself and the chamber's occupants.

"Drop the band, hero," the grey man hisses toward the blue clad man, his voice carrying an English accent Alaric cannot place. The blade at Geoffrey's neck draws a thin line of crimson. "Or I repaint these stones."

Geoffrey's eyes widen, his breathing shallow and controlled despite the steel biting at his throat. His gaze finds Alaric's, steady and apologetic.

The woman shifts her weight, but she holds position, understanding that any movement might cost Geoffrey his life. The woman's companion, Adrian, hovers his hand over the glass square on his forearm. The *band*, apparently.

The woman's eyes dart to Adrian's glowing band, fear flickering across her features for the first time since their unnatural and violent arrival. She takes a half-step toward the grey man holding Geoffrey, but Adrian's sharp gesture stops her cold.

"You can't, Brother. The timeline must come first," she cautions sharply, her voice carrying the weight of some unknown duty that binds them both.

Alaric's breath catches. *Brother.* Geoffrey's eyes widen as the implication strikes him. Whatever mission drives these strangers, his life means nothing against their greater purpose. The woman speaks of him as if he were already dead, a sacrifice acceptable for some cause beyond his understanding.

The guards surge forward, steel singing from scabbards. This time neither Alaric nor Anselm raises a hand to stop them. Geoffrey's life hangs by a thread, and these strangers speak of timelines as if the mortal men among them are merely obstacles.

But Adrian's voice cuts clean through their advancement, calm and resolute, and Alaric's men stop once again. "Let him go. You have my attention."

The grey man's grip tightens on Geoffrey's throat, the blade drawing another thin line of blood. "The band, hero. Now."

Adrian's jaw sets. His gaze never loses Geoffrey's while his fingers find the edge of the glass device, working at what appears to be its binding. A sound fills the chamber like tearing parchment, but sharper, more deliberate. The noise sets his teeth on edge, as if the very air protests being split apart.

The glass peels away from Adrian's forearm with ease. Alaric expects to see blood where such a thing had been torn free, but only a depression in his strange armor remains.

Adrian tosses the band toward the grey man. It spins through the air, its glass surface catching candlelight, before striking the flagstones by Geoffrey's feet. Alaric braces for the heavy clatter of thick crystal, but instead, it lands with a subtle thud. The sound, or lack thereof, sends unease up Alaric's spine. Thick glass that glows like captured starlight should ring like a bell when tossed onto stone floor, not settle like a dropped bread loaf.

"You can't run forever," the woman warns, her voice carrying the hint of a long pursuit.

The grey man's smile turns savage. "Watch me."

Geoffrey gasps as the blade presses deeper, crimson now trickling down his neck. The grey man's grip on Geoffrey's shoulder shifts, his voice dropping to a deadly whisper. "Pick up the band, boy. Nice and slow."

Geoffrey knees bend slowly until his trembling fingers find the device at his feet. The moment his skin touches the glass strange markings illuminate on the surface.

"Good. Now see my arm? The broken one. Remove it." The grey man instructs. "Careful now, or I open your throat."

Alaric watches Geoffrey's face go white as parchment as he works at the damaged band on the grey man's forearm. The thing comes away with that same unsettling whisper of torn air.

"Attach the new one. Press it down until you feel it... settle." Geoffrey's hands shake as he positions the device.

"Now, touch the glass. See what appears."

Geoffrey's finger hovers over the surface, then presses down. His eyes widen in sudden shock, pupils dilating as if he stares into blinding sunlight.

"Words?!" Geoffrey gasps, his voice cracking with wonder. "They appear!"

The grey man's blade presses deeper, drawing fresh blood. "Pay attention, boy. Find the marking that looks like," he glances briefly at Alaric, "like a crown with three points. Touch it."

Alaric's jaw clenches. Whatever sorcery this device contains, it responds to Geoffrey's touch as naturally as ink follows a quill. Alaric can see Geoffrey's scholarly mind waring as both terror and curiosity threaten to overcome the steel at his throat.

"There. I see it." Geoffrey's finger moves across the glass.

The band begins to pulse with steady, rhythmic light. One bright flash, then darkness. Another flash and the glow remains steady.

Beep.

The sound echoes off stone walls like a funeral bell tolling. The grey man's grip loosens slightly on Geoffrey's throat, his attention shifting to the band's heartbeat.

Beep.

"Three more," the grey man's eyes lock with Adrian's, his voice carrying satisfaction and something else, relief, perhaps. Or desperation.

Beep.

Without warning, he shoves Geoffrey away. Geoffrey stumbles forward, his legs tangling as he fights to keep balance with one hand pressed to his bleeding throat.

Beep.

Adrian launches himself across the chamber, his body flowing over Geoffrey and broken furniture. But even his unnatural speed cannot cover the distance in time.

Beep.

Light explodes around the grey man. Not the brilliant lightening of their arrival, but something softer, stranger, like the glow of a white fire. The air itself seems to fold like beaten metal, creating ripples that hurt to look at directly. The grey man's form wavers, becoming translucent as morning mist.

Then he simply... isn't. The light gone with him.

The chamber falls silent except for Geoffrey's ragged breathing and the distant crackle of torches in the corridor.

Geoffrey staggers backward until his spine hits the stone wall, his eyes fixed on the empty space where a man had stood moments before. His hand comes away from his throat now stained with blood, but the cuts are shallow reminders rather than mortal wounds.

"Saints above," Geoffrey gasps, his voice barely above a whisper. "Did he... unmake himself?"

"He fled," Alaric replies, his voice steady despite the impossibility of what he has witnessed. "And left us riddles."

Alaric's gaze shifts to the woman and her companion, Adrian, who stand motionless along the chamber's edge. Their strange garments gleam like dull blades, and their eyes hold knowledge that makes his crown feel suddenly heavy.

The woman meets his stare without flinching. Whatever fear she had shown for her companion's safety has vanished, replaced by the calculating assessment of someone who understands that survival now depends on the words spoken in the next few moments.

Adrian's hand moves to where his own time band had been, fingers finding only the shallow depth left there. His jaw sets as he takes in their changed circumstances.

Steel fills the chamber as guards surge forward, forming a tight circle around the two remaining strangers. Their blades and stances poised for a concerted attack, but Alaric raises his hand, holding them at ready distance.

The woman shifts her stance immediately. Where moments before she had moved like a predator, now her hands rise slowly, palms open in the universal gesture of peace. The transformation strikes Alaric as deliberate, trained. The difference between a warrior and a diplomat.

"We're not your enemies," she says, her voice carrying none of the clipped urgency from before. "A poor introduction, I grant."

"Understatement," Alaric's voice carries calmly, but his eyes move anxiously between the siblings.

Geoffrey slumps against the wall, one hand still pressed to his bleeding throat, but alive. That fact weighs heavily in Alaric's assessment. Adrian could have reached the grey man faster if he had simply let Geoffrey die. Instead, he chose Geoffrey's life with little hesitation.

Strangers who speak of mission objectives do not typically spare innocent bystanders when success demands it. Yet Adrian did, contradicting his partner's desire for their successful mission goal. The contradiction intrigues almost as much as the impossible arrival itself. Adrian is clearly an adept warrior, and his decision to save Geoffrey is interestingly compassionate. Compassion grows compassion.

The woman's gaze never wavers from his, steady and respectful without servility. She understands authority, recognizes the weight of his crown. Whatever these two are, they comprehend power structures.

Adrian remains silent beside her, his attention split between the guards and the doorways. A professional caution rather than panic.

The chamber holds its breath, balanced between violence and words.

Archbishop Anselm rises from his chair in an unhurried calm, his jeweled cross a glittering centerpiece on his chest as he moves between the armed guards and the two strangers. His presence fills the chamber with a quiet authority that commands attention without the need to raise voice or hand.

"Majesty, grant them breath before judgment."

The Archbishop's words carry the weight of years spent counseling restraint over impulse. Alaric feels the familiar pull of Anselm's wisdom, the gentle check against decisions made in heat rather than consideration.

Blood stains Geoffrey's tunic, a poignant reminder how close Alaric came to losing his closest friend. The impossible arrival defies every natural law, yet these two warriors chose mercy when they could have chosen success.

Alaric nods once. "Chain no one. We will hear them."

Alaric gestures toward Adrian with a measured nod. "Speak."

As a guard closes the door to prevent prying eyes, the woman steps forward, her mouth opening to respond, but Adrian's hand cuts through the air between them.

"Stand down."

The command carries an authority that stops her mid-stride. Her eyes narrow, shooting Adrian a look that could freeze ale in summer. The particular brand of irritation Alaric recognizes from watching his own courtiers when protocol overrides their intentions.

"Elaine. Consider your position," Adrian adds, his voice low but pointed. "Woman. This century."

Alaric catches Geoffrey's eye, noting the same startled recognition there. The implications settle like cold stone in his chest. If women from their time dress and fight as she does, then what manner of world do they come from? What authority do they wield that must be consciously set aside in his presence?

"My apologies, Your Majesty." Adrian glances at Alaric's crown and inclines his head with deference. "My companion forgets her manners in strange company."

The words establish hierarchy. Adrian commands, Elaine follows. Yet the tension between them suggests this arrangement chafes against their natural order. Alaric files the observation away as Elaine casts wary glances at the guards flanking them.

"We are Adrian and Elaine Rush. Agents of Time."

The phrase sounds like a title, formal as any courtly designation. Adrian's voice carries the cadence of someone accustomed to giving reports. The shared name, Rush. She called him *brother*.

"We come from the year two thousand, one hundred and ninety-three... after the birth of Christ." He gives a respectful nod in Anselm's direction, an acknowledgement of the ecclesiastical authority present.

The number hangs in the air. Nearly a thousand years hence. Alaric's mind struggles to comprehend such vastness. Generations upon generations stretching into unimaginable distance.

"A scientist in our time discovered the method for traveling through years as men travel through kingdoms. But the knowledge was stolen, made illegal. These thieves create their own devices—" Adrian gestures toward his forearm where the band once rested. "—to escape justice across time itself."

Alaric nods slowly. The concept stretches comprehension, yet the basic framework holds familiar shape: criminals fleeing authority, lawmen in pursuit. That such chase could span centuries rather than counties merely magnifies the scale.

"Our task force has gathered most of them. The escaped man, the Grey Hunter, proves our most elusive target."

Elaine motions toward Adrian's bare forearm. "We're down a ticket home."

Ralf shifts nervously behind them. "What mean you, my lady?"

"The device I surrendered was my passage back," Adrian explains, his tone matter-of-fact despite the enormity of the admission. He nods toward Elaine's forearm. "She carries the only remaining band in this time. It holds power for one."

Lord Reginald clears his throat. "Pardon, ser Adrian, was it? Should we be concerned of other... visitors from your time?"

"Unlikely." Adrian's response comes uncertain as he breathes in and prepares his next words. "This pursuit was unsanctioned. Off the mapped routes. My team cannot locate our exact position in time. We are severed from our own authority as surely as from our own century."

He pauses, measuring his words carefully.

"The device I surrendered held energy sufficient for one departure. The Grey Hunter must locate another power source to travel again. Recent years have seen such technology locked away beyond his reach."

Alaric absorbs this with growing unease. *Unlikely* means he could return.

Lord Reginald steps forward, his voice sharp with accusation as he switches to French. "Ce sont des assassins, Sire—voyez leurs armes et leurs tours." *They are assassins, Sire—look at their weapons and their tricks.*

Adrian responds in French without hesitation, "Nous ne sommes les assassins de personne. Nous poursuivions un criminel et nous avons protégé vos gens." *We are no one's assassins. We were pursuing a criminal and we protected your people.*

The fluency surprises Alaric. These future warriors speak the language of courts, yet something in their French pronunciation feels just as foreign as their English accents.

"Vous parlez tous les deux français ?" *Do you both speak French?*

"Oui, Monseigneur," Elaine replies smoothly.

Reginald, suspiciously, "Their French sits... oddly."

Alaric stands, the weight of crown and circumstance settling on his shoulders as he surveys the two strangers before him. Their impossible arrival has shattered the evening's deliberations, yet protocol must be observed, even with visitors from centuries hence.

"I am King Alaric of England. Welcome to the thirteenth century."

The formal introduction carries both authority and courtesy, establishing his position while acknowledging their strange circumstances. He gestures toward his advisors in turn.

"Lord Reginald of Redwyke, my senior counselor and chancellor to England. Lord Geoffrey, heir to Redwyke and our youngest counselor. Archbishop Anselm of Clearvale, my spiritual counselor and head of the Church in England. And Ralf Godwin, my servant man."

Geoffrey and Reginald offer slight bows toward the siblings, a clear mark of respect to acknowledge their status as guests rather than prisoners. Anselm and Ralf manage respectful nods.

"I ask your cooperation while my counselors and I deliberate this matter. You will wait in our diplomatic chambers."

Adrian inclines his head. "Of course, Your Majesty."

Alaric's gaze sharpens as he notices Ralf's attention fixed on Elaine's *garments*, his stare lingering where courtesy demands averted eyes. Alaric turns slightly toward his servant man, his voice carrying rebuke. "Ralf, keep your eyes decent."

The sharp correction echoes through the chamber, a warning to all present. Elaine's cheeks flush crimson as she shoots Ralf a fleeting glare before meeting Alaric's gaze.

"Appreciated, Sire."

The Guards escort Adrian and Elaine out first, Sir Denby providing cloaks for cover. Before the doors can close fully, Archbishop Anselm holds them ajar.

"Might I suggest, Sire, that we continue this discussion in the antechambers, while our guests await in their diplomatic chamber?" Anslem offers loud enough all in the hall to hear. His recommendation serves both to offer Alaric a more private setting and to ensure any prying eyes in the hall perceive the siblings as mere visitors, alleviating concerns over the presence of two unfamiliar faces being escorted like prisoners.

"Aye, ever the most thoughtful amongst us, Archbishop."

A Fragile Cover

- 2 -

Archbishop Anselm of Clearvale

Anselm watches the guards escort the siblings down the stone corridor, thankful Denby provided cloaks to cover their strange garments. A maid's curious glance stops on Elaine as she takes in the peculiar styled dark hair and boots escaping beyond the cloak's cover.

"Move along, Meg," one of the guards calls, his voice carrying the authority of routine. The servant startles, clutching her tray, and hurries toward the kitchens with backward glances that promise swift gossip.

Anselm leads the King and counselors to an antechamber at the halls opposite end. Anselm closes the door firmly, ensuring their deliberation remains private, while Sir Denby waits outside.

Anselm turns to face the men with whom he shares an impossible burden. Geoffrey runs both hands through his dark hair, his scholarly composure cracking. "Time travelers. In our council chamber. Speaking of centuries yet to come. What absurdity is this?"

"We must choose our story before the story chooses us. Control the *absurdity*," Anselm counsels, his voice steady despite the magnitude of their predicament. Years of navigating delicate church politics have taught him that truth, like communion wine, requires careful preparation before distribution.

Alaric paces the narrow space, his boots echoing against stone. "They cannot simply vanish. Too many witnessed their arrival. Guards, servants, ourselves."

Geoffrey considers aloud, "Guards will hold tongues when ordered and no servants were in the room to witness. The rumors of their *arrival* may be manageable."

Lord Reginald clears his throat. "The woman spoke of one device remaining. They may not both stay, Sire."

"They are siblings," Anselm observes, noting how Adrian positioned himself protectively near Elaine throughout the interrogation. "Such bonds do not break easily. If one returns to their century, both will go."

"Then we plan for their presence," Alaric decides, his tone carrying the weight of kingship. "What story serves the realm?"

Anselm studies the King's face, recognizing the careful calculation behind his words. Alaric has grown into his crown these past four years, learning to balance idealism with the harsh mathematics of governance. His wisdom often verges on that of someone in their thirties, not mid-twenties.

"French nobility," Anselm suggests, his mind already weaving possibilities. "Their accent sits strangely, but border provinces breed odd dialects. The illness sweeping across southern France could provide excuse for nobles seeking refuge beyond France's borders."

"Refugees from the continents illness." Geoffrey nods slowly, "Make the court pity their circumstances."

"And their unfamiliarity with English customs," Reginald adds, his wariness giving way to practical consideration. "French court protocols differ from ours, which may help explain their oddities until properly tutored in English etiquette."

Anselm feels the familiar weight of shepherding dangerous knowledge. The Church has long experience managing revelations that could destabilize faith. This simply adds temporal complexity to eternal concerns.

"We must craft their lineage carefully," he continues. "Noble enough to justify court residence. Obscure enough to avoid contradiction. Not too old to be unmarried."

Anselm draws himself upright, feeling the weight of his ecclesiastical authority settle around him like heavy vestments. The lie he is about to construct could unravel everything he has built. His position, his standing with Rome, perhaps even his life if discovered. Yet he sees no path forward that does not require this leap of faith.

"They are distant kin to me," he announces, his voice carrying the certainty that has guided countless sermons. "Orphaned recently by a fever that swept the mainland. As their sole remaining family, I have offered sanctuary in England."

Geoffrey's eyebrows lift slightly, recognizing the careful construction of the cover story. The Archbishop weaves the fiction with practiced skill, creating plausible threads for others to follow.

"Names?" Alaric asks, his tone sharp with attention. "Names make people."

"Sir Roland of Montbois," Anselm replies, the fabrication rolling from his tongue smoothly. "Lady Hélène of Montbois."

"*Ay-LEHN*," Alaric repeats, testing the French pronunciation with practiced fluency. His education included continental languages, and he shapes the vowels correctly. "Sounds like Elaine. But why Roland?"

Anselm allows a careful pause, as if retrieving a distant memory. "I have a cousin who bears that name. Much younger than I. A few years your senior. A capable knight, though I may have mentioned him only in passing. He serves along the southeastern borders, far from court circles. His name could provide discretion."

The Archbishop watches understanding dawn in the King's eyes. A living person whose identity they can borrow, someone remote enough to avoid immediate contradiction.

"Their lands?" Reginald inquires, his advisor's mind already calculating potential complications.

"La Brousse," Anselm states, selecting the region with deliberate care. "Remote, reclusive. Off the main courier routes where old dialects linger and customs grow peculiar."

Reginald nods slowly, approval creeping into his expression. "Few have trod those roads. Fewer can contradict you, and their odd burr and mannerisms will pass as local."

The aged lord's words carry weight beyond their surface meaning. He recognizes the risk and why Anselm takes it. Few would dare question an Archbishop's word regarding his own family, particularly Anselm, whose reputation for wisdom and integrity stands unshakeable among both court, common folk, and the Church.

"Your Grace's counsel in this matter speaks well," Alaric says, his formal address acknowledging what Anselm offers. The King understands perfectly. The Archbishop stakes his entire standing on this fiction.

Anselm feels the familiar sensation of crossing into uncharted territory, where faith and truth intersect in ways the Church's teachings cannot anticipate. Yet sometimes truth and faith are served best when wrapped in the pragmatism of necessary lies.

Anselm turns his gaze to each man in turn, letting the weight of his ecclesiastical authority settle over them like incense. "You saw only chaos and courage. Swear to that."

Geoffrey inclines his head first, his scholarly nature grasping the necessity immediately. "I will swear what I saw: they bled like us."

"Sir Roland of Montbois. Lady Hélène of Montbois," Reginald repeats carefully, testing the names against his tongue. "From La Brousse. Their parents recently deceased, and Your Grace has offered sanctuary in England."

"Their only remaining family," Anselm confirms, watching as each man commits the fiction to memory. "You understand what this requires of us all."

Ralf steps forward, his footman's training evident in his crisp bearing. "Sir Roland and Lady Hélène, Your Grace. I shall ensure the staff knows to address them properly."

Alaric looks toward the closed chamber door, his decision crystallizing into action. "Guard!"

Sir Denby enters, his hand resting casually on his sword hilt.

"Send word to the kitchens," Alaric commands, his voice carrying across the antechamber to where a footman lingers in the corridor. "Sir Roland of Montbois and his sister, Lady Hélène of

Montbois, require fresh garments, food, and drink. They await in the diplomatic chambers."

"Sir." Denby acknowledges the command with a look of understanding, then turns to the footman, who nods and moves toward a servant's passage.

As the door closes behind Denby, Anselm already sees the ordinary machinery of castle life begin to turn, weaving their fiction into its daily routine.

Anselm shifts his weight, feeling the familiar ache in his lower back that comes from long councils and longer prayers. The immediate crisis may be contained, but years of navigating court politics have taught him that every lie breeds scrutiny.

"Skepticism protects crowns," he says, his voice carrying the cadence of careful consideration. "But it also topples them when fed too soon or too little."

Geoffrey nods, understanding flickering across his scholarly features. "You speak of the court hawks."

"Lord Ranulf, our dutiful Justiciar, particularly concerns me," Anselm continues, his fingers unconsciously worrying the heavy cross at his chest. "He serves as guardian of royal interests with uncommon zeal."

Reginald's expression grows thoughtful, the lines around his eyes deepening. "Ranulf is no fool. He will sense something amiss about these siblings. Their manner, their speech, their... capabilities."

"Then we bring him into confidence," Anselm suggests, though he recognizes the risk even as he voices it. "Controlled knowledge serves better than wild speculation."

Alaric turns sharply, his young face hardening with royal authority. "No. We control the narrative by limiting those who know it. Beyond this chamber, the fiction stands complete."

"Then I shall monitor Ranulf closely," Reginald offers. "He often seeks counsel with me on matters of court security. I can guide his attention elsewhere."

Anselm acknowledges the wisdom with a slight nod, then turns to another concern. "Lord Elias Devereux presents our second challenge. His French origins make him uniquely positioned to question their lineage."

Geoffrey shifts in his chair, his practical mind already working through possibilities. "Elias has always been a court creature, never a countryside gentleman. The likelihood of him knowing the true Roland or having visited La Brousse approaches nothing."

"You will watch him?" Reginald asks, yet commands of his son.

"Closely," Geoffrey confirms.

Alaric begins pacing the narrow space again, a sign of the young King's growing anxiety. "Lord Percival troubles me less. He spends more time at court than his own lands, but his interests run toward... romantic pursuits. Elaine," he pauses and corrects himself, "the Lady Hélène may attract his attention unless her demeanor discourages such advances."

The King pauses, his expression growing more serious. "Which brings us to a larger concern. Her etiquette will require immediate attention. She lacks the deportment expected of any noblewoman, French or otherwise. Roland's etiquette can be mostly explained away due to his status as a knight."

Anselm recognizes the delicate challenge this presents. A noblewoman who cannot navigate the intricate dance of court manners will draw unwanted questions.

Alaric's expression dims as another name occurs to him. "Lord Cedric of Langmere presents a similar challenge."

The King's tone carries clear distaste. Lord Cedric is obnoxious, but harmless. He remains at court desperate for the crown's acknowledgement and a wife.

"That peacock concerns himself primarily with marriage prospects," Alaric continues. "He may view Sir Roland as unwelcome competition for eligible ladies, though he will likely dismiss Lady Hélène as beneath his consideration given her supposedly modest standing."

Geoffrey clears his throat softly. "Lord Miles of Faversham gossips freely, but his distaste for French customs may work in our favor. He already dismisses Lord Elias's mannerisms as continental oddities. He may extend the same courtesy to the Montbois siblings."

"Both Miles and Cedric bear watching nonetheless," Anselm cautions.

Ralf steps forward, his footman's instincts drawing him into the discussion. "Your Majesty, what of the staff?"

Reginald's voice sharpens immediately. "Keep their whispers contained, Ralf. Threaten their positions if necessary."

"No heads rolling," Alaric interjects firmly. "Suspension suffices for idle gossip, but harsh punishment for mere talk would suggest the gossip carries truth."

Ralf nods, understanding gleaming in his eyes. "I know precisely who can manage the kitchens, Your Majesty. Alice Whitcombe has particular skill with... guiding conversations."

"Good. But she need not know of the particulars surrounding our visitors' true nature. Give her only the fiction. Imply they are here for sanctuary."

Anselm watches this exchange with growing appreciation for the delicate web they must weave. Each thread requires careful placement and each voice must sing the same melody, or their fiction will unravel before it can take root.

Alaric stops pacing and his countenance settles into the careful resolve Anselm has learned to recognize. The King's youth sometimes breeds hesitation, but crisis sharpens his judgment.

"We keep them close," Alaric decides. "Close is safer than shadow."

Anselm feels relief wash through him like morning prayer. Proximity allows control. Scattered pieces invite dangerous speculation.

"French, not foreign," he instructs. "Unusual, not unnatural." He turns to Geoffrey. "Lady Hélène should remain largely tucked away from court until her etiquette is polished. Someone must school her in proper deportment before she makes her public debut. The Queen Dowager already expects this of foreign ladies requiring assistance in English etiquette."

"Sir Denby can manage Sir Roland," Alaric adds. "Keep him occupied with guard duties and close observation. Once Lady Hélène is released to court, he may participate in court activities as well."

Reginald shifts forward, understanding his role without explicit instruction. "I shall keep noble whispers at bay, citing your authority, Sire."

"Say only that I will answer questions regarding *my* cousins at vespers," Anselm adds, recognizing the wisdom of controlled revelation. "Shall we house them in castle chambers or at my personal residence?"

"House them here," Alaric responds. "Lord Miles's recent wed to Lady Rosamund has freed both their chambers. They have taken up residence in London. Their chambers will do."

The Archbishop watches the finality of the situation settle across their faces. Time serves their fiction. Each hour allows the impossible to become merely improbable.

Alaric calls toward the chamber door, "Sir Denby!"

The guard captain enters immediately, closing the door behind him for privacy.

"Have our visitors been clothed and fed?"

"Aye, Sire. Agnes attended them."

"You'll watch them. Not as gaolers," Alaric says, his tone carrying the weight of royal command, "as shepherds."

"Aye, Sire," Denby replies, though concern creases his brow. "The man's fighting methods... and the woman's. I've never witnessed such techniques."

Anselm steps forward, recognizing the delicate balance required. "Warrior recognizes warrior, Sir Denby. Approach both with the respect due their evident skill, not suspicion born of unfamiliarity. Sir Roland will be your charge. Lady Hélène will be kept busy elsewhere."

"Sir Roland's temperament shows him level-headed and reasonable," Alaric adds, his assessment carrying the certainty of observation. "Treat him accordingly."

The King's gaze sweeps across them and lands on Anselm. "Formal presentation comes at morning. Archbishop, inform our guests of their new identities immediately, then secure proper garments." He pauses, acknowledging the fiction they've constructed. "As family, you'll remain with them tonight."

Anselm nods, accepting both duty and burden. "Until morning, then. Silence and dignity."

The carefully laid plans settle around them like evening shadows.

Lady Hélène Montbois (Elaine Rush)

A young guard crouches before the fireplace striking flint. It only takes a few strikes for sparks to catch dry kindling and flames to begin their hesitant dance up the chimney. His companion maintains position near the door, eyes fixed on the siblings with a wariness that comes with someone accustomed to guarding fugitives.

Elaine surveys their quarters. The corridor entry opens to a modest sitting room with a fireplace. Towards the castle's outer wall extends two bedrooms with oversized windows and thick curtains. The accommodation speaks of careful hospitality rather than imprisonment, though the distinction feels speculative given their circumstances.

Old Earth. Elaine longs to peek out those windows. To see Earth as it was before industry crept in.

Roland settles into a winged back chair with unsettling ease, as though he's already accepted whatever fate medieval England might deliver. His shoulders carry none of the tension built in her own spine.

"There," the guard by the fireplace mutters, brushing soot from his hands. "Doing maids' work now, am I?"

His companion shifts toward the door. "Come. We'll wait outside."

The first guard gives Roland a curt nod of acknowledgment, warrior to warrior, while his gaze skips past Elaine entirely. The door closes and privacy settles around them at last.

Elaine examines her bodysuit beneath the borrowed cloak, fingers tracing the subtle material. Hairline fractures web across the wrist device, glowing dully in the firelight.

"Well, that's broken," she announces. "Five stars for dramatic timing."

Roland leans forward, extending his hand. "Let me see."

She moves closer, offering her arm for inspection. His fingers probe the device, testing response points that should illuminate but remain stubbornly dark.

"She's got a pulse but no brain," he mutters.

"Story of my life," Elaine drawls, though the humor feels forced in their current circumstances.

A sharp rap interrupts their examination of the device. Roland straightens as the door opens to admit a different guard—older, with weathered features and calculating eyes that miss nothing. Denby, she recalls, the same man who'd shared his cloak with her before they left the larger chamber. His thoughtful gesture then had spared them from *unwanted* stares.

"If you require food and water, then speak," he offers without preface.

"A map home would be great," Elaine quips. "Barring that, bread?"

The guard's mouth twitches, not quite a smile, but close. "Agnes", he commands to some unknown figure just outside the door. A woman appears, arms laden with fabric, her cheeks already blooming pink as she takes in their form fitting bodysuits.

"Sir Roland, for you." Agnes extends the trousers and tunic toward Adrian, determinedly fixing her gaze somewhere past his shoulder. The fabric trembles slightly in her grip as she pivots toward Elaine. "Miss, er, Lady Hélène, this will do until proper fittings."

Sir Roland. Lady Hélène. The names land like puzzle pieces clicking into place. Someone has already constructed their new identities.

"You are a saint," Elaine smiles, accepting the modest gown. "Please don't tell your saints what I was wearing."

Agnes's blush deepens, her eyes darting between the floor and Elaine's face while carefully avoiding Adrian altogether. The poor woman appears caught between propriety and fascination.

The older guard clears his throat pointedly. Agnes jolts, stepping backward toward the door, with a slight bow.

"Require you anything further?" he asks.

"We're well provided for, thank you," Roland answers.

The guard gives them both a curt nod. Respectful, measuring, equal. Elaine notes the courtesy. Unlike the younger guards who'd dismissed her entirely, this one acknowledges her as something more than decoration. The recognition feels unexpectedly valuable.

The door closes again, leaving them with new clothes and new names in a world that operates by rules they're still learning.

Elaine fingers the rough wool of the borrowed gown, testing its weight against her palm. The fabric speaks of sheep and rain and lives lived without climate control.

"Roland. Hélène," Adrian says quietly, rolling each syllable with deliberate care.

"*Ay-LEHN,*" she repeats, letting the French pronunciation settle on her tongue. "Sounds like a girl who knows which fork to use."

"You'll learn." His voice carries dry humor mixed with authority. "We both will."

They sink into chairs facing each other, the fire crackling between them like a third presence. Fireplaces have been long outdated on Earth. The open fires too unpredictable in cramped spaces. While the Mars settlements only see flames in labs.

The escape replays behind Elaine's eyes. The Grey Hunter's impossible speed, their accidental tumble though time, then their target vanishing with their only key home.

"He's loose with a band," Adrian states. "And we're playing catch with a mitt that's split."

Useless anger flickers through her. Their only equipment lies broken on her forearm and the unsanctioned time travel makes their location known only to the enemy.

"Then we stop throwing," she replies. "We survive."

Adrian nods once, sharp and decisive. "Rules of engagement: No tech talk, minimal future references, fight only if cornered."

"No spoilers," Elaine adds. "We're tourists who lost the bus."

"Correction." His mouth quirks. "We're locals who hate directions."

The sibling humor surfaces between them. Familiar language in an alien world. She grins despite everything, feeling the first solid ground beneath her feet since they landed here.

The firelight catches Adrian's blue eyes as silence settles between them. Elaine studies his features. The curly black hair short on the edges and slightly longer on top. The jawline that sets when he's calculating probabilities. The slight furrow that appears when he's weighing worst-case scenarios.

"What scares you most?" she asks quietly.

"Getting you killed."

"Wrong answer." She leans forward, elbows on knees, her hazel eyes catching his as she waits for a truer response.

He considers this, fingers drumming against the chair arm. "Watching you disappear into someone else's century. Losing Elaine to Lady Hélène."

The admission hits deeper than she expected. "If I fade here, remember me as loud."

"You don't fade," Adrian answers without hesitation. "You take up whole rooms."

She grins, but the fear has already taken up residence within her: losing Adrian to Sir Roland. They need protocols, anchors to keep them tethered to who they are.

"Hand signals," he decides, as if reading her mind. "Three fingers: retreat. Two: stall. One: lie."

"One finger is also universal," she states with a smirk.

"Please don't use that one at dinner," Adrian says, his mouth twitching.

The familiar banter continues to steady them. Whatever comes next, they'll face it as themselves, just wearing different names.

Another knock interrupts their planning. This time, the door admits Archbishop Anselm, his heavy ecclesiastical robes barely rustling as his tall and slender figure enters. The firelight catches the pectoral cross at his chest, transforming it into a constellation of jewels.

"Your Grace," Adrian rises. They both trade respectable nods.

Anselm settles into the remaining chair with the careful movements of a man who's spent long hours in council chambers. His dark and old eyes study them. Calculating, measuring, deciding what truths to share in the next moment, and what not to share.

He begins without overture. "You are my distant cousins from La Brousse, a remote holding in southwestern France. Your father, Lord Montbois, died years ago and your mother recently perished in a fever, leaving you to my care as your mother's kinsman. You've journeyed here seeking royal favor and church protection."

He pauses for a moment, allowing the details to sink in.

"You will present to court as Sir Roland of Montbois and Lady Hélène Montbois, his sister. Sir Roland is a skilled knight. For this, he will primarily remain with the guard. Lady Hélène will undergo etiquette training, before debuting to court. She cannot be seen associating with the guards."

A flicker of unease passes through Elaine at the prospect of separation from Adrian in this alien place. Adrian catches her expression and shakes his head slightly.

Elaine nods, filing away the details. Simple backstory, hard to verify, easy to remember. Good operational security, assuming anyone here understands the concept of operational security.

"How much is based in truth?" she asks, "How much is convenience?"

"Necessity breeds convenience," Anselm replies smoothly. "Your arrival... the timing coincides with illness ravaging French countrysides. Sir Roland is the sole member left in a distant family of lower noble standing. So, providence too, perhaps."

Adrian's brow furrows with that familiar intensity he gets when parsing intelligence reports for gaps and contradictions. "We're grateful for His Majesty's hospitality. Please convey our thanks."

"You may do so yourself tomorrow morning. The King plans formal introductions during court processions, before speculation takes root."

Elaine thinks of Ralf's wide stares and Agnes's curious glances at their strange attire.

"What about our clothes?" she asks. "Pretty sure bodysuits aren't standard noble wear here."

"The maid, Agnes, will return at dawn to dress you appropriately. I shall assist Sir Roland." Anselm's gaze shifts between them. "Court attire carries its own language. Best you speak it fluently."

Adrian turns toward her with a particular expression only reserved for her. Part brotherly affection, part drill sergeant patience.

"Elaine." Her real name sounds strange in this firelit room. "Repeat the story back to me. And remember, noble English lady. Keep your tongue where it belongs."

The gentle rebuke carries years of shared operations, missions where a wrong word could shatter careful covers. She straightens, adopting the posture she hopes passes for aristocratic bearing.

"Lady Hélène of Montbois, recently orphaned, seeking royal protection under Archbishop Anselm's guidance." She pauses. "How's my accent?"

Needs work," Adrian admits. "But you'll manage."

Elaine turns back to Anselm, curious about the faces they'll meet tomorrow. "What can you tell us of the royal family and the nobles at court?"

"The royal family consists of the young King Alaric and his mother, Queen Dowager Margaret. King Edward, god rest his sole, passed four years ago. As for the nobles, that is a longer discussion best stayed for another time."

Anselm rises, smoothing his robes. "To bed, *cousins*. Lady Hélène, the right chamber. Sir Roland, the left. I shall keep watch here."

"Thank you, Your Grace. Good night, Hélène." Adrian rises and retreats to the designated room with no further glances at her. His soldier nature taking root.

The formal use of her cover name feels like a gentle reminder that they're already becoming other people. She retreats toward the designated room, pausing at the threshold.

"Good night, Roland."

The door closes behind her, leaving her alone with medieval darkness and the weight of tomorrow's performance.

New Beginnings

- 3 -

Archbishop Anselm of Clearvale

The Great Hall stretches before them like a tapestry come to life, its soaring arches framing clusters of England's finest blood. Lords arrange themselves in careful hierarchies, their woolen surcoats rich with gold and silver threads that catch the morning light streaming through the eastern lancet windows. Ladies gather in fine silk, their gowns speaking languages of alliance and ambition through every embroidered vine, every pearl-sewn crest. Each stitch in their gowns and surcoats carry meaning. Family histories written in silver thread, political loyalties declared through the cut of a sleeve.

Anselm observes the siblings from his position near the dais, noting how their borrowed finery sits upon them like armor hastily donned. Roland's hair is shorter than usual, but the dark tunic and understated surcoat will pass inspection easily enough as continental restraint reads as noble dignity. But Hélène presents a more delicate challenge. While the medium length curly hair can be managed into a feminine bun, Agnes had wisely avoided forcing her into a stay, knowing that particular torment requires practiced bodies. The resulting silhouette carries a foreign looseness that Anselm prays will pass as continental country fashion rather than suspicious court ignorance.

The assembled court watches with the predatory patience of experienced courtiers. Whispers ripple through silk and wool as speculation takes root. Anselm lifts his crosier, and silence washes over the hall.

"My lords and ladies, your patience. Truth prefers a calm ear." His voice carries the capable authority of decades spent managing both souls and politics.

"I present Sir Roland of Montbois and his sister, Lady Hélène Montbois. They are of my blood from La Brousse, a quiet province many of you have never trod. God rest their parents, lost on the mainland to illness."

He sees Lord Ranulf's sharp attention, Lady Cecily's measuring gaze, and the way Lady Isolde nods with quiet approval. Then the French plague serves its purpose. Murmurs of sympathy replace suspicious whispers as grief becomes the explanation for their foreignness, their timing, their need for sanctuary.

Roland steps forward to his side with a soldier's exactness, his bow striking the perfect balance between respect and nobility. Hélène follows with a curtsy that satisfies protocol, not graceful, but adequate for a country noblewoman of humbler birth.

"Your Majesties, your welcome honors us." Her voice carries a controlled steadiness that Anselm finds reassuring.

King Alaric sits the throne in a deep blue velvet surcoat that brings out the light blue eyes set amongst wavy sand blonde hair. He receives them with his usual grace for all foreign visitors, the royal endorsement calculated to appear as if their presence was expected and to close any remaining questions.

"Kin of the Archbishop are kin of the Crown. Be at ease in my hall."

Anselm motions to the siblings to step off to the side with him. He watches the court's reactions. The subtle relaxation of shoulders, the way conversations resume their normal cadence. The performance has succeeded. Whatever strange circumstances brought these siblings to England, they are now part of the realm's fabric, woven into its story as foreign refugees under church and royal protection.

Yet beneath his relief, Anselm feels the weight of deeper questions. Time itself seemed to fracture in that council chamber. Whatever truth lies behind their arrival, it will require more than clever fiction to contain.

But just as quickly as sand puts out a fire, grease can ignite it again. The court's current leading lady, Lady Eveline Artois, a woman slightly younger than Elaine with golden tresses and blue eyes, leans toward her mother, Lady Cecily Artois, with a voice pitched to carry.

"Their French sounds... curious. Is that how they speak in La Brousse?"

Before the whisper can spread, Anselm intercedes with practiced ease. "Borders breed patois. What is odd is often merely old."

He watches relief flicker across Roland's stoic features while Hélène's jaw tightens at another lady's pointed observation about her hastily pinned hair.

"Strange visitors were seen last night," calls Lord Miles from within the crowd. He stretches his stout and short figure slightly like a peacock stretching its feathers. "Escorted by guards under cloaks not French, they say. There was fighting—"

"Indeed they arrived," Anselm interjects smoothly. "Unfortunately, their escort proved false. Attacking His Majesty under pretense of aid."

Lord Reginald steps forward. Old he may be but his dark hair and eyes barely betray his age. "I saw Sir Roland risk life for crown and my heir before I knew his name."

Lord Geoffrey, the younger image of his father, places slightly trembling hands to bandages at his throat as he adds, "Aye, steel and nerve both." Though Anselm is not sure whether the tremble is show, or if the lad still suffers with his encounter with death.

Gasps ripple through silk and wool. Queen Dowager Margaret rises from her place at Alaric's right with a stately grace. Where her son's features are light, hers are darker and clearly aged by the duties of a monarch.

"You have acted with great courage, Sir Montbois. The crown owes you a debt of gratitude."

The court's suspicion transforms into reluctant respect as the King rises and nods to Roland. But Anselm knows the court is fickle.

Roland responds with an equal nod, giving Anselm the out he needs to guide the siblings away from the center and into the hall's careful choreography.

"Come, *cousins*. There are faces to greet, bonds to forge."

He steers them toward Sir Edric Stone, a knight of Roland's years whose discretion last night earned Anselm's trust. The similarity in age might spark natural conversation, and Sir Stone's witness to the chamber fight makes him an ally worth cultivating.

Sir Stone greets Roland with soldierly directness, but his voice carries too clearly across the flagstones. "Your methods last night. Never seen their like. Will you share them with the guard?"

Anselm winces inwardly as conversations pause around them. Roland's response carries careful diplomacy.

"If His Majesty wishes it, I'll teach what I may." Sir Denby materializes by Sir Stone with a look that demands silence.

Before Anselm can redirect the discussion, the court parts as Queen Dowager Margaret approaches from Hélène's left, her royal steps commanding absolute attention. She stops precisely distant enough to assess without obligation, her sharp gaze cataloguing Hélène's posture and restrained bearing.

A subtle nod signals provisional approval before she steps closer. "We prosper when guests learn our customs, and when we learn theirs."

The Queen withdraws as swiftly as she approached, leaving the siblings barely time for proper reverence. Anselm notes the calculated brevity. Acknowledgment without commitment, acceptance without warmth.

The Queen's withdrawal creates the perfect opening. With all eyes tracking her stately exit, Anselm seizes the moment.

"Come."

He guides the siblings toward the center of the hall, their footsteps barely heard on the flagstones as conversations resume around them. Before the throne, they execute proper reverence to King Alaric. Roland's bow crisp, Hélène's curtsy adequate.

"Your Majesty, with your leave, I would see our guests settled before the day's demands claim us all." Anselm's request underpins the need to remove the siblings from prying eyes and curious questions.

Alaric inclines his head in royal blessing. "Of course, Archbishop. Let them find comfort in our hospitality. Quarter them in Lord Miles old chambers."

Anselm thanks the King for his hospitality and steers them toward the hall's great doors, his pace brisk but dignified. Behind them, he hears fresh speculation blooming like weeds. Lady Eveline's voice already picking apart Hélène's accent and curtsy, and a young noble interrogating Sir Stone over Roland's fighting methods.

The diplomatic chambers offer blessed sanctuary. Anselm pauses only long enough to ensure their immediate needs are met.

"The day is long and tongues are longer. We shall speak again when we have bread and rest."

The door closes behind him, leaving the siblings to navigate the murmurs of court as their story unfolds.

Sir Roland of Montbois (Adrian Rush)

Roland adjusts the unfamiliar weight of Geoffrey's gifted surcoat. A fine wool that will speak of royal favor without shouting it. The man, near his own age, had arrived at midday bearing garments as royal gifts. He remained to provide patient instruction on surcoat lacings, how to fasten points properly, which colors suited formal audiences, and the subtle language of sleeve length and trim.

It had been two days since their introduction to court, and Archbishop Anselm had spent every meal with them, *his cousins*. Anselm had left after the morning meal, promising to return with court notes for their review. Just as Geoffrey departed for the early evening court festivities, Agnes arrived bearing a letter from Anselm containing the promised notes. She'd also come with instructions to prepare them for dinner with the Their Majesties. A prospect that sets Roland's nerves on edge.

"Ah, from my cousin." He inclines his head toward Agnes as he takes the folded parchment. "My thanks."

Roland unfolds the letter with choreographed reverence. Playing the grateful cousin requires effort. His jaw tightens at the elaborate church seal. He was never a fan of the future's version of the Church, but Anselm shows a combination of wisdom and empathy that keeps them under protection, instead of imprisonment.

The parchment reveals Anselm's meticulous intelligence: a roster of nobles with their allegiances, feuds, and appetites. Below that, a seating chart dense with arrows and annotations, mapped like a battlefield. Roland commits names to memory, weighing each threat against their fragile cover. Lord Ranulf of Morcar's hawk-eyed loyalty; he'll scent something amiss and pry. Lord Elias Devereux's French ear, apt to test their accent, though more salon than countryside. Lord Percival of Dunmere's idle flirtations; likely to fixate on Hélène unless firmly steered. Lord Miles of Faversham's anti-French gossip; he'll brand missteps as 'continental oddities.' Lord Cedric of Langmere's peacock vanity; he'll resent Roland as marriage-market competition and dismiss Hélène for her lower noble birth. And Lady Eveline's vulture eye for protocol breaches; she'll pounce on every fumbled curtsy, every misplaced fork, turning Hélène's smallest missteps into her choicest gossip.

Across their shared quarters, Agnes works with adept efficiency, pinning Elaine's sleeves while murmuring gentle corrections about posture. Hélène, he corrects himself, no longer Elaine. The maid's loyalty runs deeper than duty; Roland sees it in how she shields his sister from curious glances in the halls, deflects awkward questions with seamless redirection. At least Geoffrey's preparation of Roland's attire spared Agnes the embarrassment of aiding Sir Montbois directly. Roland considers whether he should request a manservant, then dismisses the thought. He may not be of high enough birth to warrant his own manservant, and his fineries are not nearly as demanding as Hélène's.

"Arms up, my lady. Now breathe shallow." Agnes slips a boned contraption over Hélène's head and undergarment.

"Is bending optional?" Hélène's voice inquires. "I thought the deadly corset happened later in fashion."

"What do you mean my Lady. This is a stay. It will not harm you, I promise. Just keep you upright."

Roland keeps his eyes fixed on the parchment as Hélène picks at the contraption and mutters something that would earn stares in any century. Agnes, no longer phased by Hélène's language choices, works with deftness, layering linen, boning, and wool like armor.

The pronunciation drill has become ritual the past few days. And their last anchor to who they really are before donning medieval masks. Roland clears his throat. "Roland. Hélène."

"*ay-LEHN.*" Her voice comes out irritated as Agnes cinches another lace. "If I forget, elbow me... gently."

Through the rustling chaos, Roland studies Anselm's notes. Lord Geoffrey rates a star. *Reliable, bookish, no political ambition.* Roland finds himself almost smiling. Roland weighs Anselm's review against his own. Geoffrey has a restraint coupled with authentic kindness and a straightforward approach that is most refreshing after the court's elaborate rituals. Geoffrey might serve them well.

"Nearly finished," Agnes announces, though Hélène's grunt suggests otherwise.

Agnes steps back, surveying her work with the critical eye of a master craftsman. "There. Now sit, my lady. We must do something with this hair."

She guides Hélène to the vanity stool, fingers already assessing the damage. "Blessed saints, what happened here? The length, these layers. As if a child took shears to it."

Hélène rolls her eyes. "Something like that."

Roland crosses to her, extending Anselm's carefully annotated list. "Study this while Agnes works. Names, allegiances, what to avoid. Memorize by dinner."

" 'Your Majesty' for the King and Queen Dowager," he begins, settling into instructor mode. " 'Your Grace' for the Archbishop. Bow first, speak second."

"And breathe third?" Hélène's voice carries that familiar edge of sarcasm.

Roland's mouth quirks despite himself. Agnes continues her work with swift perfection, combing and pinning with the kind of speed that speaks to years of practice. Hélène scans the parchment, lips moving silently as she commits names to memory.

"Lord Ranulf. Suspicious of outsiders," she murmurs. "Lord Elias. French speaker, potential ally or trap." Her eyes continue down the list. "This Percival sounds like a real winner."

Agnes's hands pause in their work. "I don't know what a winner sounds like, my lady, but best stay clear of that one."

Hélène's laugh comes sharp and genuine. "Oh, I've dealt with his type before. Usually with a knee to the—"

"Elaine." Roland's voice cuts through her words like a blade, accompanied by a look that could freeze fire. *Act the part.*

Her grin doesn't fade, "It's Hélène." She resumes her review, though Roland catches the maid's suppressed laughter.

"Do you remember the table manners from basics?" Roland asks, choosing his words with care. No mention of timelines or training protocols in front of Agnes.

"Every tedious lesson." Hélène shifts as Agnes works around a particularly stubborn section. "Though I mostly passed by following others' lead."

"Good strategy," Roland concedes. "You'll need it tonight. You'll be sitting in close proximity to the Queen."

He hands her the seating chart, watching her expression shift as she absorbs the arrangement. Seven people total. A mercy, considering the alternatives.

"Small gathering," she observes.

"All who know our... circumstances," Roland confirms. "Or should know them. The Queen Dowager's awareness remains to be confirmed, but I pray she'll prove understanding of any... adjustments needed."

Agnes takes to the moment to assure Hélène that the Queen Dowager takes court etiquette seriously and ensures the necessary tutoring for visiting nobles.

Hélène nods, fingers tracing the seating positions. Roland hopes their combined preparation will suffice for the evening ahead.

Agnes's hands move to the bodice, holding up an elaborate piece worked with gilt threads and small gems that catch the candlelight like tiny stars.

Hélène eyes the ornamentation with obvious skepticism. "That's... quite the statement piece."

"Too right, you are," Agnes huffs, already reaching for a plainer alternative. The second bodice bears simple silver work. Elegant without shouting its worth.

"Much better," Hélène says, genuine relief in her voice. "Perfect for reclusive nobility."

Agnes nods approvingly as she fastens the understated piece. "This says 'born to a quiet chapel,' not 'bought in a noisy market.'"

"Bless the chapel," Hélène murmurs.

Roland seizes the moment for final preparation. "If they press about La Brousse?"

"We answer little and ask much," Hélène recites. "Listeners love themselves."

She leans closer, voice dropping to a whisper. "When in doubt, smile like the translation failed."

Roland's mouth quirks, "And if that fails, I'll pretend it did."

Roland walks over to the window, noting that the nearly set sun heralds Anselm's imminent arrival. Roland's fear of losing themselves entirely to this past creeps up again. He brushes the thought away to focus on the task at hand. They need to wrap up this session before dinner.

Roland turns back to his sister and extends his hand, fingers positioned precisely. "Two fingers—stall. Three—retreat."

Hélène mirrors the gesture, though her smile carries that familiar wicked edge. "One finger—don't tempt me."

"Keep the French simple and slow," Roland continues, ignoring her attempt at levity. "Better to seem thoughtful than stumble over complex phrases."

The humor fades from Hélène's expression. She drops her voice, vulnerability creeping through the practiced confidence. "One sentence can break a life here. His life, if we're exposed." She recognizes the risk that Anselm takes in sheltering them.

Roland's stern mask softens at her genuine fear. "Then we speak in half-sentences."

Agnes steps forward, her hands still busy with final adjustments to Hélène's sleeves. "If I may, my lady. We notice kindness and shoes. The rest is lace."

The wisdom draws a grateful nod from Hélène, who seems to steady under the maid's practical counsel. "Then fetch the kindest shoes."

A soft knock interrupts them. "My cousins?" Anselm's voice carries through the heavy wood.

Roland squares his shoulders, feeling the weight of Geoffrey's borrowed doublet settle into place. The Archbishop enters with quiet his ecclesiastical dignity.

"Time?" Hélène asks, rising from the stool.

She attempts a curtsy. Deeper this time, more controlled. "How do I look?"

Agnes surveys her work with satisfaction. "Like you intend to survive."

Lord Ranulf of Morcar

Lord Ranulf of Morcar draws his woolen cloak tighter against the late February chill as he picks his way along the garden walks. The skeletal remains of last year's roses clutch at the stone borders like gnarled fingers, their thorns still sharp despite winter's grip. Not a bloom to be found. Fitting, considering the withered state of reliable information since his return from his estates.

"Cousins appear like mushrooms after rain," he mutters under his breath, his voice cutting through the brittle air. "I dislike mushrooms."

A week of whispered fragments has left him with an incomplete picture that rankles worse than the winter wind. French nobility materializing from nowhere. An Archbishop's sudden family. Guards murmuring about drawn swords and unseemly conduct from a woman who should know better. None of it sits properly in his mind, like a poorly fitted joint in fine carpentry.

He spots Lord Reginald's familiar figure near the herb garden's dormant beds, his fellow counselor's pace steady despite the treacherous patches of frost. Ranulf quickens his step, breath forming small clouds as he closes the distance.

"Reginald, my old friend." He declares with a friendly gesture.

The Lord of Redwyke turns, his slightly aged face showing neither surprise nor particular welcome. "Ranulf. Back from Morcar, I see."

"Indeed." Ranulf falls into step beside Reginald, noting how Reginald's shoulders adjusted into an unfamiliar tension with his greeting. "I've been hearing the most peculiar stories. French cousins, sudden arrivals, unseemly disturbances. What insights might the Chancellor provide the Justiciar?"

Reginald's pace doesn't alter, but his jaw tightens almost imperceptibly. "Court life continues in your absence. Little changes."

"An attacker slipping through with their entourage suggests otherwise." Ranulf keeps his tone conversational, though his eyes remain sharp on Reginald's profile. "And reports of the lady herself taking up arms. Surely you witnessed this impropriety firsthand."

"The nobleman, yes." Reginald's response comes measured, careful. "The woman, no."

The stark contradiction to the kitchen gossip sends Ranulf's suspicion climbing higher. Reginald's reputation for precision makes such discrepancies noteworthy.

"Yet they merited a private dinner with Their Majesties." Ranulf probes deeper, watching for tells. "Curious hospitality for distant relations of questionable circumstances."

Reginald pauses at a stone bench, though he doesn't sit. "The royal family takes pity in their story. The Queen Dowager holds particular fondness for the Archbishop. Providing support to the only family Anselm has left shows proper Christian charity."

The explanation sounds rehearsed, polished smooth by repetition. Ranulf files this observation away.

"You attended this dinner with Geoffrey." He states, doesn't ask.

"We did."

"And how did they comport themselves? These mysterious Montbois?"

Reginald's gloved hands clasp behind his back. "Quiet and polite enough. Most table talk concerned winter granaries and preparing for spring planting."

Reginald's evasiveness cuts against years of shared counsel and mutual respect. The man who once dissected treaty language with surgical precision now offers platitudes about charity and granaries. Something fundamental has shifted.

"Spring brings fresh concerns," Reginald's deflection to another topic chafes Ranulf's conscious. "Princess Ysabel's arrival will demand considerable preparation. A Spanish princess requires careful protocol."

Ranulf doesn't accept this new venture, instead doubling down on the Montbois siblings. "La Brousse. Where does this appear on any decent map?"

"On roads where couriers do not race."

The cryptic response only deepens Ranulf's suspicion. He presses forward, sensing something possibly foul beneath the surface.

"Their French carries odd inflections. Foreign courts train actors well. A *patois* can be learned as easily as a lie."

Reginald's grey eyes flash with something approaching warning. "And mistrust quicker than both."

His longtime friend's rebuke lands sharp, but Ranulf's instincts have caught scent now. Something rotten lurks beneath this performance.

"The Archbishop's word carries weight." Reginald's voice hardens with caution. "If you pull one thread, my lord, you may find the tapestry at your feet."

Ranulf feels the friendly caution in Reginald's warning, but he doesn't intend to stand down where the safety of the Crown is concerned. "The Crown must remain beyond manipulation, Chancellor. If they are harmless, truth will prove it. If not, I will."

Reginald's features show disappointment rather than anger. "Ask your questions in letters, not in halls. Public accusation without proof, here or in France, will force His Majesty's hand in ways that serve no one."

Reginald adjusts his cloak with deliberate precision. "I have ledgers to review before the day's vespers. Good day, Ranulf."

As Reginald's footsteps fade on the frosty stones, movement catches Ranulf's eye. Alice Whitcombe leans against the colonnade's carved rail above, her maid's headscarf askew as if she's been straining to catch their words. Their eyes meet briefly before she bustles away with exaggerated purpose.

"A mushroom hunt she'll have then," Ranulf mutters to the empty garden.

Ranulf strides toward the castle abbey, his boots clicking sharp against the flagstones. The familiar weight of suspicion settles in his chest like winter fog. Thick, persistent, obscuring clear sight but impossible to ignore.

The cloister walk stretches before him, its covered arches providing shelter from the bitter wind as clerks and clergy bustle through the connected offices. Brother Marcus hunches over his writing desk in the scriptorium's corner, quill scratching methodically across parchment. The monk's discretion has served Ranulf well in past correspondence requiring delicate phrasing.

"Brother Marcus." Ranulf's voice echoes softly under the stone arches. "I require your services for several letters."

The monk sets down his quill without question, pulling fresh parchment toward him. Years of practice have taught him when questions are unwelcome.

"Inquiries to ecclesiastical contacts in northern France," Ranulf continues, settling onto the wooden stool beside the desk. "About a family name: Montbois, from La Brousse."

Brother Marcus dips his quill, waiting.

"Write as a friend," Ranulf instructs, watching ink pool at the nib's tip. "Casual mention in broader correspondence about regional families and their movements."

As the monk begins drafting, Ranulf's mind returns to Reginald's warning, to his friend's sudden tension and evasiveness. Something has changed and the truth will surface. It always does.

The Lady's Illness

- 4 -

Lady Hélène Montbois

The ceiling tilts like a ship caught in rough seas, stones swimming in lazy circles above Hélène's burning face. Her throat feels packed with hot sand, each breath scraping raw against her windpipe. The weight of woolen blankets presses down like lead, trapping heat that radiates from her skin in waves.

Days have passed since the royal dinner. Most were spent confined to her chambers, half spent staring longingly at the countryside through her bedroom windows and the other half studying etiquette books Archbishop Anselm provided. Proper addresses, court hierarchy, conversation subtleties. She was meant to have a proper tutor, later, but Anselm feared her severe lack of etiquette needed honing before releasing her into a tutor's care.

Now she struggles to recall anything clearly. Brief memories surface: leather volumes weighing her lap, quill scratching parchment as she practiced letters, Agnes bringing meals that cooled while Hélène memorized curtsy depths for nobility ranks., endless repetition of "Your Grace" and "My Lord" until words became meaningless sounds. All float through her consciousness like dream fragments.

Agnes's voice drifts from somewhere to her right, words floating through the thick air like bubbles rising to the surface of murky water.

"Does your castle list to starboard... or is that only my head?" Hélène's voice emerges as little more than a croak, barely recognizable as her own.

Cool fingers press against her forehead, followed by the blessed relief of damp linen across her brow. An elderly woman leans into view, her practical face creased with worry lines that seem deeper than they should be.

"Barley water, my lady." Agnes assists her weakened body into a sitting position and holds a wooden cup near her lips, a suffocating steam rising from its surface.

Hélène coughs and peers at the murky liquid with suspicion. "If it tastes as it sounds, tell it to be merciful."

The drink burns her throat going down, bitter and medicinal, but Agnes's gentle insistence proves impossible to resist. Each swallow feels like swallowing liquid fire, yet the warmth settles something restless in her chest.

"You were unawakenable all morning," Agnes murmurs, smoothing the blankets with practiced efficiency. "Sir Roland has gone in search of the Archbishop."

The words register dimly through the fever fog. Roland? No, Adrian. She begins to recall more as something important hovers just beyond her understanding, but exhaustion pulls her back toward darkness as she slips back under the covers into sleep's embrace.

The following days blur together in a haze of forced sips and Agnes's patient ministrations. Bone broth replaces barley water, marginally less offensive but still requiring coaxing. Between the gentle prodding to drink and the frequent replacement of sweat-soaked linens, Hélène catches glimpses of movement in the corner chair.

She wakes to a figure in that chair. Light blue silk catches afternoon sunlight streaming through the narrow window. An angel, surely, sent to watch over the dying. The figure's face remains indistinct, features swimming in and out of focus like reflections on troubled water.

"Did the Archbishop send you?" Hélène whispers during one lucid moment, her voice barely audible even to herself. "To take me home to Mars?"

The angel doesn't answer, but silk rustles softly in response as she slips back into dreams of orange-red landscapes and glass domes.

Finally, the room holds steady for the first time in days, walls maintaining their proper angles without the nauseating tilt that has plagued her fever dreams. Hélène sits propped against pillows, the wooden cup warming her palms as she sips the barley water with something approaching tolerance rather than resignation.

She's fully alert, but her body aches in places she'd forgotten existed. Joints protesting every small movement, muscles tender as fresh bruises. The future's advanced immunologies had made such common ailments nearly extinct, leaving her unprepared for what Agnes calls "winter's bite." Roland's earlier explanation to Archbishop Anselm echoes through her memory, his voice tight with barely concealed worry as he assured the prelate she would survive this medieval plague.

"Advanced immunologies," he'd said, the phrase meaningless to Anselm but carrying the weight of centuries of medical progress. The Archbishop's genuine concern had been endearing, his hands clasped as he offered prayers for her recovery. Agnes had eventually shooed them both away, grumbling about men cluttering the sick room and giving the lady no peace to mend.

A gentle knock interrupts her musings. The door opens to reveal a young woman with kind eyes and a graceful gait, her silks somehow familiar though Hélène cannot place from where.

"If you allow, I could read something soothing."

The voice carries the hint of a French accent, different from the one she and Roland pretend to have. The woman holds a leather-bound book against her chest, her smile tentative but genuine.

"If it ends happily, read it twice." Hélène manages a weak smile of her own, then frowns. "Forgive me, I fear my memory has gone wandering with my wits. Have we met?"

"I am the Archbishop's Angel. Lady Isolde."

The words float through the air with gentle humor, and it takes a moment for their meaning to penetrate the lingering fog in Hélène's mind. The blue silked angel in her dreams. Then she recalls her fleeting comment about Mars. The memories of her old home rush in: orange-red dust, thin atmosphere, the gleaming domes of the colonies beneath alien skies.

She tries to sit upright, but the movement nearly sends the room into a cartwheel. "The floor is persuasive today."

Soft hands steady her shoulders, guiding her back against the pillows with surprising strength. "Then we will not argue with it."

Isolde settles into the chair beside the bed and opens her book. Her voice weaves through a tale of knights and fair maidens, courtly love and grand gestures, but Hélène finds herself interrupting with observations that would make no sense in this world.

"Does the fair maiden never wonder if her knight has checked his horse's maintenance schedule?" she interjects during a particularly flowery passage about midnight rides. "Seems impractical, all this galloping about without proper logistics support."

Agnes snorts from across the room as she folds linens, "Perhaps, my Lady, there is a sonnet for 'shut up and drink your broth'?"

"I'll compose one at once," Isolde replies, her eyes twinkling with mirth.

"I see I am ruining you both."

A gentle laughter blooms in the room, but as the laughter fades, a different weight settles over the room. Hélène studies Isolde's face, noting the careful neutrality that speaks of court training.

"What do they whisper about us, my brother and I? We must provide ample fodder for court tongues."

Isolde gently folds the book over in her lap, her fingers tracing its leather binding. "They whisper because they are dull and you are not. But, please, do not let this upset you. Difference can be a kind of light in places grown too used to shadows."

"If I am to be a candle, pray someone teaches me not to set the curtains ablaze."

Isolde gives another warm smile and continues reading her knight's tale. Eventually, exhaustion creeps back like tide returning to shore, pulling Hélène toward the edges of consciousness. Her thoughts drift back to places of dry, red earth and thin, bright skies where two suns painted the horizon in shades of copper and gold. The word escapes as barely a whisper: "Mars."

Isolde leans forward, curiosity flickering in her eyes. "You have traveled far."

Hélène summons strength for one last deflection, grinning despite her weariness.

"Far enough to miss your rain," she yawns then pulls herself back underneath the covers, "and your blankets."

The room grows soft around the edges, afternoon light blurring into warm honey. Hélène's eyelids flutter as consciousness slips away.

"Lady Hélène?"

Isolde's voice sounds distant, muffled by the returning fever fog.

Hélène manages a drowsy smile. "*ay-LEHN* ...and the 'lady' can take a holiday till I stop swimming."

Isolde closes the book gently, her smile the last clear thing Hélène sees before exhaustion claims her completely.

"I will come again tomorrow, *ay-LEHN*."

Hélène murmurs, "Bring a fierce heroine, and a larger cup."

Before Isolde reaches the door, Hélène drifts back into dreams of orange-red dust and alien horizons.

Sir Roland of Montbois

The corridor's stone feels cold against Roland's back as he waits outside the King's personal antechamber, a door down from the Council Chamber they *arrived* in. It has been six days since, mostly spent under Geoffrey's patient coaching on courtly address and Anselm's lessons in medieval diplomacy, both of which have worn thin. The formal request to share his 'methods' with the guard sits heavy in his mind. Stone's invitation during their introduction provides the perfect excuse, though Roland suspects the knight meant it more as courtesy than genuine offer.

The door opens with a soft creak as Sir Denby steps out the antechamber. "His Majesty grants your request, Lord Montbois."

Denby's indifferent face shows no surprise, though Roland catches the slight emphasis on his title. Geoffrey counseled that his title would be "Sir" to indicate his status as a French knight. But Denby's use of his more formal title insinuates that the elderly guard captain is not yet ready to accept him as a fellow knight. Through the gap, he glimpses Alaric bent over parchments, quill scratching steadily. Their eyes meet briefly across the chamber. The King's nod is almost imperceptible. Acknowledgment, perhaps approval.

"The training yard awaits your... methods." Denby retreats into the antechamber, then pauses. "Can you find your own way? The King requires my attention for the armory tallies."

Roland inclines his head. "Of course."

The corridors stretch before him, finally free of the constant escort that has shadowed his every move. Staff and nobles alike pause in their tasks, curious stares following his path. He moves calmly with a straight back and face forward, his peripherals cataloguing exits and passages from habit.

Soft footsteps echo behind him, trying and failing at stealth. Roland stops without turning. "Thomas Loxley."

A sharp intake of breath, then silence.

"The King mentioned your... curiosity about foreign training methods."

Shuffling feet, then a voice cracking with adolescent embarrassment. "I meant no offense, my lord."

Without turning, Roland orders the eager youth. "Guide me to the training yard. Show me these servant passages I keep hearing whispered about. Then perhaps I will show you my... methods."

Excitement overtakes mortification. "Yes, my lord! This way. There's a passage through the kitchens that cuts past the armory, and another by the stables that—"

Roland follows the boy's eager chatter, memorizing each turn and shortcut. Information is survival, even in a castle that shelters them.

The training yard spreads before them, packed earth and sand scarred by countless drills. Sir Stone straightens from adjusting a practice post, his dust marked face breaking into something approaching a grin.

"Sir Montbois." Stone approaches with unhurried steps and a friendly smile. "Been wondering when you'd grace us with your presence. The lads have been curious about these... foreign methods."

A cluster of guards pause their own exercises, wooden wasters hanging loose in their grips. Their smirks carry the weight of a soldier's skepticism.

"Will he show us how to bow a man to death?" one jests, just loud enough to carry.

Roland's expression remains level. "I prefer he walks away unbloodied... and remembers not to try again."

The yard quiets, expectant tension replacing casual mockery. Roland's gaze shifts to the wooden wasters stacked against the armory wall, then nods toward Thomas. "Fetch those practice weapons."

More guards drift closer, forming a loose circle. The morning sun catches on mail and leather as they settle into watchful positions.

"Wooden wasters, no blades," Roland announces, his voice carrying across the yard. "Learn balance before cuts. Steel is the last answer, not the first."

"You." Roland points to the burliest guard, a thick-shouldered man whose leather jerkin strains across his chest. "Stand there."

The guard's confident gait speaks volumes. Scars cross his knuckles. Earned, not gifted.

"Charge me with your waster. Close quarters, as you would in a real fight."

Scattered laughter ripples through the circle. The burly guard grins, hefting his wooden blade.

"What'll you hold for defense, my lord?"

Roland spreads his hands, empty. "Nothing."

The mockery grows bolder. Someone whistles. Another mutters about foreign foolishness.

The guard lunges one step forward with waster raised—

Roland pivots on his heel, hips turning with left hand catching the back of the man's shoulder. Momentum and gravity become Roland's friend as the burly man continues to launch forward, chest over feet. The man loses balance and meets packed earth with a surprised grunt.

Silence blankets the yard.

Roland extends his hand. "You may have the ground back, ser."

Movement catches his peripheral vision of figures in the battlements above. Alaric leans against stone, Denby beside him with crossed arms. Geoffrey's animated gesturing suggests fascination rather than concern.

The guard accepts Roland's assistance, brushing dust from his jerkin. "How?"

"You do not lift your opponent. You borrow his stride." Roland demonstrates the shoulder grip, the pivot point where balance shifts. "A grip becomes a wheel and that wheel becomes the earth taking your enemy."

Geoffrey's delighted voice drifts down from above. "A scholar's brawl!"

Three more knights step forward, eager to understand the parry technique. Roland continues the lesson, one by one, showing how to perform the technique and how to recognize and counter it.

Roland continues training the line of soldiers, adjusting stances and demonstrating pivots, and more than a few sending Roland to meet the ground. The King steps into formation, bringing Denby with him.

"Your Majesty joins the line?" Stone's question carries no surprise, as if kings belong in training yards, not council chambers.

Alaric rolls his shoulders, working loose the tension of morning audiences. "Lord Montbois promises honesty. I require proof."

"The, er, pivot's simpler than it appears," Denby murmurs to Alaric. "Clean footwork and an honest grip, nothing more."

"Clean and honest wins wars," Alaric replies quietly.

Roland catches their exchange, barely audible over the sound of another guard meeting the packed earth. He gestures for the next man, or rather, boy.

"Loxley, your turn."

Thomas steps forward, wooden waster trembling in his grip and determination writ across his face. Roland adjusts the boy's stance, noting how his shoulder barely reaches Roland's chest. He's too small to use the technique, but he can still learn to counter it. The first attempt sends Thomas stumbling sideways, off-balance and flustered, but he doesn't hit the ground right away.

"Again." Roland steadies him. "Your size can be an advantage, not weakness. Flow like water around stone. When I pivot, make me the stone and you the water."

The boy's determination blazes brighter than his fumbling footwork. He never quite gets it, but he's gained the respect of the guards nonetheless.

Now Alaric steps forward. Roland adjusts the King's stance, heel placement, and shoulder angle. "Feel the wheel before you make it."

Alaric nods. Roland lunges with wooden waster in hand, then Alaric executes a clean pivot that sends him tumbling to one knee. Applause erupts from the circle, genuine appreciation replacing earlier skepticism.

"By God, that felt honest," Alaric grins, extending his hand.

Roland accepts the assistance, brushing dust from his tunic. "Clean and honest. A… pair…. that travels far." Alaric's brow flickers, a sign that he understood the inference to the siblings.

A young guard rushes from behind without warning. Roland flows sideways, catches the charging wrist, guides the wooden waster from slack fingers, and twist the arm, forcing the guard to kneel. He's confused, but unharmed. A few guards laugh at the boy's failed brazenness while others bristle with appreciation.

"If you must come fast, come balanced."

The guard rubs his wrist, nodding. "Aye, my lord."

Roland continues the pattern. Adjust stance, demonstrate pivot, anticipate, guide the fall. The sand and packed earth become teachers, humbling pride while preserving bones. Murmurs shift around the training yard, mockery giving way to genuine interest. Guards mirror his movements, testing footwork and grips on each other between turns.

A grizzled sergeant with silver threading his beard steps forward. "Teach me the grip you used to disarm our foolish young guard, my Lord."

"Only if you promise to call me sir, not lord."

The sergeant's eyes widen a fraction, but his smile forms into an understanding. "Aye, Sir Montbois. Call me Sir Darly."

Roland demonstrates the hold. Firm but not crushing, positioned to guide rather than force. "Twice, then you teach the third."

The sergeant nods, absorbing each detail.

Geoffrey descends from the battlements, his scholar's eyes bright with fascination. He watches two guards practice the pivot, their movements growing smoother with repetition.

"They learn when their pride survives the lesson." Geoffrey grins, then lowers his voice. "Grant me a turn, but go easy, friend. These bones serve better whole than scattered."

Roland obliges, letting Geoffrey find his balance through three careful attempts. On the fourth, Geoffrey executes a clean throw that sends Roland to the sand. Surprised cheers erupt from the watching guards.

Alaric steps forward, having observed the growing enthusiasm. "Every third bell for those who wish to keep their bones where they belong."

The announcement draws nods and scattered approval. Roland inclines his head, accepting the training schedule.

"My thanks for the lesson, Sir Montbois," Sir Stone approaches as the crowd disperses. "I'm eager to work with you again." Roland notes how the title lord has been replaced by sir. The guard's approval of Roland's status as a knight.

The training yard begins to clear out. Roland retrieves his discarded tunic and begins his solemn trek back to his quarters when Geoffrey falls into step beside him.

"You fight like a miller and think like a clerk."

"Then let us grind flour and keep good accounts."

Geoffrey chuckles. "Sir Roland, if you'll allow me to address you as such, please join my father and I for supper in our chambers. I hear your sister is still ill, and I suspect you're in need of evening company."

"Aye, Lord Geoffrey. I will take you up on the offer."

Roland's mouth quirks upward. The first genuine smile he's given to anyone besides his sister since their arrival.

King Alaric

Stone ribs arch overhead, candlelight pooling gold across worn flagstones. The chapel breathes silence as carved saints watch from their alcoves, their eyes worn smooth by centuries of prayer. Alaric kneels before the altar, the cold seeping through his hose as he rests his weight against the low bench. Guards hold the heavy oak doors against visitors. Their orders clear: only the Archbishop passes.

"Lord, grant me counsel equal to my crown."

The words echo softly against the vaulted ceiling. Uncertainty burns warmer than any faith. These *future* strangers with their strange fighting and stranger smiles possibly masking deeper currents. Roland's unusual techniques spreading through his guards like ripples from a thrown stone, each man eager to learn what cannot be unlearned. Hélène's peculiar jests to staff and Isolde.

Footsteps approach, steady and familiar. Anselm's soft-soled boots whisper across the flagstones. His ecclesiastical robes sway lightly as he comes to a stop at Alaric's side. He does not bow in God's house, only inclines his head with the respect due a king who kneels as mortal man.

"You pray to Heaven, yet summon earth to answer."

Alaric rises, brushing dust from his knees. The Archbishop's aged face holds neither judgment nor jest, only the careful attention of a counselor who has guided crowns through darker uncertainties.

"Roland's methods take root faster than weeds after rain," Alaric says, turning from the altar. "Holt speaks of nothing else. Even Stone admits the techniques have merit."

He pauses, weighing words against the chapel's listening stones. "Yet Thomas tells me our French knight has shown curious interest in every passage below stairs. Kitchen routes, granary walks. Maps a man might draw if he meant to move unseen."

Anselm's fingers trace the jeweled cross at his chest, a gesture born of long habit when considering delicate truths. "Trust requires time to season. Their arrival bore too much strangeness for easy faith."

"If they mean ill, distance arms them. If they mean well, distance wastes them."

"Then keep them near and under candlelight." Anselm steps closer, his voice dropping to confessional quiet. "Suspicion is a tool. When it rules, it becomes a sin."

"Then let it serve."

The Archbishop nods slowly, understanding passing between them like shared prayer.

"Sir Denby watches them now. A shepherd, not gaoler. His eye catches what courtesy might miss. His silence yields what questions would scatter."

Candlelight wavers in the chapel's draft. Alaric studies the dancing shadows, seeing patterns in their restless movement. Dangerous guests who might prove salvation or ruin, depending on the hand that guides them.

"Court tongues wag about accents that sit strangely on French lips," Anslem says, voice carrying the weight of unpleasant observation. "Questions arise about lineage that lacks familiar threads."

Alaric's jaw tightens. He has heard the murmurs. Servants pausing mid-task when the Montbois siblings pass, nobles exchanging glances sharp as drawn steel. They were expecting this, but navigating it is different

"La Brousse's distance serves us well," Anselm continues, stepping closer to the altar. "The remoter the road, the older the tongue. We will let it be old."

"And Ranulf?" Alaric asks, though the answer already sits heavy in his chest. "He returned a fortnight ago. Ralf reports him asking after every detail of their arrival."

"More than asking." Anselm's fingers still on his cross. "He has pressed Reginald for particulars just yesterday, sought audience with me twice. This morning I intercepted his letters to French contacts. Inquiries about the Montbois line."

The King's breath catches. Each thread of deception spawns three more, a web growing beyond any weaver's design.

"I can respond for our French allies," Anselm offers quietly. "Men who remember old favors, distant kin lost to plague and war."

"Do it." The words come swift, though conscience pricks like winter wind through mail. "Keep this from growing beyond what was intended."

What was intended. The deception bothers more than expected.

"My people deserve honesty from their King," Alaric says, the words emerging low. He grips a pew hard, knuckles white against the wood. "Yet what honesty can I give them? That I shelter those whose very presence defies understanding? That I protect secrets I myself cannot fully grasp?"

The admission hangs between them like a thread pulled taught, waiting to snap or be released.

"Honesty does not mean haste, Sire. Prudent silence serves until truth can be measured." Anselm's tone carries no reproach, only the patient wisdom of a counselor who has shepherded kings through deeper waters.

"There are those who will sniff at every seam," he warns.

"Let them sniff, but in my presence, not behind my back." Alaric's voice carries the typical weight of a new kingship. "Any challenge to the Montbois will come to me first. I'll not have whispers in corridors undermining what I have sanctioned before the realm."

Anselm's fingers still against his cross, the dark jewels catching candlelight like trapped stars. His voice carries the calculated weight of a confessor broaching delicate counsel.

"Perhaps the Queen Dowager should join our confidence."

Alaric's brow furrows, the suggestion striking like cold water against heated metal. His mother's sharp eyes miss nothing, least of all the careful choreography required to maintain their fiction. The private royal dinner soon after the Montbois arrival should have sparked questions from her, but she has remained respectfully silent.

"I have served your mother under two reigns," Anselm continues, his tone carrying decades of earned trust. "Her loyalty to crown and realm runs deeper than suspicion. Even should she harbor doubts, respect for her son would seal her lips."

"Very well." The words come slowly, pulled from consideration already half-formed. "One less soul to deceive brings its own relief."

Relief and burden both. His mother's counsel would strengthen their hand, yet another mind must grasp impossibilities dressed as French nobility.

"Lady Hélène presents... complexities," Anselm says, choosing the word like a mason selecting stones. "Her wit follows strange channels, her manner too direct for courtly expectation. The Queen Dowager's guidance might smooth these edges."

Alaric shakes his head. He has not been much in Hélène's presence, but from what he's heard he cannot imagine his mother's carefully meted instruction pairing well with Hélène's unguarded tongue.

"Direct guidance from my mother would likely sharpen what needs tempering. Better Lady Isolde first. Her patience runs deeper, her touch lighter. Once Lady Hélène finds firmer footing, then my mother's hand."

"Wisdom in that approach." Anselm nods, then his expression softens with something approaching sympathy. "The fever that laid her low, it serves our purposes, though I find myself pitying her suffering."

"As do I." The admission carries unexpected weight. Something in the woman's struggle against both illness and circumstance stirs unwelcome concern. "Yet you speak truly. Her weakness bolsters whispers of plague-touched refugees fleeing French sorrows."

The chapel settles around them. Stone and shadow the best keepers for their conspiracy. Alaric straightens, his next decision settling in his chest like a sealed vow.

"Then let this be the Crown's word as well as the Church's. No mere convenience, but royal endorsement."

"Between crozier and crown, they may yet become what we have named them."

Alaric exhales slowly, the breath carrying weeks of uncertainty into the chapel's listening stones.

Bonds of Steel

- 5 -

Sir Roland of Montbois

The third bell tolls, and the training yard holds twice its usual number this evening. Roland counts heads as he sets down his practice stave. Guards who've traded skepticism for curiosity, knights drawn by whispers of strange technique, and there, blending among the rank-and-file like he belongs, King Alaric in a plain brown gambeson. No crown, no ceremony. Just another soldier seeking instruction.

"You keep your blade sheathed again today," Roland announces. "The only blood I want is pride."

Murmurs ripple through the assembled men. Those who witnessed his earlier demonstrations lean forward with genuine interest. Others hang back near the armory wall, arms crossed, waiting for spectacle or failure.

Roland draws a triangle in the sand with precise strokes, each point marking a stance. The geometry looks simple enough to fool most into believing it decoration.

"Footwork before fury," he says, stepping his weight into the first corner. "Feet think first, or your ribs will."

He demonstrates the sequence: heel, toe, pivot. The triangle becomes a map of movement, each point offering leverage the others cannot. Some guards nod recognition. Others frown at the foreign precision.

Sir Warin Holt steps forward from the crowd, his expression that of a man who's tested every new tactic that's crossed this yard for twenty years. The lead instructor's presence commands instant attention from the assembled guards.

"If I end on my back," Holt says, voice dry, "I'll borrow your hand up."

Roland meets his gaze with something approaching respect. The man stands willing to learn in front of his subordinates. No small courage for a veteran instructor.

"You'll have it, after your lesson."

Holt steps into the triangle's center, settling into a predator's crouch. His stance speaks decades of training: balanced, alert, ready for Roland's advance. The yard quiets, breath held.

Roland doesn't attack. Instead, he waits for Holt's first move. The moment comes as Holt commits his weight forward in a testing jab. Roland steps aside, one hand batting the waster to the side and the other catching the man's arm in a controlled grip behind his back. Holt's feet move on instinct, but his footing is already lost to some unknown force. His knees hit the ground, hard in surrender.

No violence, no struggle. Just physics dressed as combat.

The yard holds its silence for three heartbeats. Then Holt grins up from the ground. "Fair fall. Again."

Roland extends his hand as promised, hauling Holt to his feet. The gesture draws appreciative nods from the watching guards. Honor kept, lesson learned.

"Now the grip that teaches without breaking." Roland positions Holt's arm at a specific angle, fingers finding the joint where leverage lives. "Pain instructs. Gentleness convinces. We'll choose conviction."

He applies pressure, not enough to injure, just sufficient to demonstrate helplessness. Holt's feet shuffle involuntarily, seeking balance his captured joint will not allow.

"Feel that?" Roland asks the crowd as much as his volunteer. "Control without cruelty. Your enemy yields because he must, not because you've maimed him."

King Alaric watches from behind a cluster of spearmen, his attention absolute. Roland catches the royal gaze and sees calculation there, not mere curiosity about technique, but assessment of what these methods might mean for his realm's defense.

Roland releases Holt's arm, watching the instructor roll his shoulder and nod grudging approval.

"Teaching moment's done," Roland announces to the yard. "Now we drill partners."

Roland steps back, letting the yard sort itself into pairs. The geometry he's drawn becomes a dozen small battlefields as guards test his triangle against familiar opponents. Grunts and laughter echo off the armory walls. That particular music of men learning something that might keep them breathing.

He circles the practice area, correcting foot placement here, adjusting grip pressure there. A spearman named Oswin has the leverage but rushes the timing. Two younger guards giggle through their attempts until Sergeant Darly's glare reminds them this isn't tavern sport.

Near the eastern corner, King Alaric pairs with a thick-shouldered spearman whose arms could span a doorway. Roland pauses his circuit to watch, inconspicuously, but close enough to intervene if royal dignity meets earth too roughly.

The King attempts Roland's opening sequence: step, pivot, redirect. His first try nets him nothing but the sergeant's amused grin and a gentle shove backward. Alaric dusts sand from his palms, adjusting his stance.

"Again," he calls, and the younger guards lean forward with obvious interest. Their King learning beside them, not above them. Roland files this detail alongside his earlier observations about Alaric's military instincts.

The second attempt flows smoother. Alaric catches the spearman's momentum and finds the precise joint that throws him off balance, but instead of hitting the ground, Alaric's smaller frame sends the larger man stumbling three steps sideways. Cheers erupt from a few guards nearby. Genuine appreciation for skill earned, not merely deference to rank.

"Your turn, Sir Garrett," Alaric tells the spearman, settling back into ready position. The trust implicit in that offer ripples through the yard. Here is a king willing to hit ground before his men.

Roland nods approval as he continues his rounds. Leadership through participation rather than proclamation. Another mark in Alaric's favor.

Movement at the yard's edge catches his attention. Thomas Loxley, the King's young esquire, receives enthusiastic encouragement from a cluster of guards. Roland recognizes the setup. Older soldiers goading youth into proving something foolish.

Loxley charges with more courage than technique, aiming to tackle Roland around the waist. Roland pivots on his heel, one shoulder turning to catch the boy's rush while his hands guide the momentum safely past. Loxley stumbles but keeps his feet.

The older guards burst into laughter. Not malicious, but the teasing that marks acceptance. Loxley's cheeks flame red beneath the attention.

"If you must be reckless, be brief," Roland tells him, steadying the esquire with a light touch on his shoulder. "Courage channeled beats courage wasted."

Loxley straightens, embarrassment shifting toward determination. "Show me the proper approach?"

Roland demonstrates the opening again, slower this time, calling out each element so the boy can follow. The watching guards nod along. They've claimed Loxley as one of their own, and his education matters to them.

Sir Holt approaches as Roland finishes the impromptu lesson. The veteran instructor's expression carries something Roland hasn't seen before. Acceptance worn openly rather than earned grudgingly.

Holt's hand lands on Roland's shoulder with the weight of acknowledgment. "We'll have fewer broken wrists this spring, Sir Montbois."

King Alaric steps away from his successful bout with Sir Garrett, approaching with sand still dusting his gambeson. Instead of the formal nod Roland expects, Alaric extends his hand for the clasp of equals.

The gesture travels through the assembled guards like ripples. Their King's handshake marking approval that transcends mere instruction.

The King's departure signals the session's end, but not its aftermath. As guards disperse toward their duties, three men linger near the armory wall. The same who kept their distance during each of Roland's drillings. Roland recognizes the type: watchers who prefer shadows to participation.

They approach with the casual swagger of men testing boundaries. The tallest, a scarred veteran labeled Holt's opposite in temperament, leads their advance.

"French techniques from a French lord," he says, voice carrying just enough volume for nearby stragglers to hear. "Yet your accent carries notes I cannot place. Which province shaped that tongue?"

Roland keeps his expression neutral, drawing from Anselm's careful coaching. "La Brousse shapes men differently than Paris or Rouen. Remote lands breed remote habits and remote patois."

The second guard, younger but no less calculating, circles closer. "And your sister, Lady Hélène? Strange for nobility to travel without proper escort. Just the two of you on such dangerous roads?"

"Fever keeps her chambers now," Roland replies, stepping back to maintain distance. "As for escort, we found England's reputation for hospitality well-earned."

Their questions probe like fingers seeking wounds. Too specific and too persistent for idle curiosity. Roland recognizes interrogation dressed as conversation, though he cannot yet identify its source.

The third guard opens his mouth to continue but freezes mid-breath. His companions follow his gaze toward the yard's entrance, expressions shifting from aggressive curiosity to wary deference.

"Begging your pardon, my lord," the tall one mutters, sketching a hasty bow. "Duties call."

They scatter like startled birds, leaving Roland alone with an approaching figure he doesn't recognize. The man is middle-aged with average and disarming features, but he moves with the predatory patience of measured steps, assessing eyes, and the bearing of someone accustomed to answers.

"The man who mocks instruction often plots defeat," the stranger says without preamble.

Roland meets his gaze steadily. "Then we shall laugh last."

A thin smile creases the man's features. "Clever response. Though I wonder if wit travels as well as technique across borders."

He circles Roland slowly, like a hunter evaluating prey. "Your methods intrigue the King. Unusual for French nobility to possess such... practical knowledge."

"Battle teaches all men the same lessons."

"Battle, yes. But which battles? Such occurrences occur on eastern borders. Curious, for a lord from western France." The man's voice carries no malice, only relentless curiosity. "And your sister's prolonged absence from court. Unusual for a lady so recently arrived to avoid... introductions."

Each question lands with surgical precision. Roland feels the ground shifting beneath his carefully constructed foundation but maintains his balance through practical deflection.

"Perhaps you might introduce yourself," Roland says, "before requiring mine."

The man's smile widens. "Lord Ranulf of Morcar. Justiciar and counselor to His Majesty—"

"Sir Roland." Sir Denby materializes at Roland's shoulder with the suddenness of a seasoned soldier recognizing danger. The familiar use of his first name meant as a warning to Roland's inquisitor. "We must discuss the training manual His Majesty commissioned. The King expects our recommendations by vespers."

Denby's intervention carries the weight of urgent necessity, though Roland suspects the manual's deadline exists only in the captain's imagination.

Ranulf's expression sours at the interruption. "Administrative matters. How... pressing." He inclines his head with minimal courtesy. "Another time, Sir Montbois. I'm certain we'll find opportunity to... continue our discussion."

The advisor withdraws with the same predatory patience he'd shown approaching. Roland watches him go, noting how the three questioning guards shadow his path toward the castle proper.

"Careful with that one," Denby murmurs once Ranulf disappears through the gatehouse. "He's not cruel, but he questions everything twice and trusts nothing once. Your story would interest him greatly."

Roland nods, remembering the guards' sudden retreat at Ranulf's approach. "Those who resent learning often serve other masters."

Denby follows Roland's meaningful glance toward the departing trio. Understanding flickers across the veteran's aged features.

"Noted," he says quietly. "Some webs catch more than flies."

Lord Ranulf of Morcar

The cloister echoes each step as Ranulf circles the courtyard, his mind churning through the morning's correspondence. Folded within his sleeve lie three letters from France whose responses arrived with a suspicious swiftness to his inquiries about the Montbois lineage.

Too swift by half. A message to France's southern border should require a fortnight's passage, yet this reply appeared days early. Distance bends to no man's urgency, regardless of station.

More troubling than speed was substance, or the deliberate lack thereof. Each response carried the hollow ring of rehearsed denial, as though scribes had prepared identical dismissals before his questions even arrived. Lords who once shared gossip freely now offered stilted courtesies and veiled warnings about meddling in distant affairs.

"The Montbois keep their own counsel," wrote one. "Perhaps such matters rest better undisturbed."

Twenty years of diplomatic correspondence had taught Ranulf to recognize the difference between ignorance and orchestrated silence. These letters bore all the marks of the latter.

He pauses beside a weathered pillar, withdrawing parchment from his sleeve marked with various heraldry. He can recall the heraldry of most noble French houses. Yet, no tree, no tower, no beast springs to mind despite hours spent ransacking his mental catalog of European nobility.

"A tree without roots is lumber, not lineage," he murmurs, studying the empty space where knowledge should reside.

For a man who prides himself on mapping every thread in the continent's tangled web of bloodlines, this void gnaws like an infected wound. The Montbois should not exist in such perfect obscurity. No family achieves sufficient prominence to approach the English throne while remaining invisible to those who trade in information.

Ranulf begins walking again, counting facts on his fingers like a merchant tallying coin. Names: Roland and Hélène. But what of parents, siblings, and ancestral holdings? Manners: the lady's informality, her brother's fighting techniques poorly disguised as French instruction. Accent: that elusive quality that shifts between recognizable and foreign with each spoken word.

Most suspicious remains the Archbishop's convenient familial connection. A claim that conveniently legitimizes their presence while discouraging deeper inquiry. Yet Anselm's authority, however vast, cannot produce verifiable records where none exist.

"When a tale arrives incomplete, it was composed in haste," Ranulf says to the empty air.

The time has come for more pointed questions. Does French knighthood claim a Sir Roland of Montbois among its ranks? Do church records in La Brousse mention Lady Hélène's birth, marriage, or inheritance? Did plague truly sweep through that remote region, conveniently eliminating witnesses to their early years?

Such inquiries will require delicate phrasing and reliable contacts, preferably men who owe him favors rather than fear his curiosity. Brother Marcus was a strategic choice for his earlier dictations. Close to the church, Anselm's rat. The quality of responses insinuates that Brother Marcus's loyalties lie with the crozier, not the crown.

Ranulf reaches his study and settles behind his oak writing desk as footsteps approach in the corridor. The familiar shuffle announces his clerk before the man appears in the doorway, parchment and ink pot balanced in hands permanently stained by years if dictations and secrets.

"You summoned me, my lord?"

"Close the door, Francis. We have delicate correspondence ahead."

The elderly clerk sets his materials upon the desk's polished surface, arranging quills with the precision of long practice. Ranulf studies the blank parchment, organizing his thoughts into careful strategy.

"Three sets of letters today. The first to French nobles who trade in hospitality and gossip alike." Ranulf leans back in his chair, fingers steepled. "I heard whispers of Archbishop Anselm having a cousin named Roland who spent years as a traveling knight. If such a man existed, someone will have encountered him or heard of him."

Francis dips his quill, waiting for dictation.

"Frame these as admiration, not inquiry. Write as if I admire them. Admiration loosens tongues." Ranulf's voice carries the lilt of experience. "Mention my interest in knightly prowess, particularly unconventional fighting techniques. Ask if they recall hosting or hearing tales of such a remarkable visitor from La Brousse."

The quill scratches across parchment as Francis captures each word. Ranulf rises, pacing to the narrow window that overlooks the outer courtyard, and the armory and training yard beyond that.

"The second set goes to men who owe me favors: port masters, merchant guilds, crossroad innkeepers. Those who see everyone and forget nothing when properly motivated." He turns back to Francis. "Request information about any French travelers matching the Montbois descriptions. Movement leaves traces, even when carefully concealed."

Francis nods, already reaching for fresh parchment.

"Finally, monasteries throughout the La Brousse region. Monks remember the dead better than courtiers remember yesterday." Ranulf returns to his seat, satisfaction creeping into his voice. "Inquire about recent illnesses, deaths among local nobility, particularly any matriarch who might have left surviving children. Frame it as concern for the Archbishop's bereaved relatives."

The clerk's quill pauses. "Shall I mention your personal interest, my lord?"

"No. Present these as routine courtesies between fellow Christians." Ranulf withdraws a small brass seal from his sleeve. Not his official sigil, but a private mark known only to trusted correspondents. "Use this cipher seal within the wax."

Francis examines the intricate design: a raven clutching a scroll.

"Even truth needs escort," Ranulf murmurs, watching the clerk prepare the sealing wax. "Begin with the first letter. We hunt rabbits with patience, not hounds."

The afternoon light slants through stone mullions as the clerk's careful script fills each page, carrying Ranulf's web of inquiry across England and the Channel.

Francis sets down his quill as the third letter nears completion, flexing cramped fingers. Ranulf studies the clerk's creased face, noting how twenty years of castle service have taught the man to observe without seeming to watch.

"Before we duplicate these," Ranulf says, "tell me what you know of our French guests. Surely the servants speak of little else."

Francis shifts uncomfortably, arranging the drafted letters with deliberate care. "I keep to my writing, my lord. Palace gossip has a way of becoming tomorrow's scandal."

"This is not gossip. I ask what you witnessed yourself." Ranulf leans forward. "Were you present when they arrived?"

"No, my lord. I was in the scriptorium when the commotion began."

"Then who actually saw their appearance?"

Francis hesitates, caught between discretion and the Justiciar's direct question. "The accounts vary considerably, my lord."

"Secondhand wonders are coin weighed in shadow. Never quite what they claim." Ranulf's voice carries a tone of skepticism. "What of firsthand accounts?"

The clerk glances toward the door before lowering his voice. "My lord, that is the peculiar thing. No one claims to have witnessed their actual arrival. The staff insist they saw nothing until the guards brought them from the Council Chambers. Yet how does one slip past the gatehouse unseen, especially bearing foreign likeness?"

"And their English guide?" Ranulf presses. "How did they come across this mysterious escort who tempted our King's fate?"

Francis spreads his hands helplessly. "Again, my lord, the tale shifts with each telling. Some say he found them on the road, others that he was sent to meet them. The scuffle in the Council Chamber, that much the servants heard true enough and the guards present swear to Sir Montbois' defense of the King and Lord Geoffrey, but what came before remains in shadow."

Ranulf drums his fingers against the desk. Such tales explain nothing while proving the court's hunger for explanation. Every retelling adds embellishment until truth drowns beneath imagination.

"A charge without proof is a sword without hilt," he murmurs, more to himself than Francis. These letters must bear fruit before he moves openly. "If they are innocent, my doubts will die easily. If not, better a friend find it than an enemy."

Francis nods, understanding the unspoken burden. Ranulf rises, moving to the window as afternoon shadows lengthen across stone.

He turns back to the clerk . "One final instruction. Note who starts befriending the newcomers too quickly. Favor is a footprint; follow it."

Ranulf settles into his chair as Francis replicates the letters for each destination. He studies the cipher seal.

Reginald, dear friend, what are you not telling me?

Lady Hélène of Montbois

The fever breaks like dawn through her chamber shutters, sudden and promising. She grips the stone mantle, forcing her legs to bear weight as footsteps approach the door. Two weeks of blankets and broths have left her muscles weak, but her mind feels sharp again, hungry for motion.

Roland enters without introduction, his dark eyes scanning her frame with clinical precision. She straightens against the fireplace, summoning what dignity remains in her borrowed kirtle.

"See? Vertical. The fashion in breathing lags behind."

"You look like you fought a siege." His voice carries the dry concern she knows to be worry disguised as observation. Her advanced immunology should have helped her recovery, but it did not.

"I lost to a blanket." She manages a weak laugh, testing her balance. "The room stays steady. Progress."

Roland crosses to her, fingers finding her wrist and pulse. His touch is cool and methodical like checking equipment before a mission. The pulse point beats steady under his thumb.

"Medieval flu," she murmurs. "Our immune systems weren't exactly programmed for thirteenth-century pathogens."

"Apparently not." He tilts her chin up, studying her eyes for signs of lingering infection. "Agnes says she'll introduce real food again today, not just her endless broths."

"Real food being relative." Hélène pulls free of his inspection, irritation flickering. Two weeks of confinement have left her restless, anxious to rejoin whatever game they're playing at court. "Tell me something useful. How goes our performance?"

Roland settles into the room's single chair, Isolde's chair, his expression shifting to something resembling satisfaction. "The Guard respects efficiency. Sir Warin Holt especially. He's warming to the training methods. They learn quickly. The King among them."

"Good." Anticipation builds in her chest, replacing the dull ache of illness. "If he trips a few lords, I'll applaud."

"Careful what you wish for." He smiles briefly at her, then the seriousness returns. "Ranulf's asking questions."

The tone in which he mentions Ranulf's suspicion sends a chill through Hélène's recovering frame. She pushes away from the mantle, pacing to the narrow window despite her unsteady legs.

"What sort of questions?"

"The sort that require answers we don't have." Roland's fingers drum against the chair arm. A tell she recognizes from their training days. Stress, barely contained. "Heraldry. Bloodlines. Why our French sounds like it learned itself from books."

Hélène turns from the window, studying her brother's face. The careful mask he wears at court has slipped, revealing the calculating soldier beneath. "Then we need better stories. Simpler ones."

"We need to stop being clever." His gaze finds hers, sharp with warning. "You especially. No more hints about distant places to Isolde. No talk of colonies or—"

"I know." The words come too quickly, defensive. She hadn't meant to let it slip. The fever muddled her mind too much.

Roland leans forward, voice dropping. "We were raised by silence, surrounded by bad roads. That's all anyone needs to know."

"And the occasional miracle bread," she adds, attempting to lighten the mood but it's forced.

His expression remains serious. "No tech terms. No prophecy about England's future. Nothing that makes us sound like we've seen tomorrow."

Hélène moves to the window again, fingers tracing the stone sill. The outer courtyard below bustles with normal life. Servants crossing with baskets, guards changing shifts. All of it moving with patterns she still struggles to read.

"Lady Eveline visited yesterday." The words emerged, carrying a weight she hadn't intended. "Well, she walked Isolde here, then lingered outside my door. Loud enough for half the corridor to hear her thoughts on my... peculiarities."

Roland's chair creaks as he shifts, attention sharpening.

"She never comes inside," Hélène continues, tone dropping further. "Just hovers like a herald, announcing every whisper about the strange French lady who curtsies shallow and speaks too plainly." Her throat tightens. "I do not mind being strange. I mind being alone."

"Then I'll be strange beside you."

The warmth and simplicity of his response steadies her more than any elaborate reassurance could. She turns from the window, finding his steady gaze.

"If they want stories, they can earn them," Roland adds, rising from the chair.

"Charge a toll in courtesy," she agrees, managing a genuine smile.

Roland moves to the door, but Hélène catches his sleeve. "Wait. The signals. We should practice."

He pauses, understanding immediately. Their survival depends on wordless communication, especially when court eyes watch too closely.

She raises three fingers against her kirtle. "Retreat."

"Stall." His hand mirrors hers with two fingers.

"One finger—" She starts to grin, then catches herself as a small cough escapes. She covers it quickly, but his sharp gaze catches everything. *The illness lingers.*

"One—smile like a saint," he finishes, deadpanned with a smirk.

The joke draws a laugh that turns into another cough. Roland's expression shifts to concerned brother, not careful soldier.

"Back to bed. Now."

"Five breaths at the window, and I'll behave." She gestures toward the narrow opening, where morning light streams across stone. Fresh air calls to her fever-dulled senses.

"Four, and I'll count."

She moves to the window, breathing deeply of the cool old Earth air. Each inhale steadies her, reminds her that recovery comes in small victories. Roland counts silently, patient as a guardian.

As he turns to leave, she calls softly, "Adrian."

He stops, hand on the door latch. "Elaine."

The sound of their true names hang between them like a bridge across centuries.

His eyes soften towards her. "We'll be who we must, until we can be who we are."

A Ride at Dawn

- 6 -

Lady Hélène Montbois

The stone floor bites cold against her bare feet, but Hélène welcomes the shock. The four walls of her bedchamber had become a cage of fever-induced dreams and endless cups of barley water. The castle now sleeps around her, wrapped in that peculiar hush before most servants wake. She moves through pre-dawn's shadows, her nightgown pooling around her ankles as hands trail stone walls.

She is anxious and starving. The kitchens lie somewhere below. She follows the scent of bread as it winds through the corridors, drawing her from her confinement. "If bread will not come to me, I shall come to bread," she whispers to the empty corridor.

A figure rounds the corner ahead, dark cloak swirling. Hélène freezes mid-step as recognition dawns. The King. They stand frozen, two night wanderers caught in collision.

Alaric's frame eases and his shocked face dissolves into a half-grin. "Ghosts in linen walk my halls?"

His voice carries gentle amusement. Hélène straightens, suddenly aware of her disheveled state but too hungry to care properly.

"Only the hungry sort."

The flat response draws a chuckle from him. She dips into what she hopes passes for an apologetic curtsy, nightgown bunching awkwardly.

"Your Majesty, I require food, trousers, and fresh air. Ideally in that order." She hopes it sounds more like a request than an order.

"A trinity I can bless." He smiles.

He guides her through a narrow door into what appears to be a storage chamber. Moonlight filters through a high window, illuminating wooden chests and folded banners. The King moves with deliberate quiet, lifting the lid of a well-worn chest.

Cloth rustles as he pulls forth a riding tunic, worn soft at the elbows, followed by a leather belt, scuffed boots, and dulled trousers. The garments smell faintly of horse and honest sweat. A welcome change from the perfumed linens that have shrouded her for days.

"If you will offend fashion, do it quickly." He instructs.

"Fashion and I were never betrothed."

She catches the bundle he tosses, grateful for anything that promises freedom of movement. The King turns his back, hands clasped behind him as he studies the far wall with sudden fascination.

The nightgown puddles at her feet. Cool air kisses fever-warmed skin as she pulls the tunic over her head. The fabric hangs loose, meant for broader shoulders and thicker legs. She works the belt around her waist, cinching until the excess cloth gathers in rough folds. The boots swallow her feet, but thick hose from the chest fill the gaps well enough.

She strikes a mock-heroic pose, one hand on hip, chin lifted in exaggerated nobility. "How do I look?"

He glances over his shoulder, eyebrows rising at the sight. "Like a squire who will gossip for weeks."

A woolen cloak emerges from deeper in the chest, followed by a simple cap and headscarf. He shakes each out before offering them.

"Best hide the hair with the scarf and cap. If anyone asks, you are a squire under my instruction."

"I shall nod as if it were true."

She accepts the cloak, pulling it around shoulders that suddenly feel steadier than they have in days. The cap and scarf tuck her hair away, transforming her from woman to anonymous youth.

"Fresh bread waits in the kitchens. We can reach the stables through the yard doors."

The stables exhale warmth and hay-sweet breath into the pre-dawn chill. She's not yet been outside the castle and has only seen horses in pictures. She finishes her honey bread as she follows the King past drowsing horses, some rousing with sleepy curiosity. He stops beside a sturdy male whose ears prick forward at their approach.

"Patient as stone, steady as sunrise."

She runs her palm along the horse's neck, fingers finding the ridge of muscle beneath winter-thick coat. The beautiful creature leans into her touch, soft lips exploring her sleeve for hidden treats.

"He has the look of a philosopher." She whispers.

"My most faithful destrier, Thunderbolt."

The King selects another from the neighboring stall.

"And you the look of a bad influence." She smiles at the grey mount.

"A patient gelding. She'll do well as your teacher."

The King prepares both mounts with the movements of someone accustomed to doing so himself. Hélène watches his technique, filing away each buckle and adjustment. When he gestures toward the mounting block, she approaches with determination masking uncertainty.

Her first attempt sends her scrambling over the grey gelding's back like an ungainly sack. She laughs hard as Alaric helps her from the hay. She makes a second attempt. The horse tolerates her graceless arrival and shifts to maintain her balance in the saddle.

"Heels down, pride up."

"Pride I have in surplus."

She adjusts her seat, absorbing his quiet corrections until balance feels less precarious. The saddle leather creaks as she settles, reins gathered in hands that remember different technologies but ready to conquer these ancient rhythms.

A stable hand emerges from the shadows, rubbing sleep from his eyes. Recognition dawns as he spots the King.

"Sire." He stands straighter.

"If anyone asks after me, I'll be in the usual spot." The stable hand relaxes and nods indicating the 'usual' to be normal.

The head out with barely a glance from early morning risers in the courtyards. A guard at the gatehouse barely lifts his head as they approach, two cloaked figures on horses that breathe silver clouds into the frigid air. Alaric raises two fingers in casual acknowledgment.

"Sire." The guard acknowledges with a casual nod.

Hélène ducks her chin deeper into the woolen folds.

"My... lord." His eyebrows raise slightly as he realizes the King's riding companion is no man, or squire.

The gates open on fields stretched pale and endless under morning starlight. Hooves bite frost-hardened earth as they move from trampled earth to open ground. The wind cuts through wool and leather as the pre-dawn sun peeks over the eastern tree line.

Alaric looks over to her. "There. Breakfast for the lungs."

King Alaric

His destrier's hooves find their rhythm against earth that yields to yesterday's early spring rain. Alaric watches Hélène from the corner of his vision, noting how her seat grows steadier with each stride. Her balance shifts naturally now, no longer fighting the horse's movement but flowing with it.

Pink bleeds across the eastern sky as they trail the hedgerows north. The familiar paths of his youth stretch ahead, worn smooth by countless rides with Geoffrey when crowns and councils seemed impossibly distant.

"You were born to mischief, not saddles."

Her laugh comes easy. A welcome reprieve from the watchful eyes and careful protocols of court life. "Heresy I will not deny."

He guides them toward a gap in the hedge where an old oak marks the entrance to deeper woods. Memory tugs at him. Races through these very trees, first on foot with scraped knees and torn hose, later mounted when Geoffrey's father gifted them matching ponies.

"Geoffrey and I wore a path through these woods as boys. Our feet first, then hooves when we grew tall enough to reach stirrups properly."

"Racing, I assume?"

"Racing, hunting, escaping tutors who despaired of our Latin."

She urges her mount forward as the path narrows, branches reaching across their route like gnarled fingers. Her riding improves moment by moment, instinct overcoming inexperience.

"What games filled your childhood?"

The question hangs between them, casual as morning mist. He watches her consider it, weighing words with the care he recognizes from council chambers.

"Roland and I grew up somewhere that believed children should be children, whatever came after. All work and no play makes for brittle adults."

"And what came after?"

"Hard lessons. Our parents served as... agents of time. We followed naturally."

Agents of time. The title sits as strangely as the first he heard it, neither fully clear nor completely opaque. "Where is home, then? I have heard it lacks the greenery we know here."

Her hands tighten slightly on the reins. "A place of red earth and sparse growth. Nothing like this abundance of leaf and flower."

He pictures vast deserts stretching beyond the known world, places where the sun beats down mercilessly and water comes dear. Isolde had whispered of Lady Hélène's fever dreams, fragments about a place called Mars. Red as rust, barren as winter fields after harvest. Some distant wasteland, perhaps, where traders venture for exotic spices or scholars seek ancient texts. Certainly not the Mars he read of in his youth's philosophy lessons. She's from another time, not the stars.

"No siblings beyond Roland?"

"None. We've always been—"

She stops abruptly, reining in her mount with the sudden precision of an experienced rider. When she faces him, her expression has shifted from easy conversation to something sharper, more direct.

"Your Majesty. I understand your curiosity, I really do, but please do not fiddle me to reveal information that would compromise the future, both yours and mine. I'll give the truth as much as time allows it."

As much as time allows it. The words carry weight beyond their courtesy. Command dressed as request, boundary drawn with velvet-wrapped steel. He would bristle at such directness from a subject, but she is not his subject and instead finds himself oddly impressed.

She protects something larger than herself, accepts responsibility that clearly weighs on narrow shoulders. The fever-weakened woman who begged for trousers and fresh air carries burdens he can only guess at.

"Understood, my lady."

A cart creaks toward them as they round a bend, drawn by a sway-backed mare that picks her way carefully over rain filled winter ruts. The old peasant at the reins nods respectfully as they approach, his weathered face breaking into the careful smile reserved for nobility glimpsed in passing.

Alaric returns the nod, noting how Hélène maintains her easy seat while offering her own acknowledgment. No tension in her shoulders, no sideways glances seeking threats in innocent encounters. Her calm strikes him as either foolishness or remarkable composure.

They round the next corner where hawthorn grows thick on both sides, branches weaving together overhead like cathedral arches. A thrush breaks from cover too suddenly, wings beating frantically against the morning air. Metal catches light in the hedgerow to their right. A blade's edge, perhaps a buckle.

Wrong. All wrong.

Alaric spurs his destrier forward and right, placing himself between Hélène and the suspected danger. Her eyebrows rise at the maneuver, surprise flickering across a bone structure that resembles Roland.

He forces his mouth into a smile while pitching his voice low enough that only she can hear. "Ride easy. Eyes right."

Three suddenly men explode from the left hedgerow instead, crashing through winter briars with perfect timing. Alaric's destrier wheels, trained for battle but caught off-guard by the misdirection.

The nearest attacker's blade whistles toward Hélène's mount. Her horse screams and drops to one knee, blood streaming from a gash along its shoulder.

"Purse or blood!"

Hélène executes a perfect roll as her mount collapses, landing on her feet with the fluid grace Roland demonstrates in the training yard. She bares her teeth at the advancing bandits.

"How economical."

Alaric wheels his destrier between her and the blades, but the attackers' next words freeze his blood.

"We know you, Majesty. Gold buys silence."

These are castle grounds and they know his face, his morning rides. How?

"Saints—"

In an unexpected move, Hélène vaults behind him with ease, settling against the cantle at his back, like she never struggled mounting at all that morning.

"Borrowing your saddle!"

The destrier's muscles bunch beneath them as Alaric drives his heels home. Branches whip past his face, catching at his cloak while mud clods spray from hammering hooves. Behind him, Hélène's weight settles against his back with surprising steadiness.

"Hold tight."

"I should like to, yes."

Hoofbeats thunder close behind. Too close. One bandit has kept pace despite the destrier's superior breeding, his mount is nimbler through the narrow gaps, but it bears the weight of two riders. Alaric fights the urge to veer into open ground where deeper mud might catch them with double weight aboard.

The track ahead curves sharply left. He leans into the turn, feeling Hélène move with him rather than against the horse's motion. Her unexpected balance speaks of experience, and he remembers ladies from her time are different.

The pursuing bandit draws alongside the right, face twisted with exertion and greed. A blade whistles past his ear.

Behind him, Hélène's arm extends past his right peripherals. Her fist closes around a dead branch jutting from the hedgerow, snapping it free. The improvised weapon cracks across the bandit's knuckles with satisfying force.

"Kindly keep your distance."

The bandit howls, nearly losing his seat. "Witch!"

She strikes again, methodical as a blacksmith working iron. Each blow finds its mark. A wrist, a forearm, the side of his head, repeatedly. The bandit's mount shies sideways, confused by its rider's flailing.

"Like a schoolroom ruler!"

Whatever that means, her tone carries unmistakable satisfaction. The mangled branch in her grip has done its work. Their pursuer tumbles from his saddle into spring's early thorns.

The track ahead narrows to nothing, choked with scrub that would trap them if they continued. Alaric's chest tightens. Open ground stretches to their right, treacherous with hidden stones and rabbit holes. Their only choice.

"Hold fast. We ride the wild ground now."

"My favorite kind."

He wheels the destrier right, trusting weight and momentum to carry them through. They cross the field quickly and into the wild growth. Thorns tear at his cloak as they plunge deeper into the woods. Branches whip across his face, drawing blood from his cheek, but each cut puts precious distance between them and pursuit. The destrier's breathing grows labored under the doubled weight, yet the animal pushes forward with the heart that made Alaric choose him.

Behind them, crashes and curses fade as their pursuers struggle through the same punishing thicket. But Alaric knows these woods, every game trail, every hidden bog, every stand of oak that marks the boundaries between the royal hunting grounds and wilder country beyond.

A final wall of brambles parts before them, thorns catching at his sleeve as they burst into open meadow. Mud spatters his legs and the destrier's flanks as they thunder across dampened grass. Not slowing down, he turns in the saddle, scanning the tree line for signs of pursuit.

Nothing. Only wind stirring budding branches and the distant call of a hawk.

Hélène's hair has escaped the scarf that held it, the cap long gone. Her dark strands whipping wild around a face speckled with mud. She leans forward and around toward the horse's neck, close enough that her breath must warm the destrier's neck.

"Easy now, beautiful. One, two, three, four..."

Her voice carries none of the breathless panic he expects. Instead, she counts with the steady rhythm of someone who understands how frightened animals respond to calm authority. The destrier's frantic gallop settles into a manageable canter, then a trot that no longer threatens to unseat them both. His own racing heartbeat begins to match the horse's steadier pace.

They reach the far hedge where hunting paths converge in familiar patterns. Alaric reins in completely, turning to study the meadow they have crossed. Long minutes pass in silence broken only by the destrier's breathing and wind through trees.

Relief bursts from his chest in laughter that would horrify his council. Unroyal, undignified, but alive with the simple joy of having escaped with whole skin.

"You vault like a devil."

"I was coached by necessity, but who coached this beautiful creature?"

He strokes the destrier's neck, feeling sweat and strength beneath his palm. "Thunderbolt earned his name today. I always wondered if he could live up to it."

The ridge rises to their east where castle towers should be visible, but no glint of mail or flash of royal colors breaks the horizon. Half the morning has passed without guard patrols finding their king missing from his chambers.

Concerning, but not unexpected. His household has grown comfortable with his independence.

"We make for the old deer path. Half the distance, twice the scratches."

"Then I shall collect scratches like jewels."

Sir Warin Holt

The morning search has stretched too long, with afternoon threatening to break through the trees. Warin guides his mount along the ridge line, scanning hedgerows that could hide a dozen ambushes. Behind him, four guardsmen spread wide across the northern fields, their mail glinting dull silver under clouded sky.

Word came at dawn. The King rode out with some unknown squire toward the southern hunting grounds. They combed every path south of the castle walls until the sun climbed high enough to mock their efforts.

Something nagged at him through all those wasted hours. A feeling that sat wrong in his gut, the kind that kept old soldiers breathing when younger men trusted what they were told. So he surrendered to his gut and moved half the men to search the northern grounds.

"Keep your eyes on the hedges. Trouble loves a thorn."

His voice carries easily across early spring's cool air. The guardsmen acknowledge with raised hands, understanding that their King's safety depends on details of bent grass, disturbed earth, and the particular way birds scatter when strangers pass.

Movement catches his attention near the eastern slope. Two riders on a single mount crest the hill. The larger sits the saddle with the easy authority Warin has watched develop over four years of kingship.

The other rider's posture tells a different story entirely. Loosely hanging off his Majesty's backside.

"Ho! Your Majesty!" He calls out.

Alaric raises his hand in acknowledgment as he approaches closer. Mud streaks his royal face and surcoat like the sky rained it.

"All well, mostly." He says firmly.

Mostly. That word carries weight Warin recognizes from battlefields and sieges. The honesty of men who have faced real danger and emerged intact through luck as much as skill.

"We thought you went south, Your Majesty."

"I told the stable hand we were going to my usual spot."

The words hit Warin like a fist to the chest. The usual spot has always been first east then up the trails to northern grounds, not the southern hunting paths where they wasted their morning. Someone gave them false information. Deliberately or through carelessness, it matters little.

The King's eyes meet his and understanding passes between them without need for words. Trust has been broken somewhere in the chain of service that keeps their sovereign safe. Warin files away a mental note to have pointed conversation with every stable hand who worked dawn duty.

His attention shifts to the second rider, and his soldier's eye catalogues details that make his jaw tighten. Lady Hélène's dark hair has escaped its proper arrangement, falling loose about her shoulders in a way that speaks of hard riding and hasty departure. Her cloak hangs open, revealing the fine fabric of a worn tunic beneath. Fabric that would mark her as nobility to any watching eye. He catches the faded markings of the crown's sigil.

"My lady," he says carefully, his voice pitched to carry only to their small group. "Perhaps it would be wise to draw your hood forward and secure your locks more closely. The castle has many eyes, and discretion serves us all when returning from... unexpected journeys."

He keeps his tone respectful but firm, the same voice he uses when instructing green recruits in the necessity of proper equipment checks. Some lessons cannot afford to be learned through failure.

They reach the castle stable's shadowed interior with only a few curious looks, but none that lingered. A small mercy. The King dismounts gracefully from the shared destrier but before he can turn to help the lady, Hélène slides out herself, but with far less grace. Her cloak catches on the saddle horn, pulling free to reveal the full extent of their morning's adventure. Her borrowed tunic hangs loose and mud-stained, the fine fabric torn at one shoulder with a minor amount of blood. Dark hair frames her face and shoulders in a portrait made of mud and twigs, every strand a contradiction to the careful arrangement expected of a court lady.

Warin studies her with the measuring eye of a man who has spent years teaching proper form. She stands with weight balanced on both feet, shoulders square, and chin level. The stance of someone comfortable in her own skin regardless of appearances. He recalls Denby's remark that both she and Roland are skilled warriors from their time. He knows this well. He was there when she… landed.

"A bold squire, my lady." He cannot quite suppress the smile tugging at his mouth. There is something refreshing about her complete lack of concern for the disaster her appearance represents.

"Promote me to apprentice."

Her cheerful response draws a quiet chuckle from him, but movement at the stable entrance cuts short any further exchange. Agnes rushes forward, her practical gown swishing against the straw-covered floor. Her hands fly to her mouth as she takes in the torn fabric and bramble scratches along Hélène's arms and thighs. Thankfully her face survived.

"My lady! Your poor legs!"

"They've survived worse ideas."

Hélène's aside carries the same dry humor Warin has begun to recognize as Roland's natural defense against concern. But Agnes's arrival changes everything unless they act swiftly. Word will spread through the castle staff like fire through dry rushes.

Before Alaric can voice whatever protest is forming behind his carefully neutral expression, Warin makes his decision. He catches the eye of young Loxley, the King's squire in training has been hovering near the grain bins.

"Go, swiftly. Words before rumors."

Loxley nods and disappears into the courtyard, understanding the urgency even if he lacks the full picture. Within minutes, the Archbishop and Sir Roland will arrive to help contain whatever story emerges from this morning's escapade.

The sound of hurried footsteps on cobblestone announces Sir Roland's arrival before Warin sees him. Future's knight moves with the focused urgency of a man who has heard whispers and drawn his own conclusions. None of them good.

Roland's eyes find his sister immediately, sweeping past Alaric and Warin as if they were merely obstacles in his path. His gaze catalogues every visible scratch, every tear in fabric, the particular way she favors her left leg when she thinks no one is watching.

Relief flickers across his features for the briefest moment before hardening into something much less forgiving.

"You rode out alone, without a guard, without *proper boots*." Roland's voice carries the controlled edge of a man barely holding his temper in check.

"I borrowed both. A guard who has and provided *proper boots*." She applies the same emphasis on proper boots and motions in Alaric's direction.

Roland ignores the retort and steps closer to Hélène, his frame engulfing her space. He gathers her loose hair, twisting it into a serviceable knot that speaks of years handling such emergencies. Hélène's protest carries a small smile that only seems to deepen Roland's scowl. He pulls her cloak forward to shadow her face, his movements sharp with suppressed anger. Warin doesn't understand the jest on proper boots, as the lady's were indeed proper, but he does see a brother worried about his sister.

Only then does Roland's attention shift to register the King's presence. "Your Majesty, I must beg your pardon for my sister's lack of—"

"Sir Roland," Alaric respectfully cuts him off, stepping forward with a faint smile, "there is no need for apologies. The fault is entirely mine."

The Archbishop's arrival brings a stillness that settles over the stable like snow. His keen eyes sweep the scene—mud-streaked King, disheveled lady, tense brother—and his expression shifts to the careful neutrality Warin has learned to recognize as diplomatic thinking.

"Lady Hélène, how do you find yourself? Given your recent confinement to bed, I confess some concern."

Hélène straightens slightly and Warin notices for the first time the remnants of her recent illness under her eyes. "I'll have a better answer once the adrenaline from this morning's adventure wears off, Your Grace."

Adrenaline. Strange term. The lady's language choices baffle the more one remains in her presence.

"Then you must take care not to let your fever creep back upon you."

Anselm's gentle warning carries the weight of genuine concern, but Alaric steps forward with the brisk authority of a king who recognizes spreading crisis.

"We need to move before word spreads. My chambers are closest and more private, until Agnes can find a more suitable garb for the lady."

Roland responds immediately, positioning himself beside Hélène and drawing her cloak more securely around her shoulders. Without hesitation, he guides her toward a narrow side door Warin barely noticed. Warin falls into step behind the King, but his attention fixes on Roland's sure navigation through corridors most nobles never see. The man moves through servant pathways with the confidence of someone who has mapped every stone, every turn, every shortcut the castle offers.

His eyes meet the King's as Roland checks a cross-passage before leading them deeper into the maze. Understanding passes between them. This is not casual knowledge. This is the thoroughness of a man who plans for every contingency, who studies ground the way seasoned soldiers study battlefields.

In the King's sitting room, Hélène accepts bread and tea with grateful hands, launching into animated description of their morning's escape. Her voice carries the bright energy of recent danger survived, words tumbling over each other in her eagerness to share the tale.

"And then the hedge tried to... negotiate..."

The words fade as she yawns and exhaustion threatens to claim her. Her head tilts back against the winged chair, eyes drifting closed. Roland's expression softens instantly.

Agnes appears with proper shoes and a floor-length lady's cloak, helping Roland gently rouse the dosing woman. Together they quickly transform the disheveled adventurer back into a lady fit for castle corridors.

"Come, sister," Roland's protective hand steady at her elbow as they shuffle her away. He nods to them as he leaves.

Warin meets Alaric's gaze across the now quiet room. "She will keep your hall lively, Sire."

"Or teach it to breathe."

Whispers of Court

- 7 -

Alice Whitecombe

Alice stirs the pot with the steady rhythm of a woman who has perfected the art of multitasking; one wooden spoon working through thick barley stew while her ears work through even thicker castle gossip.

"Needs salt," she announces to Maud, who hovers nearby with herbs, "and a pinch of 'you'll never guess who rode out at dawn.'"

Maud's eyes brighten with the particular gleam of someone who lives for such moments. "Do tell."

Before Alice can elaborate, Agnes slips through the kitchen door carrying a small bundle of linen strips and a pot of salve. The maid's movements carry a purposeful quietness, as if she hopes to complete her business without drawing attention.

Alice's keen gaze catches the telltale signs of worthy gossip immediately. Fresh bandages mean fresh wounds, and fresh wounds mean fresh stories.

"Nothing a salve can't scold," Agnes says with understatement as she catches Alice's discerning eyes. She settles her supplies on the worktable.

"Salve and scandal, our two house saints," Alice replies, her voice bright with anticipation. "Come now, Agnes, you can't arrive with bandages and expect us to pretend we haven't noticed."

Agnes glances toward the door, ensuring privacy, then leans closer. "I'm just assisting a new squire that took a tumble during a morning ride."

"A tumble?" Maud's voice carries the skepticism of someone who has heard such euphemisms before.

Before Agnes can respond, Hal bursts through the servants' entrance, his voice carrying the excited energy of a man with important news to share.

"The King returned covered in mud and scratches with what we are sure was a lady under a cloak," Hal addresses the kitchen at large.

Alice turns from her pot, wooden spoon tilted at Agnes. "Ah, so not just any squire. Your tumbling rider and the King's cloaked lady are one and the same."

Agnes shifts the bandages, gives Alice a warning look. "A certain French lady's accent carries... peculiar notes," Alice holds her stare with Agnes.

"Peculiar how?" Maud presses, abandoning her herbs entirely.

"Like a *patois* from roads that forgot they were roads," Alice declares with theatrical gravity, savoring each syllable. *Patois*. With the French sibling's arrival, then term has taken on a double meaning.

"Aye, we've noticed it in Roland's speech during his training sessions," Hal says eagerly. "We enjoy the lessons, even if the methods are as peculiar as their accent."

Agnes straightens, defensive instincts surfacing. "They weren't much at court as children. Spent years in French borderlands. Small wonder they never adopted proper noble ways. And what would you know of a French knight's methods?"

Hal raises his hands in mock surrender. Alice smiles at Agnes's defense of her lady.

"Still," Agnes adds quietly, "names stick to her. Every servant, every page. She remembers them all."

Alice's expression softens despite herself. "That's a rare habit for a lady. Rare and sticky."

The kitchen falls silent except for the gentle bubbling of stew, each weighing these small revelations against their growing collection of mysteries.

The kitchen door swings open as Hal departs, replaced by Meg and Alan entering with the tuned efficiency of servants who know their timing. Alice catches the shift in the room's energy. Agnes has drawn her protective veil back around whatever secrets surround Lady Hélène, and pressing further would yield nothing but stubborn silence.

Time to try a different thread.

"They say a Spanish princess will soon grace our halls," Alice begins, her tone carrying. "You've been named to her rooms, haven't you, Meg?"

Meg sets down a bundle of fresh rushes, her movements measured. "I've been told to be ready. Linens aired, chambers in order. I know her title, not her temper."

Alice leans against the worktable, wooden spoon still dripping stew. "No whisper of habits? Early prayers, late suppers?"

"Only the Queen Dowager's list. I'll learn the lady when I meet her."

Alan shifts his weight, curiosity overriding caution. "Think the King's already smitten? Foreign princesses have a way of turning heads."

Alice bats the suggestion away. "His Majesty is smitten with competence. It's a dangerous mistress." She stirs her pot thoughtfully. "Besides, he's never been one to fall easily for women's wiles. He's looking for a queen, not a princess. We'll have to see if this Ysabel is truly one or merely the other."

Bess emerges from her silence like a captain from her quarters, flour dusting her arms as she wipes hands on her apron. Her voice carries the weight of years spent managing temperamental ovens and even more temperamental staff.

"We follow the one who fixes the leak."

Alice turns from her pot, eyebrow arched. "Then fetch buckets. The hall is all leaks."

The kitchen erupts in soft laughter. Even Meg allows herself a smile.

But Agnes steps forward, her expression earnest beneath the humor. "Please. No thorns for her today."

Alice studies the maid's face, reading genuine concern beneath the request. She nods slowly. "Thorns pruned. I can always plant them later."

Agnes gathers her supplies and departs with visible relief. Alice watches her go, then addresses the kitchen at large.

"If we must set a table for gossip, let it be bread, not knives."

She unties her apron, preparing for her castle rounds. A tale will spread of dawn rides, mysterious cloaks, and returning laughter. But carefully, kindly. The lady has earned that much consideration.

Lady Eveline Artois

Eveline enters the royal dinner hall as the minstrels soften their chord. The timing perfected through seasons of practice. Fashionably late commands attention without rudeness. A delicate balance that separates true nobles from pretenders.

She surveys the assembled company with easy eyes. Her first goal sparkles clear as polished silver: secure proximity to His Majesty. Her second proves more intriguing: decode this peculiar French catastrophe named Montbois.

The footman approaches with intended deference, prepared to escort her toward the seat she's already purchased through careful coin and whispered promises. She floats toward the King. Every step calculated, every smile measured. She reaches her seat, positioned for intimate conversation while appearing appropriately placed by rank. The King sits in his natural place at the table's head, with Lord Geoffrey and Queen Dowager flanking him on either side. Eveline finds herself seated beside Geoffrey, the next best vantage for capturing the King's attention, as His Majesty converses most frequently with his closest confidant.

"Your Majesty," she says, pausing before the footman can seat her, "I must beg your pardon for my lateness. I was assisting my mother, Lady Artois, with correspondences from home."

Alaric nods forgiveness, and Eveline seats with satisfaction warming her chest.

When she finally settles, she leans close enough to the King to catch his attention without breaching Geoffrey's personal space. "Your Majesty, the venison smells like victory."

"Victory is patient. It prefers a long simmer."

His response carries that maddening distance she's grown to expect. Polite, short, impossible to penetrate. She presses forward with carefully crafted questions about his recent activities, but his attention drifts as Lord Miles launches into a familiar tale.

"Someone," Miles declares with pointed emphasis toward Alaric, "racing across the countryside from bandits with an English maiden in tow, disguised as a squire no less."

Eveline's pulse quickens. The English maiden. She knows exactly whom Miles means, though his French-hating sensibilities haven't yet connected the dots to Hélène, seated mere places away.

She watches Hélène listen with barely contained amusement dancing in her eyes. Roland sends silent signals. Subtle hand movements that speak a language she does not know. Then Hélène catches Alaric's gaze and offers the most discreet, knowing smirk.

That look. That shared understanding. Eveline's fingers tighten around her goblet. Eveline strikes with silk-wrapped steel.

"Lady Hélène, such courage you showed yesterday morning," her gaze catches Hélène's, "to dress so simply at dawn."

The table quiets. Miles blinks like a startled owl, finally connecting his English maiden to the French noblewoman seated before him.

"It was simple to put on," Hélène replies with maddening composure, "and simpler to muddy."

Lord Cedric of Langmere erupts in laughter, far too loud for the jest's merit. "If the hedges dared scratch you, my lady, name them and I shall duel the shrubbery."

"Spare them," Hélène responds without missing a beat. "They fought without seconds."

More laughter ripples through nearby seats. Eveline watches Lord Percival of Dunmere lean forward with newfound interest, his eyes lingering on Hélène's face with obvious appreciation. Perfect. Let him chase the peculiar French woman. Perhaps that will remind Alaric what he's overlooking.

She glances toward the King, expecting satisfaction, but finds his attention fixed on Percival with unmistakable concern. As if protecting something precious.

Eveline's chest tightens as she glances toward the Queen Dowager, seeking some sign of approval for exposing Hélène's morning escapade. The Queen rarely graces these intimate dinners among the younger courtiers, preferring formal state occasions to casual gatherings.

Their eyes meet across the polished table. The Queen raises a single eyebrow. Deliberate, pointed, unmistakable. "Conversation should clothe the room, not undress it."

The words land like the harsh rap of a fan across knuckles. Heat floods Eveline's cheeks as the Queen's meaning sets in: *stop stripping away people's dignity for sport.* Around the table, conversations pause just long enough for the rebuke to settle, then resume with careful lightness.

Eveline realizes her gambit may have backfired. Eveline reaches for her wine, fingers trembling slightly. She's miscalculated badly. Not just with Hélène wit, but with the Queen Dowager herself.

"Sir Roland," the Queen Dowager continues smoothly, "are your newly assigned quarters to your liking? And your sister's?"

"They are, Your Grace. We thank Their Majesties for such consideration."

"Having you stay with Archbishop Anselm would not have served your needs. All unattached ladies and lords in my court, English or otherwise, remain under my wing."

The message resonates clearly. The Queen Dowager's protection extends to the Archbishop's French cousins, and any who challenge them challenge her authority.

Before the silence stretches too long, Isolde leans forward, her light voice dismantling tension with the kind of ease developed from years of practice. "We were debating whether poems travel better than horses."

The strain in Alaric's shoulders eases, amusement returning to his voice and features. "Roads wear and horses tire while poems breed."

The table brightens with genuine laughter. Eveline forces a smile, grateful for Isolde's diplomatic rescue even as frustration gnaws at her chest.

Then Miles taps his goblet, recovering his composure after connecting his English maiden to the French noblewoman. His smile carries sharp edges.

"To old roads, border tongues, and *patois*." The toast hangs poisonous in the air.

Roland and Alaric exchange a brief but full look before the King raises his own cup, voice hardening. "To roads that keep their memories… and their manners."

Everyone drinks. Miles gracefully nods his defeat and turns his attention back to Isolde and Lord Elias, leaving Eveline staring into her wine, watching her evening's ambitions sink further into the red abyss.

The conversation drifts toward poems and philosophy as platters are cleared. Eveline watches Hélène's face grow distant during talk of courtly verse, her fingers tracing idle patterns on the table rather than engaging with scholarly debate. Strange. What continental noblewoman lacks education in philosophy?

The Queen Dowager rises with noble grace, offering polite farewells. The table rises in ceremony to her exit. The King sits first, signaling to all to resume their seats as well. Eveline seizes her opening. She leans closer to Alaric with a soft, carefree laugh.

"I too should like to see these roads, Sire."

"They prefer pilgrims to tourists."

Cedric erupts in another unrestrained laugh, clearly missing Alaric's meaning entirely, while Geoffrey lets out an almost undignified snort. Eveline glances toward Hélène, expecting some vapid comment, but the French woman's lips part as if to speak, then close. Instead, she leans toward Isolde.

"I have discovered a new etiquette. Silence, strategically placed."

Eveline's jaw tightens. Even Hélène's restraint sounds witty.

As servants bring the final course, Alaric addresses the table with neutral good humor, never speaking directly to Roland or Hélène. Yet the looks pass between them. Subtle glances, shared understanding that Eveline's trained eye catches easily. The entire table notices something brewing beneath courtly politeness.

Eveline maintains her brightest smiles toward the King while her eyes stay focused on Hélène. The French woman speaks more warmly to serving staff than to fellow nobles, thanking them by name with a genuine appreciation. Peculiar behavior for supposed noble birth.

When the last plates disappear, Alaric stands. "May our supper end as it began. Hungry for better company."

Eveline forces another smile, though her evening has yielded nothing but questions and failure.

Sir Roland of Montbois

Roland adjusts his grip on the practice blade, watching afternoon steam rise from the training yard's damp stones. More than a month now. Winter's bite has given way to green shoots pushing through courtyard cracks. Spring on Earth. He'd only seen pictures during the long Martian cycles, archived images of seasons that actually changed without terraforming schedules.

Strange to think they fell into snow and now stand beneath budding branches.

"Ready positions," he calls, settling into the familiar rhythm of footwork to breath, breath to grip.

"If you can't count it, you can't keep it."

Stone steps forward, demonstrating the wheel throw they've been drilling with the perfection of a seasoned instructor. His movements flow like water finding its course, using momentum instead of fighting it.

"The ground is older than you. Let it do the heavy work."

Roland grins, appreciating how quickly Stone has made Roland's forms his own.

Across the yard, Holt observes a clean joint control between two younger guards.

"That saves bones, " Holt says with a single nod that carries more weight than elaborate praise.

"It also saves explanations to widows." The young guard quips.

Roland catches Holt's dry smile in his direction. These sessions have become something more than novelty. They're building doctrine. Roland wonders if he'll be there to see it completed. He's still holding out that home will find them, preferably before the Grey Hunter does.

A young lord stumbles backward, silk sleeves tangling as he attempts what Roland demonstrated with perfect balance moments before. His velvet-trimmed cloak twists around his ankles, sending him sprawling onto the recently dampened earth.

"You fought your cloak and lost."

Color flares in the youth's cheeks. His jaw tightens as he scrambles upright, brushing mud from expensive fabric. The flash of rage burns bright. Embarrassment curdling into something uglier.

"Again," the young noble snaps at his training companion, yanking at his cloak with sharp jerks.

Roland raises one hand, voice steady. "Anger is a thief. It steals your feet first."

Stone nods from the circle's edge. "A cool temper will help you more than anger in battle."

The youth quickly settles his hurt pride and his breathing slows. Roland steps closer to adjust the boy's stance. Shoulder down, weight centered. The boy does not flinch at Roland's careful adjustments. Simply nods at each instruction.

"Lower. Your knees are your reins. Slack them, and you lose control."

Three attempts. Four. The move flows clean on the fifth try as he sends his training companion to the ground, earning approving murmurs from watching guards. The young noble straightens, then offers a hand to his companion.

"My thanks, Sir Montbois. The lesson serves."

Roland sweeps his gaze across the yard as men collect practice weapons and dust themselves off for a well-earned luncheon. The earlier tension dissolves into easy laughter as guards portion water and adjust each other's gear with the casual intimacy of shared purpose.

"Well struck today," Stone murmurs as he coils loose practice rope.

"Clean work," Holt agrees while watching two knights demonstrate the day's throws to a curious stable boy.

Thomas Loxley approaches with the eager stride that's earned him the nickname "Roland's Shadow" among the guard. The boy's initial wariness has transformed into open devotion. He trails Roland like a devoted hound.

"Sir Roland, how long will you remain at court?"

The question carries innocent curiosity, but Roland catches movement at the yard's edge. Three guards who've refused every training session suddenly find urgent business near the water barrels, ears tilted toward their conversation.

"Until I am called back home," Roland says, then adds with a grin, "or when His Majesty tires of me."

"The King would never tire of you!" Loxley protests with fierce loyalty. "But who trained you to fight as you do? None have seen such methods."

Denby materializes to Roland's left, clearly intending to redirect the questioning, but Roland waves him off.

"I left home young to serve as a traveling knight on the continent. Many French knights shared their knowledge freely. I honor their memory by passing their varied skills forward."

Denby's eyebrow climbs toward his hairline. They've been instructed by Anselm to not embellish on Roland's background. Roland tilts his head slightly toward the eavesdropping guards, now making their hasty retreat toward the castle. Denby follows with practiced discretion, ready to determine who their 'master' is.

Holt nudges Loxley toward the armory. "Come, boy. Weapons don't clean themselves."

As they walk away, Stone falls into step beside him. "The younger ones take to you like ducklings to water. You handle the green differently than the seasoned."

"Aye." Roland catches Stone's opening to cement his background to any still listening. Roland appreciates the guard's protection of his identity. Seven guards had witnessed their arrival, yet none betrayed their King's trust to keep whispers down and stories aligned, even when that meant hiding the truth from other guards.

"I've trained young and aged nobles alike."

Stone inquires no further. His mission accomplished.

They walk in shared silence to the armory hall. Roland's mind drifts to a time and place far away when he trained both young and old. Even amongst the Agents of Time, he was a skilled fighter. The agency was selective with its recruits, leaning toward families already familiar with the agency's existence. A well-hidden existence. His memory shifts to a younger Hélène amongst a sea of fresh recruits. He was seventeen and teaching his first lesson alongside their father. She was barely twelve years old. *Twelve*. A decade and many shared missions have passed since.

Lessons in Silk

- 8 -

Lady Cecily Artois

The Etiquette Chamber gleams as the morning light streams through tall windows, casting sharp reflections across polished mirrors that line the walls. Lady Cecily Artois arranges her fan while observing the three younger women seated in the circle's neatly arranged chairs.

Hélène surveys the room with obvious amusement before leaning toward Isolde and supplying one of her odd jests. "If anyone passes around herbal tea and trust exercises, I'm out."

Eveline raises an eye, ready to make a retort on Hélène's strange behavior. Cecily brings her fan down twice against her palm. Sharp, deliberate taps that command immediate attention.

"The Queen Dowager has formally assigned me to train Lady Hélène in English court etiquette. I trust each of you to remember who holds authority in this chamber."

She sweeps her gaze across each face, lingering on her daughter Eveline, who shifts uncomfortably under the scrutiny. "We begin with first principles. A lady does not conquer a room. She arranges it."

"I've been accused of rearranging furniture," Hélène murmurs.

Cecily's eyebrow arches with restrained disapproval. "Your first lesson: Wit is a garnish. Use it after the meat is served."

"Then I shall starve it till dessert," Hélène replies, her tone appropriately sober.

Isolde covers a smile behind her fan while Eveline examines her fingernails with forced indifference.

"Now then." Cecily snaps her fan closed, gaining back the room's undivided attention. "The foundation of all courtly interaction is proper forms of address."

Cecily moves to the center of the chamber, her movements measured and graceful. "Lady Hélène, you must understand that greeting establishes hierarchy. The lesser is always presented to the greater."

" 'Your Grace, may I present Lady Hélène of Montbois.' " She demonstrates with a slight inclination of her head. "We climb the stair in the right order. We descend it with care."

"And if I meet the King, or Queen Dowager?"

"Your Majesty upon first greeting, then Sire within that same exchange. In third person, always His Majesty. Never presume familiarity in public spaces."

Cecily watches Hélène absorb this information, noting the slight furrow between her brows as she matches Cecily's instruction to what she has learned in passing.

"The Queen Dowager receives Your Majesty, thereafter Your Grace. A princess or prince, should we receive either, merits Your Highness. Archbishop Anselm: Your Grace, then Archbishop or My Lord Archbishop."

Hélène nods slowly, clearly cataloguing each distinction.

"Peers require My Lord or My Lady with their place. Lord Redwyke, Lady Isolde. Among intimates, you may use Isolde, but never drop the title entirely at court."

"Knights receive Sir with given name. Sir Denby, never Sir William alone. Clergy below bishop rank: Father. Should we encounter ambassadors: Your Excellency."

Hélène attempts a playful rhyme under her breath about lords and swords that has clearly come from a children's book that Anselm provided. Eveline stifles a comment behind a subtle laugh. Cecily raises one eyebrow in warning.

"The rules exist for order, not ornament. Shall we practice with a curtsy?" Eveline prompts.

Cecily gestures for Hélène to stand beside her before the tall mirrors, their reflections multiplied in the morning light. She smooths her skirts with trained precision. Even that simple task requires etiquette. Hélène catches on and mimics the action.

"A lady bends. She does not collapse and never grovels." She demonstrates the movement with fluid grace, sinking into a deep measured curtsy before the mirror as if greeting royalty.

"Observe the line from crown to heel. Spine tall, head level. Soften the knees. Do not fold at the waist."

Hélène attempts to mirror the motion but descends too quickly, her movement brisk rather than controlled.

"Bend like a bow, not a hinge." Eveline instructs from her seat with barely concealed disdain.

"If I snap an arrow, we run."

Cecily's lips twitch despite herself, but she maintains her instructional tone. "Your footing, Lady Hélène. Slide one foot behind the other, heels close. Control your skirts with a light pinch, no swishing."

She adjusts Hélène's posture with gentle but firm corrections. Straighten the spine, lower the chin, reposition the knees.

"Depth signals respect. For His Majesty or the Queen Dowager, deeper bend. Archbishop Anselm and high peers merit moderate depth. Other nobles receive a light half-curtsy. Too low appears fawning. Too shallow reads as slight."

Hélène attempts the movement again, this time with improved control.

"Better. Pause one heartbeat at the lowest point... there. Rise in a single smooth line, no bobbing."

She demonstrates the hand placement next.

"One hand steadies the skirt. Your fan remains closed at waist level and never flutters during a curtsy. Lower your eyes to chest level, not the floor. Meet their gaze again on the rise."

Hélène executes the curtsy with proper form, earning a nod of approval.

"Remember to plant your feet, curtsy, then move. Never curtsy while walking. Should you curtsy too shallow, add a second, marginally deeper one with a soft 'Your pardon.' "

Cecily steps back, observing her student's progress before moving to the next lesson. "Now we address the art of crossing a chamber without appearing to stumble."

Isolde approaches with long strips of fabric, fastening makeshift trains to both Hélène's and Eveline's waists. The weighted cloth pools behind them like ceremonial rivers.

Eveline demonstrates the proper train walking technique, her palm brushing the fabric while her fingertips catch the hem in a delicate lift.

"Small steps. You carry the gown, not the other way round." Cecily instructs.

Hélène attempts the movement but immediately snags her foot in the trailing fabric, stumbling forward with an awkward lurch.

"Let it know who pays the rent," she mutters, regaining her balance.

Isolde presses her lips together to contain her mirth while Eveline's smile turns sharp with satisfaction.

"Again," Cecily commands.

This time Hélène does not trip, but her stride has no elegance.

"Glide, don't march." Cecily further instructs as Eveline demonstrates again. "Your train follows like a faithful hound. It should never lead you astray."

Hélène reproduces Eveline's masterful glide with precision. Her steps controlled as the fabric flows smoothly behind her.

"Much improved indeed," Cecily declares, her voice carrying the sincere satisfaction of a tutor witnessing genuine progress. She adjusts her grip on the fan, the ivory blades settling into their closed position with a soft whisper. "Your steps and curtsies have found their proper cadence, Lady Hélène. The fabric no longer commands you."

A subtle smile touches the corners of her mouth as she observes Hélène's newfound confidence in managing the weighted train and gown. Her mind frowns at Eveline's poised instructions. Too smooth to be sincere, too pointed to be kind. The afternoon's lesson has yielded fruit, though she suspects tomorrow will bring fresh challenges.

"Ladies," she continues, inclining her head with the gracious formality that marks the end of their session, "you are dismissed. Lady Hélène. I understand the Archbishop has provided papers on England's noble families. I suggest you review titles and practice the proper greetings."

As they curtsy their farewells, Hélène adds a theatrical flourish that draws chuckles from Isolde. Cecily's fan raps sharply across Hélène's knuckles.

"Save the jest until the room is already yours."

"I will spend them more dearly," Hélène replies, properly contrite as she rubs her fingers.

Eveline's smirk widens as they file toward the door.

Lady Hélène of Montbois

Hélène arrives at the Etiquette Chamber for day two, her steps measured and purposeful. She is ready to master whatever lessons await and to not allow Eveline's petty barbs dim her resolve. Upon entry, she executes a passable curtsy to Cecily, who responds with a brief nod of acknowledgment.

"Good morning, Lady Cecily. Lady Isolde. Lady Eveline."

Cecily gestures toward the center of the chamber where a small table waits, set for four with pewter plates, cups, and an array of serving dishes. Isolde and Eveline already occupy their chairs, hands folded in their laps.

"Today we dine as court demands. Take your place, but remain standing."

Hélène approaches a vacant chair but does not sit, following yesterday's lessons about waiting for permission. The table gleams with polished pewter and crisp linen, a miniature replica of the Great Hall's high table.

"We sit when His Majesty sits, and rise when he rises," Cecily instructs, settling into her own chair with fluid grace. "If Her Grace attends, we rise and sit when she does."

Hélène hovers beside her chair. "And if my knees give or my skirts tangle?"

"Then lean like ivy. Do not plant like oak."

Cecily signals for them to sit, and Hélène lowers herself carefully, watching Isolde's movements for guidance.

Beside the table, a copper ewer catches the morning light as steam rises from its surface. "Cleanse your hands first. Always," Cecily instructs.

Hélène follows Cecily's demonstration, pouring water over her fingers and drying them on the linen towel. She places the napkin across her lap, smoothing the fabric with deliberate care.

"Bread breaks. Reputations should not. Keep fingers clean." Cecily tears a portion from the dark loaf, her movements precise and controlled.

Hélène mimics the action but studies the hard remaining crust with obvious skepticism. "What if the loaf breaks me first?"

"Then you take smaller bites."

The lesson continues with the trencher placement and sauce management. Cecily demonstrates how to guide the thick pottage without allowing it to overflow onto neighboring plates. "A lady governs her sauce. Spillage is self-betrayal."

When Cecily presents the knife selection, Hélène reaches for the wrong blade before catching herself mid-motion. She swaps to the proper carving knife with smooth confidence.

"A mistake corrected is a courtesy doubled."

"Then I shall become very polite."

Her blade scrapes against the pewter with a harsh metallic sound. Cecily winces.

"Steel speaks only to the meat." Eveline's first barb.

"A pity. My knife has opinions about everything else as well." Hélène refuses to let Eveline's barbs take hold.

Isolde allows a light laugh, while Cecily provides healthier instruction to them both. "Let your words do the carving."

They settle into the lunch turned instructional. Nearing the meal's end, Cecily motions for the wine footman.

"Health first, thirsts after. When wine is offered again?" Cecily inquires as the footman leans in to pour more for Hélène.

Hélène recalls the Queen Dowager once politely saying no to more wine. She mimics by placing her palm over the cup's rim. "My cup keeps its counsel tonight."

"And so does my ledger of your good behavior." Cecily gives her a smile.

Cecily then retrieves her fan from her decorative waist belt, the ivory blades catching the light. "Now we learn a language your tongue need never speak."

They leave the table for seats in the corner. Cecily raises the fan between them like a delicate shield. "This stays within these walls. The Language of Fans belongs to ladies alone. Never shared with lords, never displayed before men who might decode our counsel."

Hélène nods, understanding the weight of sisterhood secrets.

"One tap keeps your course, two trims your sails, three stops the ship." Cecily demonstrates each signal with crisp precision. "Face up to gift your meaning, face down to soften it."

Eveline snaps her fan open with theatrical flair, executing a series of quick taps and graceful waves. Her movements flow like water, each gesture perfectly timed.

Hélène attempts to mirror the motion but nearly opens her fan backward. The ivory spokes catch awkwardly, and she fumbles to correct the grip.

"Careful. The wrong flutter can promise too much." Eveline's smirk cuts at her.

"Then I'll promise air and nothing else."

Cecily continues her instruction. "The hilt is your compass: outward asks for allies, inward keeps counsel. If Her Grace is within ten paces, keep the sea calm, no wandering gestures."

Hélène practices the basic positions, her movements improving with each repetition. The fan feels foreign in her hands. She is more accustomed to other *weapons*. Though she appreciates the tactical value in the silent communication that the fans provide.

"Never wave boredom. In this castle, boredom is treason against courtesy."

As the lesson concludes, Eveline sweeps from the chamber with practiced elegance. Cecily follows, leaving final instructions about tomorrow's lesson protocols.

Isolde lingers, moving closer to Hélène with conspiratorial warmth.

"There are signals for your maids to learn as well." Her voice drops to a whisper. "Hilt inward with one slow tap: bring cloth or note. Hilt outward toward the door with two taps: fetch guard quietly. Face down with fan to right wrist: cancel whatever you asked before."

Hélène commits each gesture to memory, grateful for practical applications. "Agnes will learn quickly?"

"Agnes learns everything that keeps you safe."

Lady Cecily Artois

The third morning brings musicians to the Etiquette Chamber. Two lute players settle beside the tall windows while a young man with a small drum arranges himself close by. Cecily adjusts her pearl-gray gown and surveys her pupils with growing satisfaction.

Hélène enters precisely at the bell's final toll, her posture markedly improved from two days prior. Isolde follows close behind, offering quiet encouragement in rapid French. Eveline sweeps through the doorway with theatrical timing, her burgundy silk catching the light like spilled wine.

"Today we speak the language of movement," Cecily announces. "In great halls, the dance reveals what words conceal."

She signals the musicians, who begin the opening notes of *St. Hugh's Measure*. A slow, stately procession that rises and falls like gentle tide.

"A lady carries a book on her head. The book must not fall."

Cecily demonstrates the proper frame, her left hand resting lightly on an imaginary partner's forearm while her right hand curves gracefully at her side. Her shoulders remain low, her chin level, her spine a perfect line from crown to heel.

Hélène mirrors the posture. Her shoulders creep upward, then drop as she corrects herself. Isolde moves fluidly beside her.

"Let your heel kiss the floor. Glide, do not stamp."

"Heel... glide," Hélène murmurs under her breath, practicing the motion.

The music swells, and Cecily counts the rhythm aloud. "One for breath, two for grace, three to arrive, four to show you meant it."

Hélène follows the count carefully, her steps gradually smoothing from mechanical obedience to something approaching natural rhythm.

"One…do not tread toes. Two…do not tread pride," she whispers to herself.

Eveline glides past with perfect form, her movements a masterpiece of controlled elegance. She catches Cecily's eye with a meaningful look.

"And yet she treads attention," Eveline murmurs low.

Cecily maintains her neutral expression, though inwardly she notes how easily Eveline's resentment surfaces. The girl's vanity remains her greatest weakness.

The final notes of *St. Hugh's Measure* fade, and Cecily nods with quiet approval at Hélène's steady improvement.

"Your frame holds true now. The spine remembers." She turns to the musicians. "The *Hall Carole*, if you please."

A livelier melody begins, all bright intervals and dancing rhythm. Cecily demonstrates the foundational step.

"Side-close, side-close. Think of it as bread to the left, bread to the right, no crumbs on the floor."

Hélène watches intently, then begins the pattern. "Side-close… side-close," she murmurs, her movements growing more confident with each repetition.

The music shifts to signal the hand chain passage. Cecily pairs with Eveline to show the gentle courtesy of fingertips meeting as couples pass.

"Eyes do the greeting. Fingers only sign your name," Isolde explains softly, as she pairs with Hélène.

Hélène nods, practicing the light touch with careful attention to the eye contact Isolde emphasizes.

As they move into the set change, Cecily guides Hélène through the forward and backward weaving.

"A feather forward, a ribbon back. Feel the lead's guidance but keep your own balance."

"Feather...ribbon. Aye." Hélène's voice carries growing confidence.

The music builds toward the end flourish and a paired bow from the waist with fans properly closed. As they prepare the movement, Eveline glides past with perfect form.

"Do try not to bow like a stable boy," she remarks cooly.

Cecily's voice remains mild but carries unmistakable correction. "And we do not coach with thorns, Lady Eveline."

The jaunt ends and Hélène executes the closing bow with near perfection. Cecily raises her hand. The chamber settles into expectant quiet, as all eyes fall on her.

"The final lesson carries the greatest weight," she begins, her tone sharpening with purpose. "You will encounter dances you have never seen. Partners who expect mastery you cannot possess. The skill lies not in knowing every step, but in following what you do not know."

She gestures for Isolde to partner with Hélène. "Watch the lead's shoulder, not their feet. Their shoulder is your compass. Their feet a map you cannot read in time."

Isolde demonstrates with fluid motion, her shoulder telegraphing direction a beat before her feet move. Hélène follows the cue, stumbling slightly but catching the rhythm.

"Feel for pressure and release on the forearm," Cecily continues. "A feather of pressure means forward or turn. A light draw calls you back. If the rein loosens, do not gallop."

Hélène nods, practicing the subtle communication through Isolde's gentle guidance.

"Keep a quiet core. Soft knees, steady ribs. Let the feet answer, not the torso."

"Like taking a strike," Hélène murmurs. "Abs still, feet clever."

Cecily's lips twitch with approval of the analogy, though she wonders why that particular parallel. "Precisely so. When lost, return to side-close, side-close at half-volume until you feel the next cue. When lost, go home. Home is side and close."

The music resumes, and Hélène whispers the count under her breath. "One-two…three-four…"

"Shall we fetch a counting slate for the lady?" Eveline's voice carries honeyed venom.

Isolde's response flows with pleasant steel. "Soldiers count to keep their comrades alive. Dancers too."

Eveline's fan snaps shut with the same sharpness her gaze gives Isolde.

"Eyes up, fan quiet," Cecily instructs with a matched sharpness. "Your eyes carry half the step. Your fan carries none." Then back to her supportive tone, "Water takes the shape of the cup, Hélène."

"And if the cup leaks?" Hélène asks, her dry humor surfacing.

Cecily allows herself a small smile. "Then you forgive him and finish the dance. We write mistakes in sand. The next measure washes them."

The final notes fade, and Cecily surveys her pupil with full satisfaction.

"Your foundation stands firm now. The training is complete, though you cannot return to court activities until Archbishop Anselm grants his approval. Practice these steps in your quarters."

Hélène curtsies with newfound grace, her form precise and respectful. "My deepest gratitude, Lady Cecily. Your patience has been my salvation."

"Time shall tell." Eveline sweeps from the chamber without a backward glance, her burgundy silk trailing indifference.

Isolde touches Hélène's arm gently. "I shall continue your practice sessions until the Archbishop speaks. The steps and curtsy will hold better with daily tending."

"Bread before bells," Hélène murmurs the wisdom.

Cecily nods approvingly, watching her pupil with quiet pride.

Allies

- 9 -

Archbishop Anselm of Clearvale

Anselm watches from his carved chair as Lady Cecily signals for the final demonstration. The solar's afternoon light catches the careful precision of Hélène's movements. Three days of Cecily's training distilled into this moment.

"The curtsy, if you please," Cecily instructs.

Hélène steps forward, her posture aligned and controlled. The descent flows smoothly, her head inclined at the proper angle, hands and fan positioned properly. She rises without tremor or haste.

"Acceptable, and nearly elegant," Cecily pronounces.

Hélène's mouth quirks under restrained mirth. "I will creep toward elegance and hope it does not notice."

Isolde stifles a laugh behind her hand while Cecily's expression remains diplomatically neutral. Anselm notes the exchange with growing concern about the girl's irreverent tongue.

"The Basse Dance, Lady Isolde," Cecily continues.

The partners move through the steps of a silent melody, Hélène following Isolde's lead with careful attention to shoulder cues and footwork. Her count remains audible but controlled, her frame steady despite the complexity.

"You still lean with your bones," Cecily observes, appraising. "Keep the counting. For now."

"By the spring ball, you will glide," Isolde adds warmly.

Hélène grins. "If I tread on a peacock, it will be by design."

Anselm clears his throat, drawing attention to his presence. The levity dims appropriately. "Lady Cecily, your assessment?"

"Lady Hélène possesses the foundation necessary for court activities, Your Grace. Her deportment will serve adequately."

Anselm nods gravely. "My gratitude for your patient instruction, Lady Cecily. You may withdraw."

Cecily curtsies to Anselm, then turns to Hélène with pointed emphasis. "Your humor disarms. Let it be the last weapon drawn."

"Last drawn, never lost," Hélène replies quietly.

After Cecily departs, Anselm fixes Hélène with a stern gaze. "Your wit cuts sharp, my dear, perhaps too sharp for comfort. Lady Cecily's counsel bears heeding. Draw upon it last."

Hélène gives a small curtsy with a downward nod. The perfect form for accepting correction.

He turns to other concerns. "While I understand your fondness for your brother's company, you are now under the Queen Dowager's wing and shall remain among the ladies."

Hélène's demeanor turns sullen, but she does not dispute.

"Lady Hélène," Isolde interjects smoothly, "perhaps you would join me for embroidery this afternoon?"

"An excellent suggestion," Anselm agrees before Hélène can respond. "You are both dismissed."

As the ladies move toward the door, the King appears in the threshold. Both women halt and execute proper curtsies.

"Your Majesty," they murmur in unison.

Alaric's smile brightens notably as his gaze settles on Hélène. "Lady Hélène, Lady Isolde."

"By your leave, Sire," Hélène says, her tone perfectly measured.

They complete their withdrawal gracefully. Anselm observes how Alaric's eyes follow Hélène's departure before the King enters and settles into the chair opposite.

"Her studies progress well?" Alaric inquires.

"Lady Cecily has pronounced her fit for full court."

Alaric chuckles. "A true lady now, no longer my dawn squire. I suppose that means no more rides through the countryside."

Anselm's expression remains stern. "A king should set the proper example, not encourage impropriety."

"Perhaps." Alaric leans forward, his brow turned serious. "Your Grace, when we needed refuge after that ride, Sir Roland guided us through servant passages to my chambers without hesitation. His knowledge of castle routes appears to serve protection, not treachery. Why else display the knowledge so brazenly?"

Anselm nods slowly. "He has earned the Guard's respect. Sir Holt speaks favorably of his methods."

"Few oppose his presence now." Alaric pauses. "They adapt quickly to circumstance."

"Indeed. Let's pray Lady Hélène adapts just as well."

Both men sit in contemplative silence, the weight of concealed truth settling between.

"They serve well," Alaric says finally, his voice quiet but certain. "Whatever their origins, Roland is proving their worth to the Crown."

Anselm inclines his head slightly. "Service often reveals character more clearly than birth or breeding. In that regard, Sir Roland has distinguished himself beyond question. As for Lady Hélène, she still has much to learn. But Lady Cecily will keep her well-tuned."

The King rises, moving to the window where he can observe the small garden between Anselm's London residence and the castle's outer courtyard wall. Town folk go about their duties on a dusty street nearby, ignorant of the world inside the castle. He considers the changes to that world since the Montbois arrival. "The realm is stronger for their presence, Your Grace. That much cannot be disputed."

"No," Anselm agrees, gathering his papers with deliberate care. "It cannot."

Lady Hélène of Montbois

The narrow stone steps spiral upward, each footfall echoing loudly in the tower's hollow core. Hélène grips the rope banister with one hand as the other adjusts the unforgiving embrace of whalebone stays.

"Why must embroidery require mountaineering?" she asks, pausing to glance up at the seemingly endless curve above.

Isolde's laugh tinkles like small bells. "This tower belongs to the ladies. We may speak freely here without fear of wandering ears."

Her eyes sparkle with mischief as she adds, "Besides, the tower offers a wonderful view of the training yard."

Hélène raises an eyebrow but continues climbing until halfway up, when her stays' merciless probing forces her to halt once more. She leans against the cool stone wall, her fan wobbling uncertainly in her hand as she struggles for breath.

"Shall I summon a physician, or Agnes?" Isolde asks with mock concern. They've developed a banter between them that nearly rivals her and Roland's. Hélène welcomes the sisterly bond.

"I have survived curtsies," Hélène manages between measured breaths. "The physicians may stand down."

Isolde produces a small cloth pouch from her sleeve, offering a sugared almond. "You learn quickly when you choose to."

Hélène accepts the sweet gratefully, savoring its crunch. "Fear is an excellent tutor."

"Perhaps." Isolde's expression grows more serious. "Though you should know, some ladies resent the King's warmth toward you. Their eyes bruise easily."

"Then I shall tread on eggs and smile at omelets." She has noticed Eveline's pointed stares when the King looks in her direction.

"Your wit serves you well, but..." Isolde touches Hélène's wrist gently. "Choose one jest, then tie it neatly. Words are like embroidery ribbons. Too many tangles spoil the pattern."

Hélène nods, understanding the careful diplomacy required. "I will keep the others in a drawer."

They resume their climb as Isolde's voice takes on the careful precision of a tutor. "Your French carries the dust of distant roads, *ma chère*. We must polish it for court."

She demonstrates with exaggerated care. "*Je vous remercie, madame.* Softly, like silk."

Hélène attempts the phrase, her tongue stumbling over vowels that feel foreign despite the cover story. "*Je vous remercie...* Like silk that survived a storm."

"Precisely the problem," Isolde laughs, though not unkindly. "You speak French like a peasant who learned it from merchants."

The accusation stings with its accuracy, though Isolde means no malice. Hélène forces a rueful smile. "The borders roughen everything, even my *patois.*"

"Then we shall smooth the edges." Isolde's eyes dance with conspiracy. "Everyone speaks, but few say anything meaningful."

"A court specialty."

"Then we will say enough for two." Isolde pauses on the next landing, demonstrating a curtsy with theatrical solemnity. "Practice makes—"

Her skirts tangle comically as intended, but she suddenly loses her balance on the step. Hélène grabs her and pulls them both backward. They collapse together against the stone wall, shoulders shaking with suppressed laughter.

They reach the upper chamber's heavy oak door, breathless but composed. Inside, afternoon light streams through tall windows, illuminating embroidery frames arranged in careful rows. Ladies bend over their work like flowers toward sun.

Eveline's gaze cuts sharp when Hélène enters. The disdain radiates from her posture. The chin lifted higher and shoulders squared in territorial warning. Hélène moves past without acknowledgment, but Lady Rosamund gives a welcoming nod, the incoming sunlight brightening the natural highlights in her copper red hair.

Isolde claims two seats near the eastern window. She gives Hélène that same twinkling look as before and giggles softly behind her fan. Below, the training yard spreads like a miniature battlefield where figures move in repeated patterns.

"He teaches men to fall without breaking," she murmurs, watching Roland demonstrate a controlled tumble that transforms potential injury into tactical advantage.

Isolde settles beside her, feeding silk through her needle's slender eye with ease. "And you teach rooms to listen without bristling."

The observation strikes deeper than expected. Hélène considers the parallel. Roland's students learning balance against her own careful navigation of court tensions. Both require precision, timing, and the wisdom to yield without surrendering strength.

"Sheathed, not surrendered," she says quietly.

"Good. Some kingdoms only open to laughter."

The words resonate with uncomfortable truth. She has always been Roland's eager pupil, following his lead, learning from his example. But Isolde sees in Hélène something different. A teacher in her own right, wielding humor like a master craftsman shapes steel.

Circumstances have removed her from her brother's shadow. A private vow forms: carry wit like a hidden blade, not a banner. Protect Roland, even if that means protecting him from her own impulsiveness.

The door swings wide. A footman's voice rings clear.

"Her Grace, Queen Dowager Margaret."

Chairs scrape stone as ladies rise in unison.

"If I fumble, push me into grace," Hélène whispers.

"Happily," Isolde breathes back.

Sir Roland of Montbois

Through the hush of morning mist, the hunting paths stretch ahead, each hoofbeat softened by new grass and damp earth. Roland adjusts his position off Sir Holt's shoulder, close enough for quick signals but distant enough to avoid clustered targets. Behind them, Sir Kingsley maintains the rear with steady vigilance.

"After the morning scrape, we ride these trails twice a day," Holt calls softly, his voice carrying the weight of new protocol. "By the King's peace, keep your eyes."

Roland's mouth quirks with dry humor. "Eyes ahead, ears behind. Forests keep two ledgers."

The phrase earns a grunt of approval from Holt, who has grown to appreciate Roland's compact wisdom. Since the bandit attack that nearly claimed the King and Hélène, Denby has doubled the watch rotations and assigned Roland to assist with perimeter sweeps.

They rein up at a small clearing where morning light filters through bare branches. A scent hits Roland. Woodsmoke, but too fresh.

A fire ring sits in the clearing's center. Ash still sending thin tendrils skyward. Boot prints stamp the earth around it like a violent dance, and bracken lies crushed along the northern edge where something heavy passed through.

Kingsley dismounts, touching the ash with trained caution. "Still warm."

Kingsley's eyes trace the prints, reading the story written in mud and broken twigs, "Four men. One favors the left foot. Two carry weight low. Food or loot."

Holt motions with two fingers, and they ease off their mounts into staggered cover.

"Triangle. I at the nose, Roland to my right, Kingsley left. No hero's charge. If they run, let them show us who whistles." Holt instructs in a whisper.

With a grim smile, Kinglsey acknowledges, "Aye, let the rabbits lead us to the warren."

A twig snaps somewhere in the bracken ahead, sharp as a bone breaking. The silence that follows stretches like a drawn bowstring, then snaps loose as two shapes burst from the brush.

"Left moving, two!" Holt's shield comes up in one smooth motion, catching the morning light on its polished steel.

The first bandit rushes Roland with wild eyes and a rusted blade, but Roland reads the attack like a textbook. He sidesteps, catches the extended wrist, binds it tight against his hip, then turns the elbow with surgical precision. His heel finds the bandit's knee, and the man crashes to earth with a strangled cry.

"Mercy!" The bandit gasps, his arm twisted at an angle that promises lasting pain if he struggles.

The second attacker rushes Kingsley, blade arcing toward the knight's exposed flank. Kingsley deflects most of the force, but steel bites through sleeve and draws blood.

"Kingsley!" Roland's voice cuts like a bell. "Hook behind the knee then twist!"

Kingsley batters the blade aside with his pommel, catches the man's jaw with the return stroke, then executes the knee twist exactly as instructed. The bandit topples with a grunt, and Kingsley pins him.

"Hold! No blood if we can help it." Holt calls over his shield.

"Another at the back!" Roland shouts, catching movement in his peripheral vision.

A third bandit emerges from deeper cover, bow drawn. Holt's shield lifts just in time to catch the arrow with a solid thunk. The archer rushes forward, swinging his bow like a club.

Holt tosses his shield to the side and executes the wheel topple with mechanical precision, using the bandit's momentum to send him sprawling into the mud.

The fallen bowman rolls over, defeat clear in his eyes, and whistles once, sharp and commanding. A shadow in the brush withdraws quickly into deeper woods.

"He calls to a handler." Roland keeps his voice low, eyes scanning the treeline where the shadow vanished.

Holt nods grimly. "We'll ask the handler's name when his boys sing."

Kinglsey binds the nearest captive swiftly with precision. He catches Roland's observation, glad to advise the fellow warrior, "Tie thumbs, not wrists. They can't wriggle loose."

Captives now restrained, they finally breathe, and Roland observes the situation. No one down, only bruises. Kingsley wipes at the cut on his upper arm, inspecting the tear with mock solemnity. "I'll tell the sleeve it died for the realm."

Roland's mouth twitches at the dry humor. "We bring them back alive. That's worth more than a tidy kill."

By noon they're back at the Armory Hall, where the air thickens with murmurs as guards gather for midday meal. The weight of recent events lingers in their whispers. In a small chamber to the hall's left, Denby listens from his scribal desk, chalice in hand, his eyes narrow as he balances discipline with discovery.

Holt stands tall, recounting the morning's chaos with pride. "Ambush set for fools. We were not fools. Montbois' grips kept blades short and men standing."

Kingsley steps forward. Calm, his words deliver the techniques that held chaos at bay. "Aye, the wheel and joint methods deliver well. Our shields ate their arrows and our grips ate their panic."

Denby's gaze shifts to Kingsley's torn sleeve, now marked by dried blood. His nod delivers a verdict, "By order of the guard, Montbois drills are now mandatory. First bell and third bell. Yard and hall."

Holt leans close to Roland, a whisper of gratitude amidst duty's solemnity. "You saved lives today."

Roland's mouth curves, almost into something that resembles a smile. "Cheaper than funerals."

Spanish Weather

- 10 -

The Court

Trumpets blare across the courtyard as the Spanish entourage crests the bridge, their pennons snapping crisp against the spring sky. Lacquered coffers gleam atop wheeled carts while gloved riders maintain perfect formation despite the road dust. The herald's voice carries clear over the bustle.

"Her Highness Princess Ysabel of Navarre!"

King Alaric stands beside Queen Dowager Margaret on the great steps, watching silk and ceremony unfold below. The Princess descends from her carriage in a cascade of crimson and gold, seed-pearls catching sunlight like scattered stars and dark hair perfectly set with pearl pins. Her smile radiates warmth, yet her dark eyes assess each face, each banner, each stone of the castle.

The Queen Dowager descends the steps first. Her posture carries the poised weight of decades at court.

"England greets us with sun and stone," Ysabel speaks first, her voice melodious yet firm.

"And hearths," the Queen Dowager replies, matching the Princess's pleasant tone.

Behind Ysabel, a second figure emerges more quietly. A young courtesan with brown curls that frame her face and freckles that dust her nose. The lady keeps her hazel eyes lowered, her French greeting barely audible above the courtyard noise.

"Je suis Dame Colette de Brissac, vos Majestés."

A chamberlain murmurs to his companion, "A pretty shadow. But why does a French lady trail our Spanish princess?"

Don Íñigo de Villaseño emerges from another carriage with courtly flourish, positioning himself at Ysabel's shoulder. His bow sweeps low, yet his gaze catalogues every noble face present.

"Spain brings friendship... and excellent penmanship," he announces with the perfect charm of an established ambassador.

Alaric steps forward, offering the courtesy due a foreign princess while maintaining the reserve befitting his crown. Her beauty strikes him as undeniable as England's spring.

"Your journey will be repaid with comfort," he states formally.

Ysabel's smile deepens, her response swift and pointed. "Comfort is a gracious coin, Sire. Fitting, as I come to the house that shall soon be *my* home."

The words settle uneasily in Alaric's mind. Neither she nor Don Íñigo have offered proper address. No "Your Majesty," no acknowledgment of rank beyond the bare minimum. More troubling still is her casual claim of ownership. *My* home. She speaks as though their betrothal were already complete, as though his crown were already shared.

He keeps his expression neutral, but unease stirs beneath the diplomatic surface. Spring has indeed arrived, yet he wonders what manner of weather this Princess brings.

Lord Geoffrey steps back into the cluster of courtiers, positioning himself where whispers flow like water between stones. Two ladies lean close beside him, their voices barely audible beneath the ceremonial fanfare.

"Such crimson," murmurs Lady Eveline. "Heavy as cathedral vestments."

"Silk like a sermon," Lady Rosamund agrees, eyes tracking the Princess's movements.

An elderly Baron shifts beside them, his face creased with disapproval. "Mark how she speaks 'my home,' as though the crown were already upon her brow."

The comment ripples through those nearby. Geoffrey feels the subtle stiffening, the shared intake of breath. A princess should court favor, not claim territory.

Lady Eveline's gaze drifts across the hall, to another figure. "And our French lady listens."

Geoffrey follows her look to where Lady Hélène stands among the court, her expression unreadable yet alert. Her attention fixes on the Spanish delegation with the intensity of someone cataloguing every gesture, every word.

Eveline's observation hangs in the air, waiting for someone else to give it meaning, but no one does. They're all too focused on the impending Spanish storm.

The Queen Dowager Margaret observes the Spanish Princess with the experienced eye of decades spent reading court currents. When Ysabel approached for the formal greeting, her bow dipped precisely, yet stopped a fraction short of the depth protocol demands. No correction with an apology. The Princess should have arrived well versed in English court protocols. Lady Faversham was sent to ensure this and missed her own son's wedding to do so. Yet, the Princess arrives with a French courtesan in her place.

Margaret's ear catches on the Spanish Princess's presumption: *my home*. The phrase sits wrong, carrying too much assumption, too little earned respect. A future queen should court favor before claiming territory.

Margaret's response flows smooth like a polished knife through warm butter, each word weighted with quiet correction. "You are welcome in my house, Your Highness."

The emphasis falls soft yet unmistakable. A gentle reminder that crown and castle remain firmly where they belong, whatever promises the future may hold.

The procession continues to unfold as the Archbishop Anselm steps to Margaret's side. Don Íñigo presents gifts of Spanish silks, Moorish silver, and documents sealed in crimson wax. Anselm nods the gifts away, then offers a blessing with his characteristic brevity of words that carry a gentle weight.

"May charity be the plainest jewel we wear."

Ysabel continues her progress through the assembled nobles, accepting each introduction with gracious nods. When she reaches Lady Hélène, modest in comparison to the nobles flanking her and with Roland at her back, Ysabel's pause stretches longer than courtesy requires. Her gaze travels deliberately from Hélène's modest slippers to the simple circlet adorning her dark hair, taking measure with the thoroughness of a merchant appraising foreign goods.

The scrutiny forces Hélène into a curtsy, her movements finding their recently learned rhythm despite the weight of royal attention. "Lady Hélène of Montbois, Your Highness. I am honored by your presence at court."

The Princess's smile brightens, yet Margaret catches the calculating gleam beneath.

"So this is Lady Hélène. The road has spoken of your... dawns. His Majesty will value such early industry in his house."

Margaret nearly flinches at such open disdain wrapped in velvet, but Hélène deflects with her own undercurrent and a perfect curtsy, neither too deep nor shallow. "Your Highness is very generous with attention."

The exchange ripples through nearby courtiers like stones dropped in still water. Margaret catches concern flash briefly across Sir Roland's features. She redirects the moment's tension by turning to present Lord Reginald, who stands not far away among the assembled nobles.

Alice Whitcombe positions herself amongst the crowd to take advantage of clear sight lines and carried voices. Her keen eye catches every nuance: the Princess's lingering assessment of Lady Hélène and the Queen Dowager's quick deflection as ripples of whispers spread through assembled nobles like wind through wheat.

When Ysabel's gaze swept Lady Hélène from slippers to circlet, Alice read the calculation beneath that brilliant smile. Ysabel measures worth by adornment and sees rivals in every corner. The pointed comment about "dawns" and "early industry" carried barbs wrapped in silk.

Alice's attention shifts to Meg Lovell. Their eyes meet briefly. A shared understanding passing between experienced staff. Meg's slight nod confirms what Alice already suspects: this Princess will bring storms.

As the procession moves up the great steps and into the inner chambers, the assembled court exhales collectively. Servants emerge from alcoves and doorways, their voices barely audible beneath the fading ceremonial music.

A footman leans close to his companion, voice pitched low enough to avoid noble ears. "Best sweep the floors and the stories both."

Alice's lips quirk upward. Fresh gossip has indeed arrived, wrapped in Spanish silk and jewels.

Queen Dowager Margaret

The closing of her solar doors brings welcome serenity from the hall's murmur. Margaret settles into her chair with stately grace, while her eyes study the Spanish princess whose many jewels catch the bright solar light like tiny suns.

"Sit, child. Travel sharpens tempers and dulls good sense."

Ysabel arranges her skirts, then waves dismissively toward her lady companion, Colette. "Fetch wine. The journey has left my throat parched."

Margaret's fan rests motionless against her palm. A neutral hold that betrays nothing. She treats her lady-in-waiting like a maid. Small wonder why Lady Faversham was not present.

"Your lady attends your person, not your pails." The correction falls soft but immovable. "Lady Colette is nobly born. In England, we observe certain customs regarding rank."

Ysabel's smile tightens. Before she can respond, Margaret gestures to the doorway where a young woman waits.

"This is Meg Lovell. She will see to linens, water, fires, and deliver small messages, for both of you. Lady Colette may help you write and dress but only fetch your drink when no servant is in the room."

Meg steps forward and bows with the trained respect of a faithful servant. "Your Grace. Your Highness. Lady Colette."

Ysabel reclines slightly with the air of a trial magistrate. Her gaze skims Meg as if assessing her worth.

"In Navarre," Ysabel begins, voice high and sweet, "a lady proves devotion by doing all. Especially where she is serving the queen."

Margaret's fan remains closed, yet the hint of steel in her voice is unmistakable. "In England, queens prove devotion by making others glad to serve."

Colette shifts uneasily, attempting her own claim to the conversation in broken English. "I... will attend... les propriétés."

Ysabel's smile flashes ivory as she interjects in English, "She struggles, poor dove."

One light tap of Margaret's fan dispels the attempt to slight. The gentle cadence resets the room's rhythm. Lady Cecily sits straighter as if summoned by a trumpet, her focus fixing on the Queen Dowager. The room waits on edge, uncertain whether Ysabel has grasped the subtle reprimand, but all else understand its depth.

"She is understood. When she speaks in French, we shall listen better." Margaret's voice, delicately woven with authority, reclaims peace.

Margaret surveys Ysabel's stubborn grandeur and Colette's shadowed humility. Margaret rises, her decision mirroring the jewel clasped to Ysabel's neck: precisely cut and unyielding.

"Lady Colette, you are released from chamber duties. Beyond dressing and writing for the Princess, your hours belong to hall and chapel now." She pauses, letting the words settle. "You will be seen where good fortune is seen."

Colette's eyes widen with a flicker of hope that is quickly suppressed as she catches Ysabel's jaw tighten almost imperceptibly.

Margaret turns to Meg with the slightest inclination of her head. The maid reads the signal perfectly. Observe, serve, report.

"Begin with a fire and plain broth. New rooms like warm beginnings."

"At once, Your Grace."

Ysabel rises, her curtsy dropping a beat deeper than protocol demands. The gesture acknowledges the correction while asserting her own breeding. "Your customs honor your halls. They shall soon be mine to keep."

Mine. Margaret's fan remains closed. Her voice carries the weight of years spent managing a kingdom. "And they will honor you, when you honor them."

The Spanish princess straightens, radiating confidence that grates against Margaret's patience. Too many assumptions. Too many reminders of a crown not yet won.

As they prepare to leave, Margaret retrieves a delicate needle wrapped in silk from her workbasket. "A queen's first lesson is to be well served. The second is to deserve it."

Ysabel accepts the gift with another curtsy, her smile brilliant and hollow. She sweeps from the solar with Colette trailing behind, leaving Margaret and Cecily alone with sunlight and calculation.

Margaret settles back into her chair, studying the embroidery frame where English roses bloom beside imported silk threads.

"Spanish weather has arrived at court", she notes to Lady Cecily.

"Aye, Your Majesty. Bright, fierce, and unpredictable."

She will need to watch this storm carefully, chart its course, and ensure it does not uproot what has taken years to cultivate. The castle will adapt, as it always does. But some seasons test more than others.

Lady Hélène of Montbois

Three days of strategic navigation through corridors, and Hélène congratulates herself on avoiding the Spanish princess entirely. The stories from the kitchens paint a clear picture: Colette dismissed like furniture, servants snapped at in rapid Castilian, demands issued as if the castle existed solely for Ysabel's comfort. Each tale kindles fresh irritation in Hélène's chest. She knows her own temper. Better to avoid the match entirely than risk setting both their reputations ablaze.

Agnes rounds the corner beside her, chattering about linens and evening arrangements. Hélène half-listens, grateful for the normalcy, until familiar voices drift from the approaching corridor.

Too late.

Ysabel sweeps toward them in crimson silk that catches torchlight like spilled wine. Colette follows two paces behind, her gaze fixed on the floor stones. Don Íñigo trails at a respectful distance, his diplomat's instincts reading the air before he melts tactfully into an alcove.

Agnes drops her voice and fall behind Hélène. "Mind the stones, my lady."

Hélène's smile comes easily, masking the sudden tension in her shoulders. "Always."

The moment arrives and Cecily's drilling takes hold. Spine straight, eyes forward, the perfect depth and duration. Hélène sinks into a curtsy that would make her etiquette tutor weep with pride.

"Your Highness honors our house."

Ysabel's dark eyes assess each line and angle as if tallying debts owed to her expectations. "You wear instruction well."

The compliment carries thorns beneath silk. Hélène's pleasant expression never wavers, though her jaw tightens imperceptibly.

"So swift a polish. Your tutors must be very patient."

"I give them much to polish."

Colette shifts behind Ysabel's shoulder, her lips parting as if to speak. The words emerge in hesitant French, barely audible. "Pardon, je… je voulais dire—"

"She muddles so charmingly."

Ysabel's tone is sweet, but it lands like a slap down the corridor, pitched for any passing ears. Colette's freckled cheeks flush scarlet, her gaze dropping further toward the stones.

Hélène's etiquette training wars with instinct as Cecily's voice urges restraint while her own sense of justice demands action. She steps forward slightly, addressing Colette in soft, precise French.

"Votre français est clair, madame. Puis-je vous aider?" *Your French is clear, madam. May I help you?*

Relief floods across Colette's features. "Vous êtes très aimable." *You are very kind.*

Ysabel's smile tightens at the exclusion, her dark eyes sharpening on Hélène's face. Why the Spanish Princess would entertain a French Lady-In-Waiting who can speak neither English nor Spanish baffles Hélène.

The Spanish princess straightens, reclaiming the corridor's attention with deliberance. "How versatile you are, Lady Hélène."

"Only as needed, Your Highness."

The words hang between them, polite but poisoned. Agnes shifts nervously beside Hélène, sensing the growing undercurrent.

"As needed." Ysabel repeats with a warm smile, but her gaze hardens on Hélène like a hunter selecting prey. "You will arrange my notes. His Majesty's household will soon be my care. You shall help me shape it."

The words drape themselves in silk, but Hélène catches the iron beneath. A cage disguised as honor. Her pulse quickens as recognition floods through her. The predator's oldest gambit: keep friends close and enemies closer.

"If Her Highness wishes it, I will serve."

Agnes's breath catches beside her, a tiny sound that speaks volumes. The maid's eyes find Hélène's briefly before dropping in deference. "I'll see that ink and paper are always near."

Hélène executes another flawless curtsy, her smile never faltering despite the trap closing around. The gesture feels like surrender disguised as grace, each fold of her skirts a banner of capitulation.

"Your Highness, I am at your call."

The words taste of ash in her mouth, but her voice remains steady, betraying nothing of the failing composure underneath. She has learned this much from Cecily's patient instruction. How to speak submission while keeping one's spine straight.

Ysabel's eyes glitter with satisfaction, dark as polished obsidian, her voice delivering a promise that carries the weight of future torment.

"I shall call often, Lady Hélène. Very often indeed."

The threat wrapped in courtesy sends ice through Hélène's veins, each syllable a small blade. The corridor suddenly feels airless. She retreats with controlled steps, Agnes hurrying beside her like a faithful shadow, both women maintaining their dignity until they round the corner. Only then does Hélène allow her shoulders to drop slightly, the weight of what has just transpired settling upon them both.

Games of Power

- 11 -

Lord Ranulf of Morcar

Ranulf spreads parchments across his oak table like a general deploying troops. Each document claims its territory. Witness accounts, court records, fragments of correspondence. The afternoon light slants through diamond-paned windows, illuminating neat columns of his careful script.

Names. Claims. Witnesses. Gaps.

"Whispers are straw. I will have grain."

He traces one finger down the witness column. Geoffrey's shaken testimony. Reginald's calculated certainty. The Archbishop's swift familial blessing. All edges too clean, corners too sharp.

His thumb works through armorial notes, pages crackling like autumn leaves. Montpelier, Montclair, Montferrat... but no Montbois. The absence gnaws at him like a splinter beneath skin.

"A noble house without a herald is a knight without a horse."

Boots echo in the corridor outside. Sir Greville enters without ceremony, dust still clinging to his surcoat. The younger knight carries himself with the eagerness of one seeking favor.

"My lord, correspondence from the French southern border."

Ranulf breaks the wax with urgency, scanning lines that tighten around his quarry like a snare. The letter is addressed to the knight. He must have inquired under his own seal. Clever.

The response speaks of a Sir Montbois trained at noble houses in southern France with an western accent. No herald provided. No sister mentioned. Though an influential cousin serves the Church in England.

Ranulf sets the letter down as the information sinks in. The cousin. Anselm himself. The Archbishop's swift intercession suddenly reeks of orchestration rather than divine guidance. A Sir Montbois exists, but the heraldry does not. Why? Is Montbois just a knight and not a Lord?

"Your seal served well, Marcus. I shall have need of it again. Fetch a clerk for me. Francis will do."

"At your command, my lord."

Beyond the window, spring gardens bloom in riotous splendor. Apple blossoms drift like snow across manicured paths where courtiers stroll in ignorant contentment. He watches a gardener prune dead wood from living branches. Soon, he will do the same for this court. Beauty masks the rot beneath.

Francis enters with quill and inkpot, settling at the smaller writing table with familiarity. The clerk's hands always remain steady despite the weight of Ranulf's dictations. A useful quality in one who transcribes sensitive correspondence.

"We shall cast a fresh net, Francis. Under Sir Greville's seal this time."

Ranulf paces behind the clerk's chair, words flowing like honey over steel. Letters to abbeys near Toulouse. Inquiries to minor nobles along southern and eastern trade routes. All seeking a "dear friend" named Roland, a traveling knight who taught grappling arts to young nobles. Urgent family news requires his swift location.

"Friendship opens doors that suspicion bars shut."

Boot steps pause outside his chamber. Reginald appears in the doorway, travel dust from a recent visit to Redwyke still clinging to his heavy velvet. The lord's slightly wrinkled face shifts to careful consideration as he spots the French heraldry on Ranulf's desk.

"Ranulf. Still toiling away over genealogy?"

"You swore them brave. Do you also swear them born?"

Reginald's mouth quirks without warmth. "I swear the Archbishop's word is heavier than mine."

"If they are true, my doubts die. If they are false, better I learn it quietly than England, or *Spain*, learns it loudly."

Reginald nods slowly, an understanding passes between them, but Ranulf cannot determine if it is mutual or something else. The Chancellor withdraws without further comment, leaving Ranulf to his careful hunt.

Francis dips his quill again, awaiting instruction.

The scratching of quill against parchment fills the chamber, steady as a heartbeat, as Ranulf finishes dictating the letters. The sweet, sharp scent of ink hangs in the air, as Francis begins drafting for the various destinations.

Ranulf takes up the wax and holds it to the candle. The steady drip forms a sanguine pool. He presses Marcus's seal into the first letter. As the wax cools, he shifts his focus.

"Francis," he begins, studying the clerk with the incisive gaze of a falcon on perch. "What murmurs grace your ear these days? I collect footprints, not stories. Tell me where the boots were set."

The clerk's hand falters, brush pausing mid-sweep. "Your Lordship, His Grace may take offense if—"

"Offense is quick. Proof is slow," Ranulf interjects, his voice slicing the air. "We will move at the speed of proof."

Francis nods, gathering his thoughts. "Sir Roland's methods, my lord, have become favored in training. His tactics, odd as they are, saved lives on patrol. There's talk that even Sir Holt speaks of their value." The clerk hesitates before continuing. "And the Lady Hélène...her transformation is notable. Lady Cecily's tutelage suits her. The staff applaud her gratitude."

A flicker of approval passes as the clerk speaks of Lady Hélène's manners. Yet it's when Francis mentions Ysabel that Ranulf's focus sharpens again.

"Colette, she seeks refuge in her own tongue with Lady Hélène. Princess Ysabel dislikes it but—"

"Ysabel is not my primary concern," Ranulf interrupts, dismissive. "She spins her own web."

Francis bows his head.

"We shall use Greville's seal," Ranulf states. "Ensure it bears uncommon wax, difficult for sleight of hand. If a letter strays, we will know which dog took it."

Francis nods, accepting the Justiciar's order with no questions asked. Ranulf's mind turns towards strategy itself.

"Who frequents the Montbois siblings?" Ranulf inquires.

Francis responds without hesitation. "The usual visitors, my lord. Lady Isolde calls upon Lady Hélène regularly, whilst Sir Denby, Sir Stone, and young Loxley attend Sir Roland."

Ranulf's fingers drum against the desk, each tap marking another thread of consideration. "Has the King shown keener interest in either sibling, particularly since his morning ride with the lady?"

"His Majesty has shown no favoritism since that morning, my lord," Francis replies steadily.

The clerk finishes applying the wax seal to the final letter, the red wax cooling into a perfect impression of Greville's seal.

"My thanks for your time this evening, Francis," Ranulf says, rising from his chair. "And for your discretion in these matters." The words carry the dual meaning of gratitude paired with warning. "The day's dictation remains between these walls, though I trust your eyes and ears remain open to all that passes in this court."

Francis inclines his head with understanding. "Of course, my lord. It has been my honor to serve in this capacity." He gathers the sealed letters, tucking them within his leather satchel. "Should you require my services again, you need only send word."

With a final bow, Francis departs, leaving Ranulf alone with his thoughts and the dying embers of the hearth.

Ranulf moves to the room's diamond window which offers a meager view into the outer courtyard below. Servants move along the shadowed edges like living extensions of the castle walls, their movements efficient and purposeful. Along the garden paths, young nobles and ladies strolled at their leisure, their bright garments catching the afternoon light as they engage in the idle conversations that mark their station.

He watches this familiar tableau unfold, reminding himself that every action he takes serves to protect the Crown, even from its young wearer, whose trusting nature might one day prove his undoing. In the delicate dance of proof and shadow, vigilance will stay his constant companion, particularly when truth lingers just beyond his grasp.

Archbishop Anselm of Clearvale

The chapel's stone walls hold their voices like cupped hands, ensuring the conversation remains between them alone. Anselm adjusts his ceremonial robes as he addresses the small gathering, his words paced as he lays out the truths before them.

"He sniffs like a hound but keeps to the hedge," Anselm begins, his gaze moving between Alaric and Roland. "Ranulf dispatches letters to France regularly with strategic care. His queries among the staff remain circumspect. No public declarations, no open accusations, yet his persistence grows."

Alaric shifts against the altar rail, his expression thoughtful. "A watchdog is useful until it barks in the throne room. Ranulf's vigilance protects the realm, but premature suspicion could shatter what we've built."

Denby stands near the chapel's entrance, his features impassive as he listens. Roland remains silent, though tension radiates from his stance.

Anselm nods slowly. "Then we must consider the torch rather than the shadow. Keep Sir Roland visible, useful, and unstartling. Familiarity dulls suspicion."

"How do you mean?" Alaric asks.

"When a man builds your bridge, you forget to ask his birthplace," Anselm replies. "Let Roland's competence speak louder than questions about his origins. Service breeds trust."

Roland shifts his weight, and the King paces as he considers the wisdom.

"Let us review what we have built," Anselm continues, settling onto the stone bench beside the altar. "Months have passed. The tale requires tending."

Roland steps forward, his voice steady. "I told the guards who questioned me that I served as a traveling knight, training young nobles across southern and eastern French provinces. Simple work, honorable purpose. Nothing that invites deeper inquiry than has already been inquired."

"Good," Anselm murmurs. "What else?"

"La Brousse remains our anchor," Roland continues. "Remote province, old dialects, sparse roads that discourage visitors. Our mother laid to rest by a strong fever, and our father having long since been dead in service to the French monarchy. We came to England seeking opportunity under distant kinship."

Anselm nods approvingly. "No embroidery beyond necessity."

"Simple story, longer life," Roland says with dry certainty.

Alaric shifts against the rail. "What happens when France responds? If they write back 'no such house' or Ranulf uncovers the real Roland, assuming he lives still in France?"

Anselm's expression remains calm, though his fingers trace the jeweled cross at his chest. "Then France lies, or France forgets. England will remember what I say." His voice carries authority and confidence. "Archives burn. Scribes err. Provincial records scatter like autumn leaves. Who will challenge an Archbishop's word about distant kin?"

"And if pressed further?" Alaric asks.

"Then grief makes men forgetful," Anselm replies simply.

Anselm turns his attention to practical measures, his tone shifting to one of careful instruction.

"Denby, you and Sir Roland will observe Lord Ranulf together. Note his messengers, his meeting places, his confidants. But observe only. Do not provoke." He fixes both men with a steady gaze. "I want rain measured, not clouds chased."

Denby nods once, understanding the distinction.

Roland steps forward slightly. "What of my own story, should he question me further?"

"Keep to your traveling knight tale but spare the details. No invented names. We know not which French nobles you might claim to know." Anselm's voice carries a quiet warning. "Let competence speak louder than words."

"I will teach, not talk," Roland promises.

"Then go. Both of you."

Roland and Denby depart, but Alaric remains beside the altar rail, his shoulders bearing weight that crowns cannot distribute. Anselm recognizes the familiar struggle of conscience warring with necessity.

"Are we deceiving too far, Archbishop?" Alaric's voice carries the burden of these recent months. "Each day builds another stone in this wall of fiction."

Anselm considers his words carefully, understanding the King's torment. "We are keeping silence where noise would harm the realm. Truth and wisdom need not always walk the same path."

"Yet the burden remains mine should this charade collapse."

"As it should," Anselm replies gently. "A king carries what others cannot."

Alaric nods, accepting the weight. "Then let us set clear bounds. If Ranulf moves to public accusation, he must bring it to my table. No ambushes in hall or feast."

"Agreed. Any quarrel comes to your table. You will carve it yourself."

Anselm rises, his joints protesting the stone's chill. He places two fingers upon his crosier and inclines his head toward the King. "Hold your post, Sire. Let time make our case."

The King's expression shifts to another concern. "The bandits Holt's patrol captured. Denby persuaded information from them."

"And what did they reveal?"

"That men beyond these walls no longer fear their young King." Alaric's voice hardens. "My father inspired little love, but bandits never dared approach the castle grounds during his reign."

Anselm sees the deeper wound. "You seek a different path than your father's."

"I refuse to rule through fear alone. Yet I cannot appear weak." Alaric meets his gaze. "I want my people's respect, not their terror."

The Archbishop's expression softens with paternal warmth. "Fear breaks easily while respect endures. Your father ruled like winter: harsh, but brittle. You can be the spring that follows."

"How does one command like spring?"

"Through steady mercy yoked to steady justice. Let your actions speak before your sword."

Anselm's words weigh visibly on the King's shoulders. The evening bell tolls across the chapel, its bronze voice calling them to dinner. Anselm brushes his robes as both men prepare to return to the world of careful words and watchful eyes.

Sir William Denby

Denby presses his shoulder against the cold stone, counting heartbeats in the corridor's gloom. The shadows here run deep. They observe from the servants' passages that branch beyond Lord Ranulf's personal advisory chambers like veins beneath skin. Roland shifts beside him, silent as morning mist.

"Men are clocks," Denby murmurs, voice barely threading the air between them. "They tell more than the hour."

Lord Ranulf emerges from the corridor's eastern side door precisely as morning vesper bells fade. The same pattern he has followed for six days running. Denby marks it: Ranulf favors the eastern passage when rain threatens, takes the main corridor when dry. Today's drizzle sends him their direction, boots clicking against worn flagstone.

Two sellsword knights follow at a respectful distance. Sir Greville and Sir Aldric. Hungry young men whose purses run lighter than their ambitions. Denby counted three visits between them this past week, each departing with coin-heavy pouches and carefully neutral expressions. The scarred veteran who questioned Roland in the training yard has yet to visit Ranulf's personal study. Presumably his wisdom has him toeing between the brotherhood of the guard and the Justiciar's purse.

Roland's breathing stays controlled, but Denby catches the subtle tension in his stance. The man tires of observation and wants action. Old habits from whatever distant service shaped him. Denby appreciates the restraint.

Ranulf pauses at his private study door, producing a key from his belt. The sellswords wait in the main corridor like patient hounds. Good. Let them grow comfortable with routine. Let them believe their movements pass unnoticed.

Time stretches. Denby's knees protest the stone floor, but he holds position. A guard learns patience before sword-work, and patience serves investigations better than steel.

Just as the study door opens, a page appears from further down the corridor. Red wax gleams in the corridor's torchlight as a sealed letter passes from Ranulf's hand to the page's leather pouch. Not Ranulf's personal crest. Denby glimpses a different design. A foreign seal, perhaps. Or borrowed authority. He'll have to review the registry of his knights' sigils.

The page departs down the corridor to resume his morning rounds. Denby notes the window of opportunity. The gatehouse guards respect him well enough as captain. A quiet word about examining outbound correspondence wouldn't raise suspicion.

Roland shifts, muscle coiling like a hunting cat's. The man's restraint costs him effort. "I have many tools," Roland says, eyes following the page. "Today we use none."

"There's plenty time to intercept at the gatehouse." Denby assures the younger man. Better to watch, learn, and wait for the moment when intervention serves purpose rather than impulse.

Ranulf retreats to his study. The sellsword knights disperse to whatever duties occupy ambitious men with recently filled purses. Time slips by and the corridor empties save for servants bearing afternoon trays.

At the midday bell, Ranulf emerges striding toward the scribal chambers with purpose that cuts through afternoon's lethargy. Denby and Roland follow at a distance, using servant traffic as cover.

Alice sweeps past them in the connecting corridor, her voice weaving through clusters of kitchen maids like thread through linen. Denby catches fragments. Something about Princess Ysabel's temperament and the Queen Dowager's patience, but the tone tells more than words. Gossip as governance, information shaped and directed.

"If kitchens were parliaments, we'd need fewer lords," Roland observes.

"And hotter debates," Denby replies.

They pause at the scribal chamber's threshold. Through the open door, Ranulf's voice carries clear: requests for specific charts with emphasis on accuracy of older markings. The scribe Brother Bennet, eager to please any noble, spreads the parchments across his copying desk, each placed to flatter. Ranulf inspects before motioning to a few and Bennet eagerly prepares them.

Ranulf departs with the rolled maps tucked beneath his arm. Denby counts twenty heartbeats before approaching the chamber. Brother Thomas remains bent over his work, quill scratching against fresh vellum.

"Weather holds fair," Denby remarks, settling into casual conversation.

The scribe glances up, grateful for another distraction. "Indeed, Sir William. May I assist?"

He uses the scribe's over familiarity to his advantage and asks after recent requests, suggesting he maintains watchful oversight of general affairs.

"Lord Ranulf seemed concerned with roads grown difficult." Brother Thomas's voice carries innocent helpfulness. "My lord sought maps with old names and routes that might avoid recent troubles."

Denby exchanges glances with Roland. "Old names fit old roads," he murmurs. "Thank you, Brother Thomas."

Brother Thomas returns to his copying with renewed focus, happy to have obliged. Denby leads Roland through the eastern corridor, following the path Ranulf's habitual stride would take toward the cloister.

The afternoon light filters through stone arches as they reach the covered walkway. Ranulf stands beside a weathered pillar, maps still tucked beneath his arm. Lord Reginald approaches from the chapel's direction.

Denby positions himself behind a supporting column, Roland close beside him. The cloister's acoustics carry voices poorly. A blessing for private conversation, a curse for observation. But men speak with more than words.

The two lords begin their customary circuit, walking with the calm tread of men unpressed by time. Ranulf gestures toward his maps, but Reginald's response comes slow, dismissive. They complete one full circuit in near silence.

"That is an argument between friends," Roland murmurs, reading the careful distance they maintain.

"Better than an agreement between enemies," Denby replies.

The second circuit proves even quieter. Ranulf's shoulders carry tension while Reginald's hands remain clasped behind his back, the posture of a man withholding judgment. When they pause near the garden entrance, their words remain too distant to capture, but their body language speaks volumes.

The meeting dissolves without ceremony. Ranulf departs through the gardens back towards his study, while Reginald approaches their direction along the cloister walk. As he passes their pillar, the older lord's eyes find theirs briefly, a knowing nod that acknowledges their presence without surprise.

Reginald's steps fade into the cloister's evening quiet. Denby watches until the lord disappears around the eastern corner, then turns to Roland.

"Nothing left worth watching," Denby says, checking the angle of shadows against stone. "His schedule runs empty until tomorrow's audience."

"The gatehouse, then." Roland suggests. "Those letters won't wait for our convenience."

They move through corridors with unseen haste, Denby cataloguing the day's observations as their boots strike worn flagstone. "Vespers timing, foreign courier, maps with old names. Eastern passages when wet, main routes when dry."

Roland matches his pace without effort. "Patterns suggest preparation, not plotting."

"Aye. He builds a case he hopes not to use." Denby considers the weight of Ranulf's newly formed habitual movements and the careful distance Reginald maintained during their cloister circuit. "Caution wearing the mask of suspicion."

The gatehouse courtyard opens before them, guards preparing to light torches for the approaching evening. Denby's steps falter as he spots the familiar figure near the main gate. Young Peter, the evening courier page, leather satchel secured across his shoulder. The boy moves with unusual urgency, already mounted and checking his reins.

"Earlier than custom," Denby murmurs. Light thunder swells in the distance. "He leaves early to beat the storm."

The satchel swings within arm's reach as Peter mounts and adjusts his stirrups. Roland's hand shifts, then stills. He meets Denby's questioning glance. "Too many eyes here."

Denby nods, watching the page ride toward darkness. "Aye."

The antechamber within the Armory Hall bears the scent of oiled leather and parchment. Denby's domain where ledgers meet steel. Seargent Godric waits beside the narrow window, his weathered hands clasped behind his back. Anselm settles into the room's single chair with his usual quiet authority.

Denby wastes no words. "Should Lord Ranulf request public audience, route it to the King first. Should he inquire on persons within the guard, particularly Sir Roland, route through me, then the King."

The sergeant's grizzled face shows no surprise. Court politics flow like winter currents, and experienced men learn to navigate without question.

"No declarations in corridors," Denby continues, meeting the captain's steady gaze. "Only in the King's ear."

Godric nods once, sharp as a blade's edge. "Understood." He departs with military obedience, leaving only the soft whisper of robes and settling shadows.

Denby turns to Anselm. Roland stands beside him like a patient hawk. "He is a flint that may spark, not yet striking." The guard captain's sun worn features settle into the steady expression of a man recounting facts rather than fears. "What I witnessed today bears telling, Your Grace."

He draws a slow breath, organizing the day's observations with the same precision he brings to inventory ledgers. "Young guards walked the corridors with purses heavier than their rank should carry. Letters passed to a page, bearing seals I could not identify from my distance. Old maps of French roads found their way from storage." His voice remains steady, then matter of fact. "I observed Lord Ranulf draw Sir Reginald aside in the cloister walk. Their words too distant to catch, but Ranulf's manner spoke of urgency. Reginald's deflections may cause spark."

Roland's voice carries plain honesty. "We keep water at hand and build bridges meanwhile."

Denby nods toward the window where Peter's departure still lingers in memory. "The evening courier departed before I could examine those letters. Too many eyes watching, as Sir Roland noted. But the pattern suggests inquiry rather than idle curiosity. Ranulf gathers threads."

Anselm's fingers drum against the chair's worn arm, considering their words with the care of a man who weighs souls alongside politics. "His motives spring from love of crown, not malice toward persons. This I know from Lord Reginald. It shall shape our response."

The Archbishop rises, joints protesting the day's length. "My thanks for this service. The realm grows stronger when watchful men guard more than walls."

Roland steps forward. "I'll see you safely home, Your Grace."

They depart into evening's embrace, leaving Denby alone with torch cast shadows and the weight of tomorrow's uncertainties. His thoughts drift to Ranulf, that careful man whose love of England drives him toward dangerous ground. How does one protect the realm from its own protectors? He settles behind his desk, quill poised above fresh parchment. The day's observations require recording of dates, times, and patterns that might serve future need.

Entanglements of the Heart

- 12 -

Lady Juliette Marchand

The Queen Dowager's solar captures the morning light through its tall lancets, illuminating neat stacks of correspondence that require Lady Juliette's careful attention. Three weeks of service have taught her the rhythm of royal correspondence. Petitions sorted by urgency, visiting lists cross-referenced with seasonal courts, seals inspected for authenticity before filing.

Her fingers move efficiently through the morning's delivery, each document finding its proper place in the mahogany cabinet's labeled compartments. The Queen Dowager's presence settles like silk against stone. Watchful but unobtrusive, allowing Juliette to demonstrate the organizational grace that has made these weeks surprisingly fulfilling.

"A steady hand is rarer than a pretty face."

Juliette glances up from the abbey petition in her hands, her chocolate eyes meeting the Queen's appraising gaze. The compliment carries weight beyond mere courtesy. A recognition earned through weeks of careful work.

"Then I shall value what is rare."

She returns to the parchment, reading aloud with clear diction. "The abbess requests a mason for her west wall."

The petition speaks of winter damage and urgent repairs, but Juliette's thoughts drift momentarily to other matters, to a certain merchant whose absence at court creates an ache she cannot voice.

"And receives him. Good walls keep good vows."

The Queen Dowager's response brings Juliette back to duty while her heart holds its questions close. She tucks a stray blonde lock behind her ear before filing the approved request. The next petition bears a merchant's seal. Juliette's voice maintains its steady cadence while her pulse quickens. Though this merchant deals in barley, not the continental provisions of the merchant that occupies her private thoughts.

"Master Oxley requests passage through the northern toll for his harvest wagons."

"Granted. Hunger serves no crown."

The Queen Dowager's swift approval flows into Juliette's notation, quill scratching against parchment in the solar's warm silence. She reaches for the third document, fingers trembling slightly as she breaks another merchant's seal. Again, not Lucien's hand, but the very sight of trade agreements stirs that persistent ache. Where does his business take him now?

The next petition bears a seal Juliette recognizes instantly. Master Aldwine's guild mark pressed deep into dark blue wax. Her fingers pause on the parchment's edge, heart quickening as she breaks the familiar seal. Aldwine works closely with many merchants, including Lucien Marecellus.

"Master Aldwine requests expanded charter rights for the eastern trade routes—"

Her voice trails as she reads his careful script and spots Lucien's name among the guild members listed for consultation. The words blur slightly as her mind wanders to harbor conversations and shared glances across crowded guild halls.

"Lady Juliette?"

The Queen Dowager's gentle prompt snaps her attention back to the duties at hand. Heat rises in her cheeks as she realizes she has missed the royal response entirely.

"Forgive me, Your Grace. The morning light—"

"Your thoughts walk faster than your feet this morning."

Margaret's observation carries no rebuke, only careful attention. Juliette sets the petition aside with lightly trembling fingers, grateful when Lady Cecily appears with a silver tray bearing a cup of cool water.

"They sometimes visit the coast."

The admission slips out before Juliette can stop it. She accepts the water gratefully, using the moment to steady herself while Cecily arranges the tray with approving precision.

"Restraint is a ribbon. When tied well, it adorns."

Juliette's thankful smile draws a scarce smile from Lady Cecily, though the Queen Dowager's watchful gaze remains unchanged. Margaret turns to the lancet window, hands clasped behind her back.

"The treasury smiles when trade breathes." The Queen Dowager's casual mention hangs in the solar's quiet air like an offered bridge.

Juliette's pulse quickens, wondering how much the Queen Dowager knows about her mother's swift decision to send her to court. Away from certain entanglements that threatened family reputation.

"Trade is... brisk, in my town." Her voice barely rises above a whisper, weighted with loss.

"We shall close the morning's correspondence here."

The Queen Dowager moves to her writing desk, sealing the last approved petition herself. The familiar ritual signals Juliette's release. She gives the proper courtesy and takes her leave, though her steps toward the door feel weighted by their unspoken questions.

Lady Cecily intercepts her path subtly, fingers barely touching Juliette's elbow as they reach the solar's threshold. "If there is a name, show it first to a friend who can carry it."

The whispered counsel stops Juliette's breath. Cecily's knowing gaze suggests depths of understanding that reach beyond morning correspondence. Juliette's eyes plead for further assistance. "I have not the acquaintances at court who would take the burden."

"I have thought of one. Lord Geoffrey has taken the burden of merchant management."

Her advice earns an approving nod from the Queen Dowager. Juliette turns back and curtsies in gratitude before leaving. One deep enough to show proper humility and steady enough to convey quiet resolve.

"Your Grace, I am content to serve."

"And to be served, in turn, by good fortune."

Alone for one heartbeat in the cool corridor, Juliette presses fingertips to a letter hidden within her bodice.

"Courage, written small."

Lord Geoffrey of Redwyke

Geoffrey looks up from his ledger as a shadow falls across the castle library's threshold into his personal study. A small and well-hidden study, but perfect for the aspiring scholar that he is. Lady Juliette hovers there, hands clasped, not presuming entry despite the door standing open. Her careful hesitation speaks well of her. Too many courtiers stride where they should step.

"Libraries fear only loud feet. Yours are honest."

"Then I will tread as a thought, not a shout."

Her smile carries nervous warmth as she enters his space, movements precise but unsure. Geoffrey sets down his quill and gestures toward the chair across from his reading table. Afternoon light slants through the narrow windows, casting geometric patterns across the scattered correspondence that chronicles merchant trade routes.

"I was counseled to find a friend who can carry a name."

The careful phrasing draws his attention fully. Geoffrey leans back, studying her composed features for signs of the weight she bears. Whatever drives this visit requires delicate handling.

"I could be that friend but must know more."

Juliette's breath catches slightly before she straightens, resolve settling across her shoulders. "There is a man, a merchant by the name of Lucien Marcellus, whose merit is larger than his birth."

The name means nothing to Geoffrey, though her careful pronunciation suggests significance and merit weighs well in his scales. He waits, letting silence invite fuller explanation.

"He pays on time and eats last."

The simple assessment draws Geoffrey's approving nod. Two behaviors that reveal character more clearly than perfumed testimonials ever could. Juliette continues with careful words, sketching a portrait of diligence and fairness that resonates with his own values.

"His workers speak well of him, his accounts balance clean, and his word holds firm across three ports."

Geoffrey processes this careful catalog, noting what she doesn't say alongside what she does. No mention of wealth or connections, only competence and integrity.

"Doors here open to names that already stand inside." He notes aloud, already anticipating the request.

"Then I ask your name, my lord." Her steady gaze meets his without flinching. A carefully crafted courage but real.

Geoffrey drums his fingers against the leather binding of his ledger as he considers the request and its implications. Court sponsorship carries weight that can crush the unwary.

"And if court frowns?"

"Then let court learn to smile at what feeds it."

Her answer strikes him as neither rash nor romantic. Sure knowledge wrapped in affection, not blind passion. Geoffrey nods slowly, decision forming.

"I will sponsor him, but conditions stand firm. Let him bring his best coat and leave his pride at the quay."

Relief floods Juliette's features, though she maintains composure. "His pride is sewn to his work, not his sleeves."

"Good. Then he understands value over vanity."

Geoffrey glances toward the window where hunting horns echo faintly across the courtyard. Perfect. When the court chases stags, they notice fewer merchants.

"When the hunting party meets, we shall meet a merchant."

"Thank you, my lord."

Her gratitude speaks to the very reason Geoffrey chooses sponsorship over caution. Merit deserves its chance, whatever the birth.

Juliette's fingers twist against her skirts, betraying the careful composure she maintains. "Might I ask one favor beyond mere sponsorship?"

Geoffrey recognizes the lilt of someone balancing between hope and propriety. He inclines his head, inviting her to lean toward hope.

"If he proves worthy of your judgment, would you speak of him to Her Grace?"

The request carries weight beyond its simple words. Speaking to the Queen Dowager signals serious intent, not mere court entertainment. Geoffrey considers the implications. A merchant seeking not just access, but endorsement from the realm's most discerning matriarch.

"Her Grace appreciates ships that carry more than noise."

"Lucien's ships carry provisions from the continent."

The response satisfies him enough. Queen Dowager values substance over spectacle, work over display. A man whose vessels feed people rather than merely profit from them deserves consideration.

Geoffrey reaches for his writing case, extracting a parchment already prepared with his seal. The ink seal bears the wheat sheaf of Redwyke. Fitting symbol for this particular introduction. He drafts the sponsorship.

"Present this to Master Marcellus as my sponsorship and see that he keeps it on his person for his arrival at court."

Juliette accepts the note with reverent care, cradling it like precious cargo. "I will guard it as I do breath and ensure its proper delivery."

She thanks him with the respect owed his standing as a court official. Then departs as she arrived: composed, hopeful, dignified. Geoffrey watches her go, musing privately: If nobles had her sense, we'd need fewer laws.

The thought brings Geoffrey pause as he settles back into his chair, considering what he has just set in motion. Supporting a match between Lady Juliette and Master Lucien means endorsing a union that will raise eyebrows throughout court. A noble lady binding herself to merchant coin rather than landed title.

Yet what alternative serves the realm better? Geoffrey has witnessed too many marriages of pure breeding produce heirs who mistake privilege for virtue, who inherit authority without earning wisdom. The established order prizes bloodline above character, as if noble birth alone could guarantee noble conduct. But Lady Juliette displays more genuine dignity in her careful courtesy than Princess Ysabel manages with all her royal prerogatives.

Master Marcellus, from what Geoffrey's ears just observed, carries himself with the quiet confidence of a man who builds rather than merely inherits. His ships provision the realm's tables by honest work that feeds families rather than simply filling coffers. Such an industry deserves recognition.

The realm's future may well depend on embracing competence wherever it flourishes, regardless of the soil from which it springs. Blood alone cannot sustain a kingdom. It requires steady hands and willing hearts, whether they bear ancient seals or calluses from honest labor.

If supporting this match helps establish such precedent, Geoffrey considers it service well rendered to both crown and kingdom.

Master Lucien Marcellus

Lucien guides his gelding through the final approach to the castle gates, rain-darkened stones rising before him like a judgment rendered in granite. A fortnight has passed since Juliette's letter arrived bearing Redwyke's seal and Lord Geoffrey's hand. Half was spent in preparation that began with selecting his least ostentatious coat and ended with polishing boots that have walked more harbor planks than castle floors. He spent the majority of the morning repolishing those boots before leaving London's heart for the Castle at its edge.

The gelding's hooves ring against cobblestones as they pass through the gatehouse and into an outer courtyard. Lucien dismounts with the sureness of habit, gathering reins while scanning faces for signs of welcome or wariness. A gatehouse guard approaches, hand resting casually on his sword hilt.

"Name and business?"

Lucien retrieves the sponsorship letter from his inner pocket, the Redwyke inked seal intact despite two journeys. "Lucien Marcellus, merchant of Fairharbor, sponsored by Lord Geoffrey of Redwyke."

The guard examines the parchment with the careful attention of a man who recognizes authentic authority. Before he can respond, Lord Geoffrey emerges from beneath a stone archway, his approach transforming the courtyard's atmosphere from suspicion to hospitality, and his crest on display for Lucien to recognize.

"Master Marcellus, I trust the road treated you fairly."

"It rained. I took it as washing."

Geoffrey's smile suggests appreciation for a response that is neither complaint nor false cheer, just acceptance of weather as weather. Lucien notes the approval and files it away as useful intelligence about his sponsor's character. Juliette's letter informed him that Lord Geoffrey holds the King's ear for merchant management.

Movement catches his attention across the stones. Juliette stands with a ledger pressed against her chest. Her eyes finding his with the precision of an arrow finding its mark. The distance between them might as well be a chasm bridged only by recognition and hope.

"Welcome," her eyes whisper.

"Found," a slight nod answers her.

Lucien turns to bow properly to Geoffrey, then toward the castle itself, acknowledging the institution as well as the man. Geoffrey's smile improves at this.

"I am grateful for the courtesy of your house."

"Courtesy grows where it is watered."

Geoffrey gestures toward the castle's main entrance. "Walk with me, Master Marcellus. I've letters for the clerks, and the path will serve as an introduction to our ways."

They move from the gatehouse and into the outer courtyard, then along a covered walkway where carved pillars frame glimpses of manicured gardens within. Lucien notes the architecture. Solid English stone with Norman flourishes that speak of wealth applied thoughtfully rather than wastefully. Juliette appears briefly in a doorway, then vanishes like morning mist, her presence more felt than seen.

The cloister walk opens onto a broader corridor where two figures approach in conversation. Geoffrey straightens slightly, a signal Lucien reads immediately.

"Lord Miles, Lady Rosamund. Permit me to present Master Lucien Marcellus of Fairharbor, sponsored by my house."

Lucien executes the bow Juliette described in her letters. Measured depth, steady eyes, hands properly placed. Lord Miles returns a perfunctory nod while Lady Rosamund offers a gracious incline of her head.

"Master Marcellus brings word from the southern markets," Geoffrey continues. "Perhaps you might share your assessment of grain weights and tolls on the south road?"

The question carries more weight than casual inquiry. Lucien straightens, meeting Geoffrey's gaze directly.

"Standard weights hold fair at six markets between here and the coast. Tolls run two pence per cartload at Millford Bridge, one penny at Crow's Crossing. Both reasonable for the road's condition."

"And if a reeve cheats by a thumb?" Geoffrey further inquires.

"I bring a scale and a witness."

Lord Miles shifts, his expression suggesting he's caught scent of something distasteful, but it is Lady Rosamund who speaks.

"How thoroughly... mercantile. All this counting of pennies," Lady Rosamund observes, her gaze moving over Lucien's dress with calculating assessment, not the disdain that colors Lord Miles's expression, but the careful consideration of one taking his true measure from the quality of his coat and the care of his boots.

"And what does your penny say to a baron?" Lord Miles adds, his voice carrying a sharper edge.

The challenge hangs in the air like incense, sharp and lingering. Lucien meets Miles's stare without flinching. His response comes without heat, his tone remaining level. "That bread rises better when all eat."

Lady Rosamund's lips twitch, whether from amusement or disapproval remains unclear. Geoffrey clears his throat diplomatically.

"Master Marcellus, we should attend to those letters before the clerks retreat for their midday meal."

"Of course, my lord."

They take their leave with proper courtesies, moving deeper into the castle's administrative quarters. A clerk glances up from his writing desk as they approach, taking in Lucien's appearance as his eyes move across Lucien's carefully maintained boots, clean but practical coat, and hands that show work without bearing stains of desperation.

"A craftsman's polish, not a peacock's," the clerk murmurs to his companion, approval evident in his tone.

Geoffrey exchanges a meaningful look with Lucien, the smallest of nods passing between them like a handshake sealed in air. Geoffrey's strategy of 'show before tell' works well in Lucien's favor.

They reach their destination in the scriptorium where a clerk manages Geoffrey's letters. Geoffrey breaks the seal on his first letter, scanning its contents before setting quill to parchment. Lucien waits, conscious of the clerks' sidelong glances and silent judgement of a merchant learning court rhythms. The scratch of quills on vellum fills the silence like rain on thatch.

"Where may a guest stand who is not yet a guest?"

Geoffrey glances up from his correspondence, smile warming his features. "Beside a friend."

The nearest clerk, a thin man with ink stained fingers, nods approvingly at the exchange. His companion murmurs something about proper humility, the words carrying no sting.

Footsteps approach along the corridor's stone flags. Juliette appears, ledger balanced against her hip, her stride purposeful as any clerk's. Her eyes meet Lucien's for the briefest moment before she offers a formal nod that would pass as any casual greeting.

"Welcome to court, Master Marcellus. How fare's my father's harbors?"

"Your welcome weighs as true as Lord Marchand's harbors."

He bows as expected of a merchant to a noble lady. She continues past without pause, but the corners of her eyes speak volumes her lips cannot voice.

Geoffrey sets aside his quill, dusting the fresh ink with sand before folding the parchment and addressing Lucien once again. "Where do you lodge tonight?"

"The Swan, not far from the castle walls."

"Nonsense." Geoffrey's tone brooks no argument, pitched to carry across the writing chamber. "You'll stay at the Redwyke lodgings as my guest. My father would find your company most agreeable, a man who speaks of markets and measures."

Several clerks pause their work to listen, the conversation now public record in the court's gossip ledgers. Geoffrey gathers his letters, then gestures toward a quieter alcove outside where stone arches muffle their words.

"Tomorrow. I'll arrange a brief presentation to the Queen Dowager. Plain words and straight backs."

"Both come easily, my lord."

Geoffrey's nod seals the arrangement like wax pressed to parchment, the die cast for whatever judgment awaits on the morrow.

Courtly Fires

- 13 -

Princess Ysabel of Navarre

The morning light catches the jeweled clasp at Ysabel's throat as she surveys the stack of parchments crowding her writing table. Petitions from wool merchants, requests from village reeves, endless tallies that make her temples throb. She traces one manicured finger along the topmost document, something tedious about bridge repairs, before pushing the entire pile toward the center of the polished oak surface.

"England drowns in parchment. We shall learn to swim by delegation." She says to Hélène and gestures toward a chair opposite with the same languid wave that summoned wine at her father's court.

Hélène settles into the indicated seat, back straight, hands folded. Seemingly every inch the dutiful attendant despite the calculating gleam in her eyes that Ysabel chooses not to examine too closely.

The first petition slides across the table with deliberate authority. Ysabel taps the margin where blank space awaits a summary, her emerald ring catching fire in the sunlight. "You will write the digest. In English, plain as porridge."

"As Your Highness commands."

The response comes smooth as silk, but Ysabel catches the barely perceptible pause before compliance. French nobility learning English bureaucracy, how deliciously fitting that even the Montbois name must bow to practicality.

Colette shifts forward from her position near the window, eager hands reaching toward the scattered documents. The girl's eagerness grates like poorly tuned lute strings. "Your French is music, dear Colette. English is accounting. Let the scribe sing in numbers."

Ysabel leans back against the silk cushions, her smile widening with satisfaction. The future spreads before her like a tapestry already half-woven, and every thread must learn its proper place.

"These trifles will soon be my trifles. It is efficient to teach my house to please me early." She says to herself rather than the room's occupants.

She watches Hélène's quill scratch across the parchment, condensing the steward's wordy complaint into something approaching clarity. The French woman's penmanship flows neat and sure. No hesitation, no scratched corrections.

"Two bridges sound, one ferryman crooked. Fines recommended, coin trailed." The summary rings crisp.

"Just so… *my words* exactly." Ysabel nods, her emerald earrings catching the light.

But mere competence deserves testing. Afterall, the girl is now her instrument and every note derived from her reflects on Ysabel's house. Ysabel straightens, arranging her features into the expression that once made Spanish courtiers stumble over precedence.

"If a duchess and an archbishop both arrive together, who begins the greeting?"

Hélène's quill pauses for the briefest moment before she sets it aside with her tutored grace. "Deference moves to rank. Hospitality moves to age. We greet both and seat wisdom first."

Perfect. Too perfect. Instructed. Not bred. *How unfortunate*, Ysabel muses. Good breeding is preferable.

The next petition concerns grain stores. Tedious tallies that blur beneath Ysabel's gaze like rain on glass. She gestures toward the remaining stack with diminishing interest. "The pattern holds. Reduce each to essence."

Hélène's quill moves with a mechanical rhythm through merchant complaints and boundary disputes, her summaries growing sharper with practice. But even competence grows stale when observed too closely. Ysabel drums her fingers against the table's edge, emerald ring clicking against the polished wood.

"Copies for King and Queen Dowager," Ysabel sighs and dismissively rolls her wrist. "They must review before a final seal touches wax."

The reminder tastes bitter as unripe fruit. Not yet permitted final authority, still watched and weighed like a merchant's daughter learning her father's ledgers. But patience yields crowns, and crowns yield everything else.

Colette springs forward as Hélène sets aside the completed documents, eager fingers reaching for the neat stack. Her French accent lilts with offered service to make the copies.

"Your letters wobble like a drunk priest's blessing."

The words slice clean as a blade through silk. Colette's hand freezes midreach, color draining swiftly from her cheeks.

Ysabel's smile sharpens at the edges. "Scribes require steady hands, not willing hearts."

"Lady Colette's French flows beautifully." Hélène's voice carries gentle firmness, her hazel eyes meeting Ysabel's with careful respect that borders on challenge. The defense comes soft but there's unmistakable steel wrapped in silk.

Colette's whispered gratitude barely disturbs the air between them, French words falling like flower petals.

"Vous êtes... très bonne." *You are… very good.*

"C'est pour la paix." *It is for peace.*

Hélène's response carries the tone of understanding between two women finding common ground. But alliances built in whispers can shift like sand, and Ysabel notes every grain. She chooses to ignore the exclusion, for now.

Once the copies are complete, Ysabel gathers them with a possessive sweep. Each page bears Hélène's neat script, but ownership flows to those who command, not those who merely transcribe. She considers her own seal once more.

"Ensure the copies are dispatched under my seal, Colette. It is a task well within your abilities."

Colette nods with downcast eyes, accepting the rebuke wrapped in royal command. Hélène rises to depart, her curtsy perfect but on the rise her gaze meets Meg's across the chamber. Something passes between maid and noblewoman.

"Lady Colette, shall I prepare fresh wax?"

Meg's inquiry to Colette carries the neutral tone of perfect service, but her blue eyes hold steady purpose in their direction to Colette and not the Princess for whom the seal bears. Ysabel's smile blooms like Spanish roses in the morning sun.

"Yes. Let England see it." She responds for Colette. A stern reminder of whose authority seals the parchments and owns the contents within.

Lady Eveline Artois

Eveline glides along the Great Hall's polished rail, her burgundy silk catching torchlight with each calculated step. The evening's gathering hums with restrained energy as nobles cluster in careful formations and sponsored merchants hover at respectful distances, their fine cloth marking newfound prosperity.

Her gaze sweeps the assembled court with practiced assessment. Strategy requires observation and tonight demands her most delicate maneuvering yet.

The King stands with his betrothed, Princess Ysabel resplendent in golden cloth and gems that shout Spanish wealth to every eye present. Lord Miles hovers nearby with Lady Rosamund, their matching blues creating the tedious harmony of the recently married. How dreary to dress like matching bookends.

But Ysabel's very excess proves Eveline's theory. The Spanish princess overdresses for every occasion. Even this simple gathering merits jewels fit for a coronation. Such desperate display speaks of insecurity, not confidence. And the court's whispered disapproval follows Ysabel like incense smoke, sweet on the surface but choking in concentration.

No. Alaric will not bind himself to his father's choice. The late king's shadow grows lighter with each passing month, and this betrothal bears that tainted legacy. Alaric seeks to rule differently. He has said as much in council and shared meals. A future queen closer to home makes perfect sense for a king determined to forge his own path.

Eveline's attention shifts to the opposing cluster where Lady Hélène converses with Sir Roland, Lady Isolde, and Lord Percival. The French woman's gown flows in simple lines of deep blue, elegant but understated, lacking the calculated threads that mark true nobility. Her brother matches her simplicity in dark wool and minimal decoration. How refreshing their modesty appears beside Ysabel's exhibitionist display. Yet modesty can hide calculation too.

Eveline notes how Lord Percival leans slightly closer to Hélène than propriety strictly demands, his practiced charm operating at full measure. The man spends more time at court than his own lands. A dangerous habit that breeds both debt and desperation. Percival's less than respectable motivations bring Eveline amusement when adorned toward Hélène. But if Lord Percival poses competition for aspiring court ladies, he pales beside a higher threat.

Lord Cedric of Langmere approaches with his characteristic swagger, gold thread gleaming in his doublet's elaborate embroidery. His father's illness makes Cedric heir to profitable holdings, transforming him from tolerated hanger-on to genuine prize. And Eveline has noticed how Alaric's jaw tightens whenever Cedric speaks overlong with Lady Hélène.

Not attraction to the French woman. Impossible. More likely distrust of Cedric's ambitions. A wise king guards against opportunists, and Cedric's transparent social climbing would naturally earn royal wariness. Lord Cedric makes a near perfect tool in Eveline's plans for gaining the King's acknowledgements.

"Lady Eveline." Cedric's greeting carries true warmth as he falls into step beside her. "You grace the evening like summer lightning."

She rewards him with a smile that could melt winter stone. "And you bring warmth to these chilly halls, my lord."

They move in synchronized elegance, her hand resting lightly on his offered arm. The positioning feels natural, two nobles of complementary rank enjoying mutual appreciation. Nothing improper, yet impossible to ignore. She feels almost guilty for using his interests for her. *Almost.*

Eveline times their approach as Alaric's group shifts closer, the King's attention momentarily free of Ysabel's golden monopoly. The Lady Rosamund speaks animatedly with the Spanish Princess about some intricate needlework pattern. Tedious feminine chatter that glazes masculine eyes.

"Your Majesty." Eveline's voice carries light respect as they near. "The upcoming hunt stirs talk of valor throughout the hall."

Alaric inclines his head with courteous warmth, though his gaze flickers briefly toward Cedric before returning to her face. "Talk often exceeds deed, Lady Eveline. The forest remembers only what strikes home."

She turns toward Cedric with admiring eyes, gifting him center stage. "And some lances never miss their mark."

Cedric straightens like a peacock sensing admiration, his chest expanding beneath the golden thread. "I rarely miss... when properly admired."

The boast rings with masculine confidence, his gaze lingering on Eveline's upturned face with unmistakable meaning. Perfect. Let every eye present witness this courtship dance.

"Whose spear flew truest last autumn?" she inquires, threading Alaric into the conversation with airy curiosity.

"The one that struck meat."

The King's response falls flatter than yesterday's bread with mild disinterest coating each syllable. But Eveline catches the slight tension in his shoulders, the way his fingers drum once against his thigh before stilling, the questioning look he gives her.

Hélène's group stands close enough that her voice carries clearly, though she speaks to Lady Isolde rather than joining the broader conversation. A sharper retort seems to spring to her lips at Alaric's flat hunting response, but she folds it into a bland smile, her fan tapping twice against her wrist in some private signal.

"New etiquette: swallow first, speak second," Hélène murmurs to Isolde, her tone carrying dry amusement.

"And live to speak third," Isolde replies with equal lightness.

Lord Percival leans closer to Hélène, positioning himself a breath too near for proper courtesy. His smile holds predatory warmth as he addresses both ladies, while also bridging his group's conversation into Alaric's comment.

"What conspiracy do the fair companions weave? Such whispered wisdom deserves wider audience."

Hélène responds with effortless grace, her wit dancing around the hunting theme without quite mocking it.

"Merely debating whether courage belongs to the hunter or the hunted, my lord. The stag that stands when the hounds bay shows remarkable... resolve."

Sir Roland's throat clears with pointed warning, his darkened blue gaze fixing on Percival with unmistakable meaning. The lord backs away slightly but maintains his challenging grin, clearly unimpressed by fraternal disapproval.

Lord Cedric's attention snaps toward Hélène's group like a hound catching scent. He pivots smoothly from Eveline's side, his voice carrying gallant authority.

"Lady Hélène speaks of hunting? Perhaps I might offer instruction in the boar-spear's proper use. A gentle hand needs a strong tutor."

Hélène's response arrives with pleasant precision. Each word perfectly courteous yet pointed as steel. "Then I shall request two tutors... one for each end of the spear."

Eveline's fingers tighten involuntarily around her fan as Cedric's attention flows toward the French woman like water seeking lower ground. The casual ease of their exchange, his immediate shift from her side to Hélène's vicinity, stings worse than open rejection.

She forces bright laughter. "We must ride out," She lays her hand a breath too long on Alaric's sleeve, a calculated touch of intimacy that marks territory before witnesses, "before the hedges lose their courage."

Alaric's response holds courteous distance, his gaze remaining fixed somewhere past her shoulder. "Hedges learn quickly."

The King's attention drifts toward Hélène's group with unmistakable interest, watching the interplay between Percival's advances, Roland's warnings, and Cedric's gallant posturing. Not jealousy. Eveline refuses to name it such. More likely the protective instincts of a host observing potential discord among guests.

"I prefer hunting verses. They bleed less." Lady Isolde interjects as she steps forward with gentle authority between Hélène and Percival. Her relocated presence dissolves the mounting tension in Roland and Alaric's gaits.

Isolde's voice carries cultured amusement, deflating masculine pride with scholarly wit. Percival's predatory grin softens into sheepish retreat, while Cedric's chest deflates slightly from its peacock expansion.

Eveline forces appreciation for the intervention while cataloging its effectiveness. Isolde wields courtesy like a blade. One sharp enough to cut through pretension yet smooth enough to leave no visible wound.

Lord Geoffrey approaches closer with Lady Juliette and the merchant Lucien Marcellus, their quiet conversation carrying just far enough for Eveline's carefully attuned ears.

"Some fish do not bite at silk." Geoffrey's tone holds dry observation as his gaze flickers from Eveline toward Alaric's distant expression.

Lady Juliette's response arrives with gentle wisdom, her words shaped by experience beyond her station. "Then silk must learn to enjoy the water."

The exchange stings deeper than intended. Geoffrey's knowing look passes to Hélène. Not conspiratorial plotting, but the easy understanding of genuine friendship. Such natural alliance highlights Eveline's own calculated maneuvering, making her feel suddenly transparent.

King Alaric shifts the conversation with calm command, his attention turning toward the Montbois knight. "Sir Roland, your recent success with the guard earns widespread praise. The bandit patrol particularly impressed Sir Holt."

Roland inclines his head with a soldier's dignity, accepting royal acknowledgment. His response holds no false modesty. "The men learn quickly, Your Majesty. Their courage needs only proper direction."

Lord Cedric inserts himself with eager politeness, his voice carrying transparent ambition. "Indeed, the realm benefits from such... foreign wisdom. Perhaps I might observe these methods firsthand?"

"Roland's training has always been open to all who would learn. Your presence would be welcome, Lord Cedric." The King's gaze shifts meaningfully toward Sir Roland. "Speaking of welcome presence, Sir Roland, join our hunting party tomorrow. Fresh eyes often spot what familiarity misses."

Lord Percival straightens with competitive interest, his earlier embarrassment forgotten. "Excellent sport ahead. Nothing tests mettle like good competition."

Alaric turns toward Cedric again, but the lean in his posture and look in his eyes suggest a deliberate aim that makes Eveline's pulse quicken. "Lord Cedric, your attentions to Lady Eveline bring warmth to these halls. Such gallantry deserves recognition."

Cedric preens visibly, his chest expanding with royal acknowledgment. The praise rings with formal approval. The sort that precedes official arrangements. Eveline's smile freezes as understanding dawns.

"Your Majesty honors my humble efforts," Cedric responds with a bow that displays his satisfaction.

Lady Eveline steps forward with graceful intent, her voice carrying the delicate precision of courtly diplomacy. "Indeed, Lord Cedric's... devotion has been most evident to all who observe." She pauses, her fan touching lightly to her left cheek. A subtle signal of agreement that masks deeper currents. "Though I confess, my own interests have grown quite... varied of late. The court offers such rich tapestry of worthy gentlemen."

Her gaze sweeps meaningfully across the assembled nobles before returning to Alaric's gaze with demure attention. "One finds oneself grateful for His Majesty's wisdom in arranging such diverse company."

Alaric inclines his head toward the assembled group, drawing Princess Ysabel closer with practiced protocol. "Court propriety demands we commune with our counselors before evening's end. Until tomorrow's hunt."

As they depart, Ysabel's gaze fixes on Eveline with the unmistakable warning of territorial marking from one rival to another. The Spanish princess recognizes the threat Eveline poses, even if Alaric pretends to be obliviously courteous.

Murmurs ripple through nearby witnesses, marking Alaric's civility, Roland's rising status, Hélène's effortless poise, and Cedric's pure interests opposing hers. Cedric basks in perceived triumph, his golden thread glinting as he straightens with renewed confidence.

Eveline's smile tightens like a pulled bowstring and her resolve hardens like winter ice.

Very well. We shall see how patience hunts.

Alice Whitcombe

Alice slips through the narrow passage between kitchen and hall. Torchlight flickers against whitewashed stone walls, casting shifting shadows that mirror the restless energy of castle life. She passes Tom the scullion hauling water buckets, his shoulders bent with purpose, and nods to Agnes hurrying past with armloads of fresh linens still warm from the pressing.

The kitchen welcomes her with the sweet smell of honey bread and the steady rhythm of Bess's paddle against dough. Flour dusts every surface like morning frost, and the great ovens breathe their ancient heat into the stone chamber.

Alice settles onto the worn bench beside the kneading table, arranging pewter cups in a precise row, each vessel ready for the careful pouring of what she knows. She pours the first cup.

"We'll pour truth while it's warm."

Bess glances up from her loaves, understanding passing between them without explanation. The baker's floured hands continue their work, but her attention sharpens toward gossip's familiar promise.

"Saw our French lady yesterday, carrying ledgers thick as prayer books into the Princess's wing. Heavy work for delicate hands."

Alice's fingers pause on the cup handles. "And the pages came out under the Spanish seal."

"Aye. Ink is loyal to whoever signs last."

Perry, the new footman, pushes through the doorway, flour smudged across his jerkin from moving grain sacks. His usual gruffness softens as he settles beside them, accepting the cup Alice offers.

"Watched our French lady thank young Peter by name for holding doors. Returned a pen to Meg proper like, with a word of gratitude." His calloused fingers drum against pewter. "She minds small things like they're big."

The kitchen falls into comfortable silence, steam rising from their cups like incense burned for quiet truths.

The kitchen door swings wide as Alan Thatcher steps through, Agnes close behind him. Flour still clings to his pressed sleeves from helping Perry move stores earlier, but his bearing carries the careful observation of one who serves wine and watches noble faces.

Alice straightens, recognizing opportunity in his arrival. Alan's duties as a head footman grant him perfect vantage for the theater of rank and desire that plays nightly in the Great Hall.

"Alan, how did the high table fare last evening?"

He settles onto the bench by Perry, accepting the cup she offers. He stares at the rising steam as he considers his words.

"Lord Cedric wore his pride like new spurs. All shine and jangle, that one. Boasted of holdings and bloodlines till the salt grew cold." Alan's voice carries dry amusement. "His Majesty smiled as if the meat had spoken."

Alice grins, understanding the delicate dismissal perfectly. "Then let the meat be well-seasoned elsewhere."

"Lord Percival made small advances toward Lady Hélène. Veiled compliments on her riding, questions about French customs." Alan's tone sharpens with disapproval. "Sir Roland's jaw went tight as a bowstring. A brother's warning, clear as chapel bells."

Perry chuckles. "French steel knows when to show its edge."

"The King praised Sir Roland's work with the guard before all assembled. Invited him to join the royal hunt next week." Alan pauses to take a sip, letting the weight settle. "Close counsel, that invitation."

Maud looks up from her bread, grinning. "Lord Geoffrey gains competition for the King's ear."

"Lady Eveline studied Lord Cedric like a merchant who knowingly weighs fake silver. Fishing for true worth elsewhere," Alan continues. "Her smile grew thin when he boasted of Langmere's acres."

Agnes's quiet voice cuts through their amusement. "If she dismisses Lord Cedric while remaining on his arm, then she uses him to shoot at higher ground."

Alice nods, understanding Eveline's calculations perfectly. The girl aims for crown and scepter, not noble holdings. She murmurs, "Bold as brass, shooting arrows at a target already claimed."

The kitchen understands ambition, but this feels different. Reckless in ways that invite whispered speculation about Lady Eveline's true understanding of court politics. The staff may find little warmth for the Spanish princess, her sharp tongue and imperious manner earning few friends below stairs, but they respect her station regardless. Ysabel wears the King's promise like armor, making Lady Eveline's pursuit seem more folly than strategy.

"But our French lady holds different ground entirely." Maud's hands still on her dough. "Watches how we work, learns our names, minds the small courtesies. Women who count our steps deserve fewer stones."

The kitchen grows thoughtful at her words. Alice recognizes truth in the baker's assessment. Hélène's attention to their names and daily labors marks her as worthy of protection.

"I'll pass the word. Let kindness be contagious."

Agnes moves closer, her expression gentle but firm. Her loyalty to Hélène runs deeper than mere duty. Weeks of dressing and tending have built genuine affection.

"If we must gossip, make it bread, not knives." She reminds Alice again to respect the Lady Hélène.

Alice places her hand over her heart, meeting Agnes's concerned gaze with warmth. The maid's request carries weight beyond mere words. She asks for fairness in a world where reputation can crumble like poorly mixed mortar.

"Warm bread it is."

The kitchen settles into comfortable understanding. Their words will shape perceptions throughout the castle's corridors, and Alice recognizes her responsibility to wield that influence with care. Truth served warm, but never bitter.

Agnes gathers her skirts and rises from the bench, her duties calling her back to the upper chambers. Perry thanks Maud for the cup and follows. Their footsteps fade down the corridor just as Meg appears in the doorway, another footman trailing behind her. Jory of the wine stores, whose tongue runs as freely as Alan's when the mood strikes him.

Alice shifts slightly, making space on the worn bench. Meg settles with her usual reserve, accepting a cup of tea but offering little warmth in return. The maid's discretion runs deeper than most, making her a puzzle Alice has yet to solve completely.

"How run the Princess's rooms?"

Meg's response comes quick and practical. "On time. With warm fires."

"A tidy answer for a tidy room."

Alice accepts the deflection, recognizing protective loyalty when she encounters it. Meg serves dual masters, the Princess and the Queen Dowager, leaving little room for careless words.

Jory leans forward, eager to share his observations from the Great Hall. "The Spanish lady grows sharp with servants who fumble wine service. Cut young Perry near to tears yesterday for trembling hands."

Alice raises her palm, stopping the flow before it turns poisonous. "Our talk should oil hinges, not burn doors. Sharp words about the Princess will spread like hearth smoke, reaching every chamber and lingering in the tapestries."

Alan nods understanding, his weathered hands folding around his cup. "Aye. We mind our work, not others' tempers. Better to speak of steady service than failing masters."

Jory shifts uncomfortably on the bench, recognizing the gentle rebuke. His eagerness for gossip wars with respect for Alice's wisdom. But he is no viper. Just a garden snake.

Bess begins stacking bowls with deliberate clatter, her signal for evening's end. "Time for honest folks to seek their beds. These ovens need rest, same as we do."

The gathering disperses with quiet farewells, leaving Alice alone among cooling stones and settling embers. She moves through the familiar ritual of closing. Wiping surfaces, final sweeps, and banking fires.

Her thoughts settle on strategy as she douses candles and torches one by one. Truth needs careful tending in castle corridors. Better to lift what deserves lifting than tear down what might fall naturally. The final wall torch remains burning by the door, its small flame a beacon for night messengers and late arrivals.

"For the night watch and the truth watch."

Hunts and Spirit

- 14 -

King Alaric

Deer slots mark the damp path. A jay scolds overhead. The party moves through morning mist, bracken, and birch at a hunting pace. King Alaric, Sir Roland, Lord Geoffrey, and Sir Hale spread in loose formation leaving behind them bruised earth from their mounts' hooves.

Alaric raises his hand, slowing the party. Geoffrey draws alongside his elbow while Roland maintains his location behind, neither pressing for favor nor retreating from notice. Sir Hale shadows at proper distance, close enough for protection but far enough to grant privacy for royal conversation.

The King slants his head in Roland's direction, not turning to meet the man's gaze, but enough to open casual conversation. "You have no faction here, Lord Roland. Tell me what my court looks like to foreign eyes."

Roland's mouth quirks with dry humor. "Foreign, yes, though not as far as some might guess."

Alaric waits, recognizing deflection when he encounters it. The man speaks truth when pressed but rarely volunteers more than necessary. A quality both maddening and equally refreshing.

"Speak plainly. I would have your assessment."

Roland obliges with a directness that Alaric has come to expect. "Reginald: spine of parchment, firm because he files it. Ranulf: hawk-sighted, he circles what he cannot name. Cecily: a seam so neat you don't see the mend. Eveline: light loves a mirror as much as she. Cedric: A peacock, a very dull one. Isolde: A saint sent from heaven to keep my sister in line."

The assessments land with the same precision as Roland's fighting techniques. Each observation cutting to character beneath courtly display. Alaric finds himself smiling despite the bluntness.

"And Geoffrey?" Alaric gives a playful look in Lord Geoffrey's direction.

"Bookish steel. Reads before he strikes."

They step over a fallen birch, its moss-covered trunk slick with morning dew.

Alaric glances back, weighing the man's honesty. "Most men sell me honey. You've brought salt."

"Food keeps longer that way."

Hale's voice carries quiet amusement from his shadowing position. "His Majesty does favor cured meats."

The exchange draws unexpected laughter from Alaric. Genuine mirth that echoes through morning stillness.

Geoffrey nudges his mount closer, his voice carrying the easy warmth of long friendship. "Speaking of court sport. Lord Percival seems quite taken with sampling French delicacies."

Roland's expression darkens with protective instinct. "He courts death, not my sister."

Laughter bursts from Alaric despite himself, but the humor carries an edge. "I've noticed his... persistent attention. A man who continuously samples what he would never buy shows poor character indeed."

The path narrows beneath overhanging hazel, forcing them into single file. Alaric's voice drops to a tone that brokers no argument. "Roland, if Percival attempts anything beyond words, inform me. I will handle it."

"Gladly, Sire."

Geoffrey clears his throat, steering conversation toward safer scandal. "Speaking of persistent attention, Eveline's flutter has drifted. Once at the sun, now at... plumage."

Roland's dry wit cuts through morning mist. "Plumage struts. Brains do not molt so easily."

"Perhaps I should give the lady what she wants: a peacock." Alaric's flat delivery draws knowing chuckles from the party.

The path widens again, allowing them to spread into comfortable formation. A rook lifts from a moss-covered stump ahead, its harsh call echoing through the bracken.

"She thinks envy is a ladder," Roland observes, studying the bird's flight.

Geoffrey's scholar's mind finds the flaw in such reasoning. "It is a rake. Teeth upward."

"Then let her find it with her foot, gently," Alaric replies, his tone suggesting consequences already planned.

The air cools as they pass beneath denser canopy, shadows playing across Roland's puzzled features. "What gives her such confidence to tilt at a crown already promised?"

Alaric considers the question with the careful attention he grants all matters touching royal prerogative. "Vanity, and the borrowed light of her mother near the Queen and her father's name in our rolls."

Roland's interest sharpens with keen curiosity. "What name, and how is it written?"

Geoffrey takes up the tale with historian's precision, his voice carrying both respect and sorrow. "Lord Artois, twelve years and more past. A peasant masked as a footman drew steel. Artois stepped between blade and king."

The memory weighs heavy in morning stillness. Alaric's words acknowledge debt without sentiment. "My father was less loved than obeyed. Artois paid for that ledger."

Roland's observation cuts to the heart of inherited burden. "Debts breed myths. Best to count them, not kneel to them."

They pause where game tracks vanish into dense fern, the hunting party temporarily forgotten beneath the weight of deeper conversation.

Alaric straightens in his saddle, conviction strengthening his voice. "I mean to be the opposite sort of king. The kind men speak to in daylight."

"You have a taste for progress, Sire, like your grandfather before you." Geoffrey's words offer the council of both a dear friend and scholar. "Go where daylight lives. Market squares, not only halls."

Hale's practical voice carries from his watchful position. "And I a taste for dry tents."

The jest breaks tension with soldier's humor.

"We shall see about those market squares," Alaric murmurs, half to himself. "Perhaps sooner than courtly halls might think."

Geoffrey's approving nod suggests the comment was heard and marked for future reference. He then shifts his reins, catching Alaric's attention with the deliberate movement. The morning's easy banter fades as his expression grows serious, weighted with purpose.

"Juliette Marchand and Lucien Marcellus. A case of worth over birth. May I sponsor the suit?"

Alaric considers the request, weighing friendship against protocol. Geoffrey's sponsorship carries weight, but the matter touches delicate ground. Class, precedent, and his mother's domain.

"Not before I speak with my mother. Lady Juliette stands beneath her eye. It is the Queen Dowager who must be persuaded, not I."

Roland's tactical mind cuts straight to strategy. "Then persuade by proof. How their union feeds the realm."

Alaric finds himself studying Roland with renewed interest. The man counsels action over ceremony, substance over spectacle. Qualities that speak to deeper wisdom than most court advisors typically provide. Alaric wonders what manner of future forged the man's soul.

A buck's harsh bark echoes ahead, freezing conversation. Sir Hale raises two fingers for silence, his weathered face alert to danger or opportunity. The party stills, breath misting in cool morning air as they wait.

Alaric catches Roland's eye with a look that almost qualifies as a smile. "Salt, then. See that you bring it again."

"I'll bring bread with it."

Geoffrey's soft murmur carries approval. "Bread before bells."

Hale's whisper cuts through morning stillness. "And bells after the shot, if you please."

Sir Roland of Montbois

The hunt ends with empty game bags but full conversation. Roland walks the forest edge alone. A ritual the castle and its guards have learned not to question. Torchlight from the walls fades behind him as he moves deeper into silver mist.

The night presses closer. Owls fall silent. Even the rustle of leaf filled limbs die to nothing, as if the world holds its breath. Roland's hand drifts toward his blade, instincts sharpened by too many hostile worlds.

"If you mean me no harm, show your hands."

Pale light shifts between the trees. A figure solidifies from shadow. Tall, graceful, with skin like moonlit water and hair that flows silver white past broad shoulders. Eyes hold depths that seem to contain starlight itself. No weapon mars the being's form, yet presence alone commands attention.

"Hands, both empty." The voice carries ancient weight without threat, like memory speaking through time itself.

Roland recognizes the being as one of the Ancients. Those who shaped the earliest paths between worlds and watch over the threads of time. He forces his shoulders to relax while maintaining ready stance.

The Ancient tilts its head with curious interest. "A signal where none should echo. We came to hear it."

"Then you know we don't belong."

"History already shaped." The Ancient pauses as the words fall like stones preceding an avalanche. "Your arrival has been woven into what must be. One thread is fixed. The loom would break if pulled."

Roland's chest tightens. The mist seems to press closer, cold against his skin. "Whose thread?"

"Hers."

The single word hits harder than any blade. Roland takes a step forward, hands clenched. "You're saying Elaine can't return."

"We are saying she will not." The Ancient's expression remains serene, untouched by Roland's rising tension. "Doors will close. We close them."

"Then we are prisoners."

"No. Stewards, misplaced."

Roland's laugh comes out harsh, bitter. "Stewards of what? A court that barely trusts us? A king who asks too many questions? An enemy who may yet return?"

The Ancient watches him impassively with those galaxy-deep eyes. "Your enemy, the one who stole your path home, when the doors are sealed, his shadow can no longer move."

"And us? What about us?"

"One foot may find a ledge when the gate falls. Only one."

Roland's voice cracks despite his efforts. "Why her?"

"Because history remembers a face."

The words hang in the air. Roland stares at the Ancient, searching for mercy in those alien features and finding only implacable certainty. The forest around them feels suddenly smaller, the weight of inevitability pressing down like stones.

The Ancient's gaze never wavers, holding Roland in place like a gentle but unbreakable chain. "She must not know. Not yet."

"What do you mean, not yet?"

"You would break what keeps her alive."

Roland's fist tightens on the hilt at his side. The unfairness of it burns in his chest. To hide his sister's fate while she plans and hopes for home. "Then I am to carry it bare?"

"Until the moment arrives when silence breaks more than speech." The Ancient extends one pale hand, fingertips barely brushing Roland's wrist. Warmth spreads from the touch. Not a gift, merely acknowledgment. A mark that this conversation happened. "You will know when the door begins to close."

"And then?"

"Then choose how to be remembered."

The mist shifts, folding inward like water finding its level. Roland blinks and the Ancient is gone. No footsteps, no rustle of leaves, simply absent as if never there. Night birds resume their calls, and the forest breathes again.

Roland stands alone in the silver darkness, pulse hammering against his temple. He stares at his wrist where the phantom warmth still lingers. The walk back to torchlight feels longer than the journey out.

Sir Roland of Montbois

Hours later with no sleep, Roland finds himself standing before the door to Hélène's bedchamber. His fingers hover over the door's metal ring. The sitting room's fire has long since perished leaving the room at the mercy of night's chill. His hand trembles, not from cold, but from the weight of what he carries. The Ancient's words echo repeatedly in his mind: *She must not know. Not yet.*

"Say it now, and ruin the morning. Say nothing, and ruin yourself."

He eases the latch with silence. Moonlight washes Hélène's face through the narrow window, her breath steady in sleep. Even unconscious, a faint frown creases her brow. The same expression she wore as a child when puzzling through lessons that came too easily to others.

"You would scold me for the frown." He whispers, then kneels by the foot of the bed, words gathering like storm clouds. The truth sits heavy on his tongue, demanding release.

"Elaine—"

It is the true name that breaks him.

Her eyelids flutter, and she shifts against the pillow with a soft murmur. "Tell the hedges I won."

The words spill drowsy and nonsensical, followed by that half smile he knows so well. The one that appears when she dreams of outrunning tutors or scaling impossible walls. Even in sleep, she finds victory in small rebellions.

Roland's chest tightens as he watches her settle back into stillness. The Ancient spoke of fixed threads, of doors sealing shut, but here lies the truth they could not voice: she is already weaving herself into this tapestry. Books and banter shared with Isolde. Patient rounds with Agnes. Those long theological debates with Anselm that leave him shaking his head in wonder. That unbreakable rib of wit that makes even Cecily grin.

"You will live this well if I hold my tongue." He leans closer, voice barely disturbing the air. "If the world must fix you here, I will still cross it."

Roland rises, forcing breath to evenness. His shoulders square against the weight of the Ancient's revelations.

"I carry it so you need not."

He draws her blanket higher with a brother's care, tucking wool around her shoulders the way their mother once did in their cramped quarters on Mars Colony Seven. The gesture feels both foreign and essential. His eyes move to a new gown Anselm gifted. Where before her gowns were simpler, this one's embroidery bears the mark of Anselm's family name from before he took the ecclesiastical oath. A protection rendered in silk and silver thread instead of kevlar, but protection nonetheless.

"Sleep, Hélène. Conquer the morrow."

She stirs slightly at his whisper, lips parting as if to answer, then settles deeper into dreams. Roland watches her face smooth into peace before turning toward the door.

He leaves their shared chambers as quietly as he came, each footfall measured against the floorboards' potential for betrayal.

The corridor's chill bites through his tunic as he straightens, already cataloguing tomorrow's demands. First and third bells will bring training. Denby expects refinements to the grappling forms. The guard rotation needs adjustment after yesterday's patrol.

"Feet first. Then the rest."

He walks toward duty, carrying secrets like stones in his chest. Each step deliberate, each breath an act of will.

Balls and Revelations

- 15 -

The Court

Candles flicker up the carved stone pillars like shadows being coaxed into existence against the backdrop of a deepening evening. Shawms and viols draw forth a steady, measured melody, weaving through the great hall as nobles arrange themselves into a tapestry of color and grace. The Spring Ball is in full bloom, each individual a thread in a grand design. The doors of oak groan softly, yielding to reveal King Alaric, adorned in a burgundy surcoat embroidered with a trio of golden lions that roar silently under the candlelight.

"His Majesty opens the dance," declares the herald, voice clear and resonant, cutting through the melodic air as if by design.

Alaric strides forward with the confidence of a young monarch who knows the weight of eyes upon him, every step a calculated ripple across the court. He finds himself beside Princess Ysabel, her dress a waterfall of matching crimson and gold, jewels gleaming like captured fire. Their bow is a scholar's delight. Perfect in form, smiles seamlessly stitched into their demeanor, though the space between them whispers of careful distance.

"Your Highness," Alaric offers, his tone a paragon of courtesy.

"Your Majesty," Ysabel returns, sweet as confections. "*Our* house keeps good time."

Our. Alaric holds back a twitch forcing its way through his careful visage. Instead, his nod carries the weight of unspoken words as the opening dance compels him to stay.

As they glide across the floor, the room hushes for a moment as a subtle change in energy ripples outward when Hélène's party joins the assembly. She enters with Lady Isolde and Archbishop Anselm. Draped in a silk gown that captures the essence of spring itself with its delicate hues and refined lines and the markings of Anselm's prior house. Agnes's handiwork, flawless as a forged blade, becomes evident in every perfectly placed hair, every graceful sway of fabric, and every stitch of Anselm's protection.

"You wear serenity," Isolde murmurs, voice soft like the brush of silk on bare skin.

"Heavily pinned," Hélène quips, eyes dancing with subdued humor.

Nearby, Lady Cecily and Baron Brightwell edge closer. The Baron's gaze alights on Hélène, and he inclines his head, the name falling from his lips with the weight of familiarity.

"Lady Elaina," his voice booms, a touch too confident, the name wrong.

The air in the vicinity momentarily stills, but Hélène's poise is practiced and true. "By your leave, My Lord," she corrects, Cecily's tutoring rushing forth in every carefully chosen word. "I am Lady Hélène; the error is mine for speaking it too swiftly before."

The Baron bows with a smile, correction mollified, chastened by the ease of her deference. "I stand corrected, my lady."

He takes his leave further into the crowd and Cecily moves to stand beside her, fan moving with whispered approval. A soft tap of affirmation barely felt, yet fully understood. "You saved his dignity and kept your own. That is court craft," she whispers, her eyes warm with praise.

Alaric catches the exchange, his heart quickening not from the dance's sway, but from the growing tapestry of Cecily's loyalty and Hélène's quicksilver wit.

Geoffrey stands amongst the bustling throng of dancers, his gaze following King Alaric as he steps smoothly into a country measure. The music transforms, vibrant but less formal than before, allowing couples to join without the same scrutiny. Cedric reaches for Eveline's hand with easy elegance, drawing several nobles into the dance including Hélène, Juliette, and Lucien.

Geoffrey steps into place beside Hélène. "My lady," he offers, tone light as the music surrounds them, "I promise not to bruise your toes."

A laugh escapes her, soft but genuine. "I should like them unbruised for running from gossip," she retorts, eyes glinting with shared mischief.

They move together, the dance guiding them close, then away. Geoffrey's curiosity stirs like autumn leaves caught in a brisk wind. Roland's sharp observations of court intrigues during their recent hunt echo in his mind, and he finds himself eager to hear Hélène's perspective on the same.

"So, tell me." He begins, voice woven between the notes, "How does Lady Hélène find English court?"

"It's..." she hesitates, weighing words as though on scales, "rife with unexpected challenges and some uncommon kindnesses."

Geoffrey's expression invites more, his steps steady and undemanding. "You speak as one who measures truth carefully," he observes, voice pitched low enough that only she might hear. "But surely you can say more without fear of judgment. Not from me, at least."

The reassurance settles something in her posture. She glances toward Roland, who observes the dancers from the edge of the floor, then back to Geoffrey. "Roland would say the court is like a chessboard where half the pieces move by rules no one explains," she murmurs, her voice carrying the dry wit that marks both siblings. "Beautiful to observe, maddening to navigate, and occasionally deadly if you step wrong."

Geoffrey appreciates that she keeps her voice low, mindful of listening ears even in the midst of revelry. Geoffrey's encouraging silence draws more from her, and Hélène's voice takes on a conspiratorial edge.

"Lady Eveline views me as competition for His Majesty's attention. Though I assure you, I seek no such thing. Lord Percival believes courtyard strolls are invitations for his... persistent company." Her tone sharpens slightly. "And Her Highness has a gift for finding tasks that require my immediate attention whenever her own duties grow tedious."

Geoffrey notes how carefully she phrases the last observation, respect for Ysabel's station tempering what could be sharper criticism. The restraint speaks well of her diplomatic instincts. She'll survive this court well if the future deems her stay permanent.

"Should Lord Percival prove too persistent," Geoffrey offers with mock gravity, "I stand ready to play knight in shining armor."

Hélène's smile brightens genuinely. "Your offer is most gallant, my Lord, though I suspect my dark knight might not wish to share such duties."

Their shared laughter mingles with the music as Geoffrey catches her fond glance toward Roland, understanding perfectly which dark knight she means.

Their rhythm falters, not due to misstep, but quiet understanding borne between them. Off to the side, two noblewomen whisper, their gossip a mere murmur compared to the lively dance.

"Beauty dazzles," one woman remarks under her breath, eyes on Ysabel.

"Competence endures," replies the second, gaze flicking to Hélène.

Geoffrey catches this in the corner of his awareness, the dance ever spiraling onward, an unbroken tapestry of music and motion.

Hours slip past like silk through eager fingers, yet Alaric has claimed only one dance from Eveline. A brief, polite circuit that left her hunger unsatisfied. She positions herself deliberately where his gaze has fallen once again toward Hélène, then draws Cedric close with deliberate ease.

"If virtue were sport, I should choose Lady Eveline as my champion," Cedric declares, voice pitched to carry across the nearby clusters of nobles.

"And lose the match for flattery," Eveline laughs, the sound bright as crystal, her eyes fixed not on Cedric but on the King's distant figure.

Yet Alaric's attention has already flickered elsewhere. Frustration burns beneath Eveline's smile as she watches Hélène execute a perfect curtsy to a passing lord, the motion graceful where once her sharp tongue would have flown unchecked. A transformation born of Artois tutelage.

"My lord," Hélène says pleasantly.

"My lady," comes the approving response.

Across the room, Cecily's fan moves in two light taps meant not for Hélène's flawless form, but a warning for Eveline's increasingly obvious display.

Princess Ysabel glides through the space between both women, her smile light but her words cut low in warning to Eveline. "England will dance well, once it learns my steps."

"Then we must listen closely," Eveline replies evenly, though her jaw tightens with the effort of restraint.

Queen Dowager Margaret's eyes sweep the ballroom with the cool calculation of a sovereign weighing her court. Each bow, each glance, each whispered word becomes another entry in the ledger she keeps within her mind. Fresh ink flowing across mental parchment as the evening unfolds.

Ysabel commands attention like a flame draws moths. Yet Lord Miles bows too deeply to Ysabel, his deference bordering on performance. While Lady Rosamund's curtsy holds the exact measure of respect due to a future queen, nothing more.

But when nobles greet Hélène, there's something different. A warmth in their acknowledgment, as though she's earned her place rather than simply inheriting it. The new addition of Anselm's prior house to her finery suggests the Archbishop believes the same.

Eveline's strategy has shifted like wind changing direction. Where once the girl openly aimed her arrows of charm at her son Alaric, now Eveline looses them toward the young Lord Cedric, who preens under the attention like a peacock in morning light. Margaret's lips thin slightly. The girl plays a dangerous game, believing she can steer Alaric's heart through jealousy.

Sir Roland stands apart, dressed appropriately for a noble guest, yet his bearing tells another story. His stance speaks of a soldier's readiness, eyes tracking movement with the alertness of one who guards rather than revels. He shadows Hélène's path, and when Lord Percival approaches with wine and practiced smiles, Roland's presence somehow materializes between them without seeming to move at all.

Reginald observes from the chamber's edge, his attention sharper than winter's bite. But what exactly holds his focus remains unclear. Another puzzle piece for her growing collection.

Archbishop Anselm moves closer, his heavy robes rustling softly against the stone.

"Faces write books," Margaret murmurs to Anselm as she keeps eyes locked on Lord Reginald.

"And some chapters warn of storms," Anselm replies, following her gaze.

As if on queue, Reginald spots the pair, strides over, and bows. His presence completing their normal trio. "Your Grace, Archbishop. The evening flows well."

"Until now." Margaret's eyes fix on the hall's edge where Ranulf emerges like a shadow given form. Notes rest folded in his palm, his gaze sweeping the dancers with the patience of a predator. The very air seems to still around him.

"Trouble finds its moment," she murmurs.

Anselm catches her meaning instantly. "Shall we fetch the weather?" he asks Reginald quietly.

Both men move with purposeful calm toward their quarry. She rises, silk rustling, and begins her approach toward Alaric. Some storms require the crown's attention before they break.

Lord Ranulf of Morcar

The letters feel like iron in Ranulf's palm, their damning silence heavier than any accusation. He watches the dancing figures blur past. The *Montbois* siblings moving through the court like they belong, like history vouches for them. But history lies silent when pressed for answers.

"When a name casts no shadow—" he begins, voice pitched low to the circle of grey-bearded lords who lean closer like conspirators.

The words die on his tongue as a shadow falls across their gathering. Archbishop Anselm's crosier catches the candlelight, its jeweled surface winking like an eye that sees too much. Behind him, Reginald and Sir Hale form a wall of silent authority.

"My lord of Morcar, walk with us, before we teach the music a discord."

Anselm's voice flows mild as water, yet immovable as bedrock. The older nobles scatter like leaves before wind, suddenly fascinated by distant conversations. Ranulf's jaw tightens, but he follows into a side chamber where candles burn lower and walls press closer.

He sets the letters on the table like daggers drawn for battle. "I serve the Crown, not a tale."

"Then serve it wisely, not loudly."

Ranulf spreads the parchments like evidence at trial. His finger traces each damning line. "One abbey knows nothing of their passing. A notary in Bordeaux hedges when pressed for records. Their heraldry appears on no roll, in no grant."

He lifts the final letter, its seal still bearing wax. "And here, the blade that cuts deepest. There is indeed a Sir Roland in that region. Yet he serves as a traveling knight of modest birth, no noble blood, no family save his only distant kin, our Archbishop."

Anselm's face remains carved stone. Reginald shifts weight from foot to foot.

"That Sir Roland yet rides the roads of France, my lord Archbishop. He has not crossed any channel, taken ship to any English shore."

Ranulf's voice drops to barely above whisper, yet carries the weight of accusation. "I seek the Crown's safety, not court scandal. Why this charade? If the siblings are false, I will stop them before they damage His Majesty further. If they are true, then provide truth stronger than words and I will stop the slander before it begins."

The Archbishop and Lord Reginald hold their gazes steady. Neither provide an answer.

"But truth or lie, my lord, your grace. Someone must answer for what walks among us."

The chamber door swings wide. King Alaric enters with authoritative steps, flanked by Denby's steady presence and Roland with a bundled burden. The cloak wrapped mystery hangs heavy in Roland's arms like secrets made manifest.

"Sir Hale, guard the door. None enter." Hale's footsteps retreat. The latch clicks with the sound of approaching finality in the now silent room.

Alaric faces Ranulf without heat, without the royal mask that distance demands. His voice carries the weight of a man choosing trust over caution. "You have long kept wolves from our doors. I prefer you inside the door now."

Ranulf's breath catches. The parchments beneath his palm seem suddenly fragile, insufficient weapons against whatever truth approaches. "Then speak plainly, Sire. What wolves circle us?"

Alaric gestures toward Roland, whose jaw tightens like a man preparing for confession.

"The French siblings are from the future. They appeared from the air whilst battling a future foe, and they chose to protect Geoffrey, myself, and others in that room at the risk of their mission, and their enemy's escape."

The words hang in the air like smoke that refuses to dissipate. Ranulf's mind reels, grasping for solid ground in a world suddenly turned fluid.

"From the future." His voice emerges flat, testing the shape of impossibility. "You ask me to believe—"

"My enemy, the Grey Hunter, still risks returning," Roland interjects, voice rough with reluctance. "Though difficult, and not in his better interests."

"What proof have you of this tale?"

Roland unwraps the bundle with careful hands. Dark blue fabric spills forth that is not quite leather, not quite cloth, but something that seems to drink the candlelight and hold it prisoner. Ranulf's fingers trace the strange weave, finding texture unlike anything in England or France.

"Peculiar work."

"Strike it hard," Alaric commands. "Watch."

Roland's fist impacts the material. Light blooms across its surface like captured lightning, racing through threads that shouldn't exist. Ranulf jerks his hand back.

"Made of fabric not yet invented. Absorbs impacts to reduce damage. A future version of mail."

Ranulf's throat works against words that won't come. His mind, trained to dissect negotiations and unravel deceptions, finds no foothold here. "Why have you not returned?"

Roland extends the forearm, revealing an empty slot worked into the strange material. "A device attaches here. One that allows travel through time. I surrendered mine to the Grey Hunter to protect Geoffrey. My sister's was damaged beyond use during the fight."

"What future can you share?"

"I must resist speaking of future events related to now, else irreparably damage everyone's fates. The greatest risk of time travel isn't being stuck in the past, it's risking the fates of those we cross."

Ranulf's justiciar instincts sharpen like blades finding their edge. "Better to lock you away than let you walk around testing fates."

Alaric steps forward, authority radiating from every line of his frame. "The siblings could have allowed my death and that of anyone else present that evening. They risked their own interests to protect us. In repayment, they stand under my protection and the Church's word. Their origin remains as Anselm named: the Montbois siblings."

His voice drops to assurance harder than granite. "On this matter, my crown and the crozier speak as one."

Ranulf studies the faces around him. Alaric's resolve, Anselm's unwavering calm, Reginald's careful acceptance. The weight of service, of loyalty tested against impossibility, settles on his shoulders. "Then my tongue will learn a new hymn."

Anselm inclines his head with satisfaction. "We ask for silence and assistance. If others sniff around, misdirect gently, don't inflame. Turn questions sideways. Let them tire."

"And if proof arrives that undoes this tale?"

Alaric's smile carries no warmth. "It will arrive to me, not to the hall."

Ranulf picks up a letter with hands that no longer shake. The parchments that seemed so damning now feel like children's games against the truth they've tried to conceal.

"Then I serve a stranger kingdom than I imagined, Sire. But I serve it still."

Denby steps forward, his steady gaze fixed on Ranulf like a captain assessing a recruit. "Words fade. Oaths endure. Speak plainly what your service entails."

Ranulf's hand hovers over the family heraldry stitched into his vest, then settles instead on the scattered letters. Two fingers press against the parchment: a negotiator's pledge, bound by wit rather than family crest.

"By my name and my judgment, I will not break your peace. The Montbois name is safe with me."

Alaric nods with satisfaction. "Good. Keep your judgment sharp. I have uses for it."

Ranulf gathers the letters and papers with patient care, folding each piece like a craftsman storing tools. The weapon becomes instrument. The hunt transforms into guardianship.

Anselm's voice flows soft as the King takes his leave. "Thank you for guarding the realm from its own appetite."

Ranulf inclines his head, the gesture carrying newfound weight. "I will watch the wolves still, just not the ones you named lambs."

The chamber door opens to spill music and laughter from the ball beyond. Ranulf steps toward the sound, carrying secrets heavier than crowns.

Sir Roland of Montbois

The last chords of the ball fade and servants begin to douse sconces. Roland finds himself at the colonnade where night air tastes of wet stone and relief.

Denby emerges from shadow, his steady presence familiar as worn leather. "A fire was banked before the curtains caught."

Roland's shoulders drop a fraction. Denby knows enough to understand the stakes, but little enough to sleep soundly. "Aye. Close work."

Ranulf passes them in the corridor, no longer hunting a stage. He catches sight of Reginald near the great doors and offers a short nod. An apology without words, understanding without surrender.

Denby's voice drops to barely audible. "Does he stand down?"

"He stands with."

Denby tips his head toward the emptying hall, where overturned goblets mark where tempers nearly sparked. "Your teachings have kept six tempers from turning to steel tonight."

Roland's mouth quirks despite exhaustion. "I accept payment in unbroken furniture."

Roland leans against the colonnade, his thoughts replaying the evening's performance. Alaric had navigated the dangerous waters of courtly expectations with deft sincerity. A word here, a nod there. Ysabel received formal grace, Eveline subtle deflection, and Hélène his genial respect, without igniting a single scandal.

Denby stands beside him, gaze following the retreating courtiers. "The King danced without feeding any wolves."

Roland chuckles, appreciating the simplicity in Denby's observation. "We should all learn that step."

Yet the memory of Ysabel's eyes linger, a predatory gleam cast over both Eveline and Hélène. He turns to Denby with furrowed brow.

"Hélène can't keep her mask forever," Roland muses, the concern tight in his chest.

Denby smiles slightly, a rare warmth. "She's stronger than you think. The staff speak of her warmly. The court sees more grace each day."

They nod, resuming silent watch as the last guests disperse.

Through the arched doorway across the courtyard, Roland catches sight of Hélène departing with Isolde and Agnes, their voices carrying softly on the night breeze. His instinct pulls him toward them, but he forces himself to study the moon's pale face instead, hands clasped behind his back.

Denby's approval comes without words. A slight nod toward Roland's restraint. "Guard her with usefulness, not noise."

"Aye."

The older knight extends his forearm, and Roland clasps it firmly. Callused palm to callused palm, a soldier's treaty sealed in silence.

"Third bell only tomorrow? Let the men recover a bit from the night's revelry?"

"Aye. Feet first, lessons second."

The court exhales around them as servants snuff the final torches and sconces. A stable boy trots past, casting moving shadows against stone in the remaining torchlight. Somewhere in the retreating darkness, an owl sings the dying chord of an evening song.

Marriage and Travels

- 16 -

Lady Eveline Artois

Eveline adjusts her emerald sleeves for the third time, the silk whispering against her wrists as she positions herself where morning light catches the gold threading. The Great Hall buzzes with uncommon energy. Nobles clustering near the dais, servants lingering by doorways instead of rushing to tasks.

A pleasantly nervous energy coils in her chest. Alaric rarely summons the entire court for announcements outside the usual morning petitions. Something significant stirs.

"Lady Eveline." Lord Cedric appears at her elbow, his surcoat gleaming with fresh gilt buttons. "You look radiant this morning."

She offers an empty smile as her attention remains fixed on the empty throne. Since the Spring Ball, the King's manner toward her has warmed. Surely he noticed her graceful partnership with Cedric, saw how effortlessly she commanded attention on the floor, how he would suite her better than Cedric, how she would suite the crown better than Ysabel.

"The King has been in fine spirits these past days," she murmurs, smoothing her skirts. "Perhaps today brings news worthy of celebration."

Lord Cedric preens slightly, mistaking her commentary for personal regard. Around them, Lord Reginald exchanges quiet words with Lord Geoffrey while Archbishop Anselm and the Queen Dowager position themselves near the throne's right side, where she should be.

Trumpets sound. The great doors swing wide.

King Alaric enters with regal stride, his burgundy surcoat rich against the morning banners. His gaze sweeps the assembled court, pausing briefly on familiar faces before settling into formal address.

"My lords and ladies, faithful servants of this realm."

The hall stills.

"In a fortnight's time," He pauses to think or for dramatic effect, to which she does not know. "I shall undertake a King's Progress across our lands. No advance riders shall herald our path. Let the people receive their sovereign as surprise brings joy."

Murmurs ripple through the hall as Alaric's words settle. A progress without ceremony, arriving unannounced in villages and holdings. Eveline nods approvingly, imagining herself at the King's side, graciously receiving the people's acclaim.

"A wise course, Your Majesty!" Lord Cedric's voice carries too loudly from her left, his enthusiasm drawing several pointed looks. "The realm shall see their sovereign's—"

"Lady Eveline." The King's clear voice cuts through Cedric's proclamation, commanding instant silence. "Step forward, if you would."

Her breath catches. Every eye in the hall fixes upon her as she glides with perfect grace toward the dais, the soft leather of her slippers whispering against the stones. Behind her, Cedric's footsteps follow at a respectful distance, his presence radiating satisfaction.

She positions herself before the throne and sinks into a perfect curtsy, her Artois etiquette evident in every graceful line. When she rises, Alaric's expression holds warmth. Surely the prelude to her heart's desire.

"My lords and ladies," Alaric continues, his hand reaching toward hers, "before we speak of journeys, there remains a second matter of joy to share with this court."

Her pulse quickens as his fingers close gently around hers. The hall holds its breath.

Queen Dowager Margaret leans forward slightly. "Your service at court has been noted, Lady Eveline. Your wit, too."

Eveline's smile deepens as she curtsies again, still maintaining Alaric's hold on her hands. "Your Majesty is gracious to notice either."

Alaric's gaze shifts past her shoulder. "Lord Cedric of Langmere."

Her mind's eyes twitches at Cedric's address. The King's words hang in the air like a blade poised to fall.

"You have my blessing in your request for Lady Eveline's hand in marriage."

The words crash over her like winter water. The hall erupts in polite applause, voices calling congratulations while her smile freezes in place. This cannot be happening.

Cedric's hands find her shoulders as Alaric's grip releases her. She is spun to face him, and the watching court. His grin spreads wide as nobles press closer with well wishes.

"My lord, I fear there has been some misunderstanding—" she manages, her voice barely audible above the celebration.

Cedric's smile twitches at the corners, his grip tightening slightly on her shoulders. "No misunderstanding at all, my lady. Your encouragement these past weeks has been most... clear."

The trap snaps shut around her, woven from her own desperate schemes.

Lady Cecily steps forward from the crowd, her composed mask slipping just enough to reveal both relief and wariness. She inclines her head toward the throne with submissive grace. "My daughter will strive to be worthy of the Crown's trust."

Queen Dowager Margaret rises from her seat, commanding the hall's attention with a single gesture. Her voice carries the weight of settled law. "A good match ends foolish noise and begins wise housekeeping."

The words land with a mental slap. Eveline's cheeks burn as she grasps the Queen Dowager's meaning. Her flirtations have been noted, catalogued, and now publicly corrected. Yet she lifts her chin, summoning every lesson in deportment her Artois heritage has provided her.

"I shall keep a tidy house, Your Grace."

The Queen Dowager's smile holds gentle. "Begin with your heart."

The continued subtle reproach cuts just as deep as the first, yet Eveline holds her curtsy until dismissed. Around her, the machinery of noble marriage clicks into motion as Lord Reginald produces prepared parchments from his sleeve.

"The dowry papers await review," Alaric announces. "Langmere waits for its lady."

Cedric practically vibrates with satisfaction. "And she shall find it eager for her step."

The timeline emerges with swift efficiency. A fortnight to marry and then ride to Langmere with the King's Progress. Away from court. Away from the King's daily presence. Away from her dreams.

As the crowd begins to disperse, Eveline moves to her mother's side with leisurely steps. Her voice drops to a whisper meant for Cecily alone. "I aimed too high and struck a different star."

Cecily's hand finds hers, squeezing gently. "Shine where you land."

The wisdom stings, yet Eveline straightens her shoulders as nobles approach with congratulations. She accepts each with perfect grace, her smile never wavering even as her heart reshapes itself around this new reality.

Lord Geoffrey offers kind words about Cedric's character. Lady Isolde wishes her joy. Even Lady Hélène approaches with genuine warmth, though Eveline notes the French lady's careful distance from the King's vicinity.

As she glides toward the hall's exit, chin high and train flowing behind her, Eveline's inner voice hardens with newfound resolve.

Very well. Let the world learn my name another way.

THROUGH TIME AND CROWN

Lady Juliette Marchand

The chapel's side aisle holds peace even as the great hall still buzzes with Eveline's sudden betrothal a week prior. Juliette kneels before the small altar, her taper flame steady in the cool air. Wax drips onto the stone as she whispers her petition.

"For safe roads and steadier hearts."

The prayer encompasses everything: the King's coming progress, Lucien's precarious position at court, and the fragile hope growing between them. She touches the simple silver cross at her throat, a reminder of simpler days before love complicated duty.

Soft footsteps pause at the chapel entrance. She knows his step by now. When she turns, Lucien stands framed in the doorway, his merchant's cap held against his chest like setting down pride itself.

"May I come as a guest who hopes to be family?"

His humility touches something deep within her chest. She rises, smoothing her skirts, and offers the smile that has grown easier each day.

"Guests who wipe their feet are halfway there."

He enters properly, bowing toward the altar before approaching. The formality between them has softened these past weeks, yet careful boundaries remain. Her station demands it, even as her heart rebels.

"The court speaks of nothing but travel preparations," he says quietly. "And marriages blessed by crowns."

She nods, watching his face in the candlelight. "Markets forgive many things. Courts forgive fewer."

The flickering light in the chapel gives way to the soft glow of the cloister walk as Juliette and Lucien step into the pale morning. The air is damp with the promise of rain yet to fall, and their footsteps echo softly against the stone floors.

"I've asked the Queen Dowager to second me to the King's traveling household," Juliette begins, hesitance barely brushing her voice. "Lucien, your petition to serve as a provisioning consultant under Geoffrey has found sympathetic ears."

Lucien's eyes brighten, a mix of ambition and affection. "If granted, we ride with the progress," he affirms. "And meet the coast as ourselves."

Juliette nods, the weight of long withheld dreams settling alongside new possibilities. Their future flickers ahead. A mosaic of hope and unknowns.

As they near the archway, Lord Geoffrey appears, his figure framed within the ancient stones, holding a folded missive. His expression is one of quiet kindness, familiar and reassuring.

"The Queen Dowager approves the match, and His Majesty concurs," Geoffrey announces, the note catching the light as he passes it to Lucien. "But due to the nature of the marriage, Alaric suggests you petition formally at Fairharbor. You are both now added to the progress lists."

Lucien offers a bow, gratitude balanced with his characteristic reserve. "Then I will start with inventories instead of speeches."

"A refreshing fashion," Geoffrey replies, clearly amused.

Juliette, her resolve now unwavering, adds, "We can wait."

In that simple assertion lies a world of meaning, anchoring their shared resolve. They part to prepare. She to lists, he to suppliers, both walking straighter.

Lucien speaks low, "Until the trumpet."

"Until the trumpet," Juliette echoes softly.

Queen Dowager Margaret

The Queen Dowager Margaret stands in the Great Hall's shadow, watching chaos bend to order. Around her, the castle transforms into a machine of departure. Wagons creak under grain sacks, harness leather gleams with fresh oil, and spare axles lean against stone walls like soldiers at attention.

"Twice counted or twice cursed!" Master Hob's voice carries above the din as quartermasters chant their endless tallies.

She observes this orchestra of logistics with satisfaction. No detail escapes notice. Not the way Juliette's hands tremble as her name appears on the traveling roster, not how Lucien straightens when listed as provisioning aide under Geoffrey's command.

King Alaric steps forward, his voice cutting through the bustle. "Service on the road is honor. Honor is work."

The herald's announcement rings clear: "Lord Cedric of Langmere and Lady Eveline Artois shall wed at first bell tomorrow. The newlyweds ride with the royal progress as far as Langmere. At Langmere, the couple remains to set their house."

Margaret notes Eveline's frozen smile, how her fan trembles in her grip. A lesson learned too late, perhaps, but learned nonetheless.

"Sir Stone and Sir Kingsley shall command the castle guard in His Majesty's and Captain Denby's absence," the herald continues. "Only traveling ladies accompany the procession: Lady Juliette Marchand and Lady Eveline Artois. Princess Ysabel of Navarre remains to observe household governance with the Queen Dowager Margaret."

The Spanish princess drifts closer, her veil catching afternoon light, tone honeyed with barely concealed disappointment. "A pity I don't display with the King."

Margaret's reply comes wrapped like a needle in silk. "A pleasure you will govern instead."

Ysabel's lips tighten, but protocol binds her tongue.

Lady Hélène approaches with parchments in hand, her manner clerklike yet respectful. "The morning rounds are in order, Your Grace. All tallies current, all rotations assigned."

"Then the house will breathe." Margaret accepts the documents with genuine approval. In her hands now lie the result of competence without pretense. Exactly what the castle needs in royal absence.

Sir Roland steps forward, offering her a proper bow, his respect genuine. His acknowledgment of Ysabel proves cooler, a nod that meets courtesy's minimum requirements as the princess surveys him with visible distaste, her gaze traveling from boots to shoulders as if cataloging faults.

When Roland reaches to pat his sister's head with playful affection, Hélène swats him lightly with her fan, the gesture so natural it draws a small smile from Margaret's lips. The siblings' easy bond remains their greatest strength, and perhaps their greatest vulnerability in a court where every gesture carries weight.

Sir Roland excuses himself with a brief bow. "By your leave, Your Grace. The preparations require attention."

Margaret nods to him with the same regal respect she provides her counselors. She turns toward her feminine companions. "Ladies, remain here. I shall return presently."

She follows at a careful distance, her presence unobtrusive yet attentive. Roland's competence deserves observation, especially before her son departs with him for three months. Near the armory, Roland joins Denby and Holt as they finalize arrangements. Maps spread across a barrel top, dotted with guard rotations and camp protocols.

"Feet first, then steel. Signal before you bleed," Roland instructs, his voice carrying the authority of experience.

Hale approaches, testing a new grappling hold with exaggerated flair. "If I twist like this, do I still look heroic?"

Roland's dry response draws chuckles from the gathered men. "Uninjured is handsomer."

"Master Lucien proves invaluable," Holt remarks when Roland inquires about the merchant. "His tallies run clean, his estimates hold true. We'll not starve nor burden the horses overmuch."

Margaret notes how easily Roland commands respect without demanding it. A quality that will serve her son well on uncertain roads.

Geoffrey arrives with parchments, seeking Lucien among the supply wagons. He presses a document into the merchant's capable hands. "Trust a miller who charges fairly and smiles rarely. These fords run honest, those marked in red less so."

Lucien accepts the guidance with genuine gratitude, his manner respectful yet confident. Margaret recognizes the bearing of a man who earns his place through merit rather than birth.

Trumpet practice pierces the evening air as tomorrow's sequence is rehearsed until precise. The herald's voice booms across the yard: "Wedding at first bell. Horses ready on the first trumpet, then departure on the second. No stragglers, not even pretty ones."

Laughter ripples through the gathered men, tension easing as preparation nears completion. Margaret observes the easy camaraderie, the respectful efficiency. Her son will travel with good men. Men who understand that competence matters more than ceremony.

Satisfied, she returns to the waiting ladies, her confidence in the journey's success considerably strengthened. The guard will see to the King's physical safety, while Sir Roland and Master Lucien will guard more. They will ensure the progress serves its purpose of strengthening the realm through visible, effective leadership.

The castle settles into its final night of a full royal presence, tomorrow promising both celebration and departure.

The Court

Silk whispers against stone as Eveline moves down the chapel aisle, her silken train pooling behind her like molten gold. The gown catches the morning light streaming through the chapel's tall narrow windows. A white silk with gold overlays, golden threading, and pearls. The gown cost more than some nobles see in a year. The Queen Dowager's own jewels rest at her throat, heavy and cold against her skin.

"Such splendor," Lady Rosamund murmurs to her companion. "The Queen Dowager has been most generous."

"A future countess deserves no less," comes the reply, though Eveline catches the undertone of calculation.

Her eyes fix ahead where Father Jerome waits beside the altar, Lord Cedric of Langmere, standing proud in his finest surcoat and cloak. His smile radiates genuine warmth. So different from the calculating expressions she'd grown accustomed to wearing herself. When did Cedric's eagerness stop seeming foolish and start appearing... endearing?

At the altar, she pauses. Cedric extends his hand with such careful reverence that her chest tightens unexpectedly. Before her stands an Earl who will give her a fine home, bountiful lands that stretch to four villages, and the title of Countess of Langmere. She may not wear England's crown, but she'll rule her own domain.

The ceremony was quicker than she imagined. Father Jerome's voice carries through the hushed chapel, concluding the sacred rites with the binding words of marriage. "In duty and in stead."

"In duty and in stead," Eveline repeats, her voice clear and unwavering.

"In duty and in stead," Cedric echoes, his tone firm with conviction.

The words settle between them like a promise neither quite expected to mean. They descend the chapel steps together, approaching the Queen Dowager's seat with proper deference. The older woman's gaze holds steady, measuring her for perhaps for the final time.

"Keep a wise house and a kinder table."

This counsel marks an ending. Eveline's chapter at court closes with these words and the stones beneath her feet. The words shut a door within her while opening another.

"I will, Your Grace."

At the chapel door, Lady Hélène waits with an expression of genuine goodwill. The rivalry that once sparked between them seems distant now, replaced by something approaching understanding. "May your laughter travel farther than your pride."

Eveline's smile feels thinner than silk, but carries surprising honesty. "And yours, my lady, find good rooms."

The King states plainly, masking deeper intentions, "Join us on the ride to Langmere. Depart with dignity." She notes the apology in his eyes.

"We will join the royal progress as far as Langmere. Thank you, Your Majesty." Cedric responds. His usual grating peacock manner replaced by a demeanor more tolerable, more respectable. Alaric nods and moves toward the assembling progression.

The chapel bells ring their passage into whatever comes next. She turns to Cedric, meeting his hopeful gaze with acceptance. Not joy, not yet, but recognition of what they might build together. His answering smile blooms with such relief that she wonders if kindness might prove easier than ambition.

Queen Dowager Margaret observes from the cool comfort of the chapel's shadow as the wedding party filters into the courtyard below, her ladies arrayed beside her like sentries in silk. Juliette stands closest, hands folded with quiet dignity, while Cecily maintains her perpetual composure. Colette hovers near Ysabel, whose predatory gaze tracks every movement in the courtyard as preparations for the King's Progress begin in earnest.

"Lady Hélène stands with her brother's mount rather than among the ladies," Ysabel notes, her voice carrying the weight of judgment. "In Spain, we understand proper station."

Margaret's expression remains neutral. "England values competence alongside ceremony, Your Highness."

She watches Hélène adjust a pack strap on Roland's horse with a soldier's efficiency. The sight stirs unexpected approval. Hélène is a woman who serves rather than simply ornaments. She wonders if all future's women conduct themselves as such.

The first trumpet's echo fades, replaced by the herald's brass voice cutting through morning air.

"Mount and muster!"

The courtyard transforms as if touched by sorcery. Denby's sharp commands organize the guard into precise columns while Holt checks weapons with methodical care. Sergeant Hale positions outriders with the eye of a man who knows ambush country. Near the supply wagons, Roland tests rope tension alongside Lucien, their movements efficient and purposeful.

Memory floods unbidden. Another courtyard, another departure. Alaric's grandfather mounting his destrier with regal bearing, leading England through rebellion into lasting peace. Twenty-three years of careful diplomacy, fair taxation, and merciful justice that strengthened the realm's foundation.

Her husband's reign had nearly crumbled those gains through indulgence and poor counsel. Conflicts waged for pride rather than intent, resources exhausted for show rather than for infrastructure and sustenance.

Now her son prepares to ride those same paths, his court balanced between tradition and innovation. She notes how naturally Geoffrey defers to Alaric's judgment, how Roland's methods already sharpen the guard's discipline.

Grant him wisdom beyond his years, she prays silently. Let him build what endures rather than what merely glitters.

Lord Geoffrey guides his mount between the assembled riders, checking positions with the methodical care his father drilled into him since boyhood. The courtyard thrums with the controlled energy of horses stamping, leather creaking, and voices calling final adjustments. He approaches the newlyweds, noting how Cedric's grin seems less performative than usual. Marriage may indeed prove the making of him.

"You peel off at the Langmere lane. No fanfare, only sense. The royal progress will not visit Langmer this year."

Cedric's laugh carries genuine warmth. "Sense is a new sport. I shall try it. We look forward to any future visits by the King."

Eveline's smile appears thinner but more honest than her usual court mask. Perhaps contentment suits her better than ambition ever did.

Geoffrey walks toward the household wagons. He catches the Queen Dowager's eye and gestures. She nods Juliette forward. Their exchange remains too distant for Geoffrey to hear, but Juliette's deep curtsy speaks volumes. The Queen's hand rests briefly on the younger woman's shoulder, a blessing disguised as dismissal.

As Geoffrey finishes settling Lady Juliette into the leading household wagon, hoofbeats approach from behind. Alaric draws alongside, leading Geoffrey's destrier with practiced ease. "Mount up. The sun climbs."

Geoffrey swings into his saddle, settling with familiar comfort. Together they ride toward the column's head, passing Lucien who stands beside the supply wagons with rope stained hands and satisfied expression.

Alaric reins in briefly. "The road eats fools. Do not feed it."

Lucien's bow carries merchant precision. "I keep a closed pantry, Sire."

As they continue forward, Lucien calls after Geoffrey with genuine gratitude. "My lord, the extra care you have provided. I shall not forget such sponsorship."

Geoffrey raises his hand in acknowledgment, warmth spreading through his chest toward his new companion. The man is proof that worth transcends birth, that competence earns respect more surely than titles ever could.

Hélène stands beside Roland's black destrier, admiring the animal's sleek lines and proud bearing. Geoffrey's generosity still amazes her. Such a magnificent mount for services rendered.

"A small payment for saving my life," Geoffrey had insisted when presenting the horse three days prior. The memory of Roland's wry protest still makes her smile.

Now her brother returns from helping secure the final supply wagon. She reaches up to brush a stubborn fleck of straw from his dark cloak, her touch deliberately fussing.

"Try not to collect arrows. They don't flatter the shoulders."

Roland's response is matter-of-fact. "I'll make do with admiration."

"Second choice: mud. It comes off."

He smiles briefly, then the smile softens, the humor fading into something deeper. "Keep the hearth breathing."

The words carry weight beyond their simple meaning. Maintain the cover, protect what they've built, and survive until he returns. Her throat tightens unexpectedly.

"Bon voyage, frère."

The French slips out naturally now. Roland's hand squeezes her shoulder once before he swings into the saddle with ease.

As the progress begins to shuffle in anticipation of departure, she steps away from her brother's spot in the column and finds her way to the Queen Dowager's party near the courtyard's edge in the safety of the Chapel's shade. The Spanish princess maintains rigid posture, her gaze tracking Hélène's every movement as she settles near Colette and turns to face the fully assembled progress.

From his position at the column's head, Alaric turns in his saddle. His eyes find hers across the assembled riders, holding steady for one beat longer than propriety suggests. Something passes between them: acknowledgment, promise, understanding. Finally, he looks toward his mother and nods.

Ysabel's voice carries just loud enough for those nearby to hear. "Such devoted attention to departures. One might wonder where such... enthusiasm truly lies."

Eveline's gaze sweeps the courtyard one final time, memorizing stones worn smooth by countless feet. These walls sheltered her through girlhood's awkward years, witnessed her first attempts at courtly grace, and harbored dreams that now feel distant as yesterday's prayers.

When Lord Artois died, the Queen Dowager's invitation to reside fully at court had transformed grief into opportunity. With her mother serving as the Queen's Lady-in-Waiting, Eveline's upbringing in court under both her mother and the Queen Dowager's guidance shaped a grieving child into a woman of standing. Now that chapter closes with wedding bells still echoing in her ears.

The second trumpet sounds. England's future thunders toward the gates in a symphony of hooves on stone. Standards lift high against morning sky as the column lurches into motion. Horses snort and stamp, riders calling final adjustments, the whole procession flowing like a released river finding its course.

She glances back once. Hélène raises two fingers in a private salute. An unexpected kindness from an unlikely source.

"Another stage," she murmurs to Cedric.

"And we are in the play," he replies, his voice carrying newfound confidence.

The herald's brass voice cuts through departure's din: "For the King. Justice on the roads!"

Trust and Stewardship

- 17 -

King Alaric

The column moves like a well-tuned instrument across Lord Miles's rolling lands, Faversham, each element finding its proper place without hurry or confusion. Wagon wheels carve steady furrows through morning mud while harness bells mark time with metallic precision. Denby rides ahead, spacing the mounted guards with seasoned judgement, while Holt maintains the rear with equal attention to formation.

Alaric draws alongside his captain, admiring the clean lines of their procession. "I like a road that looks like a sentence. Subject first, verb ready."

Denby's lined face creases into what passes for approval. "Aye, Sire. No loose words trailing behind."

As they crest a gentle rise, Highvale's timber walls recede into morning haze. The town square had stretched empty beneath yesterday's grey sky, market stalls arranged with suspicious tidiness, faces turning away when royal eyes sought them. Everything scrubbed clean, everything deliberately quiet.

Reginald urges his mount closer, ledger secured beneath his cloak against road dust. The older lord's expression carries the weight of unspoken concerns.

"Bread was plentiful, yet petitions were not," Alaric observes, his gaze lingering on the distant settlement. "Why does a fed house bar its door?"

"Fear leaves cleaner lanes than love, Sire."

The words settle heavily between them. They had held formal audience in Highvale's modest hall, bench properly arranged, herald announcing the King's willingness to hear grievances. Yet no widow stepped forward seeking justice for stolen grain. No cottar complained of excessive levies. No guild representative brought disputes over fair weights or market rights. No Lord or Lady Faversham in sight, despite having only left them at court a few days past. Alaric only half expected Miles to appear.

A wayside shrine appears ahead. Weathered stone carved with protective symbols, coins glinting in its shadowed alcove. Reginald thumbs through his ledger pages, ink entries recording an absence rather than abundance.

"We held the bench, and no widow, no cottar, no guild came forward."

Reginald's finger traces the empty columns where petitions should have been recorded. "When men do not speak in daylight, they have been taught that speech is remembered after dark."

A rider approaches from the rear guard, mud-spattered and breathless. He salutes with efficiency before delivering his report. "Word from the town reeve, Sire. Claims he 'managed' the queues yesterday. Says none formed naturally."

Alaric's jaw tightens. "Managed?"

"A courteous word for warning them off," Reginald replies grimly. "Either the lord's bailiff, or a sheriff hungry for fines. Lord Miles must have tipped them off."

"Then we shall take our hearing where managers do not stand."

A bridge appears like a riddle over water. Its timber planks spanning a swift-running beck and rails sagging with age and weather. Holt raises his fist, bringing the rear of the column to quick halt.

Denby studies the crossing. "Let the timber speak before we trust it."

Hale spurs forward, dismounting to test the planks with careful boot pressure. Water churns white beneath, carrying the scent of upland summer rains. The span will take mounted men, but only in pairs. No room for error or haste.

"Two at a time," Holt calls back. "Guards first, then the Crown."

Twigs snap from the hedgerow like startled sparrows. Three figures burst from the bracken as Hale reaches the far bank, rough wool and rusted blades catching weak sunlight. They charge toward the royal banner with desperate hunger, feet slipping on wet stone.

"To the Crown!"

Hale's shout cuts through morning air as he pivots, sword clearing its sheath. Denby's voice follows, steady amongst the sounds of hammered iron.

"Shield up, feet steady. Remember your grips."

The first bandit swings wild at Alaric's bridle. Hale intercepts the blow with his shoulder, metal ringing against mail as the impact sends him staggering. A second guard moves without orders, placing his body between threat and throne.

"You owe me a bruise, Alwin."

Hale grins through gritted teeth, rolling his shoulder. "I'll send the bill, Sire."

Roland flows past like a sparrow finding its flight. The largest bandit rushes him with raised a cudgel, but Roland steps inside the arc, hands finding shoulders and hip. The millstone turn sends the man earthward, unbroken but thoroughly disarmed.

"Stay down and keep your bones."

The bandit gasps against damp earth. "Aye, ser."

Behind them, Lucien's merchant instincts snap into action. His voice carries over the clash of steel, directing carts and coaches with crisp authority. "Circle left. Leave a gap for the King's banner."

Provision carts wheel into protective formation without panic or confusion. Juliette appears among the drivers, her presence calming skittish horses and men alike. "Hands on reins, eyes on me. Breathe like horses, slow and strong."

Holt and Denby close on the remaining attackers like twin shadows.

"Alive talks more than dead." Alaric orders.

Their adversaries lack the skill of the King's guardsmen. Making a victory without unnecessary blood a simple matter.

The progress column settles into silence broken only by running water and labored breathing. Alaric surveys his people.

Guards alert but unshaken, teamsters already checking harness and wheels, the royal banner unstained by defeat.

Alaric dismounts beside the provision carts, his boots finding solid ground after the morning's chaos. The royal banner hangs limp in still air, but the faces turned toward him shine with something fiercer than ceremony.

"Well done. The Crown remembers courage."

His words fall on Lucien first, the merchant's practical instincts having turned potential disarray into ordered defense. Juliette stands beside her intended, mud streaking her riding dress, eyes bright with shared purpose.

"Your quick thinking saved more than wagons today."

Lucien inclines his head. "The Crown's safety is all our prosperity, Sire."

Alaric turns to face his guard, men whose loyalty he has never questioned but witnessed anew in steel and blood. Hale flexes his bruised shoulder, grinning through the ache of intercepted blows.

"Today I saw men willing to stand where kings fall. That trust…" He pauses, meeting each face in turn. "Trust binds loyalty and stewardship. That is the realm's true foundation."

Stewardship, loyalty, and trust. The words settle like good mortar, binding what was already strong. Denby nods once, a simple acknowledgment that needs no flourish.

The column makes safely across the questionable bridge before wheels find their familiar rhythm again on packed earth. The column continues for another day until Faversham's country lanes divide toward distant holdings: Langmere and Thornfield. The newlyweds settle into their carriage wagon, flanked by Lord Cedric's house guard in neat formation beneath Langmere's blue and silver.

"Ride well to Langmere. Make a wise house."

Eveline's voice carries steady resolve. "We shall, Sire."

Cedric leans toward his bride, words pitched low but clear enough for royal hearing. "New venture: wisdom."

Her smile blooms genuine for the first time toward Cedric, her husband. "We'll win it."

They wheel away with bannered escort, hoofbeats fading toward Langmere's distant towers. Alaric watches until they disappear beyond the hedgerow, then signals the column forward toward Thornfield's waiting mysteries.

Sir Roland of Montbois

Roland shifts in his saddle, watching the royal column snake through morning mist like some ancient procession painted on monastery walls. Over a fortnight on English roads have shown him a medieval kingdom in motion. Not the sanitized history feeds he'd studied on Mars, but the grinding reality of governance by hoofbeat and wagon wheel.

The countryside shifts from fertile grain fields to stubbled commons where gaunt cattle nose through summer scrub. Some villages cheer genuine joy when the royal banner appears. Others watch from shuttered windows like prey studying predators.

Each township brings its own flavor of submission. Highvale's reeve read the ledgers like a speech, his face passive as if the King's arrival was like any other day, but Geoffrey noticed the too perfect writing within those ledgers. Where Highvale was a tightly rehearsed play, Westmere's guild masters pressed forward with eager smiles and showmanship, yet Lucien spotted gold changing hands beneath those bowed heads.

The camping rituals fascinate him most. No GPS coordinates or prefab shelters. Just Denby's eye for high ground and water and teamsters who can raise a traveling court from wagon beds and rope before the King's boots touch earth. It reminds him of the expeditionary protocols through the Outer Ring but powered by human muscle and medieval cunning instead of fusion cells.

The column halts where the road again meets rushing water. Ahead, a ferry crossing emerges. Thick rope stretched between wooden posts and a flat-bottomed barge moored on the near bank. An elderly man emerges from a stone hut, his weathered face splitting into a gap-toothed grin.

"Royal passage, is it? That'll be eight silver for the lot. Wagons double."

Geoffrey's spine straightens like a drawn bowstring. His voice carries the chill of noble displeasure. "Old Swithin, I presume? This ford has run free since my grandfather's day. A ford that charges is a ferry in disguise."

The ferryman spreads calloused hands with theatrical innocence. "Times press hard, my lord. Increased patrols, repairs needed." He gestures toward a tumbled causeway whose stones lie green with neglect, clearly untouched for seasons.

Geoffrey's eyebrow arches with an aristocratic disdain Roland has not yet seen grace the young man's usually humbler visage. "Stones are famous gluttons."

Lucien slides from his horse, producing leather satchels from his saddlebags with a merchant's efficiency. Weight-sticks and parchment rolls emerge. Among them last year's toll records copied from public ledgers. Figures neat as a counting house.

"Your sums breed too quickly for a thin harvest."

Old Swithin's confidence wavers as Lucien spreads tallies on his cart bed, pointing to discrepancies with steady expertise. Eight silver becomes six, then four, while the ferryman blusters about crown taxes and winter repairs.

"The stones eat wages, my lord."

From his saddle, Roland watches the negotiation unfold, recognizing patterns older than kingdoms. Power testing boundaries, commerce finding truth in numbers, authority choosing between mercy and precedent. The ferry rope sways in summer wind, waiting for royal judgment.

The first log crashes across the roadway like thunder, splintering cart wheels and sending horses rearing in panic. Roland's head snaps up from Lucien's tallies as a second timber slams behind them, boxing the column between wooden barriers thick as fortress beams.

"Circle tight! Second file on me!"

Denby's horn cuts through screaming horses and shouted commands. Masked figures pour from the treeline. Not the desperate peasants from their first encounter, but armed men with leather jerkins and proper steel. This ambush carries the stench of planning, of coin changing hands in shadowed taverns.

Roland vaults from his saddle as raiders surround the supply wagons to his immediate left. A carter stumbles, clutching his shoulder where an arrow sprouted like some deadly flower. Roland lunges forward, hauling the man toward the defensive circle just as a bandit breaks through with a notched blade.

The blade point finds the gap beneath his ribs, slicing through gambeson and shirt to scrape bone. Fire spreads across his side, but muscle memory keeps him moving. His throw lands clean as hip and shoulder drive the attacker backward until earth meets skull.

"Down. Stay down."

The words hiss between clenched teeth as Roland presses his hand to the spreading warmth beneath his ribs. The carter scrambles toward safety while Roland forces himself upright, scanning for the next threat.

Movement catches his eye near the royal guard's tight circle. Old Swithin huddles behind Hale's shield, terror painted across weathered features, or perhaps something else entirely. The ferryman's hand slides toward his belt with the smooth motion of long practice.

The blade glints beneath the midday sun as Swithin lunges toward Alaric's unguarded back. The King pivots like he's been expecting this moment since they reached the crossing, one hand catching the old man's wrist while the other strips the hidden dagger away with contemptuous ease.

"Your Majesty—"

Reginald's boot plants between Swithin's shoulders, driving him face-first into the mud. The ferryman's protests die beneath Reginald's weight as Holt and Hale compress their defensive ring, choosing submission over slaughter.

Steel rings against steel as Holt's blade meets a bandit's axe, the impact jarring both men backward. The raider recovers first, pressing forward with wild swings that Holt deflects with the ease of long training. Behind him, Stone grapples with a masked figure while two more circle like hunting wolves.

"Break left!"

Denby's shout cuts through the melee as he drives his sword through leather jerkin and ribs, dropping one attacker before wheeling to face the next. The defensive circle holds, but barely. Too many enemies, too little room to maneuver.

A horse's scream pierces the clash of weapons. Lucien's mount rears high, iron-shod hooves crashing down on a bandit who'd tried to gut the animal's belly. The man crumples with snapping bones while Lucien fights to control his terrified mount.

Another raider breaks toward the supply wagons where Juliette crouches beside overturned grain sacks. Roland pushes off from the mud, ignoring the fire spreading across his ribs. His tackle drives them both into the wagon's side, wood splintering under their combined weight.

The bandit's knee finds Roland's wound. White-hot agony explodes through his vision as he stumbles back a step. The bandit brandishes a small dagger from within his tunic and lunges at Roland, but Roland has already regained his bearing. He pivots away and his hands find the man's arm with a twist, some leverage, and the sharp crack of bone. The man stumbles away with a howl and trips amongst a splintered wagon wheel. Juliette finds the courage to toss Roland a rope. He quickly ties the man down, just as Kinglsey showed him once before.

Roland then forces himself upright, blood seeping through his fingers as he surveys the remaining scattered bandits. Two flee into the treeline while Denby and Hale secure a pair with more efficient rope work. Holt's voice carries grim satisfaction as the last raider throws down his sword.

"Keep them talking tomorrow."

Denby's voice carries the weight of hard experience. These captives hold answers about their backing. Answers the King needs before this corruption spreads further.

Roland watches Denby crouch beside their bound captives, methodical as a physician examining symptoms. The guard captain's knife works along the first bandit's belt like a surgeon, peeling back leather layers until something catches the light.

"Your thieves keep accounts."

Denby holds up a small brass token: a reeve's tally-notch. The kind used for marking grain measures and tax collections. The marking bears a familiar crest of three ravens on a field of gold. Lord Miles of Faversham's device.

Around them, Juliette moves between wounded men and spooked horses. Her voice carries the same steady authority Roland remembers from a relief coordinator on Mars Colony Seven when a dome collapsed: a calm threading through the remnants of recent chaos.

"Name your pain, then breathe past it." She guides a carter's hand to his shoulder wound, showing him how to apply pressure without panic. Near the overturned wagons, Lucien assists teamsters to secure scattered grain sacks, his merchant's eye assessing the damage.

"Hands here. Rope honest. Knot true." Hale's instructions cut through the aftermath's chaos, giving men simple tasks to master their fear. Roland marks how competence translates across centuries. Good leadership looks the same whether commanding orbital stations or medieval supply trains.

Alaric steps toward the cowering ferryman, royal authority settling around him like armor. "This ford is free until I say otherwise."

The King's voice carries absolute certainty. Old Swithin's face crumples as guards bind his hands.

Geoffrey's stare burns against Roland's side where blood darkens his tunic. The wound screams with each breath, but Roland keeps his spine straight, eyes scanning the treeline for movement.

"That cut would fell an ox."

Geoffrey's whisper carries equal measures of relief and alarm. Roland meets his gaze with a leveled certainty.

"I am not an ox. And we're not done."

Lord Geoffrey of Redwyke

By flickering torchlight, Geoffrey surveys the hastily arranged circle of torches, campfires, and benches. Tonight's camp bears no resemblance to their usual ordered rows. Instead, it has become an impromptu court. Alaric, his silhouette stark against the punishing dark, listens to brief statements, his presence demanding truth from every quivering voice.

A captured carter speaks first, eyes cast downward, recounting his side with emphatic gestures. Old Swithin, shoulders hunched and sullen, follows with calculated half-truths, knowing cunning dances behind his eyes. Finally, the captured bandits, defiant yet defeated, stand under the King's scrutiny.

"Speak plain. Lies cost double," Alaric commands, gaze unwavering.

Near the battered grain sacks, Lucien kneels, arranging mismatched tallies beside the token discovered on the bandit's belt. He stands, the weight of revelation in his words. "This notch counts coin not owed. Someone paid the wrong men to take the right purses."

Geoffrey feels the shift in the air, a sharp inhale before judgment descends.

Behind them, Juliette continues to orchestrates the quiet chaos of recovery with cool efficiency. Her voice carries the same quiet command that Geoffrey heard on the battlefield.

"Heat the cloth before you clean the wound. Men obey warmth." Her calm logistics, unexpected yet precise, restore a semblance of order. With every instruction, she proves that calm can carve order from chaos.

Geoffrey follows the tracks to the surgeon's tent, where candlelight spills through canvas gaps marked with blood. Inside, the chirurgeon peels away linen strips with careful fingers, his experienced face prepared for the worst.

Yes, the wound beneath defies expectation. Where Geoffrey anticipated torn flesh and seeping red, the gash shows edges already drawing together, the flow reduced to mere seepage.

"By the saints."

"By his will," Geoffrey murmurs, though unease prickles his spine from the speed of Roland's recovery.

Behind him, Denby and Holt share a meaningful glance.

"Some men heal like oak," Denby observes.

"Then we plant him at the front," Holt replies with grim approval.

Outside, Alaric's voice cuts through the night air like steel through silk. Geoffrey catches fragments: Lord Miles of Faversham summoned, tolls suspended, and the reeve placed under guard. The progression will not leave until the matter has been settled.

"Let the lord answer for his stones and his thieves."

The King's judgment carries the weight of mountains. Geoffrey has seen Alaric's mercy, but tonight reveals the iron beneath. Lord Miles has remained distant from his holdings, lingering at court instead. A nobleman who abandons his stewardship must still answer for what befalls his territory, and the kingdom shall not forget.

Moments later, Alaric ducks into the tent. The King moves past Geoffrey without ceremony, kneeling beside Roland's pallet. His voice drops to an intimate register, meant for one man alone.

"Rest. I prefer my teachers breathing."

Roland's mouth quirks despite his deathly pallor.

"First... and third bell, Sire."

The exchange holds warmth that Geoffrey recognizes. Not mere royal gratitude, but genuine affection forged in shared danger.

Geoffrey steps away from the tent, releasing the breath he's held since entering. The weight of what he witnessed—the impossible healing, the easy jest from a man who should be writhing—settles heavy on his shoulders.

Alaric emerges beside him, wiping his hands on a strip of linen. The King's expression remains unreadable in the dying firelight.

"He jokes with a hole in him." Geoffrey's concerned expression meets Alaric's.

"He keeps men steady with it. Let him."

Geoffrey nods, though questions multiply like sparks from the dying flames. Around them, the fires sink to coals. A watch bell sings across the camp, marking the hour. Inside the tent, Roland's breathing deepens into sleep, color returning to his face with unsettling swiftness.

Lord Reginald of Redwyke

They remained a week at camp waiting for Roland and others to heal, to fix wagons, and to deal with Faversham's transgressions. But the attack did not stop the King's Progress. No, Alaric and his Guard would not turn back so easily.

A square now opens before them like a modest prayer composed of a lime-washed chapel, weathered market boards, and a water well worn smooth by countless hands. No banners snap in welcome, no horns announce their arrival. Only the honest clatter of hooves on cobblestone and the white breath of horses in the crisp air.

Reginald adjusts his riding gloves, watching the townsfolk emerge from doorways like cautious sparrows. A blacksmith sets down his hammer. A woman clutches her shawl tighter, children peering from behind her skirts. This is Thornleigh as it truly exists. Unprepared, unpolished, and unafraid to show its modest face. Just as the way before was meant to be.

Father Beric hurries from the chapel, his cassock billowing as he approaches. Behind him, Baron Theobald shuffles forward with the careful steps of a man who has lived too many surprises. The Baron's face cycles through confusion, recognition, and mounting panic.

"Your Majesty. God keep you," Father Beric manages, his bow deep and reverent.

Baron Theobald's mouth works soundlessly before words tumble forth. "We had no word... no pennons, no..."

Reginald leans slightly in his saddle, studying the exchange with quiet approval. The truth of a place shows best without pennons. When nobles expect royal visits, they paint over cracks and hide their ledgers. When caught unaware, they reveal themselves as they are.

Alaric swings down with easy grace, passing his reins to a waiting groom. His voice carries warmth that cuts through the Baron's distress.

"Be easy, my lord. I came so because I wished to see Thornleigh as Thornleigh is."

Baron Theobald straightens slightly, something flickering in his aged features. Not pride, but the cautious hope of a man realizing he need not apologize for his honest circumstances.

"Then you see us plain, Sire. Humble, but not hungry."

Reginald notes how the Baron's answer sidesteps grandeur yet claims dignity. He answers fear with permission to be ordinary. The King has that gift of making men feel worthy without requiring them to be more than they are.

Alaric gestures toward the pack carts creaking into the square, their contents covered by travel-stained canvas. The signs of recent events well hidden.

"We brought our own board, foods, wine, and hands to lay them. Tonight we dine in *your* honor."

A ripple passes through the gathering crowd. Someone cheers under their breath. A sound quickly muffled, then echoed by another voice, and another. Reginald catches his clerk's eye and murmurs instruction.

"Mark that. Applause first for bread, not for banners."

The young man's quill scratches dutifully across parchment. These observations matter more than ceremony. When subjects cheer for sustenance over spectacle, the realm's health shows true.

Alaric steps closer to Baron Theobald, lowering his voice to the register of confidence shared between equals. "Your granaries will not be lighter for our coming. I have never heard an ill word of Thornleigh and don't expect to begin today."

The Baron's eyes brighten like morning breaking through cloud. "Your Majesty is generous."

Reginald watches the exchange with growing understanding. He steadies a hand by touching it, not by gripping it. The King offers reassurance through presence, not demands. In this small square, with its honest well and humble chapel, Alaric demonstrates kingship as service rather than spectacle.

Alaric nods to Father Beric, a crisp directive in his voice. "Send word: today and tomorrow I will sit to hear your folk. No toll, no fee. Bring only speech and truth."

Father Beric's eyes light up, the eagerness nearly tangible. "The bells will carry it, Sire. After sext, and again at vespers."

Reginald gives a slight nod, impressed by Alaric's instinct. He borrows the church's roads. Sound roads.

A mother, child tucked on her hip, bobs a shy curtsy as she passes, her face a blend of awe and hope. Near her, an old merchant doffs his cap in silent respect. Around them, the buzz of the crowd begins its subtle shift into a soft murmur of expectation. Loyalty shaped right here, minted in this small square with witnesses enough to hold it true.

"He'll hear us in the chapel, they say," murmurs a woman, her voice edged with unbelief turned hopeful.

The men move with purpose. Denby and Hale stride towards the chapel doors, efficient as a well-oiled machine.

"We'll put the bench by the rood screen. Two guards inside, two out," Denby arranges.

Father Beric gestures toward the vestry, now a temporary office. "The vestry may hold your clerks, my lord."

"Good," Reginald responds, nodding to his clerk. "Ink and sand. Names first, griefs second."

Inside the chapel, preparations quickly unfurl, setting the stage for Thornfield's tales. As the chapel fills with the soft shuffle of feet on stone, Reginald positions himself at a small table near the altar, quill ready, watching as Thornleigh's folk queue along the nave. Their faces hold the careful hope of people unused to being heard.

A grey-bearded cottar steps forward first before the King, his bow deep but dignified. "The winter past, my lord fed us from his own store. Barley to boil, cheese for the children."

Reginald's quill scratches across parchment: *charity in famine*.

A widow follows, fingers worrying her chapel veil, voice steady despite her trembling hands. "When my roof fell, his men set it right. I owe him spring."

Repairs without levy, Reginald adds. Baron Theobald shifts uncomfortably near the door, unused to such praise voiced aloud. The man governs quietly, it seems. Bread before bells, shelter before ceremony.

A forester's leather cap catches the light as he approaches, worn hands set respectful on his belt. "Only this, Sire. The coppice road breeds cutpurses now. They take from travelers after dusk."

Father Beric nods grimly from beside the rood screen. "Two carters robbed at the ford three nights past."

Alaric's expression sharpens, the easy warmth replaced by calculation and concern. "Note the ford and coppice. Sir Hale, post a patrol by dusk, and send word to Langmere for more bows."

Reginald inks swiftly: Action: patrols, bows, message to Langmere.

Reginald observes as about ten more townsfolk take their turn before the King. Their testimonies echo through the chapel like a prayer, each recounting tales of good harvests, a just baron, and the ubiquitous shadow of bandits. Each story ends with heartfelt gratitude for Baron Theobald's virtuous stewardship.

The line dwindles to none, leaving only the murmur of satisfaction in its wake. Alaric, standing before the altar like a shepherd among his flock, raises his hand for quiet. The modest crowd responds with instinctive reverence.

"Thornleigh keeps good order and better hearts. I am pleased."

Baron Theobald's shoulders drop, relief coursing through him like a benediction. The entire square seems to exhale alongside him, the shared breath of a community reassured.

Reginald closes his ledger with a sense of certainty. Alaric's words are more than ceremonial. They've forged a bond, unspoken yet steadfast, between crown and commoner. The King, promising bread and offering attentive ears, turns governance into a form of kinship.

Reginald's appreciation swells, understanding that here in Thornleigh, upon unadorned cobblestone, he witnesses the making of a king beloved by his people. A making not through grand gestures, but through acknowledgement of good stewardship and genuine trust, quietly sown.

Bread Before Bells

- 18 -

Lady Hélène of Montbois

Agnes shakes Hélène's shoulder in the grey pre-dawn, her whisper sharp with irritation.

"My lady, up now. The ovens won't wait for sunrise."

Hélène blinks awake, the stone walls swimming into focus. Outside, not even the faintest glow touches the narrow window.

"What hour is this?"

"Before prime, before sense." Agnes holds up a practical woolen gown, dyed brown with subtle green trim. "This will serve. Fine enough for a lady, sturdy enough for real work."

Hélène sits up, mind clearing as Agnes bustles about with her familiar efficiency.

"I don't understand why you should be handling Princess Ysabel's duties," Agnes mutters, wrestling with lacings. "All Queen Dowagers assign these tasks to the soon-to-be queen to familiarize them with the way of things. Yet here you are, doing her learning."

"Ysabel believes delegation shows nobility."

"Delegation." Agnes snorts. "Pretty word for lazy."

"Bread before bells."

"Aye, my lady. I'll meet you at the gatehouse."

She'd taken up Ysabel's pre-dawn duties a week after the departure of the King's Progress. Now the familiar rhythm soothes her as she slips into the servant's passage, its narrow walls still cloaked in shadow. A scullion carrying water buckets nods respectfully.

"Good morning, my lady."

"Good morning, Tom."

The kitchens pulse with heat and purpose, ovens glowing like forge mouths in the dim morning. Bess Carter stands flour-dusted before the largest hearth, sleeves rolled past her elbows.

"Morning, Bess. If the bread rises, so will the day."

"Then we'll feed you first, my lady." Bess grins, gesturing toward wooden trays lined with perfect golden rounds. "Bess has got her crew well in hand."

She stands to the side and observes the morning kitchen routine: herbs bundled for midday broth, cups and jugs rinsed and set for pouring, trenchers laid out in rows for the day's bread, dough turned out for shaping, and ovens stoked and tested for heat. Hélène breathes in yeast and warmth as she mentally catalogues what's been done and needs doing.

A sharp crack splits the air. Maud Thatcher yelps near the side ovens, pointing at a spider-web fracture spreading across fire-blackened brick.

"The whole batch'll burn crooked now!"

Hélène moves quickly, grabbing nearby cloth and lifting trays from the damaged oven. "Fire doesn't argue. Work around it. These can finish on the braziers. Flatbreads bake just as well."

"Aye," Maud nods, relief flooding her voice. "Grateful for your level head, my lady."

Crisis averted, Hélène glances toward the buttery door. The real and tedious work waits beyond. Stores to count, supplies to verify.

The buttery's cool stone shelves stretch in neat rows, barrels and tuns arranged as if the surrounding stone itself demanded order. Master Bartram stands with his ledger, ink-stained fingers tracing columns of numbers.

"Seventeen tuns of ale, my lady. Though..." He shifts uneasily, glancing toward a cloth-covered corner.

Hélène lifts the fabric, revealing a crumpled parchment wedged between two barrels. "The missing tally?"

"Aye." His face reddens. "Slipped when I was checking the seals yesterday."

"Lost paper breeds rumors. Found paper breeds breakfast."

"I'll keep better nests for my birds, my lady."

They move deeper into the stores, past sacks of grain and hanging cheese wheels. The stores reveal sturdy abundance. Grain sacks plump with winter wheat, cheese wheels aging properly, ale tuns sealed tight against spoilage. Nothing wanting, nothing wasted. The kind of plenty that speaks well of careful stewardship.

A young clerk approaches, voice pitched low with conspiracy.

"My lady, if we trim the servants' portions slightly, just for the Princess's kitchen visit next week, it would free more for..."

"Hungry hands drop plates. Feed first, flatter second."

The clerk's eager expression crumbles. "Yes, my lady."

Hélène pulls the morning ledger and a small quill from her belt. Master Bartram offers ink from his pot. Hélène makes a few quick notes.

"Master Bartram, your tallies are sound. Send the final counts to Lord Ranulf."

She bids a respectful goodbye and heads for the infirmary, where mercy meets practicality.

The infirmary's narrow windows let in pale morning light, illuminating rows of simple cots. Most stand empty, but a young maid sits hunched on one bed, cradling her bandaged hand.

"How does it fare, Milly?"

She looks up with red-rimmed eyes. "Burns fierce, my lady. Bess said to keep still."

Hélène unwraps the cloth carefully, examining the angry red mark across her palm. The skin weeps but shows no festering.

"Clean wounds heal fastest." She reaches for fresh linen from the nearby shelf. "You win today by keeping the bandage dry."

"I'll win quietly, my lady."

Hélène secures the binding, then pats Milly's shoulder. Her small smile eases the worry lines around her eyes.

"Rest now. I'll return before noon to check your progress."

She moves from the infirmary to the gatehouse nearby, where its thick walls promise different concerns. Stone steps wind upward to the wall-walk, where morning mist clings to the battlements.

Sergeant Dalry stands examining a pile of sand buckets, his summer stained face creased with disapproval.

"Good morning, Sergeant."

"My lady." He gestures toward the dampened sand buckets. "Night fog's got into everything. Makes the sand clump. Harder to use for fire prevention, though not useless."

Hélène examines the contents, noting their sodden state. "What of our bows and arrows? Are the bowstrings holding?"

"Should be safe enough, my lady. We've been keeping up with the wax wraps, given the nature of this wetter weather recently."

She nods, taking mental inventory of the quivers lined along the wall, bundles of arrows properly fletched, and spare bowstrings coiled in their protective wrappings.

"You've an eye like a quartermaster." Dalry notes.

"I borrow other people's good habits."

Hélène spots the gatehouse log nearby. She borrows the ink, pulling her own ledger from her belt again. *Oven repair mason needed by noon. Rations holding steady. Infirmary linen running low.* She adds improved sand barrels to her growing list. Each entry builds the careful picture Ysabel will claim as her own oversight.

Agnes appears at the gatehouse entrance, her own morning duties complete, a small basket of mending tucked under her arm. They pass through the training yard where Alice sweeps near the well, and Ralf instructs a footman, Perry, on Spanish protocols.

"When serving Princess Ysabel her morning meal," Ralf explains quietly, " she expects Spanish formality. Keep your eyes properly lowered and mind your bows. Both deeper than what we show our own nobility."

"My lady." Ralf's bow carries genuine warmth. "The staff speaks well of your attention this morning."

Alice's smile brightens. "Young Milley's near bursting with pride that you saw to her hand proper. Made the girl's whole day, it did."

"Small mercies cost nothing."

Back in her quarters, Agnes works swiftly, replacing the practical brown wool with a gown of deep blue silk. Fine enough for nobility, yet subdued enough that the princess would not accuse her of 'rising above her station'. Ysabel reminds Hélène daily of her lower nobility and trained mannerisms.

Agnes fits the bodice into place over the awful stays. *Stays.* Oh how she cannot wait to be back in the future where such monstrosities do not exist. She admires the fine threads on the bodice, how Agnes's intricate handwork fashioned Anselm's house into the fabric. She has come to admire the Archbishop greatly, like she once did her father. Her chest swells with pride to bear his house on her person. She aims to make him proud, like any parent.

Agnes adjusts the final sleeve as Hélène squares the ledger's ribbon, checking each entry one final time. The morning's work transforms into neat columns, ready for Ysabel's theatrical review. Everything accounted for, nothing left to chance.

"Sheathed, not surrendered," Hélène murmurs, tucking the ledger under her arm before heading toward the Spanish princess's chambers.

Princess Ysabel of Navarre

Ysabel arranges herself in her carved chair like a queen receiving supplicants, the morning light catching the gold threads woven through her crimson gown. Her fan rests closed across her lap like a scepter of authority rather than mere accessory. The English castle hums with its dull efficiency, but here in her chambers, Spanish dignity reigns supreme.

When Hélène arrives with her ledger, Ysabel doesn't rise. Let the French woman approach properly, with the deference due a future queen.

"Let us see how England arranges itself today."

The words carry just enough condescension to establish hierarchy. Ysabel watches Hélène's face for any flicker of resentment, but finds only professional composure. Disappointing. Breaking that calm reserve would provide excellent entertainment.

Hélène's report unfolds in her usual crisp, efficient phrases: repairs scheduled, stores tallied, defenses maintained. Such pedestrian concerns, spoken like a steward instead of a lady. Still, the work serves Ysabel's purposes perfectly.

"Then write it under my hand."

Ysabel's smile carries satisfaction as she gestures toward the writing desk. Delegation suits her well. She shall gain the knowledge held in such domestic duties without suffering the tedium of actual labor. Hélène earns her keep, whilst Ysabel secures credit with the Queen Dowager. Such is the nature between mistress and servant.

Colette steps forward to assist with the ledger transfer, her movements tentative as always. The girl's French accent thickens when nervous, making her English stumble worse than usual.

"The... tally for—" The hesitation stretches uncomfortably.

Ysabel's smile brightens with malicious pleasure. "She drowns in English numbers; how charming."

Colette's cheeks flush pink above her simple cream gown. Such delicious discomfort. The English court's sympathy for the struggling lady-in-waiting only enhances Ysabel's position as magnanimous princess tolerating a lesser companion's failings with gracious patience. Why else would she have brought her here?

Hélène steps closer, her voice dropping to gentle French.

"Le total est juste. Jje m'en charge." *The total is correct. I will take care of it.*

"Merci," Colette breathes, relief evident.

Ysabel's fan taps once against her wrist, irritation flickering beneath her composed exterior.

"Draft your report properly. On parchment, with solutions clearly set. Present it for my review."

Once reviewed, Ysabel makes copies in her own hand. The seal presses into warm wax with satisfying completion. Let the Queen Dowager see how swiftly England's future Queen manages castle affairs. Each solution bears Ysabel's hand and mark now, transformed from Hélène's pedestrian competence into royal oversight.

She briefly admires the sealed copies on her desk before turning to the servant. "Send to the Queen Dowager. Efficiency becomes me."

As Meg steps forward to take the sealed parchments, she dips low and mumbles to Hélène.

Ysabel's fan snaps shut. "Speak to me first."

Meg's cheeks burn slightly, and she curtsies for forgiveness, but it is Hélène who speaks for her.

"Your Highness's mercy would hearten the kitchens and lift spirits should extra loaves be sent to the scalded girl."

Ysabel considers this. Charity enhances reputation, particularly when witnessed by the right servants. After a measured pause, she inclines her head with regal benevolence.

"Very well. Let it be said."

But opportunity for refinement presents itself. She turns back to Hélène, adding silk to the steel. "Be sure the girl knows whose name feeds her."

Hélène's expression remains steady, unreadable. "She will eat better knowing she is seen."

Such diplomatic deflection. No matter. The credit flows where it belongs. Hélène shifts slightly, consulting her notes.

"Clarity saves tempers, Your Highness. Might I standardize these morning rounds into a written rota? For your approval, naturally."

Ysabel's fan taps thoughtfully against her palm. Another opportunity to claim oversight.

"Do so then bring it to me. I will make it mine."

Queen Dowager Margaret

The solar's warmth pools around Margaret's chair as Master Chamberlain reads the morning's tallies. His voice carries the steady rhythm of routine: grain stores checked, repairs scheduled, guard equipment maintained. Each item bears the same careful hand, the same practical solutions.

"Lady Hélène proposed extra bread for the scalded kitchen girl, patching scheduled for the main oven, bowstrings replaced before dampness ruins tension, infirmary restocked with clean linens..."

Margaret's fingers trace the carved armrest of her chair. A house breathes more freely when its doors are oiled. Yet the seal pressed into the wax and the penmanship within belongs to another. The Queen takes notice in how the staff give credit where it is truly due.

"Thank you, Master Chamberlain."

She waits until his footsteps fade before turning to Meg, who stands quietly by the window. "Weather, not thunder."

Meg's posture straightens slightly, understanding the distinction between idle gossip and useful intelligence. "Work was brisk; orders were plain; faces were easier by breakfast."

"And our Spanish princess? Did she handle these matters herself, or were they handed off?"

Meg's pause speaks volumes before her careful reply. "Her Highness received the report... and sent it onward."

Margaret's smile carries silk over steel as she reaches for her own correspondence. Meg's discernment with the Princess grows sharper each day. Noting not just what is done, but who truly does the doing.

The Archbishop's shadow crosses the threshold as Margaret folds the correspondence. His quiet step announces discretion rather than urgency.

"Your Grace."

"Archbishop. The house is steady. Hélène's hand shows in every corner. But keep Lord Ranulf's patience braced. He carries both his burden and Lord Reginald's whilst the King travels."

Anselm inclines his head, understanding the delicate balance required. "The Lady brings honor to my house. I will keep the Lord stable."

Margaret rises, moving to the window where afternoon light cuts clean angles across the stone floor. The outer castle below hums with purpose as kitchen boys dart between doorways with baskets of root and herb, laundresses stoop at the cistern, and a groom leads a sweating palfrey toward the stables. Beyond the bustle, the Queen's garden lies in ordered bloom of knotwork hedges, summer roses, and gravel paths treaded by courtiers in pairs, their voices low, their sleeves catching the sun.

"I mean to test both our ladies properly. Hélène will bring me facts each morning. Ysabel will bring her signature to approve them. Both will answer for the day's results."

She turns back to Meg, whose stillness speaks of complete attention. "If credit is taken, it will be taken in the light."

Meg's role requires the finest calibration. To assist without enabling, observe without baiting, and deliver honest Spanish weather each noon. "We prefer rain reported early."

"I carry a small umbrella, Your Grace."

Margaret's smile approves the metaphor. Truth sheltered, but never hidden.

"Your Grace, the extra loaves for the scalded girl, shall I credit them to Princess Ysabel's mercy?" Meg offers a test wrapped in kindness.

"If she will own mercy, let her own it."

The Archbishop's eyebrow lifts slightly, reading the layers beneath. Meg inclines her head, understanding the Queen's hand in shaping how generosity flows through the castle.

"And the house, Your Grace?"

"Let the house prefer bread to gossip."

Margaret turns to Master Chamberlain, who awaits instruction with the patience of long service. "When you speak of today's improvements, praise the work itself. We lift deeds. People will supply the names."

The distinction settles over the room like morning mist. The chamberlain nods, grasping the wisdom in letting results speak louder than signatures.

Margaret addresses Meg with renewed focus, "Does Lady Hélène keep her wit properly sheathed in company?"

A faint smile touches Meg's lips, the first crack in her careful composure. "Mostly... she polishes them instead."

Margaret's approval warms the words before they leave her tongue. "Shined steel cuts cleaner."

The Archbishop steps closer, his voice carrying the weight of unspoken understanding. "Your Grace, Lady Hélène appears to be performing admirably as an English noblewoman. Her... adjustment to court life proceeds well?"

The question hangs in the air, layered with meaning only Margaret and Anselm fully grasp. The Queen's gaze holds steady, acknowledging both the surface inquiry and its deeper currents.

"She learns swiftly and serves faithfully. Lady Isolde's continued guidance proves sound."

"Then I thank Your Grace for your attentions to my young cousin. The family is most grateful for your care." Anselm inclines his head with genuine gratitude.

His departure leaves the solar quieter. Margaret settles back into her chair and turns to her most recent embroidery work. Her needle finds its rhythm easily, silk threads catching the sun like spun gold. Her thoughts turn inward as her smile curves around the next stitch.

Time will reveal which foundation proves stronger: entitled expectation or quiet competence.

Alice Whitcombe

Alice guides the still warm loaves into clean linen, her hands quick despite the steam rising from the crust. The kitchen hums with purpose around her. Maud scraping bowls, Tom hauling water, the familiar rhythm of work that keeps a castle fed.

"Mercy travels better when it's still warm."

She speaks to the bread as much as to Bess, who watches from the proving table with flour-dusted hands and knowing eyes.

"Word is these come from Princess Ysabel's own instruction." Bess's tone carries the careful neutrality of someone who knows better than to question generosity, regardless of its source.

Alice's shrug holds layers of meaning, her smile dancing between acknowledgment and something sharper. "Praise has long legs. It will find more than one pair of feet."

Alice dispatches a boy to the infirmary with the loaves and a simple note: "From the Princess's table." Her fingers smooth the linen cover with care, though her mind already turns to the afternoon's gossip routes.

"We will let kindness write a little louder tomorrow," she murmurs to herself. Truth and credit rarely travel the same path, but both serve their purpose in keeping the castle's heart beating steady.

Meg slips through the kitchen like morning mist, her arms laden with fresh linens bound for the Princess's quarters. Alice pauses her work, her voice pitched low enough to blend with the kitchen's constant murmur.

"Work steady?" she asks.

Meg glances up, catching the careful neutrality in Alice's tone. She responds simply. No complaints, no praise, just the measured report of someone who sees much and says little.

"Good sky."

The exchange carries more weight than weather talk. Alice's silent approval settles into the space between them, an understanding that some storms pass without thunder.

Agnes appears at Alice's elbow, a tray in hand ready to fetch the usual small lunch for Lady Hélène. Her voice holds the gentle firmness of someone who tends to her lady's needs and mends more than cloth. "If you must embroider today, then stitch truth."

Alice taps the wooden counter twice, the sound sharp as a gavel in the steam-thick air. "Only practical patterns."

The promise hangs between them, an anchor against the currents that carry rumor through castle halls. Agnes nods and returns to filling her tray, satisfied that wisdom has found its proper place for the day.

Perry, newly assigned to Ysabel's staff, appears in the doorway, still catching his breath from whatever errand brought him running. His whisper carries the breathless quality of someone eager to share news before it cools.

"Lady Hélène takes tallies while Her Highness reports them beautifully."

Alice files the observation under the heading of useful optics. Her smile holds the patience of someone who knows the difference between performance and substance.

"Beauty is welcome. Bread is better."

Maud abandons her scraping to lean closer, her voice bright with the genuine admiration that follows good work well done. "The French lady knows names and numbers both. Asked after Tom's shoulder, remembered how many sacks we needed for the granary."

Alice rephrases their praise into currency that travels well through corridors where competence counts more than courtesy. "Say this: some ladies carry ledgers as well as lace."

Jory sneaks in with his weekly Spanish weather report. "There's extra sting in the Princess's compliments lately."

Alice chooses her response like selecting spices. Enough flavor to acknowledge truth, but not enough heat to burn tongues. She repeats past wisdom: "We mind our work, not others' tempers."

"Aye." Alan appears in the doorway. His demeanor now carries the weight of suppressing gossip between two houses.

"What is our creed?" He demands.

A half dozen voices rise in unison: "We follow the one who fixes the leak."

"And give the bucket to whoever asks for it," Alice muses internally.

Worth Over Birth

- 19 -

Lucien Marcellus

The salt tang hits Lucien's nose before the harbor comes into view, carried on wind that speaks of deep water and steady trade. Fairharbor spreads below them like a merchant's ledger made flesh. Warehouses lined neat as columns, counting-houses with their iron-bound shutters, and the forest of masts that marks prosperity better than any banner.

Lucien guides his horse down the cobbled approach, noting the repairs to the breakwater and the fresh timber in the pier extensions. The town sprawls comfortable and confident along the waterfront, two-story houses of good stone shouldering against shop fronts where guild signs swing in the harbor breeze. Smoke rises from a over a dozen chimneys, each marking a household that eats regular and sleeps sound.

Lord Marchand's banner hangs limp from the tower that marks his nominal authority, but the real power rests in the guild halls that cluster near the fish market. The arrangement suits all parties. His lordship draws his rents and stays clear of rope and scales, while the masters tend to tide tables and cargo manifests without noble interference.

Lucien reins in at the quays, his eyes taking automatic inventory before social pleasantries. The *Cormorant's* hull rides higher than when he left, a sign of good sales in London cloth and continental provisions. Aldwin's nets hang mended and proper. The crane arm shows new grease, and someone has reset the stones where the heaviest casks land.

"Boats talk first. men follow." His murmur reaches Juliette alone, pitched beneath the clatter of hooves on cobble and the cry of gulls wheeling overhead.

The harbor reeve approaches with stride of a man long at his post, his bow effortlessly calculated to honor the King while acknowledging Geoffrey's rank. Years of handling visiting merchants have taught him the precise depth required for each degree of authority.

"Welcome, Your Majesty."

Lucien returns a modest nod, the gesture of a man who knows his place and keeps it without apology.

"Your pilings held through the last gale. Good work." Geoffrey responds. The compliment carries the weight of someone who understands the difference between appearance and substance, between a pier that looks sound and one that can take the punishment of summer storms.

A petty alderman hovers at the edge of the royal party, his whisper meant to carry just far enough to register disapproval without courting direct confrontation. "Pennies at table with princes?"

Lucien's response comes level and unhurried, the tone of a man stating simple fact rather than defending position. "Bread rises better when all eat."

Geoffrey's voice cuts through any potential awkwardness with the calm authority of someone comfortable wielding influence on another's behalf. "This man's ships fed three parishes in a lean winter. That is coin the realm accepts."

The party dismounts near the Guild Hall. Lucien swings down with the easy motion of a man who learned to ride late but well. His boots find cobblestone worn smooth by decades of wagon wheels and salt spray.

Juliette steps beside him without flourish, her bearing neither forward nor withdrawn. The months at court have taught her the art of presence without proclamation. How to occupy space as if born to it while never claiming more than circumstance allows.

"Your town keeps good order." Her observation carries the practical authority of someone who has managed households and understands the difference between surface tidiness and deep function.

"It taught me mine." Lucien's reply holds respect for the harbor that made him what he is, that taught him reputation follows results, and that trust builds one honest transaction at a time.

They guide the royal party toward the Guild Hall through streets that know them both, though not always for the same reasons.

A fishwife pauses in her gutting to watch their progress, her knife never stopping its methodical work. "Lady Juliette returns with fine company."

Her neighbor leans closer, voice pitched to carry just far enough. "Aye, and not for the first time. My cousin works the Marchand kitchens. Says she spent more afternoons under Master Lucien's roof than her father's before court summoned her."

"Small wonder Lord Marchand packed her off to London." The reply comes with an undertone of disapproval.

A baker's apprentice cranes his neck to catch sight of the lady who supposedly chooses trade over title. "That's a pairing with consequence."

The exchange ripples through the market crowd, some muttering disapprovals and others noting the irregularity of their pairing , while neither approving nor disapproving.

Dockhands straighten as Lucien passes, caps touching foreheads in gestures worn smooth by repetition. The respect lacks ceremony but carries the weight of acknowledgment between men who know the price of honest work. "Master Marcellus."

"Keep your hands whole. Tar after rope." The warning comes automatic, born from years of watching good sailors lose fingers to careless haste.

The dockhand grins and holds up unmarked palms. "Aye, Master. Edmund's got fresh hemp if you need cordage."

"I'll see him before we leave."

A carter pauses his loading to study the royal party. More heads turn as word spreads through the working crowd. The return of their most successful merchant draws notice, but the presence of Lady Juliette at his side and the King at his front transforms routine homecoming into something worth discussing over evening ale.

The Guild Hall's oak doors swing wide to admit the royal party, hinges groaning under weight of three generations. Lucien steps across the threshold into familiar territory, where the scent of beeswax and parchment mingles with the ordered chaos of commerce conducted with scales.

The guards move through the hall with purpose, their boots echoing off stone as they arrange benches and clear space for petitioners, following the same regimen repeated in squares and halls over the past five weeks. Sir Hale directs the placement of the King's chair, while Sir Penn checks sight lines from the doors, and Reginald's scribe prepares to take notes.

"Fair timber work." Geoffrey runs his palm along a support beam, testing the grain with the eye of someone who knows good craftsmanship from hasty carpentry.

"Shipwright's hands built these walls. They know which wood bends and which breaks." Lucien's pride in his town's work carries clear in his voice, the satisfaction of a man who recognizes quality because he demands it in his own dealings.

Heavy footsteps announce Guildmaster Aldwine's arrival before his voice does. The older man enters with unspoken authority, his time-marked face taking in the royal presence with the discernment of someone who has navigated changing tides for decades.

"You've brought the King a tidy harbor, Master Marcellus?"

The question carries weight beyond its simple words. An assessment disguised as courtesy, testing whether success has bred arrogance or if steady judgment remains intact.

"Only honest scales, my lord. Tidy follows." Lucien's response draws a brief nod from Aldwine, acknowledgment that the right answer has been given.

The Guildmaster's gaze shifts to Alaric, respect measured but not obsequious. "Your Majesty honors our hall."

"Master Aldwine. Lucien speaks well of your ledgers."

Aldwine nods a respectable thank you and gestures toward a door that leads to his private chamber, where years of careful record keeping rest in locked chests. "If Your Majesty would examine our accounts?"

The smaller room holds the concentrated essence of mercantile success, with shelves lined by bound ledgers whose spines bear careful script denoting year and cargo type. A writing desk bears fresh quills and a sand-pot that has seen recent use.

Aldwine draws open the current ledger, its pages crackling as he reveals columns of precise figures and meticulous script. Lucien watches Alaric's eyes track the entries, noting the King's attention to detail.

"Clean slips, sober men. Order is the first loyalty a town owes its people." Alaric's observation carries approval as his finger traces a column of ship manifests, each entry countersigned by both captain and harbor reeve.

As the King finishes his examination, Master Aldwine shuts the ledger and questions the purpose of their arrival and the preparations underway in the main hall.

"No advance message reached us. What manner of discretion is this?" Aldwine inquires with an even voice, though his gaze pins Lucien with keen scrutiny.

The reproach stings because it holds justice. Standard protocol for royal visits demand advance notice for preparation time and proper arrangements.

"The King wants to see his people as they truly are." Reginald's intervention spares Lucien from answering directly, though the explanation does little to soften Aldwine's frown.

"Appeals find better hearing beneath timber and beside proper records." Alaric adds, the hidden complement easing Aldwine's concerns.

A guard appears in the doorway, his salute crisp. "Hall stands ready, my lord."

The party files back into the main chamber, where townspeople have begun gathering beyond the doors. Their voices carry through the oak, a blend of excited murmurs, children's questions, and the shuffle of feet as word spreads through harbor streets.

Alaric takes his seat while guards fall into position on either side. Reginald's clerk takes his place at the scribal desk while Reginald observes the growing crowd from the now open doors. The moment stretches, taut with anticipation.

"Good people of Fairharbor!" Reginald's voice carries authority that cuts through the crowd's chatter. "King Alaric receives petitions and brings royal word. Enter freely and speak your needs."

King Alaric

The hall settles into respectful hum of murmurs as Alaric raises his hand. What unfolds is not ceremony, but a meeting grounded in purpose, stripped of pageantry.

"Let us hear plain requests and plainer reasons."

The clerk's quill scratches against parchment, recording date and witness in careful script. Townspeople press closer, their faces reflecting cautious hope mixed with curiosity at this departure from expected royal formality.

Lord Geoffrey steps forward first, his voice carrying clearly through the chamber. "Your Majesty, I speak for Master Lucien Marcellus. His dealings have held steady through three seasons, from fair tolls and winter credit for fishermen to wages paid on time."

The endorsement carries weight that formal letters could never match. The future Lord of Redwyke's growing reputation for merchant judgment makes his words currency among those who matter. "He eats last. His men do not go hungry."

Alaric nods to Geoffrey, letting the endorsement settle into the watching crowd before addressing the man who prompted such praise. "Master Lucien, your sponsor speaks well. I thank you for your words regarding the state of trade in these waters."

Alaric shifts his attention deliberately, the movement calculated to draw every eye in the hall. This next moment requires ceremony. Not the gilded pomp of court, but the gravity that befits a decision already made yet needing public witness.

"Lady Juliette Marchand, step forward." He announces.

She moves with the grace her mother drilled into every curtsy, every step. Her gown is fine without being ostentatious, a deliberate choice that honors her noble birth while remaining modest enough to suit the bold request she makes.

"Your Majesty." Her voice carries clearly. "I petition leave to wed Master Lucien Marcellus and remain in honorable service to the Crown."

The hall holds its breath. This is the crux: a noblewoman asking to marry beneath her station while keeping her gentle status intact.

"I offer my recent service as a Lady to the Queen Dowager as proof I do not forget my place, even as I change it."

Clever. She frames duty as continuity, not abandonment. Alaric keeps his expression neutral, though he marks the careful phrasing.

"Master Lucien." Alaric turns his attention to the man.

The merchant moves to stand beside her, his bearing unadorned yet firm, the kind that earns respect without need for rank. "I will keep my house, my scales, and my word as one weight."

No florid vows of undying devotion. What he offers is a merchant's promise: practical, measurable, binding. The kind of oath Alaric can enforce if needed.

A guildmaster near the front benches clears his throat. His age and fine dress suggest old standing in the Guild, though Alaric knows neither his name nor his accounts.

"Should gentle blood join with trade, what becomes of rank? Stone holds by proper layers."

The guildmaster's objection echoes in the hall's silence. Alaric allows it to linger before responding, his tone steady and sure.

"Yet crumbles when the mortar weakens."

Aldwine rises from his place among the guild representatives, his practical voice cutting through any lingering tension.

"When merit builds fortune in plain sight, no man need apologize for rising above his birth. Such marriages strengthen both house and harbor."

The endorsement carries weight. A guild master backing marriage as good business speaks to broader implications than romance alone. Alaric thanks the Master Aldwine for his wisdom

He then leans forward slightly, his next inquiry directed toward Lucien's principles. "Master Lucien, when profit and fairness part ways, and they will, which serves you?"

"I keep them level." No hesitation mars the response. "A crooked profit is a debt to the future."

Sound reasoning. Alaric leans back in his chair, letting his gaze sweep the hall as if weighing competing considerations. His eyes find Geoffrey's for the briefest moment. The signal they arranged.

Geoffrey steps forward. "Your Majesty, I bear a letter from the Queen Dowager. She instructed me to present it only should a petition be made regarding this match."

Alaric accepts the parchment with every appearance of surprise, though he helped craft its contents weeks ago. He unfolds it slowly, scanning lines he memorized before leaving court, before turning to his highest counselor. "Lord Reginald, your counsel on this matter."

Reginald moves closer, reviewing the letter's formal script. Their exchange carries the weight of careful deliberation, though both know the outcome. Alaric rises, his voice carrying to every corner of the hall.

"My mother gives her blessing to this union, provided Fairharbor approves."

The response comes in murmurs that build to clear agreement. A few voices remain silent, but opposition lacks force to challenge royal will backed by local sentiment.

"Let this union be a bridge, not a theft of titles."

Lord Reginald motions Father Aberforth forward from where the priest waits near the hall's side entrance.

"Father, you will perform the ceremony in two days' time at sunset in St. Cuthbert's by the quay. The feast shall be modest, costs borne quarter by the guild, quarter by Master Lucien, and the rest by the Crown, a gift from Her Majesty. The Royal Progress departs the morning thereafter."

The practical arrangements draw nods of approval. No excessive expense, no disruption of daily commerce. Murmurs of satisfaction ripple through the crowd. The clerk sands his page with careful attention, preserving the decision for future reference.

"The floor remains open for further petitions."

What follows reveals more than formal requests for justice or favor. Speaker after speaker describes prosperity that flows from guild management, not Lord Marchand's oversight, though Lady Juliette's consistent presence is noted by many. Roads maintained by merchant coin, granaries filled through careful trade agreements, disputes settled by arbitration that serves commerce over privilege. Alaric files each detail away, weighing implications that stretch beyond this prosperous port.

When twilight deepens beyond the hall's windows, he rises to announce the last of the evening's petitions. "Tomorrow hears more petitions, then celebration and departure thereafter. Rest well."

The crowd disperses with satisfied murmurs, anticipation of the wedding mixing with approval of the day's decisions. As conversations fade into the evening air, Alaric considers how thoroughly this place thrives under stewardship that prizes competence over bloodline. Worth over birth: a lesson worth carrying forward.

Lady Juliette Marchand

Salt air mingles with beeswax as Juliette steps through the chapel doors. St. Cuthbert's bears little resemblance to Westminster's soaring stone. Here, fishing nets drape the walls like tapestries, and candles flicker in alcoves carved by generations of sea-weathered hands. Guildmasters sit beside dock workers, mothers cradle sleeping children, and the scent of tide pools drift through gaps in the timber walls.

Her father's grip tightens on her silk covered arm as they walk the narrow aisle. His face when Alaric delivered the news two evenings past, the way his voice cracked between rage and bewilderment. She knew her parents would not approve, but some choices could not wait for understanding. Lady Marchand's anger still burns fresh, but her father's now simmers as he walks his daughter down the chapel's aisle.

"Better this than becoming an ornament in some northern keep," she had told him then, watching his expression shift from fury to reluctant understanding. Her disposition was never meant for silent smiling and careful needlework while lords discussed her like livestock. Her father understood this truth, which explains why he seldom scolded her hours spent among the guildmasters' account books.

Before reaching the aisles end, Lord Marchand murmurs quietly to her. "I regret your mother declined to come. Do you truly desire this path?"

"Mother sent me to court to learn proper English manners," she murmurs to her father's sleeve. "She would never understand this choice. But you do, and I thank you."

Lucien waits at the altar, steady as harbor stone. No rich silks or golden threads, just honest cloth that speaks to earned prosperity rather than inherited privilege. His eyes find hers, and the last of her doubt dissolves.

Her father guides her to Lucien's side. Father Aberforth opens his prayer book, though the words emerge from long practice. She ought to face the priest, but she and Lucien cannot break their shared gaze. There is no longer need for secrecy. With sacred vows before them, their devotion may now be seen and honored.

"Marriage is a harbor made by hands that mend."

The priest's voice carries over hushed conversations, drawing attention back to the altar. Even his ritual adapts to Fairharbor's rhythm. Practical, enduring, and built to weather storms.

"Speak your vows."

Juliette's voice rings clear above the whispered prayers and creaking timber. "I will keep your peace and your truth."

No flowery promises of obedience or decorative devotion. Simple words that bind like well-tied knots.

Lucien's response comes without hesitation. "I will keep your courage and your bread."

Partnership, not possession. Security earned through shared effort rather than demanded through submission.

Father Aberforth nods approval and motions toward the register waiting on a simple wooden stand. King Alaric steps forward, quill steady as he signs with the weight of sovereign approval.

"Let it be remembered that work and worth can stand high together."

The royal witness transforms their union from merchant's convenience to policy statement: *Worth over birth.* Juliette watches the ink dry on parchment that will travel back to court, carrying news of precedent set in a salt-aired chapel where fishing nets hang like banners. Around them, the congregation murmurs satisfaction. Change begins in small harbors before it reaches castle halls.

The chapel doors swing wide, releasing them into afternoon light that dances off harbor waters. Dockhands abandon their nets and barrels, voices rising in honest celebration that echoes off warehouse walls. No court protocol here, just fishermen's daughters tossing flower petals while their fathers clap work-hardened hands.

Denby and Holt stand at careful distance, eyes scanning rooftops and alley mouths without dampening the joy. Their presence speaks protection rather than suspicion.

"Good noise, honest noise," Denby murmurs to Holt, who nods agreement.

Geoffrey approaches as they pause on the chapel steps, his expression warm with satisfaction. The formality that marks his court manner falls away, replaced by something deeper. "Make this town proud to have known you first."

The words carry weight beyond blessing. A charge to honor roots while building bridges. Juliette curtsies, understanding received.

At the chapel door, she and Lucien pause beside Father Aberforth's alms box. Her fingers find the small purse prepared for this moment, coins earned through ledger work and careful planning. No grand gesture, just quiet generosity.

"For hands that work and hands that wait," she whispers, letting silver pieces fall.

Lucien adds his own contribution. "And for scales that have been wrong."

The priest nods blessing as cheers continue from the harbor crowd. Through the throng, she glimpses the Guild Hall's open doors, where tables await laden with honest feast.

The Guild Hall thrums with warmth, voices weaving around tables laden with roasted fish and honeyed bread. Juliette accepts congratulations from dock workers and their wives, each handshake carrying the weight of genuine affection. These people never treated her as a delicate lady. They knew she preferred balancing ledgers in Master Aldwine's counting room to silk gowns, haggling over grain prices rather than embroidering cushions.

Master Aldwine approaches cradling a carved wooden box. Inside, brass weights nest in felt-lined compartments, each piece gleaming with careful polish.

"For scales that speak truth," he declares, placing the box in her hands. "May your measure always be fair."

The gift carries deeper meaning than ornamentation. These weights will anchor their trade, ensuring honest dealing in ports where corruption runs thick as harbor silt. She traces the carved guild mark with her fingertip, understanding received.

Geoffrey steps forward next, leading two white mounts through the hall's wide doors. Heads turn as the horses enter, their coats catching the evenings light like spun silver. Even dock workers know the mark of Redwyke breeding, where strength meets grace and lineage holds more value than coin.

"From our best stock," Geoffrey announces, offering the reins. "For roads that demand partnership."

Lucien's hand finds hers as they accept the gift, his touch steady despite the magnitude of such generosity. Redwyke mounts command prices that could buy entire warehouses. She had observed the pair repeatedly during these recent weeks among the King's retinue. They bore no riders, merely provisions. Now the purpose becomes clear. To any perceptive observer, it appeared as though Lord Geoffrey had declared his foreknowledge of this union and arrived equipped accordingly.

A fiddler strikes up from the corner, and couples begin forming on the cleared cobblestones. Lucien extends his hand with mock ceremony, grinning at her raised eyebrow. They step carefully across uneven stones, her silk slippers sliding once on worn patches.

Laughter bubbles up as she catches herself against his shoulder. "The road is never flat."

"Good. Then our feet will learn." He kisses her lightly before moving them into the dance.

Around them, other couples sway to the fiddle's rhythm. Alaric moves with royalty's grace among the guildmasters' wives and daughters, his courtesy drawing blushes and pleased whispers. Geoffrey partners with a dockmaster's daughter, his steps careful and respectful.

As evening deepens, the hall gradually empties. Children doze against their mothers' shoulders while men shake hands and make final toasts. Alaric approaches as the last dancers retreat to their homes, his expression carrying both satisfaction and the weight of tomorrow's duties.

"Thank you for your courage these past weeks," he says, clasping their joined hands. "Visit court not just for merchant business, but as friends."

The invitation carries unexpected warmth. She curtsies, understanding the honor offered.

Alaric signals Denby, who materializes from his watchful post near the doors. "Dawn will bring audits and roads again."

As the final guests depart, she and Lucien step outside the hall's main entrance. Harbor waters stretch before them, reflecting stars and torch flames in equal measure. Gulls wheel overhead, their cries mixing with the gentle slap of waves against stone. Beyond the quay, royal banners stir in the night breeze, preparing for dawn's departure.

Lucien's arm settles around her waist.

"Tomorrow, we ride through Fairharbor as one."

"Seen and the same."

Unwelcome Visitor

- 20 -

Sir Kingsley

Sir Kingsley adjusts the buckle on his vambrace, the leather warm from a day's wear. The armory settles into evening quiet with racks of spears standing sentinel and hauberks draped like sleeping mail ghosts. Through the narrow window, torchlight flickers across the training yard where sand still holds the imprint of the day's drills.

A figure slips past the doorway, rough-woven tunic snaring torchglow. Kingsley's fingers pause on his buckle. The cloth appears properly rustic, coarse weave and earth tones, yet something catches his eye. The brown dye runs too even, too rich. Real peasant garb bears patches of sun-fade and honest stains.

"New cloth taught to lie," he murmurs to himself.

The man moves past the training yard with purposeful steps, heading toward the castle's side entrances where servants and tradesmen come and go. Kingsley follows at a careful distance. His boots find the packed earth silently. A knight's training now turned to stalking prey.

The stranger's gait troubles him more than the clothing. No shuffle of exhausted labor, no careful deference of station. Instead, the man plants each step with skilled balance, weight distributed like someone accustomed to quick movement in any direction.

"You plant your weight like a duelist, not a ditcher," Kingsley breathes.

The figure approaches the service passages, slipping between shadows with unsettling familiarity. The stranger enters through the scullery door, steps sure despite what should be an unfamiliar passage. Kingsley follows, keeping to the deeper shadows cast by hanging pots and grain sacks. The man moves upward through the servant stairway, ascending toward the upper colonnade that rings the inner courtyard.

Kingsley's hand finds his sword hilt as they emerge onto the stone walkway. Torchlight dances across the arched openings, casting moving patterns on the flagstones. The stranger keeps to the outer wall, moving with an unnervingly consistent pace.

Tom the scullion rounds the corner at a run, empty bucket clanging against his leg. The collision sends both stumbling. Tom backward, the stranger briefly off-balance.

"Beg pardon, master!"

The stranger's cloak pulls wide for an instant. Light blazes along his forearm beneath the tunic sleeve, cold and blue-white, like captured starfire.

"Bright as witch-fire," Kingsley breathes.

The stranger half-turns, his profile sharp in the torchlight. His jaw is set, and one eye catches the flame with inhuman coldness. That measuring gaze sweeps past Kingsley's hiding place before the man continues walking.

Kingsley's heart pounds against his ribs. *Where have I seen you?*

Footsteps approach from behind. Loxley jogs up, breathing hard. Kingsley keeps his eyes fixed ahead, watching the cloaked figure continue down the corridor.

"Sir Kingsley—Sir Edric asks—"

Recognition lands him like a mace blow. *The Grey Hunter.*

He turns toward Loxley, his command low and urgent. "Find Sir Edric. Tell him: 'The Grey Hunter is here. Protect the Queen.' Repeat it exactly."

Loxley's face drains of color. "Aye. Grey Hunter is here. Protect the Queen."

He whips back toward the colonnade, now empty stone and dancing shadows. The man has vanished.

Kingsley grabs Loxley's shoulder. "Run. Stop for no one. Not steward, not lord, not priest. Find Sir Edric now."

The esquire bolts, bucket forgotten on the stones. Kingsley draws his sword and strides the inner corridor, choosing speed over ceremony. A doorward straightens at his approach, mouth opening for a greeting.

Kingsley lifts two fingers for silence. "No bell. Eyes sharp."

The man nods, hand moving to his own blade.

Kingsley scans the next service passage. Fresh grit scattered across the flags where water has pooled from an overturned bucket, likely Tom's doing. But pressed into the wet stone floor is a muddied bootprint too narrow for castle folk with fresh earth mingling in the recently spilled wash-water.

The passage leads toward the royal wing. Toward chambers where the Queen Dowager holds her evening councils. His boots find their rhythm on the stones as understanding dawns heavy.

"If he hunts the Montbois, he also hunts the hand that shelters them."

He runs.

Lady Hélène of Montbois

The Queen Dowager's private sitting room holds the warmth of dying embers, shadows dancing across tapestried walls. Hélène stands beside the writing desk, fingers tracing the polished wood grain while her mind wanders to the adjoining chamber where Lady Cecily pours steaming water into the oversized wooden basin.

A proper bath. The luxury still amazes her. Most in this age cleanse from bowls, yet the Queen Dowager commands hot water enough to submerge completely. Hélène's shoulders ache from weeks of washing piece by piece, cold cloth against skin that remembers sonic cleansers and thermal pools.

The gentle splash of water ceases. Queen Dowager Margaret settles into her chair with quiet elegance, silk rustling against velvet cushions. Candlelight glimmers along the silver threads of her dark gown, its glow softening her features into quiet tranquility.

Confusion tightens Hélène's chest. Why summon her here, alone, at this hour? Her thoughts spiral toward the worst possibilities. Roland injured on the roads, discovered, or captured. She clasps her hands to still their trembling.

"I know what you are, child…and I shall be discreet. Trust is my office."

The words arrive like sunlight breaking through fog. Hélène draws a careful breath, studies the Queen Dowager's composed features. No accusation lives there, only patient certainty.

"Then I am in the right office, Your Grace." She executes a wry bow, finding refuge in formality while her mind races.

Queen Dowager's lips curve slightly. "Sit. I would know more of you. What you can tell me of your life before you arrived in our time."

Hélène lowers herself onto the indicated stool, spine straight despite exhaustion. How much truth can she risk? "My brother and I were raised as Time Agents. Our parents served in the same capacity, as did their parents before them."

"You were always close, you and Sir Roland?"

"Always together. Family meant everything until…" She pauses, choosing words carefully. "Until recent events separated us from our kin."

The Queen Dowager leans forward slightly. "Where do your loyalties lie, child?"

Honesty feels dangerous, yet deception more so under that penetrating gaze. "They lie with time, Your Grace. Whatever time requires of me."

"If I did not trust you, you would not cross this threshold."

Hélène meets her eyes directly. "I will earn it, daily."

Her next question hangs unfinished as sounds erupt from the passage beyond. Scuffling feet, grunts of effort, and the sharp ring of steel on stone. Hélène's muscles coil, instinct driving her toward the door.

"Stay." The Queen's voice cuts like a blade. "Here."

More sounds filter through the heavy wood. A wet thud, something heavy striking stone. The latch shifts with deliberate slowness. Hélène's hand finds her fan, the painted silk offering little comfort.

The door swings open.

A man in peasant garb fills the threshold, coarse wool and mud-stained boots marking him as common. Yet his eyes burn with intelligence too sharp, too calculating for any farmer. Behind him, three bodies sprawl across the flagstones. Sir Kingsley's familiar form among them, crimson pooling beneath still flesh.

The Queen Dowager rises with regal composure. "Sir?"

Hélène steps between them, fan raised like a pitiful shield, as she recognizes her foe. The Grey Hunter's gaze locks onto hers with terrible recognition.

"I've come for Agents of Time. The both of you."

Ice floods her veins while warmth instinctively builds in her muscles, preparing her for the inevitable clash. She lifts her chin, voice steady as iron. "You have one."

"You insult my house." The Queen Dowager's words carry decades of authority. "Speak before you die."

A thin smile twists his features, never breaking eye contact with Hélène. "My house is ash. Yours did that. Your Agents of Time ran us to ground. I alone know where history hid you."

Her fear crystallizes. Revenge made this hunter track them across centuries, following whatever trail their arrival left. Hélène tests his resolve, probing for weakness. "So you fled the future to die in a past no one will mourn you in."

The Grey Hunter steps fully inside, closing the door deliberately slow. The latch clicks home like a coffin lid. Hatred and malice burn in his stare, consuming everything else.

Lady Cecily emerges from the bathing chamber, steam behind her silhouette. The Queen Dowager lifts her palm without turning. "Lady Cecily. Behind me. No cries."

Cecily steps back without a word, placing herself behind the Queen Dowager. Her breathing quickens, but she utters no sound. The moment she finds her place, the Grey Hunter lunges for Hélène.

Hélène catches his wrist mid-strike, twists hard against the joint's natural bend. He grunts as she drives her shoulder into his chest, sending him crashing into the writing shelf. Vellum scrolls cascade to the floor like autumn leaves, ink wells rattling against pewter.

"Not in the Queen's writing room," she hisses through gritted teeth.

He rebounds with predatory speed, fist aimed at her ribs. "Then bleed on her rug."

The blow connects. Air explodes from her lungs, ribs screaming protest, but she pivots away before he can follow through. Behind her, Cecily's sharp intake echoes through the chamber.

Another strike catches her shoulder, spinning her toward the tea service. She rebounds like the blow meant nothing, snatching a pottery cup and hurling it at his face. He ducks, and it shatters against the stone wall.

He lunges again, she pivots, but a well-placed backhand splits her lip. She tastes copper but does not falter. She grabs a heavy silver ornament from the mantel and swings it like a club. He blocks with his right forearm, metal ringing against bone, careful to not let her break the timeband on his left arm.

Cecily gasps at each impact, the sound a reminder to Hélène that more than her own skin is at stake within these walls.

Hélène seizes a lit candle from its sconce, wax spattering as she thrusts the flame toward his eyes. He jerks back, and she flows forward with an elbow strike that glances off his jaw.

He follows with a knee driven toward her stomach. She twists, takes it on her hip instead, pain lancing through muscle. The force sends her stumbling toward the chairs arranged near the hearth.

Steel whispers from concealment. A hidden blade materializes in his grip, edge gleaming with lethal promise.

Hélène grabs the nearest stool, snaps it up between them like a shield. The blade slices through oak easily, dismantling the stool with a few well placed strikes.

She throws the stool's remains between them and heel-pivots backwards, putting distance between them. "Different century, same arrogance."

His smile never wavers as he advances, blade weaving hypnotic patterns. "And the same end."

The Queen Dowager stands motionless, calculating. Cecily's breathing grows ragged behind her protector's frame.

The Grey Hunter raises his weapon, and Hélène's hand finds another ornament. A heavy brass candlestick that might serve as a club.

The door explodes inward with thunderous force. Sir Edric Stone fills the frame, short-sword gleaming in the hall's torchlight, his face set in grim determination. Behind him, young Loxley darts past like a sparrow, positioning himself squarely before Queen Dowager and Lady Cecily.

"Stand from her!" Edric's voice cuts through the chamber like a battle cry.

Hélène doesn't turn from her adversary, brass candlestick raised high. "Take his legs, not his chest!"

Sir Edric charges without hesitation, blade singing through air toward the Grey Hunter's thighs. The assassin spins to meet this new threat, his hidden weapon flashing in deadly arcs. Steel rings against steel as Edric parries a vicious downward strike.

Together they press the attack. Hélène from one side, Edric from the other. The Grey Hunter moves like liquid shadow, blocking her candlestick with his forearm while deflecting Edric's thrust with his blade. His obvious skills suggest he'll win the battle with ease, yet sweat beads his brow now, breath coming harder with each exchange. Perhaps stamina is his weakness.

Edric lunges forward, sword seeking flesh. The assassin's blade slices deep across the knight's shoulder, crimson blossoming through torn fabric. Edric staggers but keeps his feet, jaw clenched against pain.

"Still standing," he growls, raising his weapon again.

Hélène spots her chance. She feints left, drawing the Grey Hunter's attention, then pivots sharply right. Her movement drives him backward over the splintered remains of the broken stool. His ankle catches the debris, balance faltering.

Edric strikes low, sweeping the assassin's legs completely. The Grey Hunter crashes down, weapon spinning from his grasp.

Hélène surges forward, candlestick gripped in both hands like a war hammer. She brings it down with every ounce of strength her future-trained muscles possess.

CRACK.

The Grey Hunter goes still, and the only sound left in the room is the fire crackling.

Queen Dowager Margaret

Loxley's chest heaves as he turns toward her, nervous sweat glistening on his young face. "Your Grace?"

Margaret steadies herself against the writing desk, fingers finding purchase on familiar oak. "We are kept…by her."

The words carry more weight than gratitude. They acknowledge debt, loyalty earned in blood and brass.

Hélène remains astride the corpse, knuckles bone-white against the candlestick's base. Her voice emerges hollow, distant. "Stay down."

A bright chirp splits the silence. Alien, musical, wrong. Margaret's gaze snaps to the dead man's wrist where something gleams beneath torn fabric.

"Authorized user terminated. Autodestruct in ten… nine…"

The voice speaks perfect English with no accent Margaret recognizes. Hélène scrambles frantically at hidden clasps, sparks biting her fingers. Blue light pulses through the chamber like a dying heartbeat.

"No… no…NO…Please no!"

"…five… four…"

Margaret watches this girl, this woman, fight against forces beyond any court's comprehension. The air grows thick with the scent of burning metal and singed hair.

"…two… one."

The band sizzles with a sharp pop, both its internal light and voice die to silence, leaving only the scent of something burnt that Margaret cannot place.

Hélène sits motionless, legs still bracketing the Grey Hunter's still form. Her gaze fixes on the silent device as tremors begin in her shoulders, spreading downward until her whole frame shakes. She wraps both arms tight across her ribs.

Edric crouches beside her, voice low and soft. "My lady… was that your first?"

"The rule was capture. Don't kill." Hélène's words emerge flat, distant. She doesn't look up.

Margaret moves quickly with the authority of decades. "Fetch the Archbishop. Quietly. No bell, no rumor."

Loxley nods and slips toward the door.

"A hot bath. Salts. Close the shutters."

Cecily's hands flutter once, then steady. She hurries toward the bathing chamber, the water fortunately already drawn.

Margaret approaches slowly, and Cecily quickly returning to help guide Hélène upward. The girl wavers, then yields to their touch like a child surrendering to sleep.

"I broke the rule." Hélène's voice cracks small.

Margaret's arm settles firm around trembling shoulders. "You kept the vow: mine."

Steam curls in the bathing chamber, thick and merciful. Cecily works at bloodied laces with quick fingers while Margaret takes up a cloth, dipping it in warm water. She begins wiping crimson from Hélène's hair with the care of a mother tending fever. The bruises on the girl's frame already forming, a testament to both her skill and bravery.

"It is a hard mercy. It leaves a mark. We will make room for it."

Hélène's breathing slowly steadies under gentle ministrations. Her voice emerges steadier than before. "May I keep to my morning rounds? The steps help."

Margaret's hand smooths damp strands from the girl's forehead. "Bread before bells, yes. We will change no good habit today."

A soft knock interrupts. Loxley's voice carries through the door, respectful but urgent.

Margaret calls without turning. "Tell His Grace: she is safe, and I will speak with him presently."

"Aye, Your Grace."

Through the doorway, Margaret glimpses Sir Edric directing a guard to cover the still form with her sitting room rug. The sight should disturb. Fresh blood stains the intricate designs, and death lingers in the place where she gives counsel. Instead, she focuses on Hélène's damp hair against her shoulder, the steady rise and fall of breathing that speaks of life preserved.

A queen does not weep when saved. She remembers and pays her debts in full.

The Measure of Lords

- 21 -

King Alaric

The horses' hooves squelch in churned mud as they crest the hill overlooking Dunmere's green pastures, or what should have been. Alaric's gaze sweeps across the pastures and village below. Villagers gathered in clusters, their clothes bearing the careful patches of poverty made proud. Empty barn doors gape like hungry mouths. Stalks are blackened, and the green is bare.

"Want walks here wearing other shoes," he murmurs to Geoffrey, who rides close at his left shoulder.

Geoffrey follows his sight line toward the crowd. "The harvest should have filled those stores, Sire."

Children dart between their parents' legs, excitement brightening faces too thin for their years. A woman clutches a swaddled infant, her kirtle let out with mismatched thread. Men remove caps with calloused hands, bowing low as the royal standard passes.

Alaric raises his hand in acknowledgment, noting how quickly they straighten. They're eager, not servile. These people hunger for answers, not just bread.

"Court in the field," he calls to Reginald. "The flat ground there, beyond the well. And whatever bread we have to spare."

Banners snap in the wind as his retinue dismounts. The worn earth beneath their feet tells its own story of too many feet seeking too little relief. Alaric adjusts his cloak and strides toward the hastily arranged seat Denby produces.

Word spreads quickly through the gathered crowd. Lord Percival's steward should appear soon, yet something about the people's restless energy suggests more than routine petitions await.

The king's men have arranged their makeshift court and begun distributing what bread they carry when Lord Percival appears astride a magnificent destrier. He is attired and perfumed as though readied for palace halls, not for tending his own estates.

Percival sweeps into a bow that somehow manages to look casual. "Your Majesty brings weather and wonder to our humble corner."

Alaric settles into the makeshift seat, Roland on guard at his side, his voice carrying no warmth. "I bring questions."

The smile falters for a heartbeat before Percival recovers and addresses the man to Alaric's right. "A pity your sister was not able to join us for this humble gathering, Sir Roland."

Roland's response comes swift and flat. "She tends to matters of substance."

Alaric watches the exchange with distaste. Percival's endless pursuit of court ladies has become as predictable as his neglect of his own lands: always chasing, never settling, leaving broken hearts or worse in his wake.

Behind him, a lanky man in fine robes and a bailiff's chain gleaming at his throat hurries toward them, clutching scrolls like shields. Alaric motions for Percival to step aside.

The man steps forward with a confidence that sits oddly on his frame. "Your Majesty, I am Master Osbert Kett, advisor to Lord Percival, steward for the House of Dunmere, and bailiff over these lands."

Alaric's jaw tightens. Too many titles. The man speaks as though he holds the seat itself, not merely serves it.

"The harvest blight required careful management," the advisor begins, his voice reedy with rehearsed authority. "We levied additional surcharges to protect the manor's solvency during these trying—"

"You levied to protect your purse." Alaric's words puncture the explanation like a quill stabbed through vellum.

Movement catches his eye as Reginald steps forward, unfurling tally sticks with the ease of a man who lives by numbers. His voice carries clearly across the gathered crowd. "Collections rose when yields fell. That is not protection. That is predation."

Percival's laugh rings hollow against the morning air. "Your Majesty, these ledger details are beneath—"

"Beneath?" Alaric's voice sharpens.

Percival shrugs, his jeweled fingers dismissing the crowd with a casual wave. "My advisor handles such trifles. I serve at court, where my talents benefit the realm."

Geoffrey's voice cuts through the practiced charm, each word measured and cold. "A lord's first court is his fields."

The gathered villagers shift closer, sensing the tide turning in their favor. A woman pushes through the crowd, her weathered hands clutching a small wooden token. She approaches the royal seat with the determined gait of someone who has lost everything except her courage.

"I sold spring to pay winter," she says, holding up the pawn chit. Her voice breaks slightly. "My seed grain."

Alaric's jaw tightens. "Mark it," he tells Reginald.

More villagers step forward, emboldened by the widow's courage. A miller speaks of grain seized beyond the tithe. A blacksmith tells of tools confiscated for unpaid levies. Each voice adds weight to the scales of justice tilting against Percival's steward.

Reginald's finger traces down the tally marks, his expression darkening with each calculation. "The collections exceed even wartime rates," he announces, loud enough for all to hear. "Yet the manor's coffers show gaps."

Master Osbert Kett shifts behind his scrolls, sweat beading despite the cool air. "Clerical errors, perhaps."

"Too many *mistakes* for clerical error." Reginald's voice carries the authority of a man who has seen every manner of fiscal deception. "You kept two ledgers. One for your lord, one for your purse."

Alaric rises from his seat, studying the advisor's pale face. The man's robes are fine wool dyed deep blue, expensive even for most lower nobles. His rings catch the morning light, gold that should have fed families through winter.

"Lord Geoffrey."

Geoffrey steps forward with measured precision. "Sire."

"Remove Master Kett's chain of office."

The advisor stumbles backward as Geoffrey approaches, his carefully maintained composure cracking like ice in spring. "Your Majesty, surely we can discuss—"

"The time for discussion starved with these people."

Geoffrey's hands are gentle but inexorable as he lifts the bailiff's chain from Kett's shoulders. The symbol of authority lifts lighter than it should, as if the trust it represented had already fled.

Holt moves to Kett's side, his presence solid and implacable. "Hands where justice can see them."

"Mercy, please." Kett's voice breaks on the words.

Alaric's gaze never wavers from the man's face. "Mercy goes first to the hungry. You may request it afterward."

The crowd murmurs approval as Holt leads the disgraced steward away. Percival stands frozen, his court finery suddenly ridiculous against the backdrop of his people's need.

"You will remain at Dunmere," Alaric commands Percival, his voice carrying across the gathered villagers. "Learn the names you taxed. Know the faces you failed."

Percival's shoulders sag beneath his ornate cloak. "As... Your Majesty commands."

Alaric turns to address the crowd, his voice clear and strong. "From this day forward, in times of calamity, nobles pay relief tithes. Peasant taxes are suspended until yields recover. Seed and bread will flow from Crown stores and manor granaries alike."

He turns to look at Lord Percival. "The hungry will not finance their hunger."

The silence that follows stretches for a heartbeat before understanding dawns. Children peek from behind their mothers' skirts as hope kindles in withered faces. Murmurs spread like the fire that took their fields, and the queue of petitioners grows.

Hours later, the last petitioner bows and steps away, clutching a promise of grain that will see her children through winter. Alaric watches his men distribute seed from the wagons, each sack a small rebellion against the hunger that should never have taken root.

"Continue the distributions," he tells Geoffrey, whose steady hands measure portions with the precision of a man who understands scarcity. "Every family. Every need."

Percival stands apart from his people, isolated by his own negligence. The sight turns Alaric's stomach. A lord who knows his courtiers better than his tenants has forgotten his purpose entirely.

The king's thoughts drift to Redwyke, where summer afternoons of his boyhood stretched golden across well-tended fields. Reginald's lands had been a refuge then. Its orchards heavy with fruit, granaries that never emptied, and people who smiled because their bellies stayed full.

But by his own orders, Reginald serves fully at court now, as does Geoffrey. Both spend their days managing the realm's business while their own estates rely on distant oversight and occasional brief visits. What rot might fester when good men turn their backs to serve a greater good?

"Sir Denby."

Denby appears at his shoulder, ever-watchful. "Sire."

"Prepare for Redwyke. We leave at first light."

Both Reginald and Geoffrey pause in their grain distribution, shoulders stiffening as understanding dawns. They exchange a glance, but worry does not style their faces. They simply nod acceptance before returning to their work with renewed urgency.

Lord Geoffrey of Redwyke

Geoffrey's chest swells as familiar hills rise before them, green slopes dotted with fat sheep and orderly stone walls. The sight hits him like waking from a long fever, every detail sharp and precious. Apple trees hang heavy with fruit along the lane, their branches bowing under the weight of a good harvest. Small game flickers through the woodline, rabbits and grouse unafraid in lands where poaching means a fine, not a flogging.

This is how he remembers it from boyhood summers. This is how it should be.

Behind him, the column stretches forty strong: guards, clerks, camp staff, and pack animals laden with the tools of royal justice. They've seen Dunmere's lifeless fields and hollow-eyed children. Now they see what prosperity looks like when tended with care.

"The road's been mended recently," Holt observes, his horse's hooves ringing clear on fresh-laid stone.

Geoffrey nods, pride warming his voice. "Redwyke's always had the finest roads. Constant care keeps them so. Better to fix a stone than replace a wheel."

They crest the final hill, and Redwyke spreads below them like a tapestry woven from order and abundance. The town hall sits square and solid near the estate proper, its timber frame dark with age but straight as a sword. Smoke rises from cottage chimneys in neat columns. Gardens burst with late vegetables, their rows precise as soldiers on parade.

Geoffrey urges his mount closer to his father's side as they approach the hall. Reginald sits tall in his saddle, aged hands steady on the reins, but Geoffrey catches the subtle relaxation in his shoulders. Home does that to a man, reminds him what he fights to protect.

The town hall fills quickly once Alaric's banner is raised. Geoffrey positions himself where he can watch both the proceedings and his people's faces. What he sees makes his throat tight with gratitude.

Reginald dispatches a wide-eyed inn maid with instructions for Mother. Forty guests require a feast worthy of the Crown, and Lady Margery has never failed to rise to such occasions. The girl bobs a curtsy and scurries off, her steps quick with purpose rather than fear.

The first petitioner steps forward, Redwyke's head miller and local merchant Master Oxley, his face marked by years of honest work and frequent smiles.

"Your Majesty honors Redwyke with your presence. The harvest runs three days ahead of schedule, grain stores are full, and the mill wheel turns true as sunrise."

Geoffrey watches Alaric's face soften at the miller's easy confidence. Oxley is a man whose loyalty is free of groveling, his pride rooted in the craft of honest work.

More voices follow. The road warden reports bridges inspected and repaired after winter. The reeve presents ledgers that balance to the penny. No mysterious gaps or trembling explanations. A visiting merchant speaks of fair tolls and swift justice. Each testimony builds on the last, creating a picture of lands governed with steady hands and open hearts.

"Lady Redwyke keeps the grain flowing and the peace settled," an elderly farmer declares, his voice carrying the weight of decades. "Lost my Mabel this spring, and her ladyship came herself with bread and prayers. Not many nobles trouble themselves with common grief."

Geoffrey's chest tightens. Mother had written of Mabel Brewster's passing, but hearing it spoken aloud, hearing how she honored the old woman's memory, reminds him why his family's name carries respect rather than fear.

Behind him, he catches Denby's quiet observation to Holt: "A house that breathes in rhythm."

Holt's response comes equally low: "And sleeps with both eyes closed."

The assessment hits true. Redwyke functions like a well-tuned instrument, each part supporting the whole without strain or discord. Geoffrey thinks of Dunmere's frayed edges, of Percival's perfumed ignorance, and feels the contrast like a blade.

A small commotion near the door draws his attention. One of Mother's household guards enters, his livery neat but his face flushed from hard riding. The man approaches Reginald directly, bending to whisper urgently in his ear.

Geoffrey strains to hear but catches only fragments. Something about preparations and timing. His father's expression shifts from concern to satisfaction as the message concludes.

Reginald rises, commanding attention with the same quiet authority that has served three kings. "Your Majesty, once your session concludes, my people will restore this hall to order. Lady Redwyke has prepared a feast for your entire progress. All forty souls. The hospitality of Redwyke is yours."

Alaric's smile transforms his entire bearing. "Gratefully accepted. Men!" His voice carries to every corner of the hall. "Take your ease tonight. It's been well earned."

The cheer that erupts shakes the rafters. Guards who have slept on hard ground and eaten road rations whoop their approval. Even the usually stern Denby cracks a grin.

Geoffrey watches his people beam with pride at hosting the king's company. This is what stewardship means. Not extracting wealth but creating it, not demanding service but inspiring it.

The short ride from Town Hall to Redwyke Estate feels like a victory lap through Geoffrey's childhood. Every hedge shows careful tending, every gate swings true on oiled hinges. The detached dance hall that has hosted harvest festivals for three generations gleams with fresh whitewash, its oak beams dark and solid as the day they were raised.

Geoffrey watches Alaric's expression shift from royal composure to genuine appreciation as they approach the main house. The king's eyes tracks the details of a swept courtyard, polished brass fittings, and the way servants move with purpose rather than haste.

"Denby," Alaric calls, swinging down from his mount. "See our people well fed in the dance hall. I'd walk these halls once more, for memory's sake."

Geoffrey's pulse quickens. Alaric visited thrice in Geoffrey's youth, but those memories carry the weight of a boy trying not to spill wine on royal sleeves. Now he stands as witness to his family's work, ready to see it measured by his king's eye.

Lady Margery emerges from the main doors like a general taking her position. Her graying hair sits perfect beneath a simple circlet, her dark blue gown rich but unadorned. She approaches with gentile steps, her curtsy precise and respectful without servility.

"Your Majesty honors Redwyke. Welcome to a house that tries."

Alaric's smile transforms his features. "And succeeds."

"Mother, may I present Sir Roland of Montbois."

Lady Margery's keen eyes assess Roland with maternal precision. "Geoffrey wrote of your swift action against that castle intruder. You have my deepest gratitude for protecting my son."

Roland inclines his head respectfully. "I would do it again, my lady."

Geoffrey follows as they enter halls he could navigate blindfolded. Tapestries hang straight, floors gleam with beeswax, and the great hearth crackles with seasoned wood. But it's the ledgers spread across Mother's working table that catch Alaric's attention.

"Winter preparations?" the king inquires, studying the neat columns. "Never to early."

"We cut hay in thirds this summer season," Mother explains, her voice carrying the confidence of certain knowledge. "Cattle held their weight through last winter's cold snap."

"Sensible as mortar," Alaric murmurs the approval as he skims the ledgers' columns.

Geoffrey watches his mother guide the conversation with gentle expertise, each answer demonstrating mastery over lands and people alike. Pride swells in his chest again. This is what good governance looks like when nobody's watching.

The sound of light boots on stone draws Geoffrey's attention to the main hall. A figure approaches through the arched doorway. Travel cloak plain as homespun, but the stride beneath carries confidence. Geoffrey's breath catches as she pushes back her hood, revealing auburn hair braided simply and eyes the color of winter sky.

Clarissa.

Her bow is a fluid movement that bears the discipline of someone who learned courtesy as craft, not performance.

"My lord, Your Majesty."

Memory floods back of a girl of twelve summers teaching him to braid rushes while rain drummed the solar windows. Her laugh when he managed three strands without dropping them.

He moves forward slightly. An awkward smile tugs at his lips. "We were children, once."

Her expression shifts to something fond as her gaze finds his. "We are not, now."

The simple truth settles between them like a bridge built from understanding. Geoffrey straightens, feeling the weight of years and duty reshape the space around them both.

"Your Majesty," Geoffrey says, his voice finding steadier ground, "may I present Lady Clarissa Harroway, my betrothed."

Alaric's face brightens with recognition. "Ah, the Northern Beauty you mentioned. Lady Clarissa, welcome."

Clarissa inclines her head with perfect deference. "You honor me, Your Majesty."

"I confess curiosity," Alaric continues, studying her with attention he reserves for maps and treaties. "Geoffrey has spoken of you, yet you've never graced our court. Most nobles present their intended to the Crown."

Geoffrey watches Clarissa's composure hold steady as fortress walls. "I remained with the last of my family in the North, Your Majesty. My dear aunt, who raised me after my parents' passing. She died this past fall, and I have spent the winter, spring, and now summer here in Redwyke, preparing for my role as future mistress of these lands."

The explanation carries the weight of genuine grief and duty. Geoffrey catches the slight tightening around her eyes when she mentions her aunt. A loss worn smooth by months of mourning but still tender.

Alaric nods, understanding flickering across his features. "Family obligations honor those who keep them. And your preparation period, how have you found Redwyke?"

"A house that breathes in rhythm, Your Majesty. The stewardship here sets a standard worth learning."

Geoffrey feels pride warm once again in his chest. She sees it too. The careful work, the steady hands that have shaped these lands into something worthy.

"Then you should see more of the kingdom," Alaric declares. "You'll ride with our progress for the remainder of the season, then spend time at court and return before winter. Let Redwyke be seen to have chosen well."

Geoffrey's pulse quickens. Public acknowledgment of their match. More than courtesy, this. Alaric offers his royal seal on their union.

"Your Majesty," Lady Margery interjects gently, "the progress will require—"

"Arrangements will be made." Alaric's tone brooks no argument. His attention shifts to Geoffrey. "When she returns to Redwyke, you return with her. A lord belongs where decisions sleep."

The words hit Geoffrey like a physical blow. Not painful, but transformative. Here. Home. Where generations of his family have tended these lands and people.

"Yes, Your Majesty." Geoffrey's voice carries conviction he didn't know he possessed. "Gladly."

Alaric turns to Lady Margery, respect warming his formal tone. "My lady, accept the Crown's gratitude for splendid stewardship. You kept a kingdom's promise in one valley."

Geoffrey watches his mother's face soften with satisfaction earned through decades of careful work. "Promises prefer kitchens to courts, Your Majesty."

The king's laughter rings genuine as cathedral bells. "Wisdom from the source. Come. Let us rejoin the progress before Denby believes we've fallen into the wine cellars."

Lord Reginald steps forward to guide them toward the dance hall. "The feast awaits, Your Majesty. My people will have outdone themselves."

As the party moves toward the door, Geoffrey feels Clarissa's fingers brush his sleeve. A gentle signal to linger. He slows his steps, letting the others gain distance before turning to face her properly.

The hall settles around them, firelight painting warmth across stone and timber.

"You look well," she says, voice dropping to conversational warmth. "Court life hasn't spoiled you entirely."

Geoffrey grins, feeling boyhood mischief stir beneath lordly composure. "Only around the edges. I've kept most of my teeth and learned to read beyond account books."

"Impressive progress." Her smile carries genuine fondness. "But can you read the weather as well as a ledger?"

"With tutoring."

The simple exchange settles something between them. A recognition that their childhood connection has deepened into partnership built on shared understanding rather than romantic fancy.

Sir Roland of Montbois

The camp sleeps around scattered coals, horses shifting in their lines and sentries marking quiet circuits. Roland finds the King perched on a fallen log beyond the firelight, gazing at stars that pierce the forest canopy like scattered silver.

Alaric glances up as Roland approaches. "At last, a conversation without listeners."

Roland settles beside him, grateful for shadows that hide the tension he carries. The Ancient's words echo through every quiet moment. *Sealed, final, no return.* He pushes the weight down, focusing on the man beside him rather than the future that waits like a suspended blade.

"Sleep proves difficult after meeting steel," Roland observes.

"You turned blades into breath," Alaric says, his voice carrying the weight of gratitude and something deeper. "I count breath dearly."

Roland's mouth quirks into its familiar dry angle. "It spends better than blood."

The simple exchange hangs between them, honest in its understatement. Roland's hand drifts to his side where the wound should still tear with every movement, where bandages should bind torn flesh. Instead, barely marked skin lies beneath his tunic. Healing that defies the explanations of this time.

The words climb his throat like prisoners seeking escape. Accelerated cellular regeneration. Enhanced immune response. Centuries of medical advancement compressed into genetic modification. All of it useless here, dangerous to speak.

"There are..." Roland's voice drops to barely above a whisper. "Larger reasons I do not fall."

The confession hovers incomplete, heavy with implications he cannot name. His throat closes around the rest. Explanations that would sound like madness, truths that would shatter the careful fiction they've built. Silence stretches between them, filled with night sounds and the distant murmur of sleeping men. Roland swallows the words down further, locking them behind familiar restraint.

Alaric reads the hesitation without pressing, understanding written in his stillness. "Larger reasons may keep for larger nights."

The acceptance cuts deeper than questions would. Roland stares at his hands, wondering how many nights remain before duty calls him home to a future Hélène can never see.

Alaric shifts against the log, his gaze moving from stars to the sleeping camp. "The progress teaches much. Yet I suspect it teaches only what men wish me to see."

Roland catches the thread of frustration beneath controlled words. Kings live behind veils woven by others, shaped by protocol, sustained by deference, and guided by the choreography of power.

"Court performs for you," Roland says, watching Alaric's profile in starlight.

"Precisely." Alaric's voice carries quiet intensity. "I would make such journeys regular practice. Let none know when I might arrive, or which halls I choose to visit."

The desire makes sense. A young king seeking truth beneath the polish. Roland weighs the proposal, understanding its necessity and its dangers. "Then ride where silence goes first."

Alaric turns toward him, something kindling in his expression. "Before dawn. Three horses, no banners. Cloak the steel, leave orders with Denby."

"Why?" Roland asks, studying the resolve in Alaric's face.

"I caught their lands unawares during the progress. Saw rot where they showed me plenty, loyalty where they claimed weakness. Now I would catch the castle itself off guard, see what truths lie beneath the ceremony."

Roland sees the logic immediately. The same principle that revealed neglected granaries and hidden competence could expose the genuine workings of noble halls. "Then we plan this properly."

The strategy forms between them with military precision, voices low enough that even nearby sentries cannot catch their words. Roland finds himself grateful for this. Honest strategy spoken between equals rather than the careful dance of court hierarchy.

A boot scrapes against stone. Both men tense as a shadow detaches itself from the treeline, moving with the deliberate quiet of someone who has been listening.

Sir William Denby materializes from the darkness, his expression flat with the particular brand of disapproval reserved for noble folly. His weathered face shows no surprise at finding his king plotting unauthorized reconnaissance.

"Say the plan aloud so I may hate it properly."

The dry delivery carries years of experience keeping young nobles breathing despite their best efforts. Roland recognizes the tone. A captain's practical love disguised as insolence.

Alaric straightens but does not retreat from his position. "We would ride ahead. Three men, no ceremony."

"Fools' work," Denby states without heat. "If fools must ride, they will ride with a witness."

Denby demands the senior guard be Sir Alwin Hale himself, a clear route marked beforehand, and a fixed hour to signal if they miss their return.

"Your insolence preserves me," Alaric accepts, his voice carrying fond exasperation.

Denby's grunt suggests this arrangement satisfies his minimum requirements for keeping his king alive. He calls a sentry over and orders the retrieval of Hale in full guard. Then he settles onto a nearby fallen trunk, apparently prepared to supervise their continued planning.

Sir Hale emerges from the camp's shadows, already buckling a sword belt with the practiced efficiency of a man roused from sleep too many times to count. His grin cuts white through the darkness as he approaches their conspiracy.

"If I must keep you alive, Sire, I demand a raise in jokes."

"You'll be paid in silence," Roland replies, earning a snort from Hale.

The familiar banter settles something in the back of Roland's mind. The easy rhythm of soldiers preparing for work. Yet as they finalize their route and timing, his gaze drifts to the banked coals where orange light flickers like memory.

Hélène's face surfaces unbidden. Candlelight catching her concentration as she bent over ledgers in their quarters, the careful way she practiced court phrases until they felt natural. The weight of the Ancient's words presses against his frontal lobe. *Sealed. Final.*

"History remembers," he murmurs to the dying flames.

Alaric's voice comes quiet beside him. "Then we should behave."

The simple response carries layers Roland cannot untangle. Duty, legacy, the burden of choices that echo beyond their making. He swallows the confession that claws at his throat and turns toward practical preparations.

They tamp the fire carefully, sling dark cloaks over mail that might catch moonlight, and guide their mounts toward the road's edge with whispered commands. Three shadows melt into deeper darkness, ready to ride hard toward truths that ceremony conceals.

The King Returns

- 22 -

King Alaric

Dawn light filters through high windows as Alaric slips through the castle's service entrance, hood drawn against recognition. The night ride has left him road-dusty and grateful for shadows that cloak royal bearing beneath common wool. His boots find familiar stone as he follows the scent of baking bread toward the kitchens' warmth.

Heat and golden light spill from the doorway. Inside, flour hangs in the air like motes of captured sunlight, and the rhythm of work creates its own music of wooden paddles scraping stone, dough slapping boards, and the whisper of bellows feeding ovens. Bess Carter commands her domain with the authority of long years, while Hélène moves between proving drawers with careful attention.

"If the bread rises, so will we," Hélène murmurs to the baker, checking the morning's first trays.

Alaric pauses in the doorway, struck by the simple truth wrapped in her words. "A kingdom in a proverb," he says low enough that only she might catch it.

But hunger drives him forward before discretion can counsel patience. The warm loaves call with irresistible promise, and he reaches around Bess's substantial frame to pinch a heel from the nearest basket. A wooden spoon cracks against his knuckles with startling precision.

"Ned! I'll not have dirty hands on my crusts. Wash or beg!"

Bess wheels around to deliver further scolding and freezes mid-breath. Her face drains of color as recognition dawns, the spoon hanging forgotten in her grip.

"Y—Your Majesty!"

Alaric grins, rubbing his smarting knuckles with genuine amusement. The sharp crack of wood against bone still echoes in his ears, and he finds himself delighted by the baker's fierce protection of her craft.

"My crimes are hunger and poor timing."

Hélène's voice cuts through Bess's stammered apologies with perfectly placed delivery. "Promote the spoon to Captain of the Ovens."

Bess recovers with admirable speed, thrusting a hot heel toward him with renewed authority. "Then let Captain Spoon feed you proper."

Alaric bites into bread still warm from the ovens, savoring both the taste and the moment's easy humor. "The realm is well-defended."

The bread's warmth spreads through him as he watches Hélène resume her rounds, his presence not stopping her duties. She moves with quiet competence, checking supplies and speaking softly with kitchen staff who clearly expect her presence. Ysabel should be learning these rhythms, understanding how the castle's heart beats.

"Just arrived," he tells Hélène between bites. "Overnight ride with Roland and Alwin."

She nods, seemingly unsurprised by his unheralded return.

"I'll shadow your rounds, if you permit. Learn what morning teaches."

Hélène studies his travel-stained appearance with calculating eyes. "Your lackluster attire and questionable odor might pass for a delivery boy. Stay quiet, follow close."

Alaric follows her from the kitchens, savoring more than warm bread. Her easy authority, the way staff look to her with genuine respect. It stirs something deeper than admiration. *Temporary*, he reminds himself, though the word sits poorly. She and Roland return to the future eventually.

They move deeper into the kitchens where Maud Thatcher kneels beside the second oven, tracing her finger along a hairline crack that spiders across the stone. Steam escapes in thin wisps, and her face creases with worry.

"Oven's splitting again, my lady. The whole morning's bake might—"

"Fire obeys work, not wishes." Hélène's voice cuts through rising panic with calm authority. "Shift the pans."

She surveys the kitchen with swift calculation, pointing toward braziers that normally serve the scullery. "Maud, move half the loaves there. Use the flat pans for the brazier tops."

Maud's grin breaks through her worry as she scrambles to obey. "Aye, my lady."

Alaric watches Hélène orchestrate the crisis with the efficiency of a field commander redirecting troops. No wasted motion, no hesitation. The kitchen staff respond with practiced ease, accustomed to Hélène's quick decisions and comfortable taking direction from her.

A small figure catches his eye. A scullion boy hauling water buckets twice his size toward the proving area. The child notices Alaric's focused attention and freezes, recognition dawning in wide eyes.

Alaric raises a finger to his lips, asking for silence. The boy's mouth forms a mischievous circle of understanding before he nods vigorously and continues his work.

"Tom, that bucket bought us ten minutes." Hélène's praise reaches the boy as he sets down his burden, and his entire face transforms with pride.

She buys loyalty with names, Alaric thinks, filing away the lesson. Names matter. Recognition matters. This scullion will remember being seen, being valued.

They continue into the buttery where Master Bartram shuffles through parchments with increasing agitation. Papers scattered across his tally board speak of morning confusion.

"Lost the grain count from yesterday's delivery," he mutters, not noticing their approach.

Hélène spots the wayward document tucked beneath a cloth near the scales. She extracts it gently and notes the correction in a small ledger tucked into her waistbelt.

"Misfiled tallies breed doubt. Settled ledgers breed porridge."

Bartram's relief is visible as he smooths the recovered parchment. "I'll guard my counts closer, my lady."

Bartram sniffs the air in Alaric's direction, wrinkling his nose with distaste. "Stench follows some folk like shadow. Mind you don't track stable muck through my clean stores, boy."

The reeve never glances at Alaric directly, dismissing him as beneath notice. Alaric bites back laughter at being so thoroughly ignored by his own servant.

A clerk approaches with nervous deference, clutching yesterday's proposal. "My lady, about reducing staff portions to impress the Princess—"

"No." Hélène's refusal carries no anger, just finality.

"But I've brought this suggestion before, and the Princess expects—"

"Feed first, flatter second."

Alaric watches the clerk retreat, not understanding why such measures would ever be thought fitting to honor the Princess. His staff should never want for provisions.

"Feed first, flatter second," Alaric murmurs under his breath, pleased by how perfectly she captures his governing philosophy in four simple words. "My policy, spoken by another mouth."

Hélène smiles mildly at the retreating clerk and guides them toward the granary.

A kitchen girl hurries past with a bowl of flour, her path intersecting dangerously with Alaric's position. Hélène catches his arm, tugging him aside just as white powder threatens to dust his sleeve. Without pause, she taps a pinch of flour onto his cheek.

"Your face betrays your profession."

Alaric touches the flour with amused fingers. "King?"

"Hungry man. Now you're a baker's nephew."

Agnes appears from nowhere, arms laden with linens, her eyes knowing yet her expression perfectly straight-faced. "Keep him from the scullery, my lady. The buckets will revolt."

Warmth spreads through Alaric at the easy banter from one of his most trusted maids. "Promotions come quickly in your service."

He watches Agnes continue past, noting how she pauses to press a small jar of salve into Hélène's palm without a word exchanged. The unspoken language between them speaks of long understanding.

"Orders without noise," he murmurs, soft with admiration.

They move through the castle's arteries like blood through a body, Hélène's presence drawing quiet nods and murmured greetings from staff who barely register Alaric's flour-dusted form trailing behind. A scullery maid curtsies to Hélène while stepping around Alaric as if he were furniture. The invisibility amuses him. When did he last walk his own halls unseen?

They slip into the infirmary where Hélène quietly deposits Agnes's jar among the meager supplies. Alaric recognizes the salve's quality composed of rose oil and beeswax. A blend favored by nobles for cuts and burns. The castle's own stores hold only tallow-based remedies, harsh and slow to heal.

"Small mercies carried in silence," he observes, watching her arrange the gift where it might seem naturally placed.

Hélène nods without elaboration, already moving toward the door. Alaric files the moment away. The infirmary deserves better than scraps and charity. Proper healing supplies would cost little from the royal coffers but mean much to those who serve.

At the gatehouse, morning light slants through arrow slits as Hélène climbs the narrow steps to the wall-walk. Her fingers test bowstrings with practiced efficiency, finding moisture that would spell disaster when speed matters most.

"These cords are damp," she notes before instructing Sergeant Darly. "Replace them before noon."

Darly's firm features show immediate respect for her authority. "Your eye serves, my lady."

The Sergeant's gaze shifts to Alaric, recognition flickering despite the common clothes and flour smudge. Alaric raises a warning finger, requesting silence, and the man's slight nod confirms understanding.

At the stone steps' base, Hélène pauses beside an armory ledger where an inkpot sits forgotten by some clerk. She draws the small ledger from her belt, adding notes in swift strokes. Her movements recording observations while memory still holds them sharp.

Alaric stands silent, studying her concentrated expression. The morning's revelations take shape in ink: bowstrings requiring replacement, grain counts corrected, oven repairs needed. A kingdom's welfare captured in careful script.

He's almost caught off guard as Agnes materializes from the shadows at his side.

"I'm in good hands this morning," Hélène tells her maid, tucking the parchment away. "I can find my own way back to quarters."

Agnes nods, understanding the dismissal carries deeper meaning. Before leaving she throws a grin at Alaric. Her way of respecting him without exposing him.

They walk toward Hélène's quarters in comfortable silence, the morning's observations settling between them like shared secrets. Staff emerge from doorways with easy familiarity as Hélène passes.

"Good morning, Milly," Hélène calls to a weaving girl carrying fresh rushes. "Your burn mends well?"

Milly's face brightens with genuine warmth. "Much better, my lady. The salve was heaven's mercy."

A laundress balancing wet linens pauses to bob a curtsy. "Lady Hélène, the new soap recipe works wonders. My hands haven't cracked once this week."

"Small changes, great comfort," Hélène replies with a smile that transforms. Her genuine care shines for all to see.

Alaric follows half a step behind, invisible in his common wool while watching her weave connections through simple kindness. Each greeting builds something larger than courtesy. It builds allegiance earned through care rather than commanded through rank.

At the corridor's turn toward her chambers, the hall stretches empty before them. Morning light slants through narrow windows, painting the stone floor in the orange and gold of late sunrise. Alaric lets his hood fall, releasing himself from anonymity's protection.

"My thanks for this morning's education," he says quietly. "To see my castle through a traveler's eyes rather than a king's. It reveals much I've missed."

Hélène turns to face him fully, the morning light catching the subtle intelligence in her dark eyes.

"The realm benefits from your diligence," he continues, words carrying weight beyond their simple meaning. "I confess I do not look forward to the day when Elaine Rush must return to her distant home."

He reaches for her hand before wisdom can intervene, lifting it to brush his lips across her knuckles. The gesture speaks what prudence forbids him to voice directly. Her skin holds the scent of rose oil, fresh bread, and ink. A combination uniquely hers that will haunt his thoughts.

Their eyes meet and hold. His gaze carries a longing he cannot fully conceal. Her's hold questions he cannot yet answer. Time stretches between them, heavy with unspoken possibilities. He releases her hand and steps back, knowing he must leave before propriety crumbles entirely.

Hélène remains motionless in the corridor, confusion flickering across her features like shadows. Halfway down the hall, he pauses and turns back with a grin designed to cut the tension he has created.

"I should bathe away this stench before Bartram bars me from his stores permanently."

Princess Ysabel of Navarre

Ysabel glides into the Queen Dowager's solar with the grace instilled from her father's court, her crimson silk rustling against the stone floor. The fan in her jeweled fingers rests half-open at her waist. A position of confident authority she has perfected through months of careful observation.

"Your Grace—" The words halt on her lips as her gaze falls upon the King, standing beside his mother's writing desk. Her pulse quickens with surprise, though she recovers swiftly, inclining her head with regal precision. "Your Majesty. The household breathes efficiently upon your return."

She draws herself taller, grateful beyond measure that she paid attention this morning when Montbois delivered her pedestrian report. Every detail burns fresh in memory, ready for recitation.

"Bread recovered and waste avoided while the cracked oven redirected to braziers." The words flow smoothly from her tongue, each phrase delivered with the authority of personal oversight. "The kitchens maintain their rhythm and stores remain properly tallied. The infirmary wants for nothing urgent. The armory bows have been kept honest from wet weather."

Queen Dowager's expression remains pleasantly neutral, offering no hint of approval or suspicion. "Order suits you, Highness."

Ysabel's confidence swells at the measured praise. The King's unexpected presence transforms this routine audience into something far more significant. An opportunity to demonstrate her readiness for queenship before the realm's highest authority.

The King steps forward. His eyes hold a curious intensity that sends a flutter through her chest.

"Which brick, and which mason names your repair?"

The question strikes like a blade finding gaps in armor. Ysabel's fan trembles slightly before she steadies it, mind racing through details she never thought to gather. The second oven—surely it was the second? And masons... there must be dozens in the castle's employ.

"The... second oven. Mason... John?"

"We have three Johns." The Queen Dowager's voice carries mild curiosity, but her eyes glitter with something sharper.

Heat rises in Ysabel's cheeks as the King continues his inquiry. "How many loaves kept, and for which watches?"

She forces composure into her bearing, lifting her chin as she answers. "Sufficient for the... night watch."

"Which numbers?"

The question hangs unanswered in the solar's warm afternoon air. Ysabel's grip tightens on her fan, knuckles whitening beneath rings heavy with Spanish gold. Inside her chest, fury builds not at these impossible questions, but at the French mouse who should have prepared better answers. How dare Montbois leave her defenseless before the King's scrutiny?

"Names, Highness." The Queen Dowager leans forward slightly. "Names make things real."

Ysabel's smile feels brittle as parchment left too long in sun. "My authorization was... implicit."

The silence stretches between them, thick with judgment. The Queen Dowager's fan closes with a soft click that sounds thunderous in the quiet solar.

"Some mornings write themselves."

Ysabel's jaw clenches behind her frozen smile, rage coiling in her belly like a serpent preparing to strike.

The King's expression shifts to something resembling mercy, though his eyes remain watchful. "May we see the written rota that bears your seal?"

Ysabel's breath catches. Yes, a rota. She remembers Montbois volunteering to draft a formal record, and her own declaration that she would claim ownership. She never pursued the matter further, yet certainty fills her that such a document must exist. Her fan trembles briefly against her gloved hand before she commands it motionless.

"It is being... copied."

The lie tastes bitter, but she delivers it smoothly. In her mind, she sees herself penning harsh corrections for the French girl's failures. Every missing detail, every absent name will be paid for in full.

Queen Dowager inclines her head with authority. "Meg, when the rota exists, bring it. We shall read it aloud."

The maid curtsies silently from her corner, and Ysabel's stomach tightens. Another pair of eyes to witness her exposure, another mouth to carry whispers through the castle's stones.

The solar feels smaller now, its warm light harsh against her flushed cheeks. She draws herself to full height, summoning every lesson in deportment her Spanish tutors ever drilled into her bones.

"Your attention to detail honors your halls." The curtsy she offers goes a fraction deeper than usual, acknowledgment wrapped in velvet courtesy.

"And the halls honor those who keep them." The Queen Dowager's voice carries layers of meaning that slice through Ysabel's composure.

King Alaric steps forward, his tone firm but not unkind. "Come more prepared tomorrow, Highness. The realm requires precision in its stewardship."

Ysabel's curtsy encompasses both royals before she turns toward the door, spine rigid with controlled fury. Each step carries her further from humiliation and closer to retribution.

Those within her house will learn proper Spanish lessons tonight. Her mouse will discover what price comes with leaving her defenseless before the Crown's scrutiny. Every missing detail, every fumbled answer, all of it will be carved from Montbois's hide until she understands the cost of inadequate service.

Queen Dowager Margaret

The door whispers shut behind Ysabel's retreating figure, and Margaret counts heartbeats—ten, twenty, thirty—before rising from her chair. The solar's warmth presses against her skin like fever, thick with the residue of Spanish perfume and barely contained fury.

"Follow me."

She leads Alaric into the cool passage beyond her solar, where stone breathes easier and tapestries hang undisturbed. A single banner sways once in their wake, then settles into stillness. The relief of escaping that stifling chamber loosens something tight between her shoulders.

Guards and servants linger at respectful distances. She gestures with quiet authority that sends them scattering like autumn leaves, leaving mother and son alone in the corridor's gray embrace.

Alaric's voice carries the weight of judgment rendered. "You have heard enough."

"Too much and nothing of her own making."

Two paces of silence stretch between them, footsteps muffled on worn stone. The truth demands release, patient no longer.

"She is not fit to be queen."

Margaret's response comes swift and certain. "Nor to be *taught* a queen's work. Pride deafens."

They pause at a narrow window where afternoon light slants through ancient glass. Distant bells mark the hour, their bronze voices carrying across courtyards and walls to announce the day's steady passage.

Her fingers trace the stone sill, feeling centuries of weathering beneath her touch. "Spain will hiss. The Ambassador keeps a long ledger."

"Then we show our own. Inked, sealed, and merciful."

The conviction in his voice stirs something protective in her chest. Her son has grown into wisdom these past months, learned to balance strength with compassion. The realm needs such leadership, but first they must clear the path of Spanish thorns.

"Anselm must stand with us. Moral ground first."

"He will. He loves truth when it is patient." Alaric's voice holds certainty.

But there are weightier truths waiting in this corridor's shadows. Dangers Alaric knows nothing of, threats that struck at the very heart of his castle while he travelled distant roads.

They turn toward the stairs, shadows lengthening as afternoon wears toward evening. Margaret's mind sharpens, cutting through emotion to find the cleanest path forward.

"We will give Ysabel a fair task. One she *should* own. A morning circuit without Hélène's shadow."

Alaric's mouth quirks upward, grim satisfaction flickering across his features. "And a second chance to answer questions no parrot could."

Names spark in Margaret's thoughts like flint struck in darkness, each chosen for their particular strengths. The machinery of court requires careful hands to turn its wheels.

"Reginald for order, Denby for readiness, Alice for the staff's memory."

"When Alice remembers, the walls remember." His tone carries desert-dry acknowledgment of the maid's influence.

Margaret counts on her fingers, ticking off days and necessities. Protocol demands delicacy, even in dissolution.

"A private letter to Navarre, temperate and regretful. Anselm will draft. We wait one day for Ysabel's *own* report. If she rises, we gain a steward. If she falls, we have cause."

Alaric rests his hand against the stone wall, and Margaret watches decision settle into him like weight sinking into earth. The boy-king who inherited this throne four years past has learned to carry difficult truths.

"Dissolution if she cannot do the work. No scandal. No cruelty. Just daylight." His decision is clear. "And the daylight will be *hers* to face."

But darker shadows wait behind this Spanish problem. Her voice drops to barely more than breath against stone.

"Three nights past, the Grey Hunter returned."

Alaric's body goes rigid beside her, hand instinctively reaching for sword that isn't there. The color drains from his face like water from cracked pottery.

"Hélène faced him. Took blows that would fell grown men, yet stood her ground alongside Sir Edric and slew him." The words taste of iron and necessity. "She returned to her rounds the next dawn as if nothing had passed."

The concern that floods Alaric's features speaks volumes. Worry too deep for mere subjects, too personal for casual regard. Margaret files this knowledge away like a jewel wrapped in silk, precious and requiring careful handling.

"Roland knows?"

"He was with you." Her fingertips brush his sleeve, a mother's touch steadying a son's distress. "Speak quietly with Sir Roland, Anselm, and Sir Edric. Learn what this means for us all."

"But not Hélène herself?"

"Not yet. She carries enough."

Alaric nods, though his jaw works like a man swallowing bitter medicine. The way he holds himself tells Margaret everything she needs to know about where his loyalty prefers to rest.

Mercy and Order

- 23 -

Lady, Hélène of Montbois

The heavy door closes behind the last departing servant. Perfume hangs thick in the air. Spanish oils and powder that cannot quite mask the metallic scent of polished steel from the guards' mail. Two men-at-arms remain posted by the entrance, their presence transforming this solar from refuge into cage. A gesture dismissed the servants, sending them fleeing like startled birds.

Hélène stands beside the tall windows where afternoon light cuts sharp angles across Turkish carpets brought with Ysabel from Spain. Colette hovers near the writing desk, hands clasped so tightly her knuckles show white beneath pale skin. The French girl's eyes dart between floor and Princess like a sparrow watching for hawks.

Ysabel moves with deliberate grace to the center of the chamber, silk rustling with each step. Her gown, a deep crimson shot through with gold thread, catches light like spilled blood. Jewels glitter at throat and wrists. Spanish wealth made manifest in a room that suddenly feels too small.

"A house obeys its mistress." The words fall cold as winter stones. "Today, it will learn."

The change in Ysabel's bearing strikes like a blade drawn from velvet sheath. Gone is the poised princess who charmed courtiers and deferred to the Queen Dowager's authority. What remains is something poisonous, fangs exposed.

Hélène keeps her expression neutral, though her muscles tense beneath layers of lesser silk and linen. She has faced armed enemies in dark alleys and felt less threatened than she does in this perfumed chamber with its fine silk hangings and polished oak.

"Your Highness?" The question emerges carefully measured, neither defiant nor servile.

Ysabel's smile could cut glass.

"Do not feign ignorance, Lady Hélène. Your failure to inform me properly of the morning reports and your deliberate withholding of the finalized rota have led directly to my humiliation before His Majesty."

Hélène's brow furrows faintly, confusion flickering across her features. She had done precisely as Ysabel commanded, outlining the essential details. The fault lay not in her delivery but in Ysabel's habitual inattention to such matters. The duty roster had been established weeks prior. Ysabel's consistent neglect of morning briefings and household schedules had created this predicament, not any failing on Hélène's part.

"My apologies, Your Highness, for insufficient clarity in this morning's verbal summary."

"'Tis far too late, you French fool." Ysabel's barbs usually came wrapped in courtly silk, not hurled bare like stones. Hélène senses a tempest brewing. Spanish thunder rolling in to darken the chamber.

A gesture, sharp and imperious, summons a guard closer. The mail rings softly as he approaches, face carefully blank beneath steel coifs.

"Five stripes. She may keep her dress on. She'll remember why it hurts."

Hélène's veins freeze. A flogging. For a noblewoman. In personal chambers like some common servant caught stealing bread. Her ribs and shoulders still ache from the Grey Hunter's blows three nights past, purple bruises spreading beneath her dress where no one can see the marks of that desperate fight. Only the Queen Dowager, Lady Cecily, the Archbishop, young Loxley, and the guards know of that evening's events. Several guards have begun offering her subtle nods of deference when she walks past them on her dawn inspections.

The elder guard shifts his weight. His eyes find Hélène's face, then drop to study her posture. Something in her careful stillness speaks to him.

"Your Highness," he ventures, voice respectful but troubled. "The lady took a tumble down the stone steps during her morning rounds. She may still be tender from—"

"I care nothing for her clumsiness." Ysabel's voice cuts through his concern like a blade through parchment. "Proceed."

The guard's jaw tightens, but he nods. Duty is duty, even when it tastes of ashes.

Hélène's hands flex once. A brief betrayal of tension before discipline reclaims them. Ysabel's expectant smile suggests she anticipates broken dignity, perhaps tears or pleas for mercy. Instead, Hélène moves with deliberate grace to position a heavy oak chair before herself in the room's center, fingers finding purchase on its carved back.

Do not break the story. The words whisper through her mind like a prayer.

Ysabel's voice carries silk-wrapped steel. "Kneel before me."

Hélène's chin lifts fractionally. "I shall remain standing, Your Highness."

The refusal hangs between them like drawn steel. Ysabel's eyes narrow, searching for cracks in Hélène's composure, but finds only quiet resolve reflected back at her. A long moment stretches taut as bowstring. Then Ysabel's lips curve into something that might charitably be called a smile, though it holds no warmth.

Without breaking their locked gazes, the Spanish princess raises one jeweled hand, a subtle gesture toward the waiting guard to continue. Hélène meets the guard's troubled gaze directly, her look conveying both understanding and resolve. *Do your duty. I do not fault you.*

The crack of leather against fabric splits the air. Pain blooms across her shoulders. Sharp, then spreading like spilled wine through wool. Hélène counts golden threads in the Turkish carpet beneath her feet, each strand a tiny anchor against the fire racing down her spine.

"Forgive me, my lady." The guard's voice carries genuine regret.

"Do your duty." The words emerge steady through gritted teeth. "I'll do mine."

Ysabel glides closer, silk rustling with each predatory step. Her dark eyes absorb each detail, from the tension in Hélène's shoulders to the grip on the chair and the rhythm of strained breath.

"Consider this instruction an order."

The second lash follows, then a third. Each blow sends lightning through already tender flesh, but Hélène keeps her shoulders square. Her mind chants its litany: *Not here. Not this way.* The skills that could end this, the speed, the knowledge of pressure points, the dozen ways to disable an armed man, all remain locked away. To use them would shatter everything she and Roland have built.

Another strike follows before the guard's arm wavers for half a heartbeat. Perhaps mercy stirs in his weathered features, or simple distaste for his task. Ysabel's glare hardens his resolve like steel in a forge.

"Finish."

The final blow lands with grim finality. Hélène's breath comes thin but even, each inhalation a small victory over pain and fury. Blood seeps warm against her skin, hidden beneath layers of fabric that suddenly feel heavy as mail.

"Guard, summon my attendant back. You also return." Ysabel commands him with her brand of regal detachment. "Lady Hélène, prepare yourself for your usual writing duties. The afternoon correspondence will not pen itself."

Colette materializes at Hélène's side, gentle hands guiding her to the desk chair with infinite care. Colette's face has gone pale as winter morning, but her touch remains steady.

"Is Your Highness satisfied?" Hélène's voice emerges level, betraying nothing of the fire beneath her skin.

Ysabel's smile could sweeten poison. "I will be, when you're useful again."

The guard withdraws, chainmail chiming quietly in the passage outside. Meg's form emerges swiftly, while another maid's figure flickers past the doorway, with news that will spread like wildfire through stone halls no doubt.

Hélène's hand trails along the desk's polished wood, fingers finding parchment and quill. Upright, unbowed, bleeding beneath fabric that hides her wounds from Spanish eyes that hunger for her weakness.

Queen Dowager Margaret

The door to Ysabel's study swings open without ceremony. The Queen Dowager Margaret steps across the threshold, her presence filling the chamber like winter suddenly settling over summer fields. No raised voice accompanies her entrance. None is needed. The very air seems to still at her approach.

"This room is closed."

Her words carry the weight of absolute authority, spoken with the strict calm that has silenced councils and steadied kingdoms. Every figure within freezes as if caught in amber.

Margaret's gaze sweeps the scene. Hélène's careful stillness at the writing desk, shoulders held too rigid, the sheen of perspiration along her hairline despite the chamber's coolness. The guard's uncomfortable stance, loose leather still clutched in his hands. Ysabel's fan fluttering with agitated energy.

"Who ordered what?"

The guard straightens, mail catching afternoon light. His voice emerges stiff. "Her Highness, Your Grace."

Margaret's attention shifts to Ysabel, whose dark eyes flash with indignation and something sharper. Fear, perhaps, or calculation. The Spanish princess opens her mouth, but Margaret's slight lift of one hand forestalls any explanation.

"England does not correct loyalty with a whip," Margaret says, her voice bite's harsher than it ever has. "And certainly never a lady."

Ysabel's spine straightens, her fan snapping shut with unconcealed irritation. Color rises in her cheeks as she steps forward, silk rustling with each carefully measured movement.

"Your Grace, in my father's court, such disobedience requires firm correction. Spanish custom—"

"You mistake yourself." Margaret's voice cuts through the explanation. "This is England's house. England's customs. England's rules." Each word falls with the weight of iron, brooking no argument. "You were reminded of this truth on your first day. You should have remembered."

Ysabel's mouth opens, then closes. The fan trembles slightly in her grip. Irritation and pride melting into fear.

Margaret's gaze never wavers. "Actions bear consequences, Your Highness. Even royal ones."

The threat hangs in the air, unspoken yet unmistakable. Margaret turns toward Hélène, her voice softening only by degrees.

"Lady Hélène goes now to the Archbishop's care, pending the King's word. She is under my protection."

"She—" Ysabel begins, desperation creeping into her tone.

"—will walk." Margaret's words carry as final as a church bell's toll. "Unburdened. As befits her station."

Hélène rises slowly, her movements careful but dignified. The guard steps up. He unfastens his cloak with swift, respectful movements and extends it toward Hélène.

"My Lady," he says quietly, his voice rough with something that might be shame. "The blood shows through your gown. Please, allow me."

Margaret leads them through the shadowed corridor, her steps measured and deliberate. The guard falls in behind, his mail muffled against stone. Hélène steps between them with measured poise, each stride effortless despite her recent ordeal. Only the faint sheen along her temples betrays the effort.

They keep to the outer walls where fewer courtiers venture, avoiding the main passages that hum with afternoon traffic. Margaret's practiced eye notes every junction, every alcove where curious ears might lurk. The castle holds its breath around them.

At the narrow stair's head, Margaret pauses. Below, a familiar figure emerges from the shadows. Anselm, his robes dark against pale stone. Agnes hovers at his shoulder, worry etched in every line of her face.

The Archbishop's gaze lifts to meet Margaret's, then shifts to Hélène. His eyes hold both verdict and mercy, understanding written in their depths without need for explanation.

"We'll take the servants' passages to the kitchens and call for a wagon from there," Margaret commands quietly. To Anselm, "Keep her in your residence until the King says otherwise."

Anselm inclines his head. When he speaks, his voice carries the gentle authority of sanctuary offered. "My house is quieter than pain."

Agnes moves to Hélène's shoulder, her touch feather-light yet steady. Her voice drops to barely a whisper. "I have you."

Hélène's mouth curves in the faintest smile. "You always do."

The servants' entrance opens onto a narrow courtyard where autumn air carries the scent of wood smoke and bread from the kitchen within. Margaret positions herself between the doorway and the stone wall, creating a pocket of privacy while Agnes settles Hélène on a low step. The guard takes post at the courtyard's mouth, his back turned but ears alert.

A queen dowager escorting an injured noblewoman through servants' passages will set tongues wagging. Given the maid's breathless urgency when summoning Margaret, she suspects the tale will have reached every corner of the castle before the evening meal.

Margaret studies Hélène's composed features, the careful set of her shoulders, the steady rhythm of her breathing despite what she has endured. No tears, no trembling. Only that same quiet authority Margaret witnessed during the morning rounds.

"You could have stopped them."

The words fall without demand or accusation, merely observation offered in the space between judgment and understanding.

Hélène meets her gaze directly, no evasion in her voice when she answers. "A lady cannot. A weapon could. I chose the lady."

Margaret's fan rises from her belt, tapping once against her wrist. A single, deliberate motion that speaks volumes in the language only court women understand. The choice is acknowledged. The sacrifice recognized.

"We will remember this choice. Others will, too."

The wagon's wheels announce its approach across cobblestones, wood creaking under careful guidance. Agnes rises first, moving to assist as the driver pulls the horse to a stop. The guard steps forward, his movements respectful.

"My Lady," he says quietly, offering his arm. "Allow me."

Hélène accepts his support, settling onto the wagon's simple bench as Agnes arranges linens around her for comfort. The afternoon light catches the guard's agitated features as he steps back.

"If you please, sir," Hélène requests the guard, her voice carrying clearly despite its softness. "Would you see that Sir Roland comes to the Archbishop's residence? He should know where I am."

Margaret's fan stills. The realization strikes forcefully. Roland returned with Alaric in the pre-dawn hours, yet Hélène has been about her duties since first light. No reunion, no shared relief at his safe return, no discussion on the Grey Hunter. Only service, as always.

"It will be arranged," Margaret confirms, her voice gentle with new understanding.

Anselm moves into the front seat by the driver, and Agnes settles beside Hélène. As the driver takes up his reins, Margaret steps closer. Her words carry the weight of royal promise, spoken low enough for Hélène alone.

"Rest. Justice will walk at a measured pace and arrive in due course."

The wagon rolls forward, wheels finding their rhythm against stone. Margaret watches until it disappears beyond the gatehouse arch, then turns toward the castle's heart where other conversations await. And other's choices must be weighed.

King Alaric

The council chamber feels stripped of its usual ceremony this morning. No banners, no formal procession, just six men around oak scarred by years of careful decisions. Alaric settles into his chair as autumn light filters through narrow windows, casting long shadows across parchment and seal.

The memory of Hélène's composed face haunts him still. Yesterday morning he had watched her move through the castle's veins with quiet authority, solving problems that kept the realm fed and safe. Hours later, she endured punishment for that very diligence. The rage that consumed him when his Mother brought word still simmers beneath his ribs, but this moment demands precision, not passion.

He has spent the dark hours since in careful consultation under the Queen Dowager's measured counsel and Anselm's moral clarity. Each conversation carved away doubt until only necessity remained. His council's backing is essential for action against Ysabel.

"We speak plainly," Alaric begins, his voice carrying the weight of a decision already made. "The realm will feel it plainly."

Master Theobald's quill hovers over fresh parchment, ready to record what follows. Geoffrey shifts in his seat, understanding the gravity without yet knowing its shape. Both Reginald and Ranulf preserve the watchful quiet of men long-seasoned in royal counsel, yet their gazes carry unspoken inquiries.

Anselm rises with deliberate grace, his hands folded within his sleeves. When he speaks, each word falls with the precision of judgment rendered after prayer.

"Lady Hélène of Montbois was beaten yesterday on the orders of Princess Ysabel. The lady had committed no offense save the faithful execution of duties assigned. She bore five lashes with prior injury that the Princess was informed of. Yet when the lashes were done, she was callously commanded to continue her daily duties. Not one, or two, but three choices in a day that speak to the Princess's character." His pause lets that sink into the chamber's silence. "Pain was ordered where diligence stood. That is not queenship."

The Archbishop's words hang in the morning air like incense, sacred and irrefutable. Alaric feels the truth of them settle into his bones, strengthening resolve that needed no strengthening.

"I have seen what passes for governance in my absence," Alaric continues, his voice carrying the tone of royal decree. "Credit claimed for work not done. Cruelty visited upon competence. A hand that holds power only to strike those beneath it." He meets each pair of eyes in turn. "I will not set a crown upon a hand that holds a whip."

Geoffrey's sharp intake of breath is the only sound. Even Ranulf, who prizes stability above all else, nods slowly as the implications crystallize. Anselm steps forward, his voice carrying both legal certainty and pastoral care.

"The betrothal may be dissolved for grave unfitness without scandal to either crown. Canon law provides clear ground when character proves incompatible with sacred duty." His fingers touch the leather portfolio at his side. "We will write to Spain with respect, and with truth."

Reginald leans forward, his weathered hands flat against the oak. Years of negotiation have taught him to name costs before they compound. "Storms may gather, Sire. Spanish pride runs deep as their harbors. Trade agreements, shipping routes through their waters. All may feel the chill of this decision."

Alaric meets his counselor's steady gaze. Reginald speaks truth, as always, yet some foundations matter more than comfort.

"Then our roofs must be tight."

Geoffrey shifts in his chair, his voice carrying the weight of recent observation.

"The castle folk speak in whispers, but their words are clear. They have seen competence rewarded with cruelty, diligence answered with violence." His young face hardens with conviction beyond his years. "If cruelty sits the throne, men will look away when justice speaks."

The room holds that truth like a held breath. Alaric feels the rightness of it settle into his chest, joining the certainty that has grown through sleepless hours. A king who tolerates injustice breeds subjects who expect it.

He rises, and the formality of the gesture brings every man to attention. "The betrothal is to be dissolved. Her Highness will be treated with the honor due her birth and no power over my house."

The words resolve like stone set into mortar. Theobald's quill scratches across parchment, recording the decision that will reshape two kingdoms' expectations.

Anselm inclines his head with sincere approval. "Respectful parchment quells louder storms. I will write to Archbishop Rodrigo in terms that honor both crowns while speaking plainly of unfitness."

Reginald's fingers drum once against the table, his only concession to nerves, before he straightens with purpose. "I will choose ink that calms. Don Íñigo will hear measured reasons, not royal fury. The language of diplomats can soften even bitter wine."

Geoffrey nods toward the chamber's door, beyond which the castle waits for direction. "And I will choose wine that listens. The hall will know the King's justice without tasting the King's anger."

Alaric feels the machinery of governance align behind his will. Each man understands his part in the careful choreography that will transform royal decree into lived reality.

"Let it be known: mercy and order are my fashion. The court that serves this crown will reflect that truth in every chamber, every corridor, every choice made in my name."

The chamber's silence shifts like weather changing. Where tension had knotted the air, resolve now settles.

Geoffrey's voice drops to barely above a whisper. "The house will breathe."

"Then let it."

Alaric looks toward the windows where morning light grows stronger. He envisions the castle as it ought to be, its corridors alive with quiet confidence, where fear no longer shadows the work of capable hands.

Promises and Partings

- 24 -

Sir Roland of Montbois

The treeline holds Roland like a confessional. Dark enough for honesty, close enough to the castle for duty. His boots wear a familiar path through the undergrowth, ten paces out, ten paces back, marking time while his mind churns through calculations that never balance.

Five days since Hélène defeated the Grey Hunter. Two since Ysabel's whip marked her back. The numbers stack like accusations in his chest, each one proof that he's failed the most basic promise siblings make: to keep each other safe.

His fingers find the suit's collar beneath his guard's tunic, the future fabric warm against medieval wool. Instinct dressed him this way since the Hunter's attack. Half preparation and half prayer that the Ancients would finally return with answers instead of riddles.

The forest shifts around him. Owls fall silent mid-call. Mist rises from nothing, ankle-deep, carrying the scent of storms that haven't fallen.

Roland's hand finds his sword hilt as the pale figure steps from shadow like moonlight given form. The Ancient moves with that same serene grace, white hair flowing like spilled starlight, those galaxy-deep eyes fixed on Roland with terrible understanding.

"We bring what was promised."

Light blooms in the Ancient's palm. A replacement crystal for his timeband. Its crystalline surface glowing. His hands shake as he reaches for the thin blue device.

The module slides into his suit's depression like a key finding its lock. Power floods other dormant systems. For one wild moment, hope flares bright enough to burn.

"Enough energy for us both?"

His voice cracks on the question. Hope lay bare on his face. The Ancient's expression doesn't change. No pity, no comfort.

"She must stay."

Despite already knowing the answer, the words still hit like hammer blows. Roland's anger rises, hot and desperate, but he holds it tight behind his teeth. Rage won't move beings who measure time in geological epochs.

"Say why."

"Because history remembers her face."

The phrase returns like a curse made manifest. Roland tastes copper, realizes he's bitten his tongue hard enough to bleed. History's thread. Hélène woven into time itself while he remains invisible, forgettable, as it should have been for both of them.

"And forgets mine?" The bitterness cuts deeper than any blade.

The Ancient regards him with something that might be sympathy in a being capable of such emotions. "Memory chooses function. You carry the message. She carries the time."

That spot the Ancient touched weeks ago, the mark he'd almost forgotten, begins to burn hotter with each passing heartbeat.

"Doors will close. We close them."

Roland's throat tightens. "When?"

"Soon enough that your choice must be now."

The words wash over him, and the fear of losing Elaine Rush to Hélène Montbois hits his stomach's bottom once more. Roland's hands clench at his sides as he attempts to bargain with time itself.

"I'll watch over—"

"You would break what keeps her alive."

The Ancient's voice carries gentle reminder wrapped in inevitability, like a physician delivering a terminal verdict with practiced compassion. Roland feels the truth of it settling in his bones. His presence here disrupts whatever delicate weaving holds Hélène's thread intact.

His voice drops to barely a whisper. "Can I tell her? Say goodbye?"

Something shifts in those galaxy-deep eyes. Permission, perhaps. Or pity.

"The truth will no longer harm her fate."

Small mercy. Roland's chest loosens enough to draw proper breath, though the relief tastes bitter. At least he won't have to lie to her face when he disappears.

"How do I reach her afterward? Send word?"

The Ancient's head tilts slightly, considering. "Not all doors are time. Some are stone and paint, some are in a shard. Find the legal places where memory travels."

Riddles. Always riddles with these beings. Roland swallows his frustration, files the cryptic words away for later parsing. The mark grows warmer, and the time band emits a low, musical tone.

"When it chimes the second time, depart soon after. Delay breaks the bargain, and your fates."

The timeband counts down a half hour. Thirty minutes to pack a lifetime of brotherly devotion into words that won't shatter them both. Fate can be cruel. Roland squares his shoulders, meets those ancient eyes with something approaching dignity.

"I will go...and I will reach her."

The forest exhales around them, mist swirling as the pale figure begins to thin like dawn fog dissolving. Roland blinks, and the Ancient is gone, leaving only the light scent of a late summer storm.

Footsteps crunch through underbrush behind him. Roland turns to find Denby emerging from the treeline, his aged face pale as parchment, eyes wide with the shock of witnessing something that shouldn't exist.

"Fetch the King," Roland says quietly. "Have him meet me at Anselm's residence."

Denby nods without question, understanding written in the set of his shoulders. He's seen enough tonight to know some orders require no explanation.

Roland braces himself for what comes next.

Lady Hélène of Montbois

The fire burns low in the small sitting room of Archbishop Anselm's residence. Salves rest undisturbed on a side table beside folded linen and a fresh bowl of water. A testament to two days of careful recovery. Hélène's lightly reclines against cushions on the chaise, careful not to agitate the welts across her back. The welts quickly dulled from angry red to mottled purple, tender but no longer blazing.

Given her enhanced healing capabilities, she should have recovered from the Grey Hunter's assault and Ysabel's beating far more swiftly, yet she has not. She and Roland puzzle over whether the wretched fever she contracted upon their arrival might have disrupted her cellular repair nanobots. But then they contemplate the circumstances of their arrival here, an unauthorized passage of three forms thrust across centuries by a single time crystal. She remembers her body sensation as though lightning had coursed through her upon landing. Though it vanished instantly, leading her to believe her equipment had malfunctioned. Such an occurrence had never transpired during temporal transit previously, and she assumed it was due the Grey Hunter's timeband not have been calibrated for multiple travelers.

Anselm's voice carries soft and steady from his chair by the hearth, reading scripture in Latin with the same ease as speaking his mother tongue. The familiar cadence soothes her more than any salve, though she understands only fragments. Something about refuge and shelter.

A soft knock interrupts the holy words. Anselm rises, murmurs briefly with someone beyond the door, then steps aside as Roland enters. His face carries the same hard mask their father wore during combat drills: jaw set, eyes distant. But underneath, Hélène reads pain deeper than any blade could carve.

"Elaine."

Her given name falls from his lips like a prayer spoken before bad tidings. She shifts carefully against her pillows, feeling the protest of healing skin.

"Adrian."

He crosses the room in three swift strides, drops to his knees and takes her hands in his. His fingers shake against her palms, and the sight sends ice up her spine. Roland's hands never shake.

"They found a way." His voice barely holds steady. "For me. I have to go, now, to make the rest possible."

He rolls back his sleeve, and her breath catches. The timeband gleams against his forearm, its crystalline surface glowing with that familiar blue light. The sight should bring comfort, but instead all that fills her mind are his words: *I have to leave now.* Dread settles heavy in her chest.

"How long?"

Roland glances at the display. "Twenty-three minutes left."

The number hits like a physical blow. Twenty-three minutes…

"And for me?"

The question hangs between them, weighted with everything neither can say aloud. Roland's gaze holds hers, steady despite the storm she reads beneath.

"I will reach you. I don't know how yet. But I will."

She's never seen her brother in such pain. Not when their father died, not when their mother's ship disappeared beyond Martian orbit, not even during their worst missions. The sight cracks something in her chest, but Agents of Time don't break. They adapt.

"Well." She manages a crooked smile. "At least I'll have decent food while I wait. Medieval bread may be coarse, but it's not freeze-dried rations."

Relief flickers across his features at her attempt at humor. The familiar rhythm of their banter, their shared language of deflection and care. But something darker lurks behind his eyes, and the corner of his right eye twitches, barely perceptible, but she knows every tell he carries.

Fear washes over her, cold and certain. This isn't temporary separation. This is goodbye, possibly forever. The thought terrifies her, and a deep sorrow threatens to take its place. Roland wouldn't leave her side unless circumstances offered no other choice. If he must go, then time itself demands it.

"Try not to collect arrows," she says, voice dry as dust. "They still don't flatter the shoulders."

His answering smile carries genuine warmth for the first time since he entered, and he simply promises that he won't.

"At least you don't have to worry about peacocks at court anymore," he says.

"True," she replies. "No more Spanish weather to endure either."

Roland relaxes more after their sibling banter. They're quiet for a few minutes.

"Tell Trinity I said hello," she says finally. "When you see her."

"I will." His voice carries a hint of his old humor. "I'm looking forward to not cleaning up after you and her for a while."

Then his eyes turn down.

Hélène catches the weight behind those words, *for a while*, and how his gaze drops away. The sorrow settles into her bones. He is not returning for her. She permits the tears to fall, yet makes no sound. Only quiet weeping as they remain wordless together.

A quiet knock interrupts their silence. Anselm opens the door to admit Sir Denby and King Alaric, the later's gaze immediately finds the glowing timeband on Roland's arm. The King's breath draws deep, his expression shifting to one of understanding rather than surprise. A recognition that requires no explanations.

"You go with my thanks, and my expectation that your word returns," Alaric says, his voice carrying the weight of royal command wrapped in personal trust.

Roland inclines his head with the respect due a sovereign. "It will."

Anselm steps forward, producing a folded parchment bearing the Queen Dowager's seal. The red wax catches the firelight as he extends it toward Hélène.

"Her Grace requests your service as her Lady-in-Waiting. Name, room, duties. It's all here."

Hélène accepts the document with careful hands, feeling its weight. Not just parchment and ink, but purpose and place in this world that has become hers. She breathes in slowly, steadying herself.

"Then I will serve and learn to do it well."

Roland stands and moves toward her. She rises carefully, mindful of her healing back, and they face each other as they have countless times before missions that might end in separation or death. Their foreheads touch in the ritual their father taught them, the gesture that says what words cannot.

"I will find you," Roland whispers, voice low and certain.

Her response comes steady despite the tears that threaten. "I will hold the house."

The promises of siblings who have learned to trust in duty when comfort fails.

Anselm draws a small sign in the air. Not the elaborate blessing of ceremony, but something simpler and more profound. Human care wrapped in sacred gesture. "Go without fear. Stay without bitterness."

Hélène reaches beneath a cloth and withdraws a small eating-knife. Its bone handle worn smooth by countless meals. She presses the hilt into Roland's palm, watching his fingers close around it.

"In case promises need cutting free."

His mouth quirks in that familiar half-smile. "Or bread."

Roland draws her close one final time, his arms encircling her through these last precious moments. No words remain between them. The timeband chimes softly, signaling the approaching convergence of temporal pathways. Thirty heartbeats separate him from the moment he must activate the device and surrender to destiny's pull.

Roland moves to a corner of the room, away from them all. The timeband's glow intensifies, casting blue shadows on the timber walls. Hélène meets his eyes across the small space and nods once. Acceptance, permission, farewell.

He makes the fateful selection on his time band. The device begins its countdown with five clear beats. On the final, soft white light explodes around Roland's form, brilliant and brief as lightning. When it fades, the corner stands empty.

More silent tears trace down Hélène's cheeks. Alaric's hand settles gently on her shoulder, warm and steady in the sudden quiet.

Adrian Rush (Sir Roland de Montbois)

White noise fractures into meaning as his vision clears from the temporal transit. Sterile fluorescent light replaces the warm amber of Anselm's home, and his suit's HUD climbs from static snow to operational green. The familiar hum of headquarters fills his ears.

"Core restored. Temporal egress complete," announces the system's flat synthetic voice.

He steadies himself against the transit platform's rail, muscles still remembering Elaine's final embrace. The bone-handled knife rests solid in his palm. Ten centuries of separation condensed into worn ivory and steel.

Behind reinforced glass, voices carry sharp urgency through the observation deck's speakers. A passing agent acknowledges his return with a brief nod. "Rush."

Adrian Rush, he reflects inwardly. Not Roland Montbois anymore.

What strikes him most is the passing agent's casual greeting, his easy assumption of continuity. To everyone here, he departed yesterday on standard reconnaissance. They cannot see the months etched into his posture or smell the castle's wood smoke still clinging to his gear.

"Seal protocol goes live in twelve hours," a tech calls through the intercom, words clipped and professional.

The passing agent approaches a bustling technician in the control center. No inquiry proves necessary. The technician straightens, "Sergeant, every unsanctioned pathway has been terminated. All sanctioned pathways and memory lanes remain open until the seal protocol goes live."

The Ancient's warning echoes in Adrian's mind: *She must stay.* The temporal seal isn't just procedure. It's permanence.

What to do? The Ancient's words surface like bubbles breaking in dark water: *stone and paint* and *history remembers her face.*

Roland moves to the nearest database terminal, fingers finding familiar keys. The interface responds with clinical efficiency.

"Query. Artifacts from the court of King Alaric, Medieval England. Prioritize stonework and painted objects. Full provenance."

"Results: 27. Filters applied: 'stone', 'paint', 'court usage'."

The wall screen flickers to life, thumbnails cascading across its surface like scattered memories. A carved corbel with red pigment traces. Chapel plaster fragments bearing faded angels. A seal-ring catching light. Lead tokens worn smooth by centuries of handling. Tapestry cartoons sketched in charcoal and ochre.

His breath catches as one image expands unbidden. A painted oak panel, colors still vivid despite the centuries. An aged queen stands beside an equally aged Alaric. The familiarity in her eyes, the jawline, the subtle curve of her smile.

"Mother." The word escapes before he can stop it. He corrects himself, voice dropping to a whisper. "Elaine."

The metadata scrolls beneath the portrait: "Attributed: Workshop of St. Guthlac. 'King Alaric and Consort' (late reign)."

His fingers trace the screen, along the contour of her chin down to a dark gem suspended from her neck on an unadorned chain. The piece seems known to him. He'd glimpsed a similar jewel adorning an elderly woman in the castle's portraits.

"If history remembers her face, it remembered this."

Adrian's fingers hover over the console, mind racing through temporal protocols. Unsanctioned time gates remain sealed, and he won't get approval for a sanctioned one in time. But conservation work operates on different channels, threading through legal memory lanes that bypass the gates entirely.

"Not a door. A keyhole." He whispers to himself. The next query spills from his lips before he's fully thought it. "Search for a signal on the conservation pipelines."

His hands begin navigating deeper into the archival systems. Museum pulls, spectral analysis feeds, restoration workflows. All sanctioned pathways that historians use to study artifacts without temporal interference. The console chirps, a soft acknowledgment that makes his breath catch.

"Residual interface: H-Δ band. Weak but present."

Elaine's broken timeband. Even shattered, it still whispers across centuries, a faint digital heartbeat waiting for connection.

"Route a packet delivery to that signature. Trigger on the portrait's spectral scan. Twenty-five years prior."

The system accepts his commands, routing protocols falling into place like puzzle pieces. After the museum archive scans the portrait, checking pigments and analyzing brushwork to determine a more accurate creation date, his message will piggyback on the frequencies seeking the broken band's resonance approximately twenty-five years before the portrait's creation. When the woman was still young.

He opens a voice recorder, cursor blinking expectantly. Truth wars with mercy in his chest.

"Elaine, I—"

The words stick. What can he say? That she's trapped? That time itself conspired to keep her there? He stops the recording.

"No. Proof first. Words after."

He stages the transmission carefully: portrait scan triggers packet delivery to band signature. Simple. Clean. Surgical.

Footsteps echo behind him. Trinity's voice cuts through his concentration.

"Adrian. Where's Elaine?"

He turns, meeting her steady gaze. The recap tumbles out in clipped, professional terms. The Grey Hunter's attack on reconnaissance and the accidental temporal slip. Four months trapped in thirteenth-century England. The Hunter's return. His elimination. The Ancient's verdict and the sealed path home.

"Elaine's fate was already woven into time. The Ancient wouldn't permit her return."

Trinity nods, understanding flickering in her eyes. She's seen temporal paradoxes before, knows the weight of immutable threads. He shows her the screen: the portrait, the staged message, the delicate pathway through conservation channels.

"You're threading a needle."

"I'm sending a promise through the eye."

His finger hovers over the execute command. Once sent, the message will wait in digital limbo, patient as stone, until conservation channels deliver it. Though when that might reach her, Adrian cannot say. He hopes Elaine won't have to wait long for his message.

He finishes the recording, then presses the key.

The packet vanishes into the conservation pipeline, carrying hope backwards across the centuries. Somewhere in medieval England, Elaine continues her morning rounds, unaware that her brother fights time itself to reach her.

Maybe someday, he'll find another keyhole.

A House Set in Order

- 25 -

Alice Whitcombe

Alice moves through the kitchens like a shepherd through scattered sheep, her ear catching every murmur that drifts above the clatter of morning work. The word she dreads hovers at tongue-tips, *vanished*, ready to spill into something wild and untrue.

"He didn't vanish. He departed. Words are horses. Use the ones that don't bolt." Her voice carries just enough authority to turn heads without seeming sharp.

A scullion pauses mid-scrub, and Tom shifts his water buckets to listen. Agnes rolls fresh linen at the long table. No flutter in her hands, no worry creasing her brow. The very picture of a house that knows its business.

"Sir Roland returns to France. Lady Hélène stays and serves." Agnes adds with a steady voice. No hints of worry or deception.

Alice nods, letting the simple truth settle like flour through a sieve. "A house prefers facts to fairy tales."

Near the bread ovens, Maud leans close to another kitchen maid, her voice dropping to that dangerous whisper Alice knows too well. "Ran off to dodge scandal, you think?"

Alice steps closer, her tone gentle as a mother correcting a wayward child. "Royal duty concluded. Write that on your loaf, not the other thing."

Alan Thatcher arrives from his morning footman duties, wood clattering as he sets down his burden. He grins at the assembled kitchen folk.

"Bess near took some poor traveler's fingers clean off when he reached for her morning bread the other mornin'. Though word has it our 'traveler' was trailing Lady Hélène's shadow as His Majesty in disguise."

Alice cannot fathom why the King would skulk about in borrowed clothes, though other rumors have begun regarding his gentle flirtations while so disguised.

"Captain Spoon stands ready for any hungry king." Bess responds with mild theatrical gravity.

Alice feels her shoulders ease at their banter. This is the castle's true heartbeat, steady as sunrise. She moves toward Bess with the half-smile that says *all is well*.

"Promote her to Admiral if breakfast runs long."

The jest draws chuckles from the bread ovens, where Maud's earlier whispers have dissolved into the safer rhythm of kneading. Alice marks it as a small victory. Laughter over gossip, always.

Footsteps on stone announce Meg's approach, her arms laden with silver trays that catch the morning light. The younger woman's face carries that careful calm Alice has learned to read like weather signs. No storm, but clouds passing.

"Weather: calm. Work: brisk."

The coded phrase tells Alice what the castle already knows in whispers. Princess Ysabel has been confined to chambers. Alice nods, her smile warming. "Fine sailing, then."

Agnes looks up from her linen, a small scroll resting beside her work basket. The parchment bears the Queen Dowager's seal, still sharp-edged from recent breaking. "Lady-in-Waiting. Accepted."

Alice steps closer to examine the writ, though she needs no proof beyond Agnes's steady manner. The appointment surprises no one who has watched the castle's true governance these past weeks. The staff will be happy to have Lady Hélène's continued governance.

"So the ledger remembers who does the work."

Meg sets her trays on the washing table with care, each piece placed just so. When she speaks, her voice carries the weight of hard-won wisdom. "We carry bread, not knives."

Alice meets the younger woman's gaze, understanding the counsel beneath. The Princess may be caged, but caged things sometimes bite. "And slice only where needed."

Though the slice has already been made, Alice thinks, watching steam rise from fresh honey loaves. The King's blade fell clean and sure. Now comes the work of binding wounds and building anew.

She clears her throat and addresses the kitchen as whole: "What is our creed?" she demands.

"We follow the one who fixes the leak."

"Aye. Now back to it. Let the castle hear gratitude, not guesses."

The kitchen settles into its morning song, voices finding their proper pitch between duty and discretion. Alice moves toward the service passage, her voice carrying to every corner.

Lord Reginald of Redwyke

The Spanish Ambassador's diplomatic chambers carry the weight of wounded pride like thick incense, impossible to ignore. Reginald studies the two letters resting beside the leather-bound ledger, their seals already broken, contents digested and found bitter. The morning light through narrow windows illuminates dust motes that seem to hang as still as the diplomatic silence.

Don Íñigo paces in front with the stride of a man containing fury behind courtly facade. His dark eyes sweep over the assembled council. Anselm in his ecclesiastical robes, the Queen Dowager and King Alaric both in austere burgundy, Reginald himself in the heavy dark blue velvets that mark serious business.

"Your Excellency." Reginald begins, his voice firm with authority but shaped to leave the edges of the deal undefined.

"Let us call this what it is: A slight." Don Íñigo words cut sharp.

Reginald feels the familiar tightness in his chest that comes before delicate negotiations fracture into open hostility. Spain's temper has been pricked. Now comes the careful work of bloodletting without severing the vein entirely.

Anselm steps forward, his voice carrying that peculiar calm that makes even kings pause to listen. "It is a correction of fitness, not a quarrel with Spain."

The Queen Dowager's silk rustles as she moves closer to the central table, her presence adding weight to the Archbishop's words. "Her Highness departs with respect, not rebuke."

Don Íñigo's gaze shifts to the ledger, his jaw tightening as though the parchment itself has insulted his own lineage. Reginald opens the bound volume, turning pages that whisper secrets more damning than any courtly accusation.

"Rota schedules in another's hand. Staff attestations signed by those who never benefited from Her Highness's... supervision."

His finger traces the careful script documenting morning rounds, grain tallies, infirmary visits. All bearing witness to labor performed by hands other than those claiming credit.

"And here, graver still," Reginald continues, his voice dropping to the tone reserved for accusations that cannot be left unspoken. "Claims that Spanish courts permit the flogging of noble attendants for trifling faults. Testimony that Lady Colette was commanded to serve as common maid, her birth forgotten."

"These are not the customs of any court I know," Anselm interjects quietly, his voice carrying the authority of one familiar with diplomatic protocol across Christendom. "Spain honors rank as we do."

"A queen must know the weight of ledgers as well as crowns," Alaric says, his voice carrying like well-known wisdom. "Ysabel's failures prove what the realm requires. Substance, not ornament. A woman who can read the true health of granaries and guard rotas, who earns loyalty through deed rather than demand."

"Our submitted proofs will be dulled on purpose, of court. Bread tallies and duty rolls rather than *other* courtly performances." Reginald interjects.

The Ambassador's nostrils flare like a stallion scenting battle, yet Reginald watches calculation temper the fire in those dark eyes. Spain's pride demands satisfaction, but practical men know when to seek graceful retreat rather than a victory that costs more than it gives.

"Dullness can wound more than swords." Don Íñigo's fired gaze holds Reginald's, but his tone is reserved.

"And heals quicker." Anselm's voice carries the gentle authority that has counselled two kings.

The chamber holds its breath. Reginald feels the delicate balance of a moment where one wrong word could shatter careful diplomacy, yet silence might be read as contempt. Don Íñigo's fingers drum once against his belt, then still.

His nod comes slowly. Eyes hot but undeniably practical.

"We shall answer with courtesy…and prompt coaches."

The soft rustle of fabric draws Reginald's attention to the corner where Lady Colette has sat silent as stone throughout the proceedings. Her hands rest folded in her lap, yet something shifts in her posture. A straightening of shoulders that speaks of resolve gathering like water behind a dam.

"Je… I request… Angleterre protection."

The words stumble forth in broken and heavily accented English, each syllable carefully formed yet trembling with effort. Reginald watches the Queen Dowager's expression soften with understanding.

"En français, mon enfant. Quelle est votre requête?"

Relief floods Colette's features as she straightens, finding her voice in her native tongue.

"Je supplie Votre Grâce de me permettre de demeurer en Angleterre sous votre protection, plutôt que de retourner en Espagne."

The young French noblewoman requests sanctuary in English court. The Queen Dowager's eyes flick toward King Alaric, a momentary consultation, to which he nods approval.

"Lady Colette de Brissac shall remain at court under my protection. Your conduct recommends you to our favour."

The declaration rings with royal authority, ensuring all present understand the grant of sanctuary. Reginald notes the careful phrasing. No criticism of Spain implied, merely acknowledgment of service rendered. Don Íñigo's expression remains neutral, though his shoulders ease fractionally.

"Lady Colette, you shall take English lessons with Lady Hélène, as she is the only French noblewoman still remaining at court."

Reginald turns back to the council ledger to ink the day's final decisions. "Ink that calms has been chosen."

The Ambassador exhales slowly, the sound carrying nights of accumulated tension. "Then let it dry quickly."

Anselm steps forward, his voice carrying the particular authority that only one prelate addressing another can convey. "A message to Spain's Archbishop. Brother to brother. Truth without bile."

Reginald recognizes the careful distinction. Diplomacy for courts, honesty for clerics. Spain's Archbishop will know exactly why Princess Ysabel departs, stripped of the gentle euphemisms that preserve royal dignity.

The clerk appears as though summoned by invisible signal, sprinkling sand across the fresh documents. Parchment whispers as pages settle into permanence. Reginald follows the Queen Dowager toward the door, noting how the chamber's atmosphere shifts as authority withdraws.

In the hallway's cooler air, Margaret's voice drops to the intimate register reserved for trusted advisors. "Storm diverted, rain gathered."

Reginald nods, understanding flooding through him. The crisis has passed, but consequences remain. They fall gently now, no longer in torrents that could drown kingdoms.

Lady Hélène of Montbois

The Queen Dowager's solar holds a quality of light that seems to approve of honest work. Afternoon sun slants through tall windows, warming the writing desk where Hélène bends over fresh parchment, quill scratching methodically across the surface. Each line of the updated rota carries weight. Not just duty assignments, but the architecture of a household that actually functions.

The Queen Dowager watches from her embroidery frame, needle pausing mid-stitch as Hélène's suggestions take shape in careful script. Hélène has settled well into the role of Lady-In-Waiting these past three weeks. The Queen no longer hovers during their late morning rota review. Ysabel still remains locked in her quarters. The Spanish monarch having delayed the retrieval of his daughter, though Hélène is not sure whether it was to punish Ysabel or in hopes England would change its mind.

"A complaint coffer," Hélène murmurs, glancing up. "Simple wooden box in the great hall. Fair complaint slips, signed or anonymous."

The Queen Dowager's eyebrows lift with interest. "Justice needs a small door."

Meg, arranging fresh linens nearby, catches the exchange and adds quietly, "And a lock that opens."

Hélène nods, already moving to the next item. Her quill dips again, forming letters that will reshape castle routine. "Numbered tags for every sack in stores. Missing tallies outlawed entirely. No exceptions, no excuses."

The logic flows as easily as ink. Too many mysteries hide in unmarked grain, too many questions arise when counts go missing. "Lost paper breeds rumors. Found paper breeds dinner."

Agnes, entering with afternoon refreshments, catches the phrase and her face brightens with genuine pleasure. "The kitchens will eat that proverb."

The warmth in the maid's voice confirms what Hélène already knows. Staff hunger for clarity as much as bread. She continues writing, momentum building as each improvement suggests the next.

"Infirmary standards for clean linen stocked daily and all salves logged with dates and sources. Request better quality supplies from the herbalist in town rather than making do with castle-grown remedies."

The Queen Dowager's needle resumes its steady rhythm, approval radiating from her composed silence.

"Sand barrels in the granaries and armory replaced every few months. Dampness makes the sand clump, and clumped sand won't smother flames."

Hélène sets down her quill, satisfaction warming her chest as the Queen nods approvingly at the completed suggestions.

"Your competence in such matters grows daily," the Queen Dowager says, her tone carrying genuine respect. "These improvements will serve the castle well."

Hélène cannot resist the quip. The scars still too fresh. "Better than certain Spanish approaches to household—"

The Queen Dowager's fan taps once against her wrist, sharp and precise. The signal stops Hélène mid-sentence.

"One jest per hour," she says dryly, though her eyes hold amusement. "We've already spent yours on yesterday's bread rationing comment."

Hélène grins, unrepentant. "I'll write them smaller next time. Fit more into the allowance."

The Queen Dowager's mouth quirks upward despite herself.

The solar's door opens with a soft creak, and Alaric steps inside. His boots carry traces of mud from the training yard, and his doublet bears the wrinkled evidence of a morning spent reviewing guard rotations. The Queen Dowager's eyes narrow slightly at his informal appearance. This is her domain, where protocol matters.

Alaric pauses, clearly reading his mother's expression, then straightens with visible effort. "Mother, I've just signed the provisioning charter for Master Lucien's routes. The merchant networks will serve the crown's needs well."

His gaze flickers toward Hélène, and something softens his features. Then vanishes as quickly as it came.

The Queen Dowager's fan rests motionless against her wrist. "Indeed. And you chose to share this news in person because...?"

"The matter seemed worthy of immediate report."

The explanation sounds thin even to Hélène's ears, but the Queen Dowager merely inclines her head with regal patience. "Since you are here, perhaps you would review Lady Hélène's suggestions for the household rota."

Hélène lifts the parchment, her voice steady as she reads aloud the improvements for complaint coffers, tagged stores, infirmary standards, and fresh sand barrels. Each item receives Alaric's thoughtful attention, his nods growing more frequent as the list progresses.

"Sensible measures," he says when she finishes. "The castle will run more smoothly."

The Queen Dowager's seal finds warm wax, pressing the royal approval into permanence. The rota becomes law with that simple gesture.

"I'll carry this to Lord Reginald," Alaric offers, accepting the sealed document. "He'll want to coordinate implementation with the senior staff."

The Queen Dowager's slight smile suggests she recognizes the offer as something more. Yet she merely waves her hand in dismissal. "Go then. Duty calls."

After Alaric departs, Hélène turns to her remaining tasks with brisk efficiency. The afternoon's work requires delegation, and she has learned to trust the right hands.

"Meg, the noon weather needs your attention. Note staff temperature and any brewing concerns."

"Yes, my lady."

"Agnes, double-check the infirmary ledger against actual supplies. Make note of any discrepancies."

Agnes curtsies. "At once."

The Queen Dowager eyes find hers with a thankful smile. "You are released, " she says as she waves them toward the door.

Hélène, Agnes, and Meg step into the corridor together, the afternoon light streaming through lancet windows to pattern the stone floor. The castle hums with quiet purpose around them. A house in order, work proceeding without drama.

"Bread before bells," Hélène murmurs as they part ways.

King Alaric

The armory hall stretches before Alaric, its stone walls lined with racks of spears and hauberks that catch the afternoon light streaming through high windows. Practice posts bear the scars of countless training sessions, their surfaces worn smooth by repeated strikes. The assembled guard stands in neat formation, faces expectant beneath mail coifs.

Denby's voice cuts through the crisp authority of seasoned command. "Breathe first. Then stand."

The line straightens, shoulders squaring as veterans and recruits alike find their center. Alaric surveys the ranks, noting the easy confidence that has replaced the initial skepticism Roland's methods once faced. These men have seen those techniques save lives on muddy roads and narrow bridges.

"Courage on the road, order at home. I am pleased." Alaric begins. The words carry weight without ornament. Alaric has never believed in gilding simple truths, and the guard's steady attention tells him none is needed here. They have earned his respect through blood and dedication.

From beneath his arm, Alaric draws forth a slim manual. Its pages bound in leather and marked with the royal seal. Its contents drafted by Denby and Holt to retain Roland's knowledge. He raises it for all to see.

"By my word, these holds and footings are the King's Grips. Sir Holt oversees instruction. Sir Denby writes the book."

Holt steps forward, his gruff features betraying a flicker of pride. "I'll keep it clean."

Denby's response comes without pause. "And short."

A ripple of quiet laughter runs through the ranks. These men know both knights well. Holt's exacting standards and Denby's preference for economy in all things.

Alaric's gaze finds Alwin Hale, whose bruised shoulder no longer bears witness to the bridge crossing. The knight's willingness to take a blow meant for his king has not been forgotten.

"Sir Alwin Hale stood where I should have been struck."

Hale's grin breaks across his face, boyish despite his knightly bearing. "I prefer applause to stitches, Sire."

The assembly's approval rumbles through the hall. Not boisterous cheering, but the deeper satisfaction of warriors acknowledging courage in their ranks. Alaric nods thanks to Hale, letting the moment settle before continuing.

Denby receives the manual with careful hands, tucking the item inside his jerkin with the care due a precious thing. His lips move in silent words meant for no ears but his own.

"Ink keeps better than boasting."

The ceremony draws to its close as Alaric raises his hand for attention. Protocol demands dismissal, but the warmth in his voice transforms duty into invitation.

"Back to posts. Let practice make habit."

The guard begins to disperse, conversations resuming in low murmurs as they file toward doors and duties. Alaric, Denby, and Holt merge seamlessly with the throng of perspiration, mail, and iron, as they move swiftly across the grounds toward their subsequent duty.

The Great Hall opens before them like a canvas stretched for proclamation, its high banners stirring in drafts that carry the scent of rushes and old stone. Alaric strides toward the dais with Denby and Holt flanking him, their footsteps echoing against vaulted walls where nobles and staff gather in expectant clusters. A very different hall for a very different sort.

Denby's voice reaches him in a low murmur as they climb the steps. "Lucien and Juliette arrived safely this morning. The bandit troubles have quieted. Fewer reports, cleaner roads."

Alaric nods, filing the intelligence away. Order spreads outward from the center when the center holds firm.

The hall settles as he takes his place beneath the great windows, late afternoon light casting colored patterns across the assembly.

Lords adjust their positions while servants hover near pillars, all waiting for the royal word that will shape their understanding.

"In two day's time, the Princess of Navarre departs to sew her household elsewhere." The announcement falls delicately. Alaric keeps his tone flat, offering no offense to distant crowns while making his meaning clear.

Whispers ripple through the crowd, nobles exchange glances, and staff shift positions as they process what has been left unsaid. Ysabel's confinement for the past two fortnights brought many questions that none dared speak.

A messenger's arrival cuts through the murmurs, his travel-stained cloak marking him as fresh from the road. The man approaches with a scroll bearing Dunmere's seal, his travel-stained face failing to conceal satisfaction beneath formal deference.

"Your Majesty, the relief tithe was implemented in Dunmere. The fraudulent advisor stands remanded, and seed has been issued to every holding. Hunger will not finance hunger."

"Let that be said often." Alaric lets the echo carry his approval through the hall. Simple truths deserve repetition until they become habit.

His gaze finds Geoffrey and Clarissa among the assembled nobles, their quiet dignity a welcome contrast to the morning's theatrics. "Lord Geoffrey, Lady Clarissa. Return to Redwyke within a fortnight. We would welcome an invitation to your wedding."

Geoffrey bows deeply while Clarissa's smile brightens the space around them.

"A lord belongs where decisions sleep." Alaric will be sad to see his dear friend go, but proper stewardship demands his presence in Redwyke.

The modest seal for coastal provisioning passes from Alaric's hands to Lucien's, its weight small but its meaning vast. The merchant's fingers close around the charter with respectful care.

"Worth not birth." Again, Alaric lets the hall echo his words.

Juliette steps forward to her husband's side with the grace that once made her indispensable in his mother's court. Lucien's bow speaks of gratitude earned rather than entitled. "We will balance the scale."

Honest applause fills the hall, not the calculated thunder of courtly display, but the steady approval of people witnessing competence rewarded. Guards tap spear hafts against stone in rhythm with clapping hands.

Denby's voice barely reaches Holt beside him. "Good noise."

"True noise."

Alaric dismisses court and the hall empties in waves. Nobles flowing toward chambers, servants toward duties, guards toward posts that never sleep. Alaric remains on the dais until the last footstep fades, watching order reassert itself like water finding its level.

Early evening creeps through the windows, and somewhere in the depths of the castle, candles and wall torches begin their nightly bloom. He descends the steps slowly, letting the day's weight settle into memory, and turns toward the inner halls where past's kings and queens watch from gilded frames.

The portrait gallery stretches before him. Generations of crowns in their painted glory. He stops before his grandmother's likeness, her eyes still sharp beneath the artist's careful hand. The painter caught her in her prime, when wit and wisdom balanced on her tongue like birds preparing to take flight. Even captured in pigment, she seems ready to speak.

The dark garnet hanging from her neck draws his gaze, the detail in its painted surface reflecting the nearest candle like a captured star. She never removed that necklace, not in all his childhood memories of her. It rests with her still, buried beneath stone and ceremony where earthly concerns no longer reach.

How much Hélène reminds him of her. The same quick intelligence, the same ability to cut through pretense with a glance. Though his grandmother never possessed Hélène's gift for turning gravity into gentle laughter, never offered the unexpected jest that somehow made hard wisdom more palatable.

He moves from the gallery into the upper colonnade that wraps the inner courtyard. At the overpass, he stops, positioning himself like a king surveying his realm as movement below draws his eye through the arched windows. Three figures emerge from the service entrance, and he leans closer to observe. Hélène walks between Meg and Agnes, their heads bent together in conversation that sparks one quick laugh before purpose reasserts itself.

Even from this distance, he can see the careful way she moves, still favoring her back where Ysabel's cruelty left its mark, though she carries herself with the same gentle authority that has won the castle's heart.

"Hold the house." The words slip from his lips like a prayer, too low for any ear but his own.

The Council Antechamber waits in candlelight, shadows pooling in corners where daylight surrenders to evening. Loxley stands beside Alaric's desk, a scroll held with the careful devotion of one who carries the castle's daily pulse.

The boy bows as Alaric enters, extending the parchment with steady hands. "Today's measure, Sire."

Alaric accepts the report. Each line speaks of order maintained, of a household that breathes in steady rhythm even when ceremony sleeps. The numbers align like soldiers in formation. Bread enough for winter's reach, medicinals sufficient for autumn's ailments, men posted where walls require their vigilance. At the bottom, space waits for royal approval. The moment when measurement becomes mandate.

He dips his quill and signs with deliberate strokes as he whispers, "Mercy and order remain my fashion."

The ink settles into parchment as he turns toward the great windows, where night begins to trace the forest's edges. His gaze lingers northeast, towards Fairharbor, where vows once transformed merchant and lady into husband and wife. Tomorrow's tide will carry them toward their chartered routes, honest scales measuring honest trade.

"Let honest scales be our embassy." The words drift soft as candleflame, meant for no ear but the night's.

His thoughts move southward, following roads that lead to Redwyke's gentle valleys where Geoffrey and Clarissa will soon rebuild what time and distance tested. Good stewardship returns to good soil. The oldest treaty between crown and land. *Good roofs, good sleep.*

Dunmere waits within his thoughts' western reach, where autumn's harvest will tell true tales of reform's first fruits. He makes a mental note: return unannounced when grain stands ready for cutting, when honest accounting shows its worth. *Trust, then verify.*

The page shifts slightly. "Will there be more, Sire?"

Alaric glances at the remaining documents, at correspondence that waits like patient courtiers for royal attention. Work flows without end. Turn one stone, and three more wait beneath, each requiring its own careful consideration.

"Always."

The boy bows and withdraws, leaving Alaric alone with the demanding weight of governance. Along the walls, flames dance in their sconces, as the castle breathes around him, settling into evening's slower rhythm.

"The house is almost ready."

Lady Hélène of Montbois

The chime pierces sleep like silver threading through velvet. Soft, insistent, unmistakable. Hélène's eyes snap open to predawn shadows, her hand already moving to the band circling her wrist. She'd been wearing it every night, waiting for her brother's promised message. Beneath her fingertips, light flickers through hairline cracks in ways that have nothing to do with candleflame. She needs to be quick, for there is not much energy left in its crystal reserves.

"Not a dream this time."

Footsteps approach from the outer chamber. Agnes arriving with morning's first duties. The door opens and Agnes stops short, taking in her mistress's already alert form and the strange glow emanating from the band at her wrist. She too knows what this means.

"Meg." Agnes calls toward the adjoining chamber where sounds of fire-building drift through stone walls. "Their Majesties. Now."

"Privacy is required. We'll meet in the Queen's chambers." Hélène adds as she swings her legs from the bed, bare feet meeting cold stone.

They clothe her in her usual predawn duties attire. Hélène's fingers shake as she assists Agnes with fastenings, bindings, and tresses. Completely garbed as though facing an ordinary morning, she draws breathe deeply and strides quickly toward her chamber's entrance.

The corridors stretch empty in pre-dawn's early hush. Guards nod respectfully as they pass, eyes sliding away from whatever urgent business carries the Lady Hélène through shadows toward royal chambers.

Queen Dowager Margaret receives them already dressed in deep burgundy, gold glinting at throat and wrist as if she expected dawn to bring correspondence requiring immediate attention.

"Close the shutters. Let the room belong to us."

The shutters close softly, sealing them within walls that have heard confessions and shaped kingdoms. Hélène moves to the center table, her damaged timeband catching the light from the hearth as she lays it in the center.

A light knock precedes the door's careful opening. Meg enters with quiet steps, followed by two figures in plain doublet rather than ceremonial dress. Alaric and Reginald, arriving without fanfare or announcement as to not wake curious ears. Not long after, Anselm arrives in full ecclesiastical robes, completing the private assembly.

"Whatever comes, we will hear it cleanly." Anselm's voice carries the steadiness of crozier and conviction, gentling the room's racing heartbeat as surely as morning prayer settles restless souls.

Reginald unrolls fresh parchment across the Queen Dowager's writing desk, his hands smoothing the surface. "Truth is a better scribe when ink is ready."

Queen Dowager turns toward Meg and Agnes.

"No one comes in unless they carry a prayer."

Both women nod once and retreat through the doorway, their steps growing distant as they assume their watch outside the chamber with the guards. Those remaining gather around the center table, prepared to receive future's words.

Hélène extends her hand, fingers steady despite the tremor she feels beneath her ribs. She taps the timeband's surface. It flickers with static washing across its cracked display before settling into a loading sigil that pulses with alien rhythm.

Alaric meets Hélène's eyes across the table's width. His gaze holds questions, concern, and something deeper. Trust given without reservation. Her finger hovers above the activation control.

The band's glow turns constant, almost peaceful. A soft tone signals the packet has found its destination, traveled impossible distance to reach this room, this moment.

"Let truth be kind." Hélène's quiet voice settles over them like incense.

Hélène presses the control. The tiny screen wavers once, then forms a shimmering projection of Roland's features, unchanged from his departure weeks past. The gathered witnesses, taken aback by the floating image, withdraw a pace. Hélène draws nearer, with Alaric matching her movement.

"Adrian." Her murmur lost beneath the transmission.

"Elaine…if you can hear me…"

Stone and Paint Remember

- 26 -

Lady Hélène of Montbois

"Elaine… if you can hear me…I kept something from you." Roland's voice carries the weight of confession.

"The Ancient said 'She must stay.' I didn't say it before because I didn't know how to let it be true."

Hélène's breath catches, but she doesn't step back from the projection. Beside her, she hears Alaric's quiet intake, Anselm's whispered prayer.

"The Ancients have sealed time. No more sanctioned or unsanctioned corridors. You will not be found again. No one can."

The revelation strikes her chest like a physical blow. No rescue missions. No temporal extraction. The future has closed its doors, leaving her stranded in stone and candlelight forever. Her fingers find the edge of the table, gripping until her knuckles pale.

"They told me 'stone and paint.' I searched artifacts from Alaric's court. Conservation scans moved through legal channels. I tied this packet to a scan of an artifact."

Roland's ingenuity sparks familiar pride. Her brother, finding solutions where others see walls. The projection flickers, then shifts to show something that steals her breath entirely.

A portrait fills the projection's display as if it were there in real time: An aged Alaric in rich ceremonial robes beside a woman whose face mirrors one she lost many years ago. Around the familiar woman's throat hangs a large dark stone on a modest dark chain.

"I almost called her Mother. Then I saw it was you."

Roland's voice softens with wonder, and Hélène understands. This isn't prophecy. It's proof. History already holds her story, written in pigment and memory across decades she has yet to live.

"It isn't a cage. It's a home you build. History remembers your face because you make it worth remembering."

The words settle like prophecy, transforming prison into possibility. She feels Alaric's presence at her shoulder, steady as heartbeat.

Roland speaks to the room now, the change in his tone seeming to pierce through time itself, but the projection remains on the portrait, enhancing itself on the dark stone at her neck.

"If the King is with you…Alaric, when you see this, you'll know the message is true."

The necklace in the portrait gleams with promise, a bridge between now and then. Hélène's fingers drift to her bare throat, already feeling its weight.

"She is brave enough for a crown that means work. Treat her as such."

The projection steadies back onto Roland, his expression shifting from messenger to brother again.

"Elaine… No, Hélène… Live. Take what your heart has already chosen. I will write when the law lets memory travel."

His tone holds the warmth she recalls from their stolen interludes between assignments. When they would not speak of partings.

"I am not leaving you. I am keeping my promise differently."

The words reshape everything. Not abandonment, but adaptation. A brother's love finding new channels when the old ones close.

The projection wavers, then fades to darkness. The room returns to candlelight and shadow, the scent of ink and parchment replacing the strange sterile glow.

Soft chime…

Her timeband falls silent, its faint luminescence dying like an ember in snow.

Hélène draws one deep breath, feeling centuries of possibility settle into her bones. Her spine straightens as if receiving orders, then relaxes as she accepts what was always true.

"All right, Agent Rush. Final order received."

King Alaric

The silence following Roland's message stretches like a held breath. Alaric watches Hélène's shoulders settle, her spine finding its natural pose as she releases something she'd carried too long. The cracked timeband lies dark on the table. A relic now, no longer a lifeline.

He reaches into the folds of his robe, his fingers finding a hidden pocket before drawing out a small casket, its presence deliberate yet unassuming. His hands know its weight, the smooth grain of its wood. He's carried it through councils and correspondence, waiting for clarity that never seemed to come.

Until now.

"I had this made before I knew why it should exist."

The casket opens with a soft whisper of hinges. Inside, nestled in midnight velvet, lies the necklace. Dark stone on modest chain, exactly as Roland's projection promised. The weight of prophecy made manifest settles in the room like incense.

Hélène's voice comes soft as prayer. "Stone and paint."

Queen Dowager steps closer, her approval carrying the authority of decades. "And work. You'd take up the prior Queen Dowager's mantle."

Alaric's pulse steadies as purpose aligns with possibility. The portrait showed truth, but choice makes it real. He does not reach for the necklace, does not presume. A king who governs by consent must ask, not take.

"Lady Hélène of Montbois, will you enter formal courtship with me, to seek a betrothal when the spring turns again?"

The words carry weight beyond ceremony. A vow to build rather than claim, to court not just a woman but a partnership that history will remember.

Anselm's voice carries warmth tempered by wisdom. "A vow grows best when it is watered by days."

Queen Dowager adds her measured counsel. "And trimmed by duty."

Hélène meets his gaze with the directness he's come to treasure, her answer balancing heart with house as she always does. "Yes, if the work comes first and the crown remembers bread before bells."

Relief floods through him like spring water. Not just acceptance, but understanding. She knows what she asks as he knows what he promises. "Bread, before and after."

His smile feels like armor falling away, revealing the man beneath the crown. Reginald's quill scratches against parchment, recording the moment with his characteristic precision. "Clarity is mercy in ink."

Alaric lifts the necklace from its silken rest, the stone cool against his palm. Hélène turns slightly, offering her throat with trust that humbles him. The chain settles where Roland's projection promised it would rest. Not an ornament, but the seal of a purpose shared.

Queen Dowager's satisfaction carries final approval. "Fits like truth."

Alaric steps back the proper distance, offering a brief bow that acknowledges both her rank and the gravity of what they've begun. Protocol matters, especially when hearts are involved.

"We will proceed properly."

Hélène's smile is small but genuine. She straightens, breathes in deeply, wipes at the tears on her cheeks, then gives a slight curtsy.

"I promise one joke per hour, Your Majesty."

His mother chuckles lightly from behind. He nods approval as he moves toward the chamber doors. The castle waits beyond. Staff and nobles, responsibilities and rhythms that shape a realm. No fanfare needed, no grand announcements. Truth travels best through steady action.

"Come. Let the house hear truth, not trumpets."

---- ◈ ----

Alice Whitcombe

Alice positions herself near the service door where shadows meet stone, close enough to catch every word yet distant enough to seem invisible. Her fingers worry the edge of her apron as she watches the King and Lady Hélène stand the proper distance apart. Close enough to show intent, far enough to honor propriety. The Queen Dowager and Archbishop flank them like pillars, their faces carrying the gravity of witnessed promises.

The herald's voice cuts through morning stillness, clear as chapel bells.

"Hear the King."

Alice's pulse quickens. She's seen this moment building through whispered conferences and careful glances, but watching history unfold still steals her breath.

Alaric's voice carries neither flourish nor hesitation. "We begin a formal courtship toward betrothal with Lady Hélène of Montbois. We will let the house test us."

A ripple passes through the assembled court. Surprise tempered by inevitability. Alice catches Lord Geoffrey's satisfied nod, Lady Isolde's warm smile. Even stern-faced Ranulf offers grudging approval, though his eyes hold warning. The King's choice will face scrutiny, but it will not face rebellion.

"Our fashion remains mercy with order and bread before bells."

Bread before bells. The familiar phrase settles like a blessing. Alice has heard it spoken in council chambers and kitchen corners, watched it shape grain distributions and guard rotations. Now it frames a royal courtship. Work before spectacle, always.

Hélène takes her place by the Queen Dowager, the movement natural as breathing. No ceremony needed, just the quiet assumption of duty. Alice notes how the positioning speaks: not consort-in-waiting, but partner-in-governance.

Lord Reginald steps forward and continues the days proceedings. "Dunmere: relief enacted, audits set."

Geoffrey follows, his voice carrying satisfaction. "Redwyke: stewardship resumes within a fortnight."

Anselm's diplomatic tone closes foreign concerns. "Letters with Spain: courteous and closed."

The rhythm of good governance flows like water finding its course, demonstrating how a realm should breathe.

King Alaric's attention turns to the guards, recognition due where service was given. "The King's Grips are law. Holt instructs. Denby writes. Hale is commended."

Sir Hale murmurs to Holt with dry humor. "I'll accept applause as armor."

Holt's flat response draws chuckles from nearby guards. "Don't dent it."

Even ceremony needs breathing room, Alice thinks. The King understands that formality serves best when it doesn't suffocate warmth.

"Juliette Marchand and Lucien Marcellus hold a provisioning charter. We cherish worth that rises over birth."

The merchant couple exchange quiet words, their faces glowing with vindicated hope.

"Balance kept," Juliette whispers.

"And paid," Lucien replies.

Alice's attention shifts to the murmur passing through servants and nobles alike. Recognition dawning as they notice the necklace at Hélène's throat. The design echoes the old Queen's jewelry, the one who fed orphans from her own purse and died beloved by kitchen maids and courtiers alike. The older court understands that this choice honors legacy through service, not bloodline through spectacle.

Bess Carter appears at Alice's elbow, flour still dusting her sleeves. "Stone and paint, love. It suits her."

Alice nods, watching how the dark stone necklace catches light without demanding it.

"Tell it right," she whispers to Bess, setting the day's narrative. "The King chose work, then love."

Anselm raises his hand, his blessing carrying the weight of ancient authority. "May this house keep bread at the front and knives sheathed."

Applause rises like gentle rain, honest sound without theater. Queen Dowager leans close to her son, satisfaction evident in her measured words.

The formal declarations conclude, but Alice lingers, watching how naturally court business resumes. Hélène doesn't retreat to ladies' quarters but remains beside the King as petitioners approach. Work continues, as it should.

Alice commits every detail to memory, knowing this moment will shape countless retellings. The corridor conversations have already begun, servants catching each other's eyes with approval. By evening, every pantry and stable will know: the King chose competence over ornament, partnership over possession.

Lady Hélène of Montbois

The stone balcony edge feels cool beneath her palms as twilight deepens into darkness. Stars emerge one by one, pinpricks of ancient light that watched other worlds before they found this one. Hélène draws her knees up, settling into the familiar comfort of sky-watching, though these constellations still feel foreign compared to the twin moons she once knew.

Her fingers find the necklace above her chest. The dark stone is warm from her skin. Beneath her sleeve, the cracked time crystal rests silent against her wrist. She wears it not from hope but from habit, a tether to what was rather than what might be again. The last message drained its final spark. She knows Adrian would reach her if physics allowed, but the universe has closed that door. She destroyed the suit to preserve history, but she wasn't ready to let go of the crystal. Not yet.

A half-smile touches her lips as distant Mars whispers across memory's gulf. Red dust and glass domes, a childhood spent learning atmosphere recyclers and hydroponics before she ever saw natural rain.

"I always meant to learn one planet well."

The words drift into evening air, meant for no ears but her own. She touches the time crystal's cold surface through her sleeve, whispering to the silence where her brother's voice once lived.

"Try not to collect arrows, Adrian."

Warmth settles around her shoulders like a familiar cloak. The quiet holds no expectation of response, no demand for impossible connection. Just the peace of words offered to love that distance cannot diminish.

Footsteps echo along the colonnade's stone and halt behind her. She turns enough to see Alaric framed in the archway, that comfortable smile softening his features. It's an expression she's grown to recognize over the past month. The genuine warmth he wears when duty allows honesty.

He approaches with the easy confidence of someone who belongs in her space, who has earned the right to interrupt her stargazing.

"The rota reads like a vow."

His voice carries gentle teasing, recognition of how she's shaped the castle's daily rhythm into something dependable. She turns fully to face him, responding to both his words and his presence.

"Then the day will keep it."

The promise settles between them, simple as shared bread. Work first, always work first. The foundation that makes everything else possible.

"Work first," he confirms, stepping closer.

"Then love, properly."

He inclines his head in acknowledgment, fingers brushing the necklace at her throat. His kiss lands light as he withdraws, leaving her to her thoughts and the stars that remember longer stories than theirs.

She whispers to the dark stone against her skin.

"History, do your best."

Stone and paint remember.

Bread before bells.

Mercy with order.

Worth over birth.